The Crescent

Arlene Johnston

Pine Lake Books
Canada

First Printing, 2019

ISBN 978-1-989322-09-3

Pine Lake Books

West Guilford, ON

Canada

www.pinelakebooks.ca

For all my family and friends, past, present and future.

The Crescent

GARNET MURRAY INHALED deeply, the last trace of white paper up in smoke. Bob Barker's soothing voice emanated throughout the living room as the acrid smoke filled her lungs. *He's the most handsome man in the world.* Her face burned with racy thoughts tossing the cigarette butt into the smoke glass ashtray, anchored on the brass stand beside her chair. She eyed the collection of butts accumulated since rising this morning; with a notion to quit the disgusting habit, she walked across the worn area rug confident, once again, it wouldn't be today. She loved her cigs as much as she loved her kids, sometimes more. She paused and reflected, watching the neighbourhood kids play kickball on the road out front, the tension easing in her neck and head. She tucked a loose strand of black grey streaked hair behind her right ear rather than undoing her signature scrawny ponytail and starting all over again. Her stained toothy smile quickly evaporated; the muffled cries from up the stairs averted her attention back to the television. Increasing the volume, she settled back in her chair, reaching for her cigarettes.

It was unanimous; the group decided more players were needed if they were going to have a decent game of kickball. The kids sat on the curb debating who they should invite. Ronald, the tallest and oldest wasted no time suggesting Evelyn.

Daniel quickly turned to face him. 'You know damn well she wouldn't play a stupid game of kickball. You just want to ask her because you've got the hots for her.'

Ronald felt his face redden. Ever since he was twelve years old he'd had a huge crush on Evelyn. 'If you weren't my best friend I'd punch you out,' he said calmly, reaching for a stone.

Ronald's younger brother, Timothy, as always, picked up on his brother's angst. 'It's better if we stay down at this end of the street to avoid Crabby Appleton. He's already got two of my Indian rubber balls.'

No one had any idea what Crabby Appleton's real name was, just the rotten reputation he had of stealing any ball that landed on his well-manicured front lawn.

'I bet that SOB's got quite a stash,' Ronald said sarcastically. 'The freak of nature stands behind his living room sheers just waiting for something to land on his precious grass and out he runs wearing the same baggy beige pants and plaid shirt. I wonder if his wife ever washes them,' he added, holding his nose.

The kids laughed heartily. They had all witnessed this tall, lanky man with a squished head sporting a reddish brown brush cut, quickly run out, grab a ball then run back inside with it. The kids, shocked by his behaviour, would torment him from the curb. Depending on his mood, he'd reluctantly give the ball back, but not before reciting the same boring speech regarding the need to respect other people's property. Needless to say, all the kids hated his guts.

It was beginning to get hot. 'If we're going to play, hurry up and decide,' Cathy said, searching her legs for peeling skin from previous sunburns. 'I'm getting burnt to a crisp,' she sighed, peeling off a large strip of dead skin.

'We could ask Glenn or Jimmy,' Andrea said, looking toward their house on the corner.

David shook his head. 'Naw, he's gotta look after his mother.' He tried to balance the dirty white volleyball on his fingertip, but it fell onto the road. 'And Jimmy's gotta help out too. So the Smythe kids are out,' he said, retrieving the ball.

'What's wrong with their mom?' Dana said.

Andrea spoke first. 'I heard my mom telling Mrs. McPherson that Mrs. Smythe takes lots of pills for her condition.'

'With a house full of kids running 'round all day I'd take pills too,' Ronald said, knocking the ball off David's middle finger.

'You creep! I just got it spinning,' David yelled, retrieving the ball from the middle of the road.

'Don't be such a whiner,' Ronald said, tucking his hands behind his head, laying back on the grass.

Once again, Anne Smythe slept through the alarm. She could feel someone tugging at the sheet covering her flabby body. 'Mommy up, Mommy up,' the tiny voice encouraged.

Anne rolled away, tugging hard at the sheet pulling her young daughter, Katherine, into the side of the bed.

'Where's your brother?' she barked, turning back, tucking the sheet around her. Katherine stared wide-eyed at her mother.

Anne, suppressing the sudden urge to shake her daughter opted for the bottle of pills sitting on the nightstand beside her bed. Expertly, she flipped the lid off catching it with her left hand, popping two valium into her stale mouth, chasing them with a mouthful of water.

Katherine continued coaxing her to get out of bed, but she ignored her pleas tucking the sheet closer to her squishy body; years of child bearing had taken its toll not only physically, but mentally. Her thirty-four year old body was a flabby mess, her mind messier still.

She turned toward Katherine, the second youngest of five, waiting patiently beside her. 'You need your hair washed,' she said, reaching a hand out from under the sheet, running her fingers through the tangled blond curls. 'You're a mess.'

Katherine, oblivious to her comment, widened her bright blue eyes, smiled broadly, lifting her arms and twirling around in circles. Falling to the floor, she kicked up into the air. It was then Anne focused on the stained diaper and the stench that rose with each kick.

Her head pounded, turning sharply away, focusing on the ceiling waiting for the pills to take hold.

Katherine righted herself, moving closer to the bed. 'Bad girl!' she said, slapping her mother's face.

'What do you think you are doing? Get out of here!' she screamed. As her daughter scurried out of sight Anne focused on the ceiling praying, *Dear God, please make me barren.*

Katherine ran screaming down the hall, her diaper heading south. Her older brother, Glenn, scooped her up in his arms.

'Me hungry,' she whined as her brother hoisted her up onto the change table. 'Me want Sucar Cisp and Mommy won't get up,' she cried, rubbing her eyes vigorously.

Glenn smiled tenderly reaching for the last clean diaper. 'Mommy's just tired,' he said patiently, holding back a gag, gently cleaning her bottom. The foul smelling contents had hardened into the folds of her skin.

'You're all set,' he said, pulling up the white rubber pants, placing her on the floor. She ran full tilt to the kitchen while he finished tidying up. He was surprised all her racket hadn't disturbed Rose, the youngest, sleeping soundly in the crib. He spoke quietly to Sherry, the oldest of the three girls, lying on the top bunk reading *Black Beauty.* 'Do you know where Mark is?'

Without looking at her brother she replied, 'probably doing some stupid experiment in the basement.' Lately, Mark spent his free time working on experiments he had learned in science class in his makeshift lab downstairs.

'Have you had breakfast yet?'

She looked up from her novel. 'No, and I'm not hungry.'

'Are you feeling okay?'

'I'm waiting until Mom gets up, whenever that will be,' she said, rolling her eyes toward the ceiling.

'If you change your mind, I'm getting breakfast ready for Kath,' he said, watching her turn the page.

Glenn dumped the contents of the soiled diaper into the toilet and flushed. He continued to thrash it against the porcelain; the running water removing most of the hardened excrement. He thought he was beyond the gagging, but today's load was horribly ripe. With watery eyes, he squeezed the water out, tossing it on top of the overflowing diaper pail. He debated taking the pail downstairs to wash, but Katherine's demanding cries guided his next move.

Ronald eyed the second hand on his new Timex watch, a gift for his 14th birthday. 'Do you realize, with each passing second, we've lost that time and it's gone forever?'

Dana said, 'I've never thought of that. It sounds so morbid.'

'Only stating the facts, therefore, I refuse to waste any more of my precious time. If you don't hurry up and think of…hey Daniel, go ask George.'

Daniel turned toward Murray's driveway. 'Not happening.'

'He's not as bad as his twin sister, Gloria,' Sharon said, bringing her hands five inches from her face, fiercely rubbing the tips of both thumbs against the tips of her fingers with paisley green eyes locked intently on the task, transporting her elsewhere.

'Why do you do that?' Dana asked sarcastically, watching Sharon working feverously with her fingertips.

'Do what?' she said, jarring her hands down to her sides, quickly running off.

'Speaking of retards,' Timothy concluded.

Garnet sat in a cloud of smoke; mesmerized by the Price is Right. *Garnet Murray! Come on down! You're the next contestant on the Price is Right! She ran quickly toward the stage sending the audience into frenzy, walking excitedly toward Bob Barker smiling like the Cheshire cat watching her approach. Standing mere inches from him she couldn't resist the urge to clamp her skinny arms around his neck, hugging him tightly. No kiss though. Bob Barker didn't like women kissing him.* Her heart pounded wildly. With eyes closed, she raised her nicotine stained fingers to her nose, inhaling the scent deeply; the remedy when cigarettes were beyond her reach. The persistent knock on the front door interrupted her fantasy. 'George! Get the goddamn door!'

Daniel's loud excessive knocking could be heard at the curb where the others waited.

Theresa craned her neck to see what was taking so long. 'Why isn't anyone answering?'

'Who knows? The old lady's probably sittin' smoking cigarettes, totally oblivious to what goes on in that house,' Ronald said, spitting as far as he could into the middle of the road; the gob splashing heavily onto the pavement.

'That's disgusting!' Janice said, eyeing the glistening wad.

'Now don't go getting all silly now. The sun will evaporate it like it always does,' he said, lying back down on the grass.

George angrily tossed the magazine under the bed, walking slowly down the stairs watching his mother whiff her two fingers stuffed under her nose. *Stupid bitch is probably out of cigs.*

'Didn't ya hear me calling ya? Someone's been banging on the door for ten minutes now.'

'I was busy,' he said, walking toward it. He stared vaguely at Daniel through the screen door.

'We gotta game of kicker goin'. Wanna join us?'

George didn't blink. 'Naw.'

Daniel said, 'What about Barry?'

A weird look crossed George's face. 'He's helping my sister.'

Daniel smiled. 'No sense asking if Gloria can join in then.'

'No sense,' he said, slamming the door.

'George! How many times have I told you not to slam the damn door? Mommy's got a headache. Now, be a good boy and get Mommy's cigarettes for me.' She didn't want to miss one second of the Price is Right.

'Yes Mommy,' he said, reaching on top of the fridge. He handed her the new pack, then ran back upstairs, two at a time, slamming his bedroom door.

She lit a much needed cigarette, inhaling deeply. *I honestly don't know what gets into that kid sometimes.*

Barry sat on the edge of the bed perspiring profusely, his face buried in his hands. He tried wiping the perspiration off his face, rubbing briskly with his hands. 'Please stop crying, Gloria. Mommy will get really angry and we don't want that.'

Though it was over 80 degrees in the bedroom, Gloria lay in bed wrapped tightly in the thick princess eiderdown, a gift from Grandma Perkins for her eighth birthday. *See all the pretty pink princesses. One day you will be a princess* her grandmother had promised. Gloria wiped her blue eyes and runny nose on a princess, whimpering at the snotty mess she left behind. She always seemed to make a mess of everything lately.

Barry stood, running his fingers through his hair as he walked to the other side of the bed where his tightly cocooned sister lay on her side. 'I'm going to go to my room now so you can sleep.'

George looked up when the bedroom door opened. 'Where's Gloria?' he asked in a concerned tone.

'Sleeping,' Barry said, lying on his bed. He reached underneath for the magazine with curled edges, turning to the centerfold, feeling an instant rush.

Daniel took his time walking back down the driveway. 'None of the Murrays can come out,' he said, sitting down beside Theresa.

Timothy spoke first. 'Barry too?'

'He's helping his sister,' Daniel said, pulling on a piece of long grass, sucking on the end.

'Helping her with what?' he persisted.

Lately, Barry rarely came outside. 'How the heck should I know. I gotta go. It's too hot for kickball now anyway,' he said, pitching the grass, walking away quickly.

As if on cue, the other boys ran off in different directions.

'Game over,' Theresa smiled.

Garnet turned off the television watching the boys run away, leaving the girls sitting on the curb. She could tell by their smiles they were having a good time. *I used to have fun when we lived downtown. My best friend Thelma, god I miss her; her and I would sit and drink coffee while our kids played.* A smile crossed her face reminiscing about their days together.

I hate it here. It was all Ben's stupid idea to move to the suburbs. He claims it's better for the family. What's he know? The neighbours here are unsociable, so stuffy. Not like Thelma. She was the best. She thought about Gloria upstairs in her room on such a beautiful summer day. *She was such a happy child until this stupid move.*

Gloria waited for the bedroom door to close. *I hate you Barry.* Unable to hold back the tears she sobbed into her pillow, wishing she was dead.

Chapter Two

MAC PUSHED OPEN the front door ushering his 6'2" frame into the clutter and chaos that has always been the McConnell household trademark. He never had to announce his arrival; invariably someone would sense his presence, today was no different.

'Daddy!' Rebecca cried, launching herself toward his broad chest. 'I'm so glad you're home,' she said, hugging him tightly around the neck. He kissed her cheek, asking after her mother.

'Probably doing laundry.'

'Should I head to the basement and surprise her? What do you think?' He enjoyed watching the kids' faces whenever he asked for their input.

'Yeah!' she giggled. 'Mom would like that. But don't scare her too much,' Rebecca said, pointing at her stomach.

'Right,' he said, with a wink.

With the 6th McConnell offspring due in a few weeks, Veronica was finding the bend to sort laundry strewn across the basement floor challenging. She placed the white clothes into the top loader, filled the soap dispenser, closed the lid feeling two strong arms envelope her gently across her swollen belly.

'It's about time,' she said, pushing the start button. His caress was warm and sensual as his hands travelled up to her swollen breasts. 'Mac, what about the kids…before she could finish the sentence he spun her round, kissing her with the passion of a man in the crazy throes of love.

Veronica drew a deep breath. 'Welcome home,' she smiled, moving her forefinger gently across his lips. 'That shade of lipstick isn't your best,' she smiled, wiping her finger on a dirty towel. 'It took you long enough to get down here.'

He looked at her quizzically. 'How did you know I was home?'

'I could feel your presence,' she smiled admiringly. 'Besides, the front door is right up there,' she said, pointing toward the wooden rafters. 'I may be in the basement, but I'm always in tune.'

'Does that mean you don't want me to finish off the laundry room?'

'I didn't say that,' she said, reaching for his hand, resting on her shoulder. 'How long are you home for?'

He guided her toward the stairs giving her a loving pat on the bottom; at the top of the stairs he hugged her tightly. 'A few days, you know how it is, V,' he said, kissing the top of her head, breathing in her perfumed hair. In his eyes, she was the most beautiful woman in the world with her rich black hair and dark brown eyes, but it was her radiant smile that attracted him when they first met at a mutual friend's birthday party. It still amazed him that after five and a half kids, her smile continued to make him mushy.

When they married 18 years ago, Veronica graciously accepted that his engineering projects would take him away, at times for months, to some of the most exotic places in the world. Presently, he was a consulting engineer on a construction project in Columbia. Throughout the years, she unwaveringly supported his career and his determination, offering their children the opportunity to attend university.

Veronica smiled warmly at her handsome man with the wavy brown hair and mischievous brown eyes. 'I guess you won't be home for the baby's arrival in a few weeks.'

He sighed, glancing at the ceiling. 'I can try, but I doubt it. There are other engineers working alongside of me who haven't been home in months.' Kissing her lips gently, he promised her an early retirement with a decent nest egg. 'But until then, I gotta make hay while the sun shines.'

When the dinner bell sounded, the family gathered on two long benches Mac had designed and built into a corner of the kitchen when they first bought the house. At the time, there were only three kids. But now with five kids, another due shortly and two adults they had almost outgrown the dinner table. *We need a bigger house* he concluded, gazing around the table at his beloved family.

There was a mutual respect felt by all members of the family, every voice counted. He was filled with an overwhelming sense of pride, listening intently to each of his offspring. In moments like this, he was positive he was the luckiest man on Earth.

When it was Mac's turn to speak, the kids listened keenly to his every word. Their dad was known for his zany, exciting stories from abroad and today was no different.

'A few weeks ago, our group, needing some downtime, embarked on a guided hike through an area of rainforest known to have excellent sightings of some of the rarest animals in the world. It was close to 100 degrees when we left our camp with Luiz, our guide. Short in stature with youngish looks belying his real age, he walks around with a cigarette anchored in the space where a front tooth used to be. When he's finished a cigarette, he pushes it out with his tongue, replacing it with another. He's been a guide for 35 years beginning at age of 12. Always with a smile, he's a comical little four and a half foot character.

'Luiz showed us how to find and spear tarantulas to cook over the fire. They are a delicacy; a good source of protein.'

'Did you eat one?' Susan asked squeamishly.

'I must say, I didn't partake this time, but if the opportunity arises again, I probably will.'

'We were astounded by the variety of animals and exotic birds, Luiz, who knows exactly where to look, introduced us to. He's an expert on preferred habitats and eating schedules. We saw anteaters, armadillos (related to the anteater and sloth), jaguars, red-eyed frogs, egrets, herons, lizards, night monkeys, boa constrictors, crocodiles, dolphins, parrots, umbrella birds and kinkajous. Luiz's idea of a shore lunch is fried piranha which we all indulged in. The tour was memorable, but it would have been better if all of you had been there with me trudging through the muck.'

They sat quietly anticipating what he would say next.

'We also saw some of the largest trees in the world, the canopy tree. These trees are huge; housing anteaters, crabs, porcupines, even kangaroos. Animals I always associated as ground dwellers.'

'Wow! I'd like to see a kangaroo,' Susan smiled.

'Someday,' he said, waiting patiently for someone to break the silence.

Tommy said, 'Any souvenirs?'

Dad glanced at his watch. 'As a matter of fact, it's due to arrive in 12 hours, 14 minutes and 38 seconds,' he said. 'In the meantime, you can clean up the dishes for your mom. I need some Mom time,' he said, leading Veronica out the backdoor. It was a perfect evening that had the makings of a tequila sunrise.

Chapter Three

GARNET DECIDED DR. Fletcher was the handsomest man in the world. She felt all fuzzy and warm as he read the diagnosis. 'You have terminal…She cursed under her breath, turning away from the Tide commercial, listening to the goings on in the kitchen. 'Don't you two mess up my kitchen,' she said tersely. 'I haven't got time to be cleaning up after you two.' Her mind raced wondering what Sally's diagnosis could possibly be and couldn't afford to miss one second of *The Guiding Light*. 'What are you two doing?' She lit a cigarette filling her lungs with acrid smoke.

'Just getting some lunch, Mom,' Barry said. 'It is after one.' He watched George slap a slice of baloney between two pieces of white bread. 'Don't you want any mustard on that?'

George snapped. 'If I wanted mustard, I would have put it on,' he said, taking a huge bite.

Too many damn ads Garnet decided getting even more annoyed with the boys. 'Don't you two start fightin'. Just eat your lunch and get outside. It's too nice of a day to be stuck in here.' Turning her attention back to the television she focused on Dr. Fletcher's blond patient. *I'm prettier than Sally. What a plain, simple name* she concluded smugly. *Garnet is more of a star's name. It's a beautiful name for a beautiful girl my mom used to say.* But for most of her life, she hated her name. The kids would taunt her. After she met Brian Anderson the taunts became unbearable.

Shortly after Garnet's 13th birthday, her mother invited Brian, a boy from the neighbourhood, to visit. Though she would protest her mother's extended invitations, her mother knew what was best for her quiet, shy daughter, ignoring her pleas, encouraging him to visit more often. 'Brian is such a nice, good looking young man.

For the likes of someone like you, you should be flattered he wants to visit with you.' Her mother was right, in that, all the neighbourhood girls had a crush on him. His charismatic personality, sky blue eyes and wavy blond hair made him by far, the most popular boy on the block. In contrast, she was skinny, dull and unpopular.

One afternoon, her mother went grocery shopping leaving the pair sitting side by side on the chesterfield. As soon as Brian heard the door latch, he kissed her gently on the lips. She felt an odd, yet pleasurable sensation. He smiled tenderly, kissing her more intently. After a few passionate kisses he tried persuading her to remove her panties, but Garnet balked at his request. Gently, he ran his hands through her long black hair, staring into her hazel eyes, convincing her it was okay to remove them. 'This is what good girls do.'

She felt silly and vulnerable removing them, but at the same time safe in the knowledge that Brian, two years older, would know what good girls do. He encouraged her to lie back on the chesterfield, yearning to look between her legs. Red faced, she confessed she had never shown her private parts to anyone. He smiled wickedly, 'I bet they are beautiful, like you.'

And for the first time in her life, she felt truly beautiful spreading her legs wide, watching his wide-eyed reaction. She asked him again, 'do you really think I'm beautiful, Brian?'

'You are the most beautiful girl I've ever seen.'

Expertly, his fingers probed her vagina. She wanted to protest but found his touch exciting, feeling things she had never experienced before. 'Beautiful things need to be touched' he gasped, penetrating her deeply with his middle finger. She felt anxious, but reassured herself this is what good girls do.

Perspiration dripped from his forehead, instructing her to close her eyes. 'I have a big surprise for you, my beautiful princess,' he said hoarsely, quickly pulling down his shorts.

Willingly, she shut them, content she was his princess, but when she felt the weight of his rigid body on top of her, she flashed them open again. Brian's scarlet face, mere inches from hers, ordered her to close her goddamn eyes. Quickly she obliged, feeling a sharp pain, squeezing them tighter still, willing herself not to cry out. She trembled uncontrollably as he continued thrusting deep inside; his fast, hot, stinky breath turned into a long drawn out moan. Breathing deeply, he lay spent on top of her, rolling sideways.

Garnet, eyes shut tightly, lay very still listening to him dress. He mumbled he had to go; he'd see her tomorrow, walking hurriedly out of the living room.

Tears ran down her cheeks reaching between her legs; wet, gooey liquid spilled out of her privates. Vigorously she wiped the area with a wad of tissue. When she stood up she discovered a wet patch, tinged red, in the center of the cushion. Unsure of what to do, she flipped it over.

Sitting on the edge of her bed, she wiped the tears, listening to her mother call out to come help with the groceries.

'There you are,' Mother said, not bothering to knock. 'Didn't you hear me calling you?'

Garnet wiped her sweaty palms on her shorts and began shuffling the books on her desk. 'I didn't know you were home. I've been busy tidying up my room.'

A stunned look crossed her face. 'Well, that's unusual; I didn't have to nag you for a change. Did you have a nice time with Brian? I hope you didn't chase him away. He's such a nice boy.'

Garnet felt a cold shiver in the oppressive heat.

Her mother walked toward her. 'Are you sure you're alright? It looks like you've been crying.'

'I'm just hot,' she said, feeling her face burn. 'I'm fine.'

'You don't look fine. Did something happen?'

Yes Mother. That nice boy Brian you kept encouraging to come 'round had his way with me. 'Nothing happened,' she mumbled.

'You need a bath. Then you'll feel better. Would you like me to run it for you?'

Garnet awoke with a start, she had fallen asleep, missing Sally's diagnosis. 'George, you in here?' With no response, she rested her head on the back of her chair, wiped her sweaty palms on the flowered upholstery then lit a cigarette.

Gloria sat up with a start, sweating profusely in the oppressive heat. Even with the windows wide open her bedroom resembled a hot oven. She threw back her princess comforter, reaching between her legs for the sticky goo her brother had anointed her with. Vigorously, she rubbed herself with a wad of tissue, tossing it to the floor beside her bed. She rubbed her sweaty palms on the white sheet feeling violated, hateful. Cringing at the sound of her mother's voice, she laid back down, pulling the comforter up.

Her mother knocked steadily on the door. 'Gloria, you asleep in there?' she said, hoping she was outside with her brothers. When she got no response, she swung it open. 'It's so hot in here,' she said, picking up the wad of tissue. 'Aren't you feeling well, again?' she said, placing her hand on her daughter's forehead.

Gloria flinched at the touch of her cool hand, watching with satisfaction as her mother wiped her nose with the wad of tissue.

'You don't have a fever,' she sighed, reaching for the comforter.

'Don't touch me,' Gloria hissed, gripping it tightly.

'Girl, what's gotten into you?' She anchored her two fingers under her nose breathing deeply. 'You can tell me, I'm your mother.'

Gloria felt angry tears sting her eyes. 'If you were my mother, you wouldn't let your son near me.' A look of confusion settled on her mother's brow, wiping beads of perspiration. 'Your son comes to my room to keep me quiet so I won't upset you,' she said angrily, watching for her reaction, but her mother continued wiping her forehead. 'I used those tissues to wipe my private parts,' she smirked.

Her mother squeezed the wad tightly. 'Gloria, you need to take a bath then you will feel better. I'm going to run the water for you.'

'I don't need a bath! I need you to look after me! I hate you!' she yelled, watching her mom leave the room.

Garnet sniffed the tissues, tucking them in her pant pocket. She stood mesmerized watching the steady stream of water fill the tub. *You just need a bath. Then you will feel better. I know how much you love taking a bubble bath so I added a little extra. Do you know why I named you Garnet? Because you are a rare beauty, like the red stone I named you after.*

The bathroom door swung widely, interrupting her thoughts.

'I told you I don't want a bath! It won't make me feel better,' Gloria said tersely, watching her mother turn off the tap.

Garnet reached for a container. 'Would you like me to add some of my special bubble bath?'

'No! Get away from me!' she yelled.

Unfazed by the outburst, she glanced at her watch. 'Hurry on now. Daddy will be home soon and we can all have supper together.' She closed the door behind her. *Gloria is not a good girl.*

Benjamin Murray turned into his driveway, parking his Ford Falcon just outside the carport. The early morning departure and drive from Montreal had left him drained and exhausted. All he wanted now was a shower, shave and a dry martini. He collected his suitcase from the trunk focusing on the bottle of vermouth tucked in the back of the kitchen cupboard closest to the sink. If not, a drier vodka martini would suffice. 'Hello, I'm home,' he called out, eyeing the blaring television and no one nearby. He stood his suitcase at the base of the stairs, switching off the TV. 'Anybody home?' he said, walking toward the backdoor. 'Garnet? Are you out there?'

Garnet's presence at the kitchen entrance startled him. 'There you are. Didn't you hear me calling?' Before she could answer he made it clear, once again, that if no one is watching the television it's to be turned off.

Garnet put her two fingers under her nose, inhaling deeply thinking of days gone by when he would hold her in his arms and kiss her hello upon his return. 'I was watching my show, but had to tend to Gloria's bath.'

Ben began fixing himself a much needed drink. He splashed the remaining mouthful of vermouth into a glass half filled with vodka. 'What's wrong with Gloria? Isn't she capable of turning on the taps?'

Garnet tucked her hands in her pockets, squeezing the wad of tissues. 'She's just gettin' up.'

Ben tipped back the last of his drink. 'Is she sick?' He reached into the new Kelvinator refrigerator for more ice, christening the cubes with a hefty shot of vodka.

'No, she's just experiencing some girly issues,' she said, hoping he would extend an invitation to join him. She couldn't remember the last time they spent some time together chatting with a drink.

Ben began sorting through the mail. 'Nothing but bills,' he said resignedly. 'Do you know if she's out of the bathroom yet?' He tore open the electricity bill, chucking it in the pile of unpaid bills. 'The electricity bill is ridiculous this month. Another reason to make sure the television is off when no one is watching it.'

Garnet sighed deeply. *What did I ever see in this man?* 'I believe Gloria is in her bedroom now.'

He placed the pile of mail on the counter. 'Where are the boys?'

'Out somewhere,' she said, opening a package of thawed hamburger meat.

Ben sipped his drink nearby. 'You're getting too skinny, Gar. You need to give up those damn cigarettes,' he said, downing the last of his martini. 'Now for a long hot shower, and I don't want to be disturbed.'

Garnet raised her two fingers to her nose breathing deeply, browning the meat. When she heard the bathroom door close, she lit a cigarette.

George sat down at the table and scooped a heaping spoonful of mashed potatoes, plopping them on his plate, turning to his sister. 'Want some?' he asked, offering to hold the bowl.

'No.'

Dad looked up from his dinner. 'No what,' he said, watching his daughter move what little food was on her plate around.

'No thank you,' she said obstinately, staring down at her plate.

'That's better. I don't want you to forget your manners. It's important that ladies maintain their dignity...' Gloria's fork dropped heavily onto the plate. 'With good manners at all times,' he continued. He sensed something was wrong, suppressing the urge to ask. If it was a girl issue, as her mother suggested, it would be inappropriate to discuss such matters in front of her brothers. He recalled Garnet had been quite moody when he first started dating her, concluding Gloria must be following in her mother's footsteps.

He focused on his sons. 'So Barry, what have you been up to?'

Gloria's eyes quickly shifted from her plate to her brother.

He half-grinned looking up from his plate, averting his sister's hardened gaze. 'Nothing much,' he shrugged.

Gloria said sarcastically, 'That's not true. You've been busy keeping me quiet so we don't disturb Mommy.'

'Is that true, son?' Dad said commendably. 'We don't want to get on the wrong side of Mom.'

He watched his wife place her knife and fork on the edge of her plate, pushing back her chair. 'If you'll excuse me, I'll start the dishes,' she said, placing her plate on the counter, reaching for the cigarettes.

'George, what about you?' Dad said encouragingly.

'Nothin' much.' He looked at his twin sister.

Dad suggested, 'Gloria, maybe you could play with your brother...'

Gloria pushed her chair back against the wall. 'May I be excused?'

'Jesus Gloria, watch the paint. You're lucky you didn't take a hunk out of the drywall,' Dad scolded, leaning over for a closer look. He watched her stomp out of the kitchen, suppressing the urge to ask his sons if they knew what was troubling her.

After dinner, Ben helped Garnet with the dishes. 'Are you sure it's just girl problems and nothing more with Gloria? She seemed downright miserable at supper tonight.'

Garnet stopped scrubbing the frying pan with the SOS pad. 'It is, I'll have a talk with her,' she said conclusively.

'Good,' he said, hanging up the towel and exiting the kitchen.

Garnet removed her rubber glove. Placing her two fingers under her nose, she breathed deeply, detesting the smell of rubber.

Chapter Four

EXOTIC CARIBBEAN MUSIC on hot air wafted into the bedroom. 'Mac must be home,' Ken said, offering to shut the window.

Bea threw back the cover. 'It'll be too damn hot,' she said, pulling up the sheet, adjusting her sheer black baby-doll pyjamas, lying idle in an effort to cool down.

Ken Rowan was a worrier; tonight was no different as he tossed and turned, worrying about how tired he was going to be getting up for work.

At forty-two, the responsibilities of holding a steady job and fatherhood overwhelmed him at times; he was content leaving the child rearing to his wife, Bea, while he assumed the role of breadwinner. Each morning, he made the hour long drive to Bathurst and Yonge to work as a purchasing agent for the city's transit commission. He was a diligent, conscientious employee with a work ethic that didn't go unnoticed by the upper echelon. He was offered a senior management position, but after little consideration, turned it down flatly due to the high level of stress the promotion incurred. At times, his job was stressful enough.

After the Second War ended, Ken and his new war bride, Bea, returned to Toronto to live with his parents in a semi-detached home located off Danforth Ave. His cousin, Muriel, and her parents occupied the other half of the structure; a communal door in the dividing wall gave anyone unlimited access day or night. Needless to say, this arrangement didn't sit well with Bea, who was constantly voicing the lack of privacy. She barely tolerated sharing the kitchen with his parents residing upstairs, not to mention, rather cramped quarters the newlyweds had to endure downstairs. It was no surprise, after the birth of their first child, Gregory, Bea took it upon herself to permanently nail the adjoining door shut, thus ending the constant flow of well-meaning relatives. After the birth of their second child, Theresa, Bea wanted to move, but they couldn't afford a house of their own. Ken took on part time evening work for extra earnings, but the end result was a nervous breakdown. Fortunately, he recovered quickly after terminating his evening usher job at Maple Leaf Gardens.

Shortly after the birth of their second daughter, Tamara, they had saved enough for a down payment on a detached home in the suburbs.

The move prompted Ken's parents to sell their half of the semi and move to a tiny two bedroom house with no indoor plumbing in rural Pickering. Everyone was content with the move, except Theresa. *It's bad enough they live on a dirt road with no street lights, but they have no running water, not to mention a flush toilet.*

Ken tried in vain to convince his daughter that her grandparents were quite content with their new home. 'They have a huge garden to grow their own vegetables...'

Theresa interrupted, 'And a stupid hand-pump well to fetch water. It must be lots of fun traipsing through a foot of snow in winter when all we have to do is turn on the tap.'

At the time, his parents seemed quite happy with their new abode and to his knowledge, content with their decision. 'There's a hand pump at the kitchen sink,' he offered, hoping to end the confrontation.

But Theresa became even more adamant. 'Does it run hot water too? How do they keep themselves clean? They don't even have a bathtub.'

He hadn't given much thought to his parent's living conditions until she broached the subject. 'They have a gas stove to heat the water they need.'

Theresa looked him in the eye. 'Don't you feel any guilt? All you have to do is turn on a hot water tap. How would you feel if you had to boil water every time you needed it? And then there's the toilet. How does a stinky, tiny outhouse, attached to the back porch sound every time you need to go to the bathroom? I bet it's tons of fun in the dead of winter in sub-zero temperatures. Not to mention, the disgusting stench that greets you every time you lift the lid. Imagine sitting on a toilet that never flushes.' Her stomach soured just thinking about it. 'These are your parents, for goodness sake, and they aren't getting any younger. I think it's disgusting. I certainly wouldn't want my parents living like that, especially in this day and age.'

Of all the kids, Theresa caused him the most angst. This lanky, opinionated girl with dark brown-black eyes, able to penetrate deep inside her target, was determined to make the world a better place. In the meantime, he found confrontations of this nature frustrating and very stressful, but assured her he would speak to his folks.

Ken rolled over as the alarm sounded. He had no idea what time he fell asleep, wearily dressing for work.

Theresa stretched languidly in the brightly sunlit bedroom she shared with her sister, Tammy. She listened for her father to leave for work, dressing quietly. She had a busy day ahead collecting bundles of newspapers with the McConnel kids; the last thing she needed was Tammy tagging along. She quickly ate a heaping bowl of Sugar Crisp, brushed her teeth and hopped on her bike.

For Theresa's eighth birthday, her parents had surprised her with a bicycle suitable for an adult. She had no idea what they had been thinking purchasing a bike she could only sit on with one foot anchored to the curb. They tried to convince her not to be too dismayed; she would eventually grow into it.

The Crescent kids had made fun of her attempts to master it, but this only fueled her determination. By the end of the summer, sporting multiple scrapes and bruises, she had mastered the big blue beast, as she fondly referred to it.

Riding past Alexander's house, reminiscing about the time her brother took a major tumble off his bike, she chuckled to herself.

Greg had convinced her to join him for a bike ride after supper, but once they hit the road, it was obvious it wasn't a leisurely brother and sister outing, but a race to see who could circle the Crescent the fastest. Being a young novice, she knew she could never keep up with him riding at her own pace, he quickly sped off. After finally realizing she couldn't keep up, he returned, boasting of his winning. He was about to take off again when his foot slipped off the pedal, instantaneously contorting his face with the pain of crotch colliding with crossbar, sending him tumbling toward the road in front of Alexander's well-kept bungalow. Stooped in pain, he hovered above the pavement cupping his privates, crying out in agony. Theresa wasn't sure if it was the look on his face or his ranting trying to convince her, and the rest of the neighbourhood, his wiener was ruined for life and any hopes of conceiving children had been shot to hell, which induced fits of laughter she couldn't hold back. Complicating things even more, he left his bike in the middle of the road, gingerly walking away, hands cradling his crotch, leaving her to juggle the bikes back home. Needless to say, they hadn't ridden together since.

Theresa rode around the neighbourhood spotting neatly tied bundles of newspapers sitting by the curb within a four block radius. But time was of the essence, the stinky, noisy garbage truck was making the rounds throughout the neighbourhood.

Rebecca swung the door wide, ushering Theresa inside. The messy living room looked like a tornado had decimated the area. Books, magazines, newspapers, articles of clothing, shoes, games, puzzles and dirty dishes were strewn about. She scarcely remembered a time it was in any sort of order. She watched Rebecca wade through the muddle, locating her Black Beauty novel. 'Tommy! Theresa's here,' she yelled, sitting down comfortably on the cluttered chesterfield.

Tommy rounded the corner with his hands in his pockets, shirt randomly buttoned. When he saw Theresa, he ran a hand through his disheveled thick, black hair. 'Hi T, what brings you to my door this early in the day?'

Theresa shook her head, breaking into a wide grin. At thirteen, he was definitely a younger version of his dad; tall, slim build and dark brown eyes. He was serious, funny, intelligent, sensible and trustworthy. The two had been classmates since grade two. 'Did you forget it's garbage day today? The garbage men are picking up bundles of newspapers as we speak.'

He slapped his forehead. 'Darn, I forgot. Janice, come quick.'

Janice, a year younger, appeared at his side. 'You summoned me?'

'Yeah, we need to collect newspapers today. You up for it?'

'I just have to get my shoes,' she said, moving quickly toward an odd conglomeration of objects piled beside the chesterfield.

Theresa chuckled, watching Janice dodge the clutter to retrieve her running shoes. One thing about the McConnel clan, they may live in total disarray, but they are the classic example of how to function efficiently in organized chaos.

The threesome dragged wagons around the neighbourhood loading them to capacity with bundled *Telegram* newspapers. Returning to McConnel's carport, they spent the remainder of the morning meticulously scouring every page of each section, searching for of the coveted Fun Cheques. The task was both tedious (the cheques were never in the same section twice) yet rewarding.

Tommy smiled after neatly cutting out a cheque. 'We managed to locate 96 cheques this time round. That's 32 each; for sure our biggest haul to date.' He gazed around the paper strewn carport. 'Now all we have to do is re-bundle them, hopefully before the garbage truck returns.'

They worked feverously completing the task as the truck rounded the corner.

'Must be Tely Fun cheque time,' the garbage man said, picking up a couple of bundles.

Tommy volunteered in an effort to lessen the chore. Within minutes, the papers were collected and compacted in the back of the truck. The garbage man expressed his appreciation hopping up on the back ledge of the truck. 'See you next week.'

Theresa heard her mom calling her for lunch. They made a pact to meet after for a game of kickball. She held the Fun Cheques tightly, barely able to contain her excitement walking home. It was the first summer she was allowed to go to the CNE with friends; she could hardly wait.

'Hello love,' Mom said. Theresa slid between her mother and the Weston's Bread delivery man. 'Just two loaves of bread today, thanks love.' (Mom called everyone love, including the breadman.)

Theresa stood by watching him pull two fresh loaves of white bread from a large metal basket filled with a selection of butter tarts, cupcakes, cookies and other baked goods. Her mouth watered, but she knew better than to make a request. '*I can do my own baking*' was Mom's standard reply. Still, it would be nice to have the odd treat once in a while. She was sure her classmate, Steven Grant, the breadman's son, would have all the baked goods he could possibly eat.

After a quick lunch, Theresa ran over to Tommy's and found him sitting on the front step waiting for her. 'I've got something to show you that is totally amazing. This way,' he said, with a bowing gesture.

'Tada.' He pointed at a long, wide, dark olive, black spotted oval object spanning the wood panelled basement wall.

Theresa stared wide-eyed trying to figure out what it was; Tommy encouraged her to take a guess.

She inched closer. 'It looks like a huge snakeskin.' She had found a garter snakeskin in a grassy field last summer. She reached out, touching the huge specimen.

'Well done, T,' he said, proceeding to tell her how it ended up on the basement wall. 'Mac arrived home yesterday; needless to say, supper was quite entertaining with all his adventure stories. When I asked if he brought souvenirs, he usually does, it would be delivered at eight this morning. By the way, you had just missed it earlier on. So this huge wooden crate arrives; took two guys to bring it into the house and down into the basement,' he said, pointing to the container. 'Mac left us kids to wrestle it open with a crowbar, encouraging the younger ones to help drag it out. Susan was a bit squeamish, but Rebecca just kept pulling the tightly rolled skin; we all pitched in to unwind it while Mac filled in the details.

'The group had been walking beside the Amazon River when their guide, Luiz, spotted an almost thirty foot anaconda. Casually, Luiz asked if any of the group had ever thought about wrestling one. It was no surprise Dad was first to volunteer, followed by his buddy Doug. It didn't take long for the others join in. Can you imagine wrestling a huge snake in the all that muck? A difficult challenge to say the least; it took the strength of ten very strong men to keep the snake steady enough for Luiz and his assistant Gomes to cut off the head then skin it. Dad was first to claim the prize, mainly because none of the others wanted an anaconda snakeskin. And there it is,' he smiled, staring admiringly at the newly mounted specimen.

Theresa decided then and there, the McConnel kids had the best dad in the world. 'Has anyone else seen it?'

'Nope, you're the first,' Tommy smiled. She doubted she'd be the last. The McConnel house was a welcoming gathering place for any curious kid in the neighbourhood interested in Mac's amazing adventures. Smiling enviously, Theresa secretly wished Mac was her dad.

The rest of the afternoon Janice, Tommy and Theresa planned their upcoming day at the Canadian National Exhibition.

'We'll get a huge discount on all our ride tickets,' Janice said, waving her stack of fun cheques. 'And there's still a few more garbage days left before the grand opening. Hopefully, we can increase the wad.'

Chapter Five

GLORIA SAT ON the edge of her parent's bed watching her dad pack his suitcase. He had been home for nearly a week, but once again had to leave on business. 'I wish you didn't have to go away to work all the time,' she said, eyes full of tears. 'Why can't you be like other dads and work closer to home?'

Her father looked up from his packing. 'I wish I could, but unfortunately travelling is part of my job,' he said, watching tears spill down her cheeks. 'Hey, what's this all about?' Since his arrival, other than sleeping, she had been a constant at his side. He sat down on the bed, hugging her. 'I don't like to see my little girl upset. I'll be home before you know it.'

'I don't want you to go, Daddy,' she cried, holding him tightly.

'I promise I will be back as soon as I can. In the meantime, you've got Mommy, your twin George and big brother Barry.' He felt her body tense when he mentioned Barry. 'Gloria, is something going on I should know about?'

Gloria sat back thinking of her mother's condition and how she had to be good and not upset her. 'The condition that Mom has, what is it?'

Ben stood with a furrowed brow pondering what to say. She had had a mental breakdown many years ago, before they had met, involving a neighbourhood boy.

'I'm not sure how to explain it to you. Something traumatic happened when she was your age and she had a nervous breakdown...'

'Please can I go with you,' she pleaded.

He was thankful she interrupted; he really wasn't in the mood to talk about Garnet's past, especially with his daughter. It was getting late and he should have left much earlier. 'I'm afraid not. Travelling the road with a young girl isn't safe. You're better off here with your family. I have to make so many calls every day; I wouldn't be able to spend any time with you. It just isn't feasible.' He glanced at his watch. 'I'm already late. I wanted to be out of here by nine at the latest.' He kissed the top of her head with a promise to be home soon.

Gloria felt tears stinging her eyes watching him exit the bedroom. She quickly ran to her room, jimmying a chair tightly under the doorknob.

Ben looked toward the smoke filled living room listening to Garnet chastise herself for being so careless. *Damn cigarettes burned a hole in my good chair.*

'Gar, I'm leaving now,' he said, watching her scrawny fingers pick at the hole. After a few moments she turned toward him, her face void of any expression when he pecked her cheek. 'Take care of our baby girl. There's something not right. Are you sure there's nothing more than girl problems?'

Garnet raised her two fingers to her nose, breathing deeply. 'Do you still think I'm beautiful? There was a time you thought I was the most beautiful girl you had ever met.'

Ben was momentarily stunned by her response. He had never thought of her as beautiful, more of a lost soul in need of saving. He had first met her through a friend. At the time, he had been drawn to her quiet, shy self. He had asked her for a date; she was reluctant at first, but after a few tries they started dating and married the following year. 'Can we talk about this another time? I'm really running late. Bid good-bye to the boys for me and *please* keep an eye on Gloria.'

Garnet smirked wickedly. *Brian thinks I'm beautiful.*

When Theresa entered the kitchen, it was no surprise her mother, an avid reader, had her nose in a book with a cigarette burning nearby. 'Morning love,' she said, looking up from her novel. 'How are you this morning?'

'Morning, fine thanks,' she smiled, remembering her manners. It was probably the most important criteria Bea had instilled in her kids. *Remember your manners and you'll go places.* She sat down and poured a heaping bowl of Sugar Crisp.

Mom closed her book, pouring another cup of hot tea. 'Your Aunt Audrey is coming over later today. Your father and I have a wedding to attend this evening.'

Theresa looked up from her bowl. 'Who's getting married?'

'One of your dad's co-workers will be tying the knot today at five.'

She questioned why her aunt was coming to look after them. 'I'll be thirteen in August. Where's Greg going to be? He's quite capable of taking charge.'

Bea side-glanced her daughter, 'You give your brother more credit than I do. I never know when, or if, he'll be home; I can't depend on him. Besides, Aunt Audrey jumped at the chance to visit and prepare supper for you and Tammy.'

Theresa looked up from her cereal. 'I could do it, Mom. Remember when you worked at Reitman's last year? I was the one who came home every night after school to make supper.'

'I'm sure you can, love, but I'd feel better with my sister here to keep an eye on your sister. This way, you can come and go as you please.'

'Any idea what's she's making for supper?'

'She's, the cat's meow,' Mom said, lifting her head high. 'Auntie will be preparing your favourite, hot dogs and French fries.'

Theresa's eyes lit up. Friday night was usually fish and chips. 'Can I still go to Bellevue Pool with Judy at three?'

'I don't see why not, as long as you're back by five for supper. I'll tell Aunt Audrey where you will be.'

It's going to be a good day after all, she thought, hoisting her bowl to her lips.

Judy knocked on the screen door just before three. Theresa grabbed her towel running for the door. 'Have you got your bathing suit on?'

'Yeah, under my shorts and top,' Judy smiled, flashing the strap.

'Good, it gives us more time to swim not having to change first.'

They had been best friends since Theresa moved to the Crescent seven years ago. Judy had been blessed with carrot-coloured hair she hated, tons of freckles and a weak bladder; often peeing her pants if she laughed too hard. Theresa would stop making her laugh whenever Judy began crossing her legs in an effort to stop the flow of urine. But often it was too late with Judy having to run home and change.

On the way to the pool, Theresa spoke about a funny show she had seen on TV. Judy laughed so hard, the fidgeting and leg crossing couldn't stop her pee. With her face as red as her hair, she wanted to go home and change.

'Why? You're wearing your bathing suit and it's going to get wet anyway.'

She twirled around. 'Can you see any wet spots on my white shorts?'

'No. Besides, we still have a couple blocks to go; you'll be dry by then.'

On sunny, hot days, it was no surprise the pool was very crowded. They had to search for a vacant grassy area. 'This place is packed,' Theresa said, scanning faces to see if she knew anybody.

Judy pointed to a small grassy area. Moving quickly in single file they claimed it, spreading their towels wide.

'Maybe we should go to the change rooms to get undressed,' Judy said, sensing all eyes watching.

Therese undid her cotton blouse revealing a padded fuchsia, black striped bathing suit top. The thick padding gave the illusion of small breasts on her otherwise flat chest. 'Why bother? You've got your bathing suit on already.'

Voicing her opposition, Judy felt odd undressing in front of strangers.

Theresa chucked, 'I'm sure no one is watching,' she said, dropping her shorts revealing the matching pink bottom of her two-piece suit. Her mom had sewn elastic around the legs because her thighs were too skinny.

Judy quickly removed her clothes, lying down on her towel. They chatted until it got too hot, scurrying off to the pool to cool themselves. The pool was so crowded swimming was not an option; they jumped in and out, running back to their towels.

Theresa rolled over onto her stomach resting her chin on folded arms, thoroughly enjoying the hot sun drying her back.

Judy lay on her back gazing up at the cloudless blue sky. 'When I grow up, I want to marry a handsome man who will work hard to buy me all the things I desire. I want to have lots of kids too. I don't want to go to work when I finish school,' she sighed, thinking of her mom getting up very early each day to travel downtown to work in an office; her father quit his teaching job years ago, staying home to take care of household chores.

Angela Patterson, a short, fiery redhead was born with a stunted neck; her head slanted permanently to the left. Surprisingly, her physical disability seemed to strengthen her determination. Her mother was friendly and outgoing, whereas, her dad, Allan, chose the introverted life. The tall, skinny, prematurely grey, laid-back chain smoker preferred life behind closed doors. Judy often wondered if his rotten front teeth, coupled with his refusal to visit the dentist had anything to do with his lifestyle choice. At any rate, Angie was content being the breadwinner.

Theresa was surprised Judy didn't want to work after school. 'Personally, I think it would be great to have a job, earning my own money. I want to be a teacher when I grow up.'

Judy turned to face her. 'Yuk! I'd never be a teacher. All those bratty kids every day…'

'And you want lots of your own?' she interrupted.

She turned back. 'That's different, of course. My husband will buy me a big house with lots of bedrooms to send them to.'

Theresa chuckled, turning her attention back toward the pool. Feeling content and relaxed she closed her eyes for a few moments. When she opened them, the landscape had changed. A goofy-grinning older man was lying horizontally a few yards away blocking her view of the pool; his lecherous smirk made her skin crawl. Curiously, her eyes followed the gentle nudging of his head.

Theresa gasped loudly burying her head into her arms, breathing raggedly; the image of his fingers manipulating his exposed penis under the hem of his swim trunks and the lecherous grin seared permanently in her mind. 'Oh my god Judy!'

Sleepily, she rolled over to face her. 'What?'

'There's an ugly old man lying in the grass playing with his dick!' she whispered hysterically.

'What?'

'There's some guy playing with his dick nearby!'

Judy sat up and looked around. 'Are you sure?'

'Yes, I'm sure! I saw it with my own eyes. He's about three yards in front of me on the grass.'

'What colour is his towel?'

'Oh for Christ sake! He doesn't have a towel. He's lying on the grass.'

Judy craned her neck. 'Well I can't see him.'

Theresa slowly raised her head, immediately spotting the pervert. 'Oh god, he's still there.' She quickly stood up, grabbed her things and ran off; the sneaky pervert inconspicuously disappeared into the crowd.

Theresa ran halfway home with Judy running breathlessly behind. 'You could have waited,' she huffed, finally catching up. 'What's the matter with you?'

Theresa, holding back tears, picked up her pace. 'I don't want to talk about it.'

Judy grabbed her arm. 'Does it have anything to do with that man?'

She yanked her arm away. 'Of course it does! He was playing with his goddamn dick and I had the good fortune of watching him do it.'

A puzzled look crossed her face. 'I wouldn't say you were fortunate.'

'Oh for crying out loud, I'm being sarcastic. It was absolutely horrible! I wanted you to see it too, so I'm not the only one feeling like I could puke.'

Judy stared blankly trying to imagine what it would be like, concluding it would be disgusting. 'I'm glad I didn't see him.'

'I feel sick,' Theresa said, walking faster.

Judy said, 'I've never seen a man's dick before.'

'It was disgusting. It looked like a one-eyed over-boiled wiener.'

Judy's faced soured walking quickly beside her best friend.

Theresa walked quietly to her room. Feeling nauseated, she sat on her bed with the image of the disgusting man touching himself deeply embedded in her mind, haunting her for the rest of her life.

Aunt Audrey knocked gently on the door. 'Theresa, are you in there?'

She jumped off the bed. 'Yes Auntie, I'm just changing out of my wet suit.'

'I will leave you to it then, dear. Don't forget to hang it on the clothesline.'

Theresa sat down to supper, feeling ill staring at the contents on her plate.

Tammy smacked her lips. 'Mmmm hotdogs and fries, my most favourite supper of all. Thanks Auntie.'

'You're welcome,' she smiled, sitting down in Mom's chair. 'Your brother won't be joining us. He's dining at Jim's tonight. Would you like some mustard and relish, Theresa?'

She swallowed hard. 'No thank you.'

Her aunt smiled warmly, 'Aren't you hungry, dear?'

She felt her face burn and stomach churn. 'I think I got too much sun this afternoon at the pool. I don't feel like eating…'

'More for me,' Tammy said, reaching for the hot dog, sending the wiener cascading into her sister's lap.

'Ahhh!' Theresa gasped, jumping up, running out of the kitchen.

Tammy scooted under the table, retrieved the wiener, stuffing it in her mouth. 'Delicious,' she said, biting off the end.

Aunt Audrey proceeded to discipline her rudeness. 'If Theresa comes back, I'll cook her another wiener. 'Do you know if something is bothering her?'

Tammy continued to cut up the rest of the wiener. 'She's grumpy about something. I always know when something is up because she won't let me in the bedroom.'

Aunt Audrey sighed. 'Maybe she's not feeling well. It's quite unusual for her to miss her favourite supper.'

Theresa buried her head in the pillow muffling her cries. What happened today was way worse than Daniel's invite into his tent last summer to play a game of doctor. *I will be the doctor, you can be the nurse. First, we need to take off our clothes.* She had told him in no uncertain terms she was having no part of his stupid game. He kissed her lips, but she still wanted no part of disrobing. *Can't we play doctor with our clothes on?* But Daniel insisted you can't have a game of doctor fully dressed. After a few more unconvincing attempts he said frankly, *I'll show you mine, if you show me yours.* She felt her stomach knot, shoving him hard and running out of the tent. He never suggested the game again.

Today, she was able to run away, but not from the searing image cemented in her mind. She wondered if she had done something to encourage the creep, wishing now she had listened to Judy and used the change rooms.

Theresa ran a hot bath, scrubbing herself vigorously, but still felt dirty. After drying off, she climbed into bed, falling into a deep, restless sleep.

Audrey looked up from her novel when she heard the door. 'How was the wedding? You both look like you've had a good time,' she smiled, closing her book.

'It was lovely. Short and sweet,' Bea smiled, asking after the kids.

'Gregory arrived home a few minutes ago. He had supper at Jim's. And a reluctant Tammy went to bed about an hour ago. Theresa went to bed rather early. She may have gotten too much sun at the pool today and didn't want supper.'

Bea stepped out of her high heels. 'That's better,' she said, storing them neatly in the hall cupboard. 'That's unusual for Theresa to miss supper, especially when it comes to hot dogs and fries.'

'I tried to talk to her, but as I said, she retired early. I'll be on my way now.'

Bea thanked her with a quick hug, locking the door behind her. Weddings tend to enhance her more amorous feelings; reaching for Ken's hand she led him willingly down the hall.

Garnet quickly butted out her cigarette, the annoying knock on the front door growing more intense. 'Oh it's you,' she said, opening it a crack. 'You've got quite the knock there, Dana. I'm assuming you're here for Gloria.'

Dana stood near the doorway. 'Yes, Mrs. Murray. Can she come out?'

'It's not raining,' she said, breaking into a wide yellow grin. 'I don't see why not. In fact, I think it's just what my Gloria needs. That girl spends far too much time in her room.' She moved to the bottom of the stairs. 'Gloria.' She waited for a response. 'Gloria, there's someone here to see you. Maybe you should head upstairs and ask her yourself.' Garnet moved quickly to her chair as the intro to the Price is Right filled the living room.

Dana moved past the boy's closed door. Glancing into the master bedroom, she noticed an ashtray teeming with cigarette butts on the bedside table. Thankful her mom didn't smoke, she knocked on Gloria's door.

Gloria sat up with a start. 'Go away!'

Dana was just about to reply when Barry's door flew open. 'What are doing?'

She jumped at the brusque sound of his voice. 'I was just seeing if Gloria could come out and...'

He cut her off midsentence. 'I don't think she wants to go outside,' he said authoritatively. 'I was planning on spending some time with her this morning.'

Dana felt uncomfortable with his peculiar tone, not to mention, the creepy look on his face. 'I asked your mom and she said it was okay. Maybe we should let Gloria decide.' She knocked again. 'It's me, Dana...'

The door flew open; Gloria grabbed her arm pulling her into the room, jimmying the chair under the doorknob.

Barry tried the door. 'Is everything okay in there?'

Gloria squeezed her eyes shut, covering her ears. 'I hate his goddamn guts.'

Dana was taken aback by her best friend's hatred of her brother. She had never felt that way about Daniel, on the contrary, loved her brother very much.

'Going somewhere?' Barry said, gripping Gloria's arm tightly as she passed by. 'Have fun. I'll see you later,' he smiled, releasing her arm.

Mrs. Murray sat rigid in her chair, engulfed in a thick cloud of smoke watching the loud television. Dana yelled, 'Aren't you going to say good-bye to your mom?'

'No. She wouldn't miss me anyway,' she said, running out the door.

George woke up to the slamming of the bedroom door. He eyed his brother moving quickly toward his bed. 'Where's Gloria?'

'Out,' Barry replied gruffly.

He turned away from his brother. 'Good. I hope she's having some fun for a change.'

Garnet watched the two girls quickly run off down the road, disappearing around the bend. Gloria rarely went outside. She was pleased Dana had called on her daughter. *The sunshine will do her good.* The thought triggered memories of the last time her best friend, Roxanne, called on her. *Roxanne is here to see you, Garnet. You need to go outside. The sunshine will do you good* her mother had said, shuffling her out the door.

Garnet hadn't seen Roxanne or Brian, for that matter, since he forced himself on her a few weeks ago. As they walked toward the bridge over the creek in Willow Martin Park, Garnet was anxious to tell her about Brian, but first she asked if she had seen him around. *I see Brian all the time. He's dating my best friend, Cathy.* The pain of knowing Brian had a new girlfriend *and* Roxanne had a new best friend had torn her apart. Garnet proceeded to tell her about Brian's visit. He kissed me and thinks I'm the most beautiful girl he's ever seen.

Staring out the window, Garnet inhaled her two fingers vividly remembering the look on Roxanne's face; her face burned, as it had then. She would never forget the look on her best friend's face when she told her what Brian had done or Roxanne's reply. *I thought it was just a dirty rumor. I came to your defense, Garnet; my best friend would never do anything like that, even when the kids labelled you a slut I stood steadfast.* She had tried reasoning with her best friend. I'm not a slut, you have to believe me. Brian said it was okay, it's was what good girls do. He told me I'm the most beautiful girl he has ever seen.

Sitting down in her chair, Garnet's hand shook uncontrollably lighting a cigarette, inhaling deeply, recalling vividly the disgusted look on her best friend's face and the anguishing pain she had felt watching her run away.

Gloria, placing her hands on her knees to catch her breath, waited for Dana to catch up.

'What the heck is going on?' Dana gasped, hugging the wooden post sporting a metal caution sign.

'Come on,' Gloria said, grabbing her arm, forcing her to keep up.

The two friends sat down on a large grey rock beside the creek behind the school breathing deeply, watching the calming, soothing water flow. Gloria, feeling warm sunshine on her face, felt peaceful sitting by the water with her best friend, but it wouldn't last.

'Now will you please tell me what's going on?' Dana said, turning to face her.

'Why did we have to run all the way to the school? I don't even run that fast when it's on,' she said matter-of-factly.

Gloria felt her inner peace fade to angst. Recklessly, she ripped a leaf off a milkweed plant, vigorously tearing it into pieces, tossing them into the water. She watched pieces of leaf drift downstream with the exception of a rather insignificant tiny piece held captive against a large slimy grey rock. With an eye on the tiny specimen she said, 'I needed to get away from Barry. Running fast makes me forget.'

'Forget what?'

She turned abruptly, 'does Daniel ever do things to your privates?'

Dana felt her insides somersault wondering if she had heard her best friend correctly. 'What are you saying?'

Gloria spoke as it was an everyday occurrence between a brother and sister. 'Like, you know, touch your privates with his.'

42

Dana looked skyward, 'Are you serious?' she said, sensing there was no way she could be making this up.

Gloria shrugged. 'Why of course.'

Dana grabbed her arm. 'This is so sick! My brother has never touched my private parts and would *never*. He hasn't even seen me bare and naked.'

Gloria, feeling a sense of betrayal, yanked her arm away. 'Don't you ever grab my arm like that again,' she said threateningly.

Dana, on the verge of hysterics said, 'I'm sorry, it's just I'm so upset, I want to shake some sense into you. This is not right at all. It's so sick.'

Tears flowed down Gloria's cheeks. 'Shaking me probably wouldn't do any good anyway,' she said, describing her ordeal in minute detail. 'Barry told me it's what all good girls do.' She paused briefly watching the small piece of leaf continue its struggle to get away from the rock, seemingly holding it in place. 'The worst is when he puts his private part in mine.'

Dana jumped to her feet. 'Oh my god! Didn't you scream? Didn't you tell your mother?' she cried, feeling sick to her stomach.

Gloria thought of her recent attempt to tell her mother. *You need a bath and then you'll feel better.* She stared straight ahead. 'I can't tell my mom because of her condition.'

'Her condition, what condition?'

'She has a nervous condition; she's not allowed to get upset, so I can't talk to her about it.'

Dana threw back her head. 'I still can't believe you don't scream when Barry comes near you.'

'I try, but if I do he just puts his hand over my mouth,' she said, drawing a deep breath, sensing the suffocating hold. 'He said I have to be real quiet so I don't upset Mother because of her condition.' She turned her attention back to the large rock harbouring the small piece of leaf.

Dana paced back and forth like a caged animal. 'This is not right. It's all so very wrong. You need to tell somebody who can help you immediately. But most of all, you need to get out of that house and away from your sicko brother.' She stopped in her tracks. 'What about your dad?' Dana thought about how lucky she was; she could talk to her father about anything. 'You need to tell him. He will help you.'

Gloria had thought about telling him this morning watching him pack, pleading with him to take her along. 'He's away. He's always away because of his job.' *I'll be back soon.* She looked forlornly into the distance. 'I don't know when he'll be back. He doesn't like to talk about girl stuff and tells me to talk to my mother because she's the expert on all this stuff.'

Dana sat down beside her. 'This is much more than girlie stuff,' she said emphatically. 'Your brother is very sick and needs help. What he does to you is totally wrong. You must go to your mother and tell her immediately what's been…'

Gloria interrupted. 'Talking to my mother is out of the question. 'I hate her goddamn guts.'

'You don't mean that…'

'Yes I do,' she hissed. 'I hate her with a passion. I hate Barry's guts too.' Her shoulders heaved, sobbing uncontrollably into her cupped hands. 'I didn't do anything wrong. I don't understand why this is happening to me. I'm so scared. I don't know what to do.'

Dana hugged her tightly. 'We are going to get to the bottom of this, I promise.'

Gloria clenched her eyes shut, halting the flow of tears. When she opened them, the small piece of leaf broke free, floating swiftly downstream.

Chapter Six

THE ROYAL LEPAGE sign cast a warped shadow of itself in the middle of the lawn at number 45. In the first light of day, an agent had quietly driven in and out of the Crescent, staking a claim on Donaldson's front lawn. The perpetrator was long gone when Ken Rowan left for work at 7:30. Backing out of his driveway he was curious, wondering when the sign had been posted, but more so, why the Donaldson's were moving away.

Theresa sat down across from Gregory watching Mom mix up pancake batter for Tammy's breakfast.

Greg looked up from his cereal. 'It looks like I'll be losing a friend.'

Theresa looked up from her bowl of Sugar Crisp. 'What's that supposed to mean?'

'There's a 'for sale' sign on Donaldson's lawn,' Tammy said, running into the kitchen.

Theresa wondered if her sister ever walked. She was sure it wasn't there last night when she came in at 8:30.

Greg said, 'Knowing the real estate, someone sneaked in when everyone was sleeping. They tend to be a crooked bunch.' He lifted the bowl to his lips downing the remaining milk. 'It probably has something to do with Mrs. Donaldson's death. Ever since she kicked, the house has never been in order. The inside is a regular pig pen.'

Mom stopped stirring the batter. 'You mean worse than your room?'

'Ha, ha, my room is neat and tidy in comparison. Gotta run. I'm helping Ralph with the appliance deliveries today.'

Mom said in a suspicious tone, 'I hope he's paying you well. You seem to be helping him out a lot these days.'

'He pays me well,' Greg smiled, placing his bowl on the counter, pecking her cheek.

'You need to brush your teeth before you go, Son. The dental bills are on the rise in this house,' she huffed, side-glancing her eldest daughter.

Theresa's insatiable sweet tooth and lack of dental hygiene were taking a toll on her pearly whites. Lately, every trip to the dentist warranted one or two fillings and a promise on her part to do a better cleaning job. She spent all her allowance on sugary treats. During school, Brad, her ever obliging classmate, would return from lunch with boxes of wine gums and jellies that he willingly shared.

After breakfast, Theresa spent more time brushing her teeth before heading outside. She noticed William and Michael standing on their front lawn in the bright sunshine, crossing the street to join them. 'It looks like you're going to lose your next door neighbours,' she said disappointedly.

William was the first to speak. 'No loss. Their father is seldom home to look after the boys anyway. Basically, they've been on their own since Mrs. D died.'

Theresa squinted. 'He's an engineer with the railroad, keeping him away for long periods, travelling the mainline back and forth across the country.'

William turned to face her. 'Which leaves Ronald in charge, not the best option,' he said, rolling his blue eyes.

Michael playfully shoved his older brother. 'Ever since Mrs. Donaldson died, that house hasn't been the same,' he concluded, instigating a game of chase around the for sale sign.

William, in an effort to escape his younger brother, hoisted himself onto the hood of their dark green four-door Chevrolet Impala parked outside the carport and discovered too late it wasn't a good idea when his bare legs touched the hot metal, sending him tumbling toward the driveway, slamming his left arm into the pavement.

Theresa witnessed the fall, running toward William lying on the driveway hugging his arm, crying out in agony.

His dad, hearing his son's cries, came running out of the house, glancing harshly at Theresa. 'Where does it hurt, son?'

'My arm, I think it's broken,' William said tearfully.

Gingerly, Mr. Johnson lifted him into the backseat of the car stating pointedly, 'whenever anything bad happens around here, it seems there's always a rotten Rowan kid nearby.'

Theresa, feeling the guilt for something she had no part of, walked quickly across Donaldson's lawn, knocking on the door.

Timothy, clad in Superman pyjamas, swung the door open wide. He stared at Theresa with a blank look on his face.

'Who's at the door?' a voice boomed from within.

'It's only Theresa,' he yelled back.'

Ronald appeared instantly. 'I bet you want to know why we're moving,' he smirked, but his troubled green eyes portrayed a different tale. 'I'd ask you in but the old man's got company, if you know what I mean.'

She had no idea what he meant as Ronald promised to be out shortly and said to meet him in front of Daniel's house.

It was going to be scorcher, Theresa thought sitting down on the cool grass in front of Daniel's. After a few minutes, Daniel and Dana joined her at the curb. 'Did you notice the for sale sign on Ronald's front lawn?'

Daniel met her gaze. 'What are you talking about? Ron's my best friend. Don't you think I'd be the first person he'd tell if he was moving?'

Theresa hugged her knees to her chest. 'See for yourself.'

In a flash, Daniel sprang to his feet, with Dana close behind. Ronald had been his best friend since he moved onto the Crescent ten years ago. With only a month separating their birthdays, they were more like brothers, remaining a constant in each other's lives throughout the years.

Ronald hurried his brother to get dressed, but Tim was still buttoning his shirt walking toward the group settled on the curb in front of Daniel's house.

Ronald sat down beside his best friend, Timothy to his right. 'We are moving. I'm sure most of the neighbours know it by now. It's my old man; wants to make a fresh start.' He lowered his head scraping at the dirt under his fingernails. 'Things have been so different since our mother died,' he said sadly, wiping a line of black crud on his grubby shorts.

They sat silently remembering where they were when they had heard the news of her death.

Daniel got the first call from Ronald. *My mom died last night. God took her home to heaven to be with Him.* It was the one and only time his best friend had broken down and cried his heart out.

Shortly before Mrs. Donaldson's death, Theresa had asked her mom why she was always taking meals over to the Donaldson's. *Mrs. Donaldson is very sick. She has a disease; it's very doubtful she will ever get better.* Two weeks later, Mrs. Donaldson died. Theresa had felt overwhelming sorrow for Tim and Ronald losing their mom at such a young age. She couldn't imagine what life would be like without a mother.

When Daniel broke the news to Dana, she cried and cried. She too couldn't imagine a life without her mother.

Ronald broke the silence. 'The old man has a new girlfriend.'

'My dad says we need a new mom to take care of things that women take care of that men don't,' Timothy added.

'Yeah, she's our new stepmother,' Ronald said indignantly. 'Instant family,' he sighed, lying back on the grass.

Daniel's biggest concern was where they were moving to.

'The old man said somewhere near Ottawa, because of *her* job.'

'Can't she work around here?' Dana said.

Ronald sat up, spitting out the blade of grass he'd been gnawing on. 'That's what I said. But she's got some high ranking position with the government.'

Daniel sighed deeply. Ottawa was four hours away, far enough that he would seldom see his best friend and phone calls would be too costly, especially since they were used to talking daily. 'This sucks man.'

'You're telling me. It's like he has no regard for his kids, just the new gal he wants to marry.'

'Maybe your house won't sell,' Theresa said, feeling the loss. Ronald was more like an older brother to her than Gregory.

For a brief moment everyone seemed hopeful.

Ronald was not so hopeful. 'Already there are five families coming to see it today. The Crescent is a great street to raise kids; nice and quiet, close to schools, a bus stop five minutes away, grocery stores nearby and so on. It'll sell pretty quickly I'm sure.'

Dana thought of her best friend, Gloria. She hadn't seen her since she spilled her guts at the creek, wondering if she had spoken to her mother. In the meantime, she had spoken to Daniel about Gloria's accusations and was totally shocked by his response. *Gloria is a drama queen. She's George's twin, who is not the swiftest wiener in the package and maybe she has a bit of that too. I know Barry, and he would never do anything like that.* She spotted Mr. Murray's car parked just outside the carport. Content with the knowledge he'd look after Gloria, she decided not to visit her today. She'd had enough upset for one day.

Ronald jumped up with Timothy, his constant shadow, following close behind. 'We've got to go. Our new stepmother is cleaning the house and we have to help. Our mother used to do it all on her own, but this one's more liberated.'

Without a word, Daniel ran off in the opposite direction.

'Your brother is really upset,' Theresa said, as he disappeared out of sight.

'Yeah, they've been best friends for as long as I can remember.'

Theresa spotted the Johnson's car pulling into the driveway. 'I'm off too. I want to see how William is doing. He may have a broken arm.'

Anne Smythe stood at the dining room window tightening the belt of her housecoat. She ran her hands through her long black wavy hair, in dire need of a wash. She was about to head to the shower when she noticed one of the Johnson kids gingerly exiting the car.

'Glenn, come quick. Is that a cast on William's left arm?'

'Looks like it,' he said, pondering what happened.

Anne watched his mom gingerly walk him up the driveway. 'Renee is always doting on that kid, clearly her favourite. For goodness sake, it's just a broken arm.' She let out a loud tut, turning away. 'I'm going to have a shower and wash my dirty mop,' she said, scratching her head. 'Your dad is coming home tonight. Can you tidy up, please? It'll be all I can do to clean myself up. I didn't sleep very well again last night.'

Glenn called Jimmy up from the basement to help, protesting all the way.

'Why do we always have to do the damn cleaning?' Jimmy said, tossing toys into a beat up old laundry basket. 'Other kids don't have to do this stuff.'

Glenn ignored his continual ranting, moving pill bottles to the chesterfield, dusting the coffee table, unaware of Katherine sneaking up behind.

'Rattle, rattle,' she said, shaking a bottle in each hand, trying to remove the lids.

Glenn quickly scooped them out of her hands. 'No touching,' he said. 'These are Mommy's pills.'

'Me want candy,' she said, snatching them from the chester-field, shaking them defiantly. 'Me want, me want,' she said rhythmically.

Glenn was shocked by how fast she retrieved the bottles, more so, by her determination to remove the lids. He had a heck of a time prying them from her little hands.

'Me want candy!' she protested, banging her hands on the chesterfield.

Patiently, he explained that pills were not candy, and she was not to touch them, placing them on top of the oak hutch, out of harm's way.

Michael waved, running toward Theresa standing at the bottom of the driveway. 'Will broke his arm in two places,' he said, running a hand through his thick blond hair. His expressive sky blue eyes widened. 'I was first to sign the cast that he'll have to wear for at least six weeks,' he smiled, revealing a mouthful of straight white teeth.

'He'll be going back to school in September with it on,' Theresa added.

'Yup, and that's going to be a problem, he's left handed. He's going to have to become pretty creative when it comes to everyday stuff, not to mention school work.'

They both turned anticipating William's approach. Theresa asked if his arm hurt.

'Not really. Now that the cast is on, I can't move it.' William, like his father, Ian, tended to be more serious, whereas Michael was outgoing and bubbly like his mom, Renee. William's hair was darker than his brother's and he wore braces on his teeth. He had a huge dimple on his right cheek that came and went with a smile, which was seldom. 'Would you like to sign my cast?' He handed her a pen.

Theresa printed her message on the bottom of the cast then walked away.

'What does it say, Mikey?'

'Not guilty this time, Mr. J, Theresa, 'R' is for Rowan, in case you forgot.'

William scrunched his face. 'I wonder what that means.'

Michael smiled knowingly. 'I'm pretty sure it's a tart message for our name-calling Dad.'

Robert Smythe parked his car in the carport and locked it. It was good to be home, if only for the weekend. Though he considered himself an expert in the pharmaceutical drugs he was commissioned to sell across Canada, often for weeks at a time, the downside was very little time at home with his family.

It was a beautiful summer afternoon; he wondered why the kids weren't outside in the backyard enjoying it. He spotted some toys partially hidden in the tall grass; the plywood sandbox cover tilted to one side of the box. *Why was the yard so unkempt?* He made a mental note to get the boys to cut the grass and tidy it up. The house was quiet when he opened the screen door, announcing his arrival.

'Da, Da,' Rose said, running headfirst into his crotch. He picked up his youngest daughter. 'How are you doing?' he smiled.

It didn't take long for the others to congregate around him, each vying for his attention. He put Rose down, but she continued to hold on tightly to his leg. He scooped Katherine into his arms, listening intently while the older kids took turns filling him in on what's been going on in his absence. It was total bedlam, but he enjoyed his children very much.

He stood Katherine beside his black sample case, turning his attention toward Jimmy. 'How are you, Son?'

He shrugged, 'okay, I guess.'

'Still working on your scientific experiments in the basement? Hopefully you're not going to blow the place up,' he chuckled. 'You seem down in the dumps, Jimmy. Is something troubling you?'

He fought the urge to tell his father what really goes on in his absence, deciding now was not the time; he had turned his attention to Katherine wrestling with the case, trying to open it.

'No Katy. Don't touch. They are all the samples Daddy has to cart around,' he said, pulling her away. Once again, she charged toward it. 'Me want candy,' she whined, tugging the handle.

'No, Katherine,' he said firmly. 'There's no candy in there, just medicine to help people get better.' She squirmed defiantly in his arms. 'Let's go find Mommy.'

She buried her head in his shoulder wanting no part of her mother when Anne appeared at his side. He stood her on the floor, asking Sherry to look after her sisters, following Anne into the living room. He pecked her cheek when she was settled in her chair. 'How are you?'

Anne's skin tingled searching the congested coffee table for her pills. 'I need to find my pills,' she said abruptly, tightly furrowing her brow. 'Glenn, have you seen my pills?' Her palms started sweating and her heart beat erratically, scanning the area.

Glenn said, walking toward the hutch, 'I put them on top here; Katherine got a hold of them with a notion in that sweet little head of hers that they're candy.'

'Pass them to me please, saves me getting up, and a glass of water.'

She turned toward her husband. 'What were you saying?' Her head felt heavy and her hand trembled grasping the glass. She searched the bottles in pursuit of her anxiety pills, mentally chastising herself for not knowing which bottle they were in. After what seemed like forever, she flipped the lid with one hand, popping two pills into her parched, stale mouth, chasing them with a mouthful of water. One pill stuck in her dry throat; she downed the rest of the water sending it on its way, longing for the relief that would follow.

Robert quickly sensed his wife's struggle and asked the boys to take the girls outside to the backyard. When the door closed, he turned toward Anne noticing, as if for the first time, the dark circles under her once vibrant green eyes. Her thick black hair had lost all its sheen; tiny lines around her eyes belied her biological 34 years. He reached across the table for her hand, eyeing the fingernails that used to be immaculately manicured, chewed to the quick. The guilt of always being away from home took its toll, tears filled his eyes. 'I'm so sorry, Anne.'

It was like she had been reading his mind. Abruptly, she turned to face him. 'Sorry for what? Sorry your wife isn't pretty anymore, or she's fat and flabby. Or she needs bottles of pills to get through her endless nightmare days. Or she hates all aspects motherhood. Or, how about hates her life in general. Now tell me what the hell you're sorry about,' she said, indignantly pulling her hand away, wiping streams of saliva spilling out the corners of her mouth.

Robert was aghast by her sudden outburst. Obviously, he had no idea of her present mental state. He paced the floor facing this new reality trying to figure out a solution. 'You're a mess, Annie. I hate to be so blunt, but look at you. I'm not talking about your appearance, but your mindset. Is your life really that bad?' he said, running his hands through his wavy black hair. 'I have never heard you talk like this before. I believe you're a good, strong, loving, Catholic woman determined to provide a good, moral life for your family. I just don't get it. Everything I do is for you and the kids,' he said defensively.

He hasn't called me Annie since we first met in high school after I invited him to the Sadie Hawkins dance she sighed, watching her lean, handsome husband meticulously polish his gold wire-framed glasses with a tissue. Ironically, she couldn't remember when she entered the depths of hell, but things definitely went to pot literally, after the birth of their fifth child, Rose. Or maybe it was her husband's career change a few years ago and having to deal with his continual absence and lack of support. She leaned her head back savouring a brief moment of calm as the meds kicked in. Standing on trembling legs, she walked determinedly toward him.

The kids were enjoying a game of soccer in the backyard. After working all morning cleaning the house for Dad's arrival, it was a welcome outing.

'Nice catch, Sherry,' Jimmy said, watching her cock her head to one side.

A confused look crossed her face. 'Is that Mom?'

Glenn tuned into the yelling too, choosing to ignore the altercation going on inside, encouraging her to throw the ball.

Sherry threw the ball toward him, grabbed her crotch and ran quickly out of the yard. 'I have to pee.'

Mere inches separated Anne and her husband as she spoke with a confidence she hadn't realized for a long time. 'Well Mr. on the road all the time,' she said indignantly, 'you need to be more present in a house you choose to drop in on periodically, and during one of those rare visits, be much more observant of the disarray around here. The paint is chipped on every corner of every wall. The tap in the bathtub drips a steady rhythm day and night. The curtains in the girls' room are torn, not to mention the shit stains on the well-worn carpet. There are mildew stains in all corners of the bathroom. The kitchen ceiling is sagging and has been since some of the shingles blew off during the last storm. The screen in the backdoor is ripped, introducing all kinds of bugs into the establishment, bugs I've never even seen before. The bathroom window doesn't shut properly. Most of the floor tiles in the kitchen are cracked or broken. The inside of the refrigerator stinks to high heaven. The oven is so coated with crap the house fills with smoke every time it's turned on. The chesterfield cushions are stained with juice, pee, jam, poop and who knows what else. Shall I continue?' Without waiting for a response she said, 'And then there are the children. Our children, I might add. I am with them, in this god forsaken house, day in and day out while you're gallivanting across the country selling magic pills, leaving me with total responsibility of raising them; a task I find overwhelming at the best of times. Now ask me again if my life is really that bad.'

Sherry quietly opened the backdoor, tiptoeing through the kitchen, crouching down on the floor near the entrance to the living room.

Robert promptly decided the house repairs were incidental, fixable. But he had to admit, his wife's current mental state caught him totally unaware. He had no idea how bad she was. 'Anne, I will have all these things repaired. I'll hire someone immediately to do the work...'

She raised both hands in protest. 'You just don't get it, do you? YOU are what's missing from this god forsaken house. You go away for weeks on end, reappear for a short time when it's convenient, then disappear for weeks on end,' she said, covering her face with her hands. Her head throbbed. She yearned for the comfort of her bed, her only solace these days.

Exasperated, Robert sighed deeply. Time and time again, he had explained that travel was a necessary component of his job. After years at the bottom, he was now one of the top five sales reps of pharmaceuticals in Canada.

Ironically, especially at times like this, he was thankful he was on the road. Fighting the urge to give his wife a good shake, he opened his sample case. 'Anne, this is our newest anxiety medication. It's not even on the market yet,' he said, embracing her with his sales pitch. 'These meds will enable you to carry on with your day to day functions with very few side effects. You won't be as irritable or drowsy,' he added, watching her flip the lid in a single hand motion; a skill she had mastered hundreds of pills ago.

Sherry watched her mom draw the bottle rim to her lips and swallow a dose of pills without water. She didn't understand why Dad was always giving her pills to make her feel better, but decided *he's like a doctor because he gives pills to people too.*

Robert watched her stuff the coveted bottle into her housecoat pocket. 'Also, these pills are faster acting with longer lasting effects,' he smiled warmly, thinking she looked better already. 'You look like you could use a hug.'

Sherry couldn't remember the last time she saw her parents embrace. Quietly, she slipped out the backdoor, smiling contentedly.

After a few moments, Robert said, 'Would you like me to hire someone to help around the house until you get back on your feet again? We can afford a housekeeper you know. I will do some of the repairs when I'm home and hire workers for the bigger jobs,' he said reassuringly.

Anne, feeling the full effect of the new pills, felt better than she had in days. Dreamily, she stared up into her husband's handsome face. It was the first time in months he had held her in his arms and it felt like heaven. 'You don't have to hire a housekeeper. I can do it and what about the kids? They can certainly pitch in.'

Robert stepped back, almost throwing her off-balance; grabbing her arms to steady her. 'Good idea. I'll go have a talk with them.'

Anne sighed contentedly watching him leave. 'Hurry back, my love.'

Jimmy slammed the soccer ball to the ground with such force it flew high into the air, ricocheting off the side of Katherine's head, sending her wailing toward her father. 'I'm sick and tired of doing all the damn work around here. I don't have any life at all. I never get to be with my friends because I've got to stay home to cook and clean or look after my sisters while Mom stays in bed. I hate it. I wish I was an only child,' he yelled, covering his face with dirty hands.

Once again, Robert hadn't realized the toll his absence was taking on everyone. 'It's just for a while until your mom gets better. I need you, Glenn and Sherry to help your mother as much as possible. She's on the mend...'

'Is she ever going to get better?' Jimmy interrupted, stuffing his hands in the pockets of his grubby shorts. 'What's the matter with her anyway? Why can't she be like a normal mother?' He kicked the ground hard, forcing his hands further into his pockets.

'Yes, of course she'll get better. She just needs more time. Hopefully, she'll be back to her old self soon,' Dad said reassuringly. He was confident this latest batch of pills he had given her would aid the process.

The joy Sherry had felt earlier dissipated with her brother's anger. 'I hate this house so much I can hardly wait for school to start. And I don't even like school.'

Dad put his hands on her shoulders. 'We just have to give Mom a chance. She's sick, not in the sense that you can see physically, but inside her head things aren't right. That's why we all have to help her and then she will get better. I'm sure of it,' he said confidently.

He looked toward Glenn for support. 'I know I can count on you, son, being the oldest; the man of the house when I'm away,' he said, in a flattering tone, insinuating it was some great reward. 'We all need you to take charge. Can I count on you?'

Reluctantly, Glenn promised, though he too was fed up, choosing not to voice his own frustrations.

Dad promised to be home more often. I have a great idea. Let's go eat dinner at a restaurant, like a real family.' Without waiting for a response he said, 'let's go find your mother.'

Chapter Seven

TAMMY COUNTED THE steps down the hall to answer the persistent knocking on the front door. 'Oh, it's you,' she said, studying the freckled face on the other side of the screen. 'Have you ever taken the time to count the freckles on your face?' She eyed her bare arms and legs. 'I bet there's close to a million freckles on your whole body, and then there are the ones I can't see; must be a billion. Is my sister expecting you? I hope so. It took me eleven giant steps to get here and I wouldn't want to think they were wasted.'

Judy's face was as red as her curly hair. 'Your sister is expecting me.'

'You can come in then. T, my new nickname for my sister, is lying on her bed reading. By the way, if you ever do a freckle count, I'd really like to know the numbers. I care you know.'

Tammy counted each step toward the bedroom, announcing Judy's arrival.

Theresa closed her book as Judy sat on the edge of the bed. It was the first time they'd seen each other since the encounter with the pool pervert.

Judy whispered, 'How are you doing since, you know what?'

Tammy stopped bouncing on her bed. 'Since what?' she said curiously, hoping to find the answer to her sister's moodiness after the hot dog incident.

Theresa asked her to leave and it was no surprise Tammy ignored the request, continuing to bounce; her sun bleached light brown bob spread out with each descent. Coming to a sudden stop she said matter-of-factly, 'It's my bedroom too. I don't have to leave.'

Rather than arguing, Theresa ushered Judy outside.

'Your sister is so hyper.'

Theresa nodded, 'tell me about it.'

Tammy, a going concern, seldom walked, choosing to sprint everywhere. Most nights, she was so wound up she would have trouble falling asleep. During these times, she would be her utmost bothersome, singing or talking loudly. Mom would threaten her with a good whipping with her slipper if she didn't quiet down, but the threats only intensified Tammy's annoying game of wits and patience, testing the waters to see how much she could get away with. Whenever she heard Mom's footsteps approaching, she hid under the covers, tucking them tightly, making it impossible to penetrate with Mom's soft soled slipper; she would whack the lump in the middle of the bed, a futile attempt at disciplining the annoying little bugger. Tammy's faked cry would put an end to Mom's thrashing with a promise of more of the same should her infernal racket continue. When Mom left the room, Tammy would quietly commence singing herself to sleep as if nothing had happened.

Judy and Theresa stretched out on matching green and beige striped chaise lounges on the flagstone patio, under a massive grapevine growing wildly over the top of the wooden trellis; nature's umbrella shielding them from the hot sun.

Judy suggested it would be a great day to go to the pool for a swim. 'Hot and sunny, doesn't get any better than a day like today.'

Theresa tensed with the thought; the memory of the pervert playing with himself, still vivid in her mind, as if it happened yesterday. Since that day, she had experienced sleepless nights, a total aversion to hotdogs vowing never to eat them again, and lost time spent convincing herself she was the victim of a sick man's fantasy. 'I never want to go back there,' she said adamantly.

Judy turned sharply, 'Because of what happened?'

Theresa drew a deep breath. 'Yes, I'm still trying to get over it.' The experience had left her so traumatised, she wondered if it would haunt her for the rest of her life.

'Get over what?' a voice boomed from the bedroom window.

Theresa spotted Tammy's distorted face pressed tightly against the dirty, black screen. 'You goddamn little brat,' she said, moving quickly toward her. 'Get lost you little jerk,' she said, pushing Tammy's face. 'See what I have to put up with,' she said, picking up her chaise, moving it to a grassy area in front of her parent's bedroom window. 'She's not allowed in my parent's room.'

Judy placed her chair next to hers. 'I want you to know I'm there for you. Am I still your best friend?'

'Of course you are,' she half smiled. 'It's been a huge struggle to keep that horrid memory at bay. I'm better than I was, but periodically it creeps back to haunt me.'

'I feel sorry for you. Have you talked to your mom about what happened?'

Theresa shook her head. She was so embarrassed she hadn't spoken to anyone, especially her mother. *Hey Mom. You're never going to guess what happened at the pool. Some old, creepy man decided I needed to see his wiener.* The incident was so bazaar, she doubted anyone would believe her. Sadly, there was nothing anyone could do to lessen her trauma. The ordeal had taught her that unless it happened to you, one has absolutely no idea what a person goes through. 'I don't trust any males, other than my dad.'

Judy gave a sympathetic sigh. 'I had no idea it was this bad.' She couldn't begin to imagine how it would have affected her. 'Usually, you are the strongest person I know, springing back quickly from life's ups and downs; I honestly thought you'd be over it by now. It wasn't your fault at all. Since then, I've heard these awful things usually happen to innocent people these creeps don't know. Unfortunately, you were in the wrong place at the wrong time. I really hope you can get over it soon. I've missed all the fun we have when we're together.'

It seemed like forever since Theresa had had any fun. It was time to make a concerted effort to distance the memory. Like everything else, it will fade with time. She turned to Judy, 'I've been missing all our fun times too, except swimming. We are still best friends and always will be. Remember when my mom pricked our fingers so we could rub them together making us blood sisters?' She studied the end of her middle finger for any telltale sign.

Judy chuckled, 'My finger hurt for days afterward. It was worth it though. It not only makes us best friends but...'

They both jumped with the crashing sound emanating from her parent's bedroom, followed by Bea's angry voice. 'What the hell do you think you're doing you little bugger? Look at my sewing machine table. You've bloody well busted it. Get to your room.'

Judy and Theresa huddled together stifling their laughter listening to Bea curse and swear trying to right the heavy mahogany table housing her Singer sewing machine. 'God damn it, Tamara. You've busted the wooden extension. I can't close the bloody lid now. You had better hope your dad can fix the damn thing. In the meantime, stay in your room.'

Tammy waited until Mom left the room then checked out the damage. *It's not that bad. Dad can fix it. Hell, I could fix it.* She ran back to her bedroom, jumping on her bed.

Judy's eyes widened, 'Your sister is absolutely wild!'

'She's a pain in the butt,' Theresa sighed.

'You're not kidding. I'd better be going. But don't forget to call me.'

'You too,' Theresa smiled, pulling the chaise lounges over to the patio, feeling lighter than she had in days.

Gloria hugged her father tightly. Her mood had been noticeably better since his arrival a week ago, but it was time for him to get back to work.

'I'll be home soon,' he said, pulling away.

'Why can't I go with you? I promise I will be good,' she pleaded.

'Sweetheart, we've been through this a million times. The answer is still no. Why don't you go outside, enjoy the lovely sunny day while I finish packing.'

Gloria crossed her arms, sitting down hard beside his suitcase.

'Women,' he sighed. 'If I live to be a hundred, I will never understand them.'

Gloria followed him downstairs, watching him move toward her mother sitting in a thick cloud of smoke, engrossed in *The Price is Right* blaring throughout the room.

He turned down the volume, pecking her cheek. 'I have a lot of territory to cover this trip and will be away a bit longer. I'll call when I can.'

Garnet, eyes riveted to the television, made no comment.

He kissed Gloria gently on top of her head. 'Daddy loves you, sweetheart. Be good and help Mom out. I will be home soon.'

She watched him close the door, scurrying up the stairs.

Garnet wiped her cheek with a tissue walking toward the television, cranking up the volume.

George opened the screen door, eyeing his mother's smoky silhouette, asking after his father.

Garnet, thankful it was a commercial break; she hated any interruptions when her favourite shows were airing, said dryly, 'Can you not see his car is gone? He left about ten minutes ago and will be away indefinitely. Where have you been all morning?'

He had left the house early to run an errand. 'Out, I had to do some stuff,' he said evasively. 'Where's Bar?'

Garnet lit a cigarette, inhaling deeply, feeling the acrid smoke soothe her edginess. 'He said he was going over to Daniel's. I imagine that's where he is. I never seem to know where my sons go, or what they're up to,' she added warily.

'Well I'm home now,' he said, running upstairs, two at a time, shutting his bedroom door behind him. He pulled a small white box, dotted with dirty fingerprints, from under his shirt and stood it on the bed. Spitting into his grimy hands, he rubbed them vigorously on his pants before picking up the box, inhaling the sweet fragrance within. Gingerly, he opened the lid, removing the clear plastic container housing a diamond-eyed, black cat wearing a tiny pearl necklace; a small bottle of *Fabrege Sophisti-Cat Perfume* housed between its front legs. He was tempted to open the bottle for a whiff, but decided against it. He stroked the statuesque cat's head. *Gloria's going to love you, she really loves cats.* Gently, he replaced the cylinder. Spitting on his finger, he rubbed the fingerprints on the box.

Guardedly, Gloria pulled the princess comforter up to her neck. 'Go away.'

George tried the door knob. 'It's me, George. Can I come in?'

She threw back the blanket, pulling back the chair jimmied against it. 'What do you want?' she said suspiciously.

He kept his hands behind his back. 'I have something for you,' he smiled.

Untrustingly, she stepped back. The only male she trusted was her father.

George screwed up his face. 'What's wrong? You look like you're afraid of me or something?'

Deep down, Gloria knew George would never do anything to harm her and felt bad for overreacting. 'I'm not afraid of you,' she said calmly.

'I hope not, because, I have a present for you, but ya gotta pick a hand.'

She rolled her green eyes, pointing to his left.

'Wrong. I knew you'd get it wrong,' he said, egging her on. 'I'll give you one more chance.'

She couldn't help but smile. Even as a young child, her fraternal twin, always the kidder, liked to play silly games given the opportunity and today was no different.

'Last try,' he smiled, curious to see if she'd get it this time.

Gloria knew her twin well enough, pointing to his left hand.

Spraying saliva excitedly he asked how she knew.

'Lucky guess.'

He thrust the package toward her. 'I didn't wrap it because the white box is like it's already wrapped.'

A perplexed look crossed her face. 'What is it?'

His eyes widened leaning forward, filling the space between them. 'Open it and see, dummy.'

She flipped the lid. 'George, where did you get this?' The black cat stared ominously at her through the clear plastic.

'From the store, silly goose. Isn't that where you get things from? Do you like it? I know how much you love cats,' he smiled, watching her hastily thrust it back into the box, shoving it toward him.

'Black cats bring nothing but bad luck,' she said, returning to her bed.

His mind raced trying to convince her it wasn't unlucky. 'It's not a real black cat. It's only pretend. You can throw the damn cat away and just use the perfume. But I still think it would look nice sitting on your dresser.'

'Thanks for being so thoughtful, but I don't want it,' she said, pulling up the comforter.

The kids stopped their game of kickball, moving toward the curb watching a police car drive by slowly, intriguing the group.

Barry snickered, 'Better look out Ronald, the cops are coming for you.'

Ronald was not amused. From the moment he had met Barry there was something about him that made his skin crawl. 'It looks like they're coming to take you away, *asshole*,' he smiled confidently, watching the car turn into Murray's driveway.

Tammy bound quickly down the hall. 'There's a cop car driving slowly by our house,' she said excitedly.

Theresa held the extension of the sewing machine table steady for her father. 'Maybe it's come for you.'

Tammy screwed up her face stating she wasn't a criminal for standing on the extension. 'I had to stand on something to see out the window. If that stupid table wasn't so heavy to move, I could have moved it under the window. By the way, are you and Judy still best friends?'

Theresa rolled her eyes wondering how much she had heard of their conversation. 'Yes Miss Nosey.'

'Good, because I really like her sister, Christine, my new best friend,' she said, beginning to twirl her arms. 'Look Daddy, I'm a windmill.'

He turned briefly watching her whip her arms around. 'Clever. But can you make one arm spin one way while spinning the other arm in the opposite direction?'

Tammy contemplated his request. 'Miss Cordello, my grade three teacher, would probably like that. One day when I was spinning my arms, she made me stand beside my desk and show the class how it's done. The only problem was she forgot to tell me when to stop. I had to tell her my arms were getting really sore, but she still didn't ask me to stop, so I just stopped and sat back down. I don't think she liked me at times.'

Dad said, 'I still think you should practice spinning your arms in opposite directions.'

Tammy ran out of the room, arms flailing.

'That should keep her occupied for about ten minutes,' he said, tightening the screws.

In less than a minute, Tammy returned. 'You are not going to believe this. George, the retard, is being taken away by the police. This I gotta see,' she said, running full tilt down the hall.

Barry fired the volleyball toward Daniel, sprinting up his driveway to confront the officer gripping his brother's arm. 'Officer, what's going on?'

The officer tightened his grip. 'Who are you?'

'My name is Barry Murray, his older brother, sir.'

Garnett, arms folded across her chest had made a rare appearance outside, stepping inconspicuously around the carport. 'He's in charge,' she said, taking her place beside him. 'This is my oldest son. In his father's absence, he is the man of the house.'

Suddenly, Barry's mind raced trying to think of why George was being questioned. *He wouldn't say anything about me and Gloria. I'm sure he hasn't got a clue.* He swallowed, composing himself. 'What seems to be the problem, officer?'

Garnet placed two trembling fingers under her nose inhaling deeply.

The officer said, 'Your brother was seen shoplifting at the Towers store located at Midland and Lawrence.'

Barry thought back to earlier this morning when he woke to find George's bed already made. With a sense of relief, coupled with authority, he said, 'Is this true, George? Did you steal something?'

George's voice was barely audible. He shuffled his feet hoping the officer would ease the grip on his arm. 'Yeah, I did. But it was all in vain. Gloria doesn't like damn black cats. She said they bring nothin' but bad luck. Now I know it's true,' he added.

Garnet gasped loudly. 'I will not have you using profanity in my house.'

'Sorry Mother, but I went to all the trouble for nothin'. It was a gift to make her feel better.' Focusing on his brother's crimson face, he said, 'My sister's been down in the dumps lately. I thought it would cheer her up.'

The officer eyed the crowd congregating across the road; releasing his grip on George's arm he suggested they go inside, away from prying eyes.

Garnet led the way, the three shuffled inside behind her. She motioned the officer toward the chesterfield. 'George, you are to stand beside my chair,' she said, sitting down, lighting a much needed cigarette.

The officer pulled out a small notepad. With pen poised he said, 'I hope you realize stealing is against the law, son. It is a felony that can lead to jail time; at the very least, a criminal record. Do you understand?'

George bowed his head in shame. 'Yes sir.'

The officer droned on with a well-rehearsed dialogue, 'I am not going to press charges this time. But mark my words, if it ever happens again, you will be charged with theft and penalized in a court of law. Do you understand?'

George felt a heavy weight roll off his shoulders. 'Yes sir. I promise never to steal again.'

Garnet, eyes closed, took one last drag of her cigarette, butting it out quickly around the ashtray while the officer made notes.

'I have spoken to the manager at Towers. He assured me he will not press charges, but only if the item is returned promptly to him. Do you understand, George?'

He felt a sense of dread having to return the perfume to the store manager, but it was better than the alternative. 'Yes sir. I have it upstairs in my room.' He was thankful Gloria didn't want the perfume. The last thing he wanted was to alienate his twin.

The officer addressed Garnet when George left the room. 'Normally in cases like this, being a first offence, we don't hold them criminally responsible. But if it happens again, he will be arrested and charged with theft.'

Garnet apologized for her son's behaviour, reassuring the officer it wouldn't happen again. 'My George is a good boy, a little slow at times, but a nice, kind, sensitive young man.' *He gets it from his mother* she wanted to add.

Garnet stood at the window watching Barry escort the officer to his cruiser; not the least bit surprised by the gathering of noisy neighbours milling around on the other side of the street. *Well, well. If it isn't that sorry excuse of a mother, Anne Smythe, dressed in pants and a blouse no less, standing front and center. Quite a change from the raggedy old housecoat she lives in, that is, if she manages to drag her big fat ass out of bed. Miss nosey busybody herself managed to dress up for the occasion. Nothing like a cop car parked in the driveway to draw out the riff raff.* A disgusted look crossed her face. She had never noticed before, but Anne had the uncanny resemblance and stature to her mother's best friend, Agnes Parker, the neighbourhood snitch from her childhood. Like Anne, Agnes loved sticking her long, crooked nose into everybody's business. Though it was close to 80 degrees, a chill ran down her spine recalling her last encounter with Agnes, shortly after her 13th birthday.

Hello Garnett. I haven't seen you around lately. Come to think of it, I haven't seen Brian sitting on your porch lately either. Garnet's face reddened studying the satisfied look on Mrs. Parker's ugly face. *Why, I do believe you are blushing, my dear girl.* Garnet trembled standing motionless at the entrance to the kitchen; the relentless woman, smiling wickedly, continued her assault until her mother chimed in.

Agnes is right. I haven't seen Brian around here for some time now. He was always here visiting. It seems like he vanished into thin air.

Garnet said defensively, *I have no idea where he's gotten too. Can I please go to my room?*

Her mother lit a cigarette, inhaling deeply. *Not before you bid Mrs. Parker a good day. That would be very rude if you didn't, and you know better than that.* She obliged, walking quickly out the kitchen, remaining close by to eavesdrop on their conversation.

You know, Patricia, there's a rumour going around the neighbourhood that your daughter is, you know, promiscuous.

Patricia tensed. *What do you mean, Agnes?*

Agnes leaned forward relishing the moment. *I mean, I have heard from a very reliable source that your daughter let Brian go all the way, if you know what I mean. THAT'S why he never comes around here anymore.* She sat back smugly in her chair.

Poised as ever, Patricia leaned toward her. *Agnes Parker, my daughter would never do anything like that. She is a lady through and through. I can take credit for her high standard morals. And besides, Brian is such a nice boy; he would never take advantage of my daughter.*

Agnes raised her eyebrow, guzzling the last mouthful of coffee. *I've got to be on my way. My husband wants beef stew for supper; it needs to cook for hours. Thanks for the coffee. Oh, and if it was my daughter, I would ask if there was any truth to the rumour. Cheerio, darling.*

Patricia's hand shook lighting a cigarette. She inhaled a few drags deeply, summing Garnet to the kitchen. *Sit down in Mrs. Parker's chair, please.* Timidly she sat cringing inside sensing the heat from Mrs. Parker's departed fat ass emanating from the foam chair cushion. Her mother dragged heavily on the cigarette. *I'll get right to the point. Why hasn't Brian been around lately?*

Garnet felt like her face was on fire. *I don't know, Mother.*

Patricia butted the cigarette around the ashtray. She was very adept at reading her daughter; Garnet had always been an open book. *Well, let me tell you about the rumour that's going around the neighbourhood. Rumour has it you let Brian go all the way with you. Is there any truth to this appalling gossip?* Her tone insinuated if it was true, it was all her doing.

Of course not, Mother. I would never do anything like that.

Her mother sighed contentedly sitting back in her chair. *That's what I thought. My daughter would never do anything like that. She's not a slut.*

Garnet remained at the window long enough to watch Anne Smythe waddle back inside and the neighbours disperse when the cop drove off. *I hate nosey neighbours.*

Barry shut the bedroom door behind him. 'What the hell were you thinking, George, stealing like that? Are you crazy? There are private dicks moving around the stores all the time just looking for stupid people like you.'

George stared down at his dirty hands. 'I didn't know about the dicks.'

Barry sat down across from him. 'Then why would you do such a stupid thing?'

George shot his brother a suspicious look. 'I did it to try to cheer up my sister. Ever since you been helpin' her, she ain't been happy, not one bit. I thought the black cat, 'cause she loves cats, holding some perfume for her to wear would make her feel better. You know how she loves cats. She's always bugging Mom to buy one, but Mom don't like cats because they affect her breathing. The real reason Gloria didn't want it was because black cats bring nothin' but bad luck. She's right about that,' he added, rubbing his arm.

Barry stood, pacing the floor between them. 'Well you did a very stupid thing. Now all the neighbours are going to have a good time with it. I won't be able to show my face outside the damn door. And when Dad hears about this, look out.' He moved toward him. 'In the meantime, go take the damn thing back to the store.'

George stood face to face with his brother. 'Don't tell me what to do. You are not my father.'

Barry said, 'to hell I'm not. When Dad's away, I'm the *man* of the house. You heard what Mom said.'

George shoved his brother onto the bed, hurrying out the room.

'George, come here, please,' Mom said, butting out her smoke.

Damn. With a loud huff, he stomped into the living room watching her light a cigarette, inhaling deeply. 'You realize you have shamed this family by being so foolish,' she said, focusing on the television.

He looked down at the white box that had caused him so much grief. 'Yes Mother.'

She dragged her smoke. 'And you realize when your father hears about this he will be very upset and angry. Why would you do such a foolish thing?'

He was getting tired of explaining his motive. 'I did it for Gloria because she's not happy. She always stays in her room and cries.' *While you sit in your chair all day smoking cigarettes and watching television.* 'I thought it would make her happy. The cat has her green eyes. Remember, she loves cats, but not black ones, they bring nothin' but bad luck.'

'Nothing,' Garnet corrected. She turned to face him, looking him in the eye. 'I want you to promise me you will *never* do anything like this again.'

He sighed deeply, promising.

'Now, I don't want you worrying about your sister. She's just going through a girly phase and like everything else, it will pass. You better get to the store. You've got some fixin' to do.'

Gloria cringed at the sound of her mother's voice. It was all her fault George was in the mess he was in. Now she had to convince her mother she had nothing to do with it.

'Don't make me come up there to get you,' Mom said tersely, lighting a cigarette. Garnet watched Bob Barker quiz his next contestant. *Where are you from?* The over-exuberant woman continued jumping up and down. *I'm from Columbus, Georgia. Can I kiss you?* Bob glanced skyward, *only if you stop jumping up and down.* She watched the heavy set woman plant a kiss on Bob's cheek, jumping up and down, professing her accomplishment. *Stupid twit* she thought watching him wipe his cheek with the back of his hand. 'Did you have anything to do with your brother stealing the perfume?'

Gloria's felt her eyes tearing. It was no surprise her mother would think this. 'No Mother. I didn't ask him to steal it. I would never do anything like that,' she said, covering her face with her hands.

'Good. I wouldn't want to think my daughter would encourage her brother to do bad things,' she said, focusing on the television. 'You may go back to your room now.'

Gloria quickly ran upstairs.

George stood outside the store entrance catching his breath. He had run all the way hoping to rid himself of guilt, although he still believed it was an act of kindness on his part; his sister had not been herself lately. With a sense of dread, he watched the customers enter and exit the store.

Gloria wedged the chair under the doorknob.

'What are you doing?'

The sound of Barry's voice sent shivers down her spine. Her stomach lurched watching him step out from behind the drapes. 'How did you get in here?'

He smiled kindly, a smile she had grown to hate.

'I want you out of here now,' she hissed, wrestling with the chair.

He moved toward her. 'No need to move it,' he said, wedging it tightly. 'This way, we won't be disturbed. I'm here as the supportive big brother, not like George. He did a very stupid thing. He's lucky the cop didn't haul him off to the slammer; mainly because I was able to convince him our brother is a good kid and won't steal ever again. Fortunately, I was home to be of assistance, like now,' he said confidently.

Gloria's heart pounded erratically. 'If you touch me, I'll scream so loud the whole neighbourhood will hear me.'

Barry shook his head, 'You know very well we must always remember Mom's condition; we mustn't upset her.' He glanced at his watch. 'Besides, she's busy watching her precious Bob Barker. And we both know, nothing takes her away from The Price is Right. She's content to sit in her chair all day, cigs nearby; it would take the house going up in flames to move her,' he smiled knowingly. 'Gloria, I'm here to comfort you, make sure you aren't upset by your twin's foolishness. He said he stole the perfume to make you happy. Aren't you happy? Come on now, you can talk to me. I'm your big brother and I want to help you.'

George's heart raced walking toward the Courtesy Desk. The lady behind the counter looked up from her magazine. 'Can I help you?' she said, flipping through the pages for the article on *bettering yourself.*

'I'd like to see the manager,' George said resolutely. *Might as well get this over with.*

Promptly, she shut the magazine, stuffing it under the counter. 'May I ask why?' she blushed, tucking a strand of brown hair behind her ear.

'It's personal.'

'Are you applying for a job?' she said politely, hoping he wouldn't rat on her to the manager. It wouldn't be the first time she was reprimanded for slacking off.

A smirk crossed his face. *Yeah right, lady. Like they'd really hire me, a common thief.* 'Look, can you just get me the manager,' he said impatiently.

She moved quickly toward the opposite counter, dialing a three digit extension. After a brief conversation she returned. 'Mr. Benson will be with you in a moment,' she said, transferring the magazine to the return bin.

George leaned against the counter trying to identify the manager. His heart began thumping watching a short, surly, young man with reddish-brown curly hair and dark rimmed glasses approach the counter. After conversing with his employee he ordered George to follow him.

Little shit she sniggered, fetching the magazine.

Gloria, anxious with worry about George's pending confrontation with the manager, coupled with Barry's presence, broke down sobbing.

'There, there,' he whispered, collapsing her into his arms. 'Big brother Barry is here. Everything is going to be alright.'

Reluctantly, she welcomed the comfort of his arms, holding on tightly to a lifeline. Feeling at peace, she rested her head on his chest.

Barry closed his eyes savouring the warmth of her closeness; breathing in the fresh scent of her hair, gently stroking her head he tightened his grip.

The manager led George to his office, a tiny, windowless room beside the stock room. 'Have a seat, young man,' he ordered, pointing to a tatter-edged black vinyl chrome chair that had seen better days.

George sat down with a thud, his hand perspiring profusely holding onto the white box; transferring it to his other hand. He had hoped to hand over the perfume and leave, but the manager continued to stall, shuffling papers on his desk before sitting down; the chair creaking in opposition. Wheeling closer to his desk, he briefly read the sheet in front of him. He looked up from his notes; his fingers forming a steeple in front of his face. 'You know this is a very serious offence.' He watched with interest as George sat up straighter.

'Yes sir, I do.'

The manager asked him his name.

'George Murray, sir.' He sat quietly while the manager wrote something on the paper in front of him.

'Do you have the merchandise?'

'Yes sir, right here.' He placed the box on the desk, thankful to be free of the demon, rubbing his sweaty hands along the sides of his grubby blue shorts.

The manager picked up the box like it was contaminated. In his mind, it was. 'It's covered with fingerprints,' he said disgustedly.

George stared down at his filthy hands, explaining how he had tried to keep it clean so he wouldn't have to wrap it for his sister.

The manager's tone intensified. 'A gift for your sister, if you hadn't taken it in the first place...I doubt I can sell the damn thing now. I certainly can't put it on the shelf looking like that,' he huffed, dropping it on the desk.

George suggested getting rid of the box. 'The cat is encased in plastic; you can put it on the shelf without the box.'

The manager, resting his elbows on the desk, rubbed his face briskly. It was obvious the young man had no clue about marketing or sales. 'When people make a purchase, packaging is a huge part of what attracts them to an item in the first place. In other words, they want a brand new item, not one that has been run all over Scarborough.'

Remorsefully, George lowered his head. All he wanted was to get out of here. 'I said I am sorry. I don't know what else to do.'

Sensing he was dealing with a developmentally challenged individual, he said, 'Son, I want you to promise me you will never steal anything from this store, or from any store, ever again.'

George eagerly obliged. 'Can I please go now?'

The manager nodded watching him jump to his feet. 'Remember, if this ever happens again, you will be arrested.'

Again, George felt a huge weight roll off his shoulders. 'It will never happen again, sir. I promise,' he said, running out of the office leaving the door ajar.

The manager tossed the box into the garbage can, reapplying the price tag onto the plastic container.

'Courtesy Desk, Alice speaking,' she said, leafing through the magazine.

'I have an item on my desk that needs to be placed on the shelf in cosmetics,' the manager said curtly. 'You are to come to my office immediately. Oh, and bring the magazine with you.' Smugly, he sat back in his chair, anticipating her dismissal.

Gloria, pulling back from her brother's embrace, felt his grip tighten. 'You don't want me to let go because I love you. I love you very much,' he whispered.

She struggled to break free as he yanked her top up, exposing her breasts. Instinctively, she tried to cover them but he pulled the top down pinning her arms, rendering them useless. With her arms pinned to her sides, he manoeuvred the top, releasing her ample breasts. Crazed with passion, he sucked eagerly, yanking her shorts down. Muffling her screams, he shoved her onto the bed, stepping out of his shorts, pinning her down with his body, stifling her screams with his sweaty hand. 'Don't scream. Please don't scream. I don't want to hurt you. We mustn't upset Mother,' he whispered, feeling her body go limp beneath him.

Garnet focused on the black and white scene unfolding in front of her. *'Please stop! Amanda cried.* Dr. Young tightened his embrace. *You want this too,' he whispered,* as the screen went blank.

Garnett, breaking out in a cold sweat, lit a smoke with a trembling hand. *Slut.*

George ran quickly past some kids playing handball in front of Wilkinson's driveway, ignoring an invitation to join them. Running full speed toward his driveway, he had never been happier to see his house.

Ronald said, 'He won't join us; too busy living a life of crime. You need to pray more often,' he yelled, watching him run up the driveway. 'Scumbag.'

George stood at the bottom of the stairs catching his breath, eyeing his mother's outline sitting rigid in her chair in a cloud of smoke.

'Did everything go okay?' she said, eyes riveted to the television.

'It's done.'

'That's a good boy, George. Now, promise me you won't do anything like that again.'

'I promise,' he said tersely, ascending the stairs.

Barry pulled up his shorts consoling his sister. 'Don't cry Gloria. Go to sleep,' he said, covering her with the comforter. Exiting her room, he was surprised to see George standing there, and even more surprised by the confrontation that ensued.

'What were you doing in Gloria's room?' he asked suspiciously, listening to his twin's muffled cries.

Barry put his finger to his lips, running a hand through his disheveled hair, leading him into their bedroom, but George persisted. 'What were you doing in her room? And why is your face beet red?'

'For your information, asshole, I was calming her down so she wouldn't disturb Mom.'

George wrinkled his brow. 'Calming her down? Why?'

Barry put his face mere inches from his. 'Because of your stealing escapade, dumb ass. See how much upset you've caused her? You must promise you will never steal again.'

George lost any patience he had. 'I am so sick of promising everyone,' he yelled.

'Don't yell!' Barry scolded. 'You have to be quiet because of Mom's condition. You know she can't get upset.'

George sat down hard on the bed covering his face with his dirty hands, wishing he had never gone near the damn store.

Barry ordered him to take a nap. 'Then you'll feel better. In the meantime, I'm going out.'

He listened for the screen door to latch before knocking on his sister's door. 'It's me, George. Can I come in?'

She rolled onto her back answering feebly, pulling the comforter up around her neck.

George stared wide-eyed at his sister's flushed face, trying to ignore the pungent odour of body sweat permeating the steamy room. Gingerly, he sat on the edge of her bed. 'I've returned the perfume. It's gone, and I didn't get into too much trouble,' he smiled humbly, but it quickly vanished with her sudden tears. 'Oh god, I'm so sorry. I didn't mean to upset you. I promise I won't ever steal again. I mean it Gloria. I won't ever do it again. I'd better go,' he said remorsefully.

She reached for his arm. 'Don't go. It's not you George, it's me. Everything is a mess because of me.'

A confused look crossed his face. 'That's not true,' he said, sitting back down trying to pull back the covers.

'Don't do that!' She tightened her hold on the comforter.

'I'm sorry. I was just trying to hold your hand to make you feel better. I love you.'

His words sent a cold shiver through her, tucking the comforter tighter.

Guilt overwhelmed him; tears stung his eyes. Vigorously he rubbed his face. 'I'm sorry,' he cried.

Gloria sat up, hugging him tightly. 'It's okay. Please don't cry.'

He wrapped his arms around her sobbing hysterically into her shoulder. 'This is all my fault,' he sobbed. 'Can you ever forgive me?'

'It's okay, George. I forgive you.'

He pulled back, wiping his tear stained face. 'Then will you be happy and go outside with your friends more often?'

Gloria threw back the cover and sat down beside him. It was clear he had absolutely no idea what his older brother did to her behind closed doors. 'This isn't about you stealing the perfume.'

Barry entered Daniel's yard and stood watching his two friends flip through a magazine.

Ronald looked up, giving him an inquisitive eye. 'Well, don't we look like the cat that just swallowed the canary?'

Daniel snickered. ''What you been up to, Bar?'

He shrugged, 'Nothin' much. What are you guys looking at?' He peered over Ronald's shoulder, sitting down next to him at the wooden picnic table.

'Naked ladies.' Ronald hoisted the magazine up to his face. 'Here, have a good look,' he said, fighting the urge to shove Barry's face into the centerfold crease.

Barry smirked, 'That's nothing.'

Ronald closed the magazine, crossing his arms across his chest, turning toward him. 'Really,' he said sarcastically. 'And I suppose you've seen something more titillating. Judging by that look on your face…'

Barry held up a hand. 'Let's just say, I've gone a bit further than just looking, if you know what I mean.'

'No actually, I don't know what you mean. But I'm sure you will oblige us with the details, right Danny?'

Daniel leaned in closer.

Barry's voice a mere whisper, 'I've done it.'

Ronald and Daniel looked at each other, saying in unison, 'Done what?'

'Fucked.'

Ronald reeled back; Daniel leaned in closer still. 'You've done that?' To date, his sex life consisted of a magazine and a tight hand grip in the comfort of his bedroom.

Ronald rubbed his hands together briskly. 'Hot diggity dog! Who's the girl?' he said, sensing some reluctance. 'Come on Mr. Stud, don't keep us in suspense.'

Barry's face grew serious. 'Do you both promise not to tell anyone?'

Daniel nodded, raising his hand.

'Scout's honour,' Ronald said, with a salute.

Gloria held on tightly to George's hand. 'Barry has been doing things to me...'

He interrupted, 'Like what?'

She sighed dejectedly, 'Things a brother shouldn't do to his sister.'

George thought of the times he had witnessed Barry coming out of her room, furrowing his brow. 'He told me he was helping you.'

She could tell by his confused look, he had absolutely no clue what his older brother was doing during those visits. 'Do you know what sex is?'

George thought of the dog-eared nudie magazine tucked under Barry's bed; an awkward grin crossed his face. 'Sort of,' he said sheepishly. He often looked through it when he was alone in the room.

Gloria's mouth was so dry, it was difficult to speak. 'Barry does sexual things to me.'

George ran his hand over the top of his brush cut, tickling the palm of his hand. 'Such as?'

She swallowed what little saliva was in her mouth, 'He puts his private part into my private part.'

He raised his eyebrows trying to comprehend the scenario. 'Where your pee pee comes out?'

She nodded.

He threw his head back. 'My wiener, that's my private part. Barry asked me once if I get a funny feeling in it when I look at pictures of a woman's,' he paused, pointing toward her chest. 'I told him my wiener starts to grow bigger sometimes.' He could tell the admission didn't sit well with her. 'But I don't look at dirty pictures or get a funny feeling down there very often.'

She lowered her head in shame. 'Barry puts his wiener inside my private part.'

Finally the dots connected; George jumped to his feet. 'Oh my god! He shouldn't be doing that. That's disgusting. I'm telling Mom.'

Barry, knowing he finally had something over the righteous, pompous Ronald, leaned in closer. 'Gloria.'

'Gloria. Who the hell's Gloria?' Ronald said, watching Barry squirm. 'Wait a minute, you don't mean your sister, do you?'

He nodded briefly.

Ronald stood up with such force the table shifted with him. 'Oh my god! You're having sex with your sister! Are you bloody crazy?'

Daniel covered his face, reeling back in stunned silence.

'You goddamn frickin' pervert. I always figured you weren't quite right. Now I know it for sure.' Ronald felt the bile rising. 'How could you do that to your own sister?'

Barry's face reddened, folding his arms across his chest. 'You're just jealous you don't have a sister. I see nothin' wrong with a little brotherly love.'

It was all Ronald could do not to punch him in the head. 'Oh my god. You just don't get it. Even if I had a sister, I wouldn't be having sex with her, for Christ's sake. You are sick in the head you goddamn perverted whacko.'

Daniel felt physically ill thinking of his recent conversation with Dana, siding with Barry, labelling Gloria a drama queen. 'I have a sister, your sister's best friend. Sex with Dana has never ever crossed my mind. You are a very, very sick person. You need help. In the meantime, stay the hell away from me.'

'You are disgusting pig,' Ronald spat, running after Daniel.

Gloria grabbed George's arm. 'No! You can't tell Mom because of her condition. This has to be kept secret,' she said, wishing she hadn't told him.

George thought of their mother. It was true; they had to do their utmost not to upset her. 'I won't tell Mom, but I'm going to talk to Barry...'

Gloria tugged his arm forcefully. 'No! I don't want you to get involved. He hasn't done anything to you. I don't want this coming between the two of you. I know how much you love Barry and look up to him. This is my problem. I have to figure out what to do.'

George wasn't sure he could ever regard his brother the same; very reluctantly he agreed. 'If that's what you want, I won't say a word to anyone.'

'Promise,' she pleaded.

He looked into his sister's puffy eyes and nodded.

Barry, head downcast, walked home quickly. He greeted his mother sitting in a cloud of smoke watching television then raced upstairs to George's icy glare. 'What?' he said indignantly, moving toward his bed.

George asked where he had been.

'Why? You a cop all of a sudden, or are you writing my book? I don't think it's any of your damn business, but for your information, I was hanging out with Daniel and Ronald.'

'Ronald? You hate his guts.'

Barry reached under the bed for his magazine. 'Let's just say, I hate his guts even more now.'

Disgustedly, George watched Barry flip through the girly magazine, knowing in his heart he would never feel the same about the brother he once admired and looked up to.

Chapter Eight

BEA PLACED THE warm dinner plates on the table, summoning the family for supper.

Tammy sat down first, inquiring about Gregory's whereabouts, screwing up her face gawking at her plate. 'You know I don't like green beans,' she said, pushing them to the left side of her plate. At every meal it was the same performance of dividing her plate into food for consumption and crap, as she called it, to be shipped overseas to the starving.

Mom was in no mood for her shenanigans. 'Just eat the bloody stuff.'

'T, do you know where Greg is?'

'No, I haven't seen him all day,' she said, suspiciously. It was no secret; Greg had little tolerance for his youngest sibling.

Mom cut a piece of roast beef topping it with a smear of horseradish. 'I believe he's making deliveries with Ralph.'

Tammy looked up from her plate. 'That sounds like him now. Either that or we've got a robber joining us for supper.'

Gregory hurried into the kitchen. 'Sorry I'm late.'

Without looking up from her dinner, Mom suggested he wash his hands before sitting down at the table.

'Where were you?' Tammy said, mashing her potatoes with her fork, watching him pull up his chair.

'Making deliveries with Ralph.'

Mom glanced at the clock. 'You're usually home long before this. You know what time dinner is,' she said, raising an eyebrow. Dinner was always at 5:30 every evening with little exception.

Gregory cut a piece of meat. 'Today was busier than normal.'

Dad sopped up the gravy with a piece of bread. 'When you've finished dinner, Greg, how would you like to go over to the schoolyard and play catch? We can break in that new glove of yours.'

Gregory washed down his mouthful with a sip of milk. 'Sure Dad,' he said, placing the glass on the table.

Tammy, sensing his lack of enthusiasm said, 'By the way, where is your baseball glove? I haven't seen it around for a while.'

Gregory stared her down, adamantly stating it was in his room.

Funny, I was in your room this afternoon and didn't see it. 'Where?'

He scrunched up his face. 'None of your business, Miss Nosey.'

Tammy smirked, 'Yesterday, when I was over on Brendon Avenue visiting my best friend Diane, her brother Rickie was play- ing catch with a baseball glove that looked exactly like yours.'

Greg felt the back of his neck warm. 'People can have the same baseball glove,' he said defensively.

'Well, I was in your room...'

Greg dropped his fork onto the plate. 'You little brat.' He looked toward Mom for support. 'Can't I have any privacy? I need a damn lock on my door.'

Mom looked up from her plate. 'Gregory, I will not have you use profanity in this house. Tamara, you are not to go into your brother's room. Do you understand?'

She continued stacking green beans on the crap side of her plate, nodding.

After the dishes were cleared away, Dad knocked on Greg's door. 'Son, ready to play catch?'

Greg sighed, 'I have a confession, Dad. I've lost my baseball glove. I remember having it a couple of weeks ago at school, but I guess I must have left it there after a game of baseball,' he said re- morsefully.

85

Dad ran his hand through his hair, a nervous habit he acquired at a young age whenever he was upset. 'Did you check with your friends to see if they might have picked it up for you?' It was difficult to hide his disappointment. The leather glove had been costly, but he made the investment hoping his son would follow in his footsteps.

On Ken's return to Canada after the war, he joined a baseball league and was undoubtedly the Eddie Black team's star pitcher for three straight seasons. He had hoped to spend father/son time with Greg, something he never shared with his father, a self-centered man more focused on the bottle than child rearing.

'I've already checked with them; they don't have it. I guess it's lost,' he shrugged.

'I hope you can find it, Greg,' he said disappointedly, shutting the door behind him.

Less than ten seconds later, there was a tap on his door.

'What the hell do you want, you little troublemaker?'

Tammy wasted no time sitting down at his desk, enquiring about the magazine he was reading.

'Did I ask you to sit down?'

She ignored his belligerent tone. 'We need to talk. I know for a fact the baseball glove Rickie has is yours.'

He fired the magazine in her direction. 'It isn't.'

She persisted, 'Liar.'

'Did anyone ever tell you you're a pain in the ass?'

Tammy crossed her arms in defiance. 'There are so many things I could tell Mom about you. Starting with the swear words. Not to mention, the magazine full of bare and naked ladies.'

'I'm sure Mom doesn't give a shit what magazines I read. And swear words, my word against yours, jackass.'

'Fine, I'll let that go, but the baseball glove, not so fast.'

'I lost my glove. I've already talked to Dad about it,' he said angrily.

She jumped up from the chair. 'I know what happened, Greg. You sold it to Rickie for fifteen bucks.'

'No, I didn't,' he said calmly. 'Like I said at dinner, there are others who can have the same glove.'

'True. But Rickie was playing catch with the glove Dad bought especially for you.'

'Jesus Christ! It's not my glove,' he said emphatically.

Tammy placed her hands on her hips. 'He told Diane, his sister, my new best friend, he bought it from you for fifteen dollars.'

'Diane is full of shit.'

'Another swear word...'

'Get out of my room.'

'Whatever you want. Seeing I'm done talking to you, I'll go talk to Dad...'

He grabbed her skinny sun tanned arm. 'Rickie does not have my glove, got it.'

She stuck out her chin defiantly. 'The glove has your name and phone number written on the inside of the strap.'

Greg knew how hurt Dad would be if he found out he had indeed sold it to Rickie. He remembered how happy his father had been; wishing now, he hadn't been so foolish. *It's genuine cowhide leather, guaranteed to last for many years. We can go to the schoolyard, just the two of us, and play catch. I'll teach you how to pitch a fast one.*

An early morning thunderstorm did little to deter Tammy's mindset of finding out the real reason Greg had sold his baseball glove. After their brief meeting last night, she agreed to keep quiet, for now. He was hiding something she decided, hoisting her bowl and gulping down the last mouthfuls of milk.

Mom looked up from her novel with a tut. 'I'll never make a lady out of you,' she said, competing with a clap of thunder.

Tammy clanged her spoon into the empty bowl. 'You wouldn't want me to waste any. You're always going on about people starving around the world. Besides, you wouldn't let me have any more cereal to soak it up.'

Mom turned back to her novel wondering what she had done to deserve such a pain in the butt.

Tammy hurriedly brushed her teeth. Standing at the screen door she counted the seconds between the lightning and thunder. 'One steamboat, two steamboat, three steamboat, four steamboat,' she said, continuing until she counted twelve steamboats before the next rumble. Her best friend, Christine swore, if you count the seconds between thunders, the storm was that number of miles away. By her calculations, the storm was twelve miles from here. *Here goes nothing!* She swung the door wide, running swiftly down the driveway, across the road, up Johnson's driveway, through their rain soaked yard, scaling the four foot fence into McBride's backyard, running toward the carport, pausing briefly to catch her breath. Her new running shoes were full of water but she didn't care. She had cheated death by lightning.

Mr. Johnson shook his head watching Tammy climb the white wooden fence he had painted last week. He was tempted to bang on the bedroom window. Reluctantly, he shoved his hands into the pockets of his avocado green Bermuda shorts, cursing under his breath, *Rotten Rowan kid.*

The rain picked up as Tammy ran toward Diane's house, but nothing could stop her now.

Bea plugged in the kettle for a cup of tea, listening to the urgent knock on the front door. She smiled, opening the screen door. 'Is Greg supposed to be helping you with deliveries today?'

Ralph, eyes cast downward said, 'Actually, Mrs. Rowan, it's you I've come to speak with.'

Tammy knocked harder on the door. She didn't like being ignored.

'Oh it's you. I know you're anxious to see my sister, but do you have to keep knocking like that?' Rickie said. 'I'll get Diane.'

'Actually, it's you I've come to see,' Tammy said quietly.

Rickie screwed up his face. 'Me. What does a pint size,' he paused trying to find the right word, 'princess like you want with me.'

Tammy rolled her eyes. 'Cut the crap. You know I'm no princess, nor do I ever want to be. Is there somewhere we can talk in private?'

Rickie, taken aback by her straight forwardness, pointed to the chairs in the carport. 'Have a seat. Now, what can I do for you?'

Tammy got right to the point. 'I need to know why my brother sold his baseball glove to you.' He rolled his eyes sitting back hard in his chair. 'Without any friend protection bullshit,' she added.

Rickie half chuckled. 'It seems your brother needed some ready cash.'

'For what?'

Rickie shrugged. 'Didn't say.'

'Bullshit.'

'Christ you're obnoxious. Have you always been this frank?'

'Only when I need answers, or, if I feel like a person is hiding something,' she added suspiciously.

Rickie grinned, shaking his head. 'Well detective Tammy, I'm afraid I can't add anymore to your case.'

She looked him in the eye. 'I'm willing to pay you for information.'

'Wow! You are like your brother, always wanting to make a deal.'

She smirked, 'It's in the blood.'

'Look kid, why don't you just ask Greg. I really have no idea why he needed the cash.' He stood, walking toward the door. 'Let's just say, it's not in the cards.'

Bea ushered Ralph into the kitchen offering him a coffee. 'How do you like you coffee?' she said, pouring a steaming cup.

'Black, thank you. I have to make this quick before Greg finds out I'm here,' he said, resting his hand on the cup.

His comment perked her curiosity, more so than his impromptu visit. Bea looked up from her cup. 'You don't have to worry; he was up and out of here early this morning.'

The answer hit Tammy like a bolt of early morning lightning. Anxious to get back home, she picked up her pace, stopping suddenly eyeing Ralph's van parked out front.

'Have you been encouraging this?' Bea questioned in an accusatory tone.

Ralph looked up from his cup. 'In the beginning I thought it was harmless fun, but recently it's gotten way out of hand,' he said remorsefully.

Bea looked him in the eye. 'You realize this could cost you your job.'

He nodded dismally.

After a brief silence Bea said, 'I will get to the bottom of this. In the meantime, you are to have no further contact with my son.'

Tammy scooted out of the carport and around the corner of the house waiting for Ralph to drive off. Unsure of what the conversation was about, she felt it was her duty, as a loving sister, to warn her brother. She stepped inside announcing her arrival.

'I'm downstairs doing the laundry,' Mom said, loading the washing machine.

'Just wondering where you are.'

Tammy shut Greg's door quietly behind her. The room was tidy for a change; nothing seemed out of place with the exception of underneath his bed.

Bea placed the basket of wet laundry on the table, in need of a hot cup of tea before hanging it outside. 'Tammy, would you come here please. She caught the mischievous look on her daughter's face. 'You look like the cat that just swallowed the canary,' she said, raising a brow.

Tammy had a habit of screwing her face up when she wasn't sure what something meant, more so with her mother's dumb sayings. 'What does that mean?'

She unplugged the kettle. 'It means, whatever you've been up to you've been successful. It's written all over your face.'

Tammy beamed. 'Do you happen to know where Greg is?'

She was quite curious about Tammy's sudden interest in her brother; the two were barely civil at the best of times. 'I was just going to ask you.'

Greg knocked gently on the screen door.

'Hey Gregor, want to come in?' Rickie said, his younger sister, Diane, appeared at his side.

Greg shook his head. 'No, I can't stay long. I need to talk to you, in private.'

The two sat on the wooden fence at the back of the yard. Rickie picked at a piece of rotting fencing. 'What's up?'

'I need to buy back my baseball glove,' he said adamantly.

Rickie threw his head back. 'Ah, the baseball glove; seems to be a hot topic with your family right now.'

Greg turned to face him, knowing the answer.

'Your kid sister, aka the brat, came 'round early this morning trying to get answers out of me.'

It didn't surprise him. 'Mom's the word, right?' he said, raising his black bushy eyebrows.

'Now what kind of friend would I be if I sided with the enemy? I didn't tell her nothin'. She's quite a *determined* girl.'

'She's a royal pain in the ass,' Greg sighed, focusing on last night's confrontation. *I know for a fact you sold your glove to Rickie, so stop lying. Now, we can crack up a deal, and I'll keep my mouth shut or...Every Saturday morning for the next three months, when you go to KO's, bring me back a Jersey Milk chocolate bar, a box of Macintosh Toffee, five pieces of red licorice, (make sure they're fresh, please. I hate the stale stuff) and five pieces of Double Bub-*

ble gum. Since you're my brother, I'm letting you off easy. I could make it longer. He wondered why the hell he had agreed, but it was imperative she keep her mouth shut. Presently, Tammy was the least of his concerns. 'I need to buy back my glove, Rick.'

Tammy bounced on her bed trying to figure out where Greg might be; hopefully far enough away for her to search his desk for a piece of gum.

She tiptoed to his room, rummaging through the top drawer of his desk, tossing aside bits of folded paper. *IOU $15, signed Lou. IOU $75 signed Lou. IOU $30 signed Lou.* She had no idea what they meant. *Bingo!* Her mouth watered in anticipation tearing off the Bazooka gum wrapper.

Greg stood at his bedroom door watching Tammy rummage through his drawer. 'What the hell are you doing?'

She slammed it shut. 'You scared the wits out of me!'

He quickly shut the door. 'You fucking little bugger. What are you doing?'

She turned to face him. 'You are in enough trouble without adding swearing to the list. Have you seen Mom yet?'

'No.'

She sat in the chair. 'Gregory, you are in deep trouble, and as your best sister, it is my duty to warn you.'

He reached for the doorknob. 'You need to get the hell out of my room.'

'Not so fast. Your good friend Ralph was here this morning chatting with Mom. Let's just say, it was not a social call.'

The colour drained from his face. 'Where were you during the chat?'

'Standing at the screen door in the carport. Mom asked if he had encouraged your behaviour.'

He could tell by the puzzled look on her face she didn't have a clue, asking cautiously if there was anything else.

'Ralph said something about in the beginning it was harmless fun, but now it's gotten out of hand. It must be serious because Mom said he could lose his job. She also assured him she'd get to the bottom of it.'

'Did you hear anything else?'

Tammy shook her head. She had only heard snippets of conversation.

A smirk crossed his face. 'Looks like you have nothing to hold over me anymore.'

Chewing her gum keenly she said, 'true, but I have something of yours.'

She returned with her hands behind her back. 'This,' she said, jutting the plastic bag of poker chips and a deck of cards toward him.

Greg swallowed, 'give me the bag,' he said in even tone.

'Not so fast,' she said, swinging it behind her back. Though she had absolutely no idea why he'd want a bag of coloured circles, she caught his flushing cheeks. 'Do you still promise to fulfill my candy request?'

It was all he could do not to wring her neck. 'Yes, now hand it over.'

'I can still tell Dad about the baseball glove, should you decide to stop.'

'I will get your bloody candy,' he said, through gritted teeth. 'Now drop the bag and get out.'

'That includes being nice to me,' she smiled, tossing it on the bed.

It had been a hell of a day. In the end, Rickie had sold the baseball glove to his cousin, for an even higher price. He was angry at Ralph, his supposed friend, for going behind his back and snitching to his mother, not to mention his sister's continual threats. But the biggest challenge would be facing his mother's wrath.

Tammy was familiar with a deck of cards. Mom had taught her to play *Go Fish*, *Beat the Clock and Concentration*, but the colourful plastic discs remained a mystery.

Supper was quite subdued. Theresa was down the street attending a birthday celebration for Judy. Bea had spoken briefly to Ken before dinner about Ralph's visit. Needless to say, he was dreading the confrontation, more so than Greg. And Tammy sat quietly making faces on her plate with shrivelled, cold peas, the vegetable she hated most.

Before leaving the table, Mom instructed her to stay put until every pea had been consumed. The timing couldn't be better, offering a front row seat to what was being said in the living room.

After a brief preamble Mom said, 'I was absolutely flabbergasted to think my son was gambling. Are you that hard up for money? Your father and I have tried to instill, in all of you kids, nothing comes without working hard to earn it. I need to know all about your sudden interest in gambling.'

Greg pushed his glasses up onto the bridge of his nose, focusing just above his mother's head. He decided earlier on to put the onus on Ralph for corrupting him. 'It was all harmless fun, Mom. I have no idea why Ralph thinks I'm the one with the problem; it was all his idea in the first place to play a few games of *friendly* poker. He's the card shark who taught me the game, for crying out loud.'

Mom didn't believe he was that naïve. She knew her eldest well; the consummate artist of pinning the blame elsewhere. 'Ralph claims the games started getting out of hand with you wanting to play for higher stakes, gambling with money you hadn't even earned yet.'

He had lost some of his wages, working for free on occasion, but he wasn't going to admit it. 'Ralph is exaggerating, like he always does. In the end, I broke even, and gained some poker skills,' he said a little too confidently.

Mom was not amused. 'The question is; are you going to continue your gambling ways? It's an addiction, not a solution.'

He had given this a lot of thought lately. 'No Mom. I've decided to quit my job; wash my hands of Ralph and his gambling ways. You have my word, I will not gamble with him anymore.'

Dreading the answer, Dad asked him if he owed Ralph any money.

'I am not indebted to him, Dad. I'm sorry for any grief I may have caused you both. May I go to my room now?'

When Bea heard his bedroom door close, she grit her teeth, 'Lying bugger.'

Tammy quietly placed her plate on the counter then tiptoed down the hall to her room wondering if the plastic discs he wanted back so badly had anything to do with cards.

Dad knocked on her door. 'How are you doing, Tam? I see by your empty plate you ate all your peas.'

She turned up her nose, 'I hate peas.'

'I know, but they are good for you.'

She wanted to leave dinner talk behind her. The last thing she wanted to chat about was disgusting green peas. 'Dad, what are these?' she said, opening her hand. She had thought to pull a few out of the bag before handing them over to her brother.

He eyed the red, blue and white chips wondering where she had gotten them from. 'They're poker chips. I believe each colour has a monetary value. The blue chip may be worth ten dollars, red chip five dollars. To be honest, I don't know much about the chips or the game.'

Tammy's eyes widened. *Damn. There must have been 30 blue chips in that plastic bag. No wonder he wanted it back so badly.*

'Where did you get them from?' he asked curiously.

The question caught her off-guard; she wasn't quite ready to rat on her brother. 'I was playing store with my best friend, Lucy; we used them in place of real money. Neither of us has *any* money,' she said, hedging toward a raise in allowance.

Dad said humorously, 'It's not in the cards. In the meantime, I'm glad you ate all your peas. Mom will be very happy.'

That was the second time today she had heard the phrase *it's not in the cards,* surmising like her mother, others were into dumb sayings too.

Greg rolled his eyes hearing the knock on the door. He had grown all too familiar with Tammy's insistent knock.

'Just making sure you're going to keep up the bargain you made with me,' she said, eyeing the bag on his desk.

'Why should I? Mom and Dad know about my gambling.'

Tammy asked if he'd bother to mention the baseball glove.

He had forgotten, knowing the glove was gone for good; there was no way he could tell Dad.

'How could I forget, for Christ sake, with your continual banging on my door to remind me?'

She walked to his desk and picked up the poker chips. 'Since you've given up gambling, can I have these?'

He grabbed the bag, tossing it in the garbage. 'I've learned that gambling causes nothing but trouble. I'm done with it. Now get the hell out.'

Bea plugged in the kettle for tea. 'I don't trust him,' she said, measuring two tablespoons of dried tea leaves. 'He's a sneaky bugger,' she said, heating the teapot.

Ken was hoping to avoid any more stress before bed. 'Hopefully, Greg has seen the light and won't do it again. It's commendable he's eliminating temptation by quitting his job with Ralph.'

Bea poured the tea, 'I trust him about as far as I can throw him,' she said, handing him the mug.

Theresa arrived home shortly after eight.

'How was the birthday dinner?' Mom smiled.

'Good thanks. Mrs. Patterson made Judy's favourite baked chicken dish. I don't know how she does it, working full time. But the best part was the birthday cake she picked up from a bakery near her work. The chocolate icing had to be an inch thick. It was so delicious.'

Bea had often thought about returning to work, but decided her family was more important. 'If you like, I can make the cake for your birthday.'

Theresa's eyes widened at the prospect. 'Nah, I still love your golden cake with chocolate icing, but thanks, Mom, you're the best.' Reluctantly she asked where Tammy was.

'She said she was going to have a bath and go to bed early.'

Theresa sighed knowing a sudden change in Tammy's behaviour usually meant she was up to something. 'And Greg?'

The look on her Mom's face changed even more so. 'I believe he's at Jim's house.'

Tammy stacked blue chips on the desk. *There's got to be over a hundred dollars.* Her mouth salivated thinking of how much chocolate she could buy, counting the red chips and white chips, stacking them neatly.

'Where did you get those?' Theresa said.

Tammy jumped, 'I found them,' she said, quickly scooping them into the bag.

Therese shook her head. 'I thought you were in bed asleep.'

'I was,' she said, climbing back into bed. 'Where are you going?'

Theresa turned on her heel, closing the door behind her.

Tammy stuffed the bag of chips into her bright pink Barbie purse, last year's Christmas gift from Aunt Muriel and hung the strap on the hanger with her winter coat. *Nobody will ever find them.* She jumped into bed singing happily, pulling up the covers. 'You are my sunshine, my only sunshine…'

'Go to sleep, Tamara.'

'You make me happy when skies are grey, you'll never know dear how much I love you, please don't take my sunshine away. I've finished singing now, Mom. Good night.'

There was no reply.

Chapter Nine

BEA BALANCED THE wicker basket of wet laundry on her hip, ascending the basement stairs. Halfway up, she spotted a row of shrivelled peas lined up neatly along the back of the wooden step. *That little bugger.*

Tammy pumped her legs harder and harder in the warm sunshine until the swing was as high as it would go. She was surprised no one was around, that is, until she spotted George, the retard, as she fondly referred to him, walking quickly toward her.

'Hi George, I did have all the swings all to myself until you came along. You can join me if you want,' she said, watching him occupy the swing to her right, pumping his legs fiercely to catch up.

After a few minutes of silent swinging, Tammy coasted to the ground with George following suit. When the swing stopped, he sat forlornly staring at the dirt groove beneath him.

Tammy suggested they walk over to the creek to catch frogs.

He continued staring at the ground. 'Naw.'

She had spent enough time with him to know when something was troubling him. 'Okay, what's bothering you?'

'Nothin'.'

'Bull crap.' She could tell by his face he was hiding something, in need of more coaxing she continued. 'If you tell me, I can probably help you.'

He turned toward her so quickly, it startled her. 'If I tell you something, do you promise not to tell anybody? And I mean anybody.'

Tammy's green eyes widened with curiosity 'cross my heart and hope to die,' she said, drawing a big X across her chest.

Barry knocked harder still on Ronald's front door, totally convinced he was in there.

'Don't answer it, Tim,' Ronald whispered. 'It's that sicko, pervert Barry.'

Tim was confused. 'I thought he was your best friend.'

Ronald said disgustedly, 'He's never been my best friend, for crying out loud. And furthermore, I don't ever want to see that frickin' creep ever again. That scumbag turns my gut. The only best friend I have is Daniel.'

Barry hurried down the driveway rubbing his aching knuckles, unaware of the audience behind the white sheers.

Timothy turned to his brother, 'Finally, he's gone.'

A disgusted look crossed Ronald's face. 'Good riddance, filthy pig.'

Totally confused, Timothy furrowed his bushy brown eyebrows. 'What in the world happened between you two?'

Ronald pointed to the grey swivel chair. 'Have a seat, little brother.'

Barry walked quickly toward Daniel's house hoping Ronald was there. He knocked steadily on the door.

'Oh, Barry, it's you.'

'Hello Mrs. Fleming. Is Daniel here?'

She peered at him through the crack. 'I'm sorry. What did you say?'

'Is Daniel home?'

'Yes, right, Daniel.' She rubbed her temples, her mind in disarray. 'Actually, he's gone somewhere. If you'll excuse me,' she said, hastily closing the door.

Barry's stomach flipped. *Damn.*

Daniel sat against the old willow tree focusing on the fragmented remnants of a charred rope swaying back and forth in the warm summer breeze. He thought of Ronald wading waist deep into the creek to retrieve an old tire wedged in the mud and silt; Barry's discovery of some heavy rope tied around a makeshift raft anchored downstream. Together they secured the rope around the tire. He had climbed the tree, securing the rope tightly to a large limb jutting out over the creek. They had spent endless hours swinging back and forth over the water, but unfortunately it didn't take long for others to follow suit. Barry and Daniel were okay with others using the swing when they weren't around, but Ronald was fiercely opposed, so much so, he set it ablaze with newspaper, turning the tire into an inferno sending black acrid smoke high into the air; the fire truck's siren sent them scurrying behind the school. There was nothing left but a smoldering charred rope when the fire department arrived. The three friends vowed never to tell anybody.

Daniel rested his head on his folded arms. So much had changed since that day; his life would never be the same.

'There you are,' Barry said, gasping for breath.

Daniel winced at the sound of his voice.

Still trembling from the run, he sat down beside him, giving him a friendly nudge. 'Hey buddy, a penny for your thoughts.'

Reluctantly, Daniel raised his head, focusing straight ahead.

Barry's voice trembled. 'I know you mustn't think much of me now. To tell you the truth, I don't think much of myself either. But it just happened, man,' he said, rubbing his sweaty face vigorously. After a few moments he continued. 'It was really strange. All I did was hug her to calm her down and then suddenly this uncontrollable sensation filled me,' he said, verging on tears. 'I fought this demon inside of me.' He paused, looking skyward into a cloudless sky. 'But the warmth of Gloria's body against mine almost drove me insane until,' he paused looking toward his friend, 'the next thing I knew I was having sex with her.' A wicked smile crossed his face, 'sex is amazing. I just know you would love it too. Hell, what guy wouldn't? It's what we do, isn't it? It began so innocently, you have to believe me. All I was doing was trying to keep her calm so she wouldn't upset our mom, because of her condition. She can't get upset, you know,' he added matter-of-factly. 'Can we please keep...' his mouth clamped shut watching Daniel tear off across the field.

Katie Fleming turned up the cuffs of her denim jeans, tucking in her red and white checked gingham shirt. What should have been an easy task morphed into a frustrating struggle with the top button and zipper. Her once slim figure, much more rounded now, forced her to make several attempts at sucking in her stomach enough to fasten the button and move the zipper, though only halfway. She decided then and there a diet was in order, vowing to cut back on her baking. Short in stature, she had always prided herself in being in the best shape possible. That is until Daniel and Dana came along and she literally went to pot.

Moving toward the bathroom, she ran a hand through her short, grey-flecked, pixie cut that at one time cascaded down her back in long, brown, luxurious waves, the way her beloved husband, Perry, liked it. Shortly after Dana's birth, she decided a short haircut would be easier to manage with two young children occupying all of her time. She reached for the comb recalling her husband's reaction. *I begged you not to cut your hair. Why did you do it, Katie, when I forbid you to do so?* It seemed from that moment on their relationship changed; he became quite indifferent toward her. She dabbed some rouge on her already flushed cheeks, reaching for the new tube of red lipstick. Removing the lid, she contemplated wearing it. After the children were born, she would only wear lipstick on special occasions, preferring a more natural look.

Perry Fleming eased his dark grey Austin Mini into the driveway parking it just shy of the carport, sliding his impeccably dressed, slim physique, across the light grey leather seat. Moving toward the trunk, his piercing blue eyes rapidly scanned the front yard eyeing the long tufts of grass and weeds sprouting throughout the burnt out lawn; the driveway in need of a good sweep. But it was his prized yellow burgundy tipped Hybrid Tea roses that upset him most; the blooms wilting and dying in the afternoon sun. He sighed deeply reaching for his brown leather suitcase.

Contemplating the chipped, peeling paint above the brass doorknob Perry opened the door, stepping determinedly inside.

A smiling Katie greeted him, offering to take his suitcase upstairs.

'I can do it,' he said, curtly, tightening his grip on the handle. 'Where are the children?'

Katie, hoping for a peck on the lips or a warm hug like in the old days after extended business trips, reluctantly stepped back rubbing her forehead; a motion she did a lot lately, helping her to focus. 'I'm not sure where Daniel is. But I do know that Dana will be returning home shortly.'

He stared intently into her hazel eyes.

Katie, feeling somewhat flustered continued, 'Yesterday evening, Dana had supper at Catherine's house; the two slept in a tent, in the backyard, of course,' she half smiled, hoping they had enjoyed the experience. 'It was Dana's first time sleeping in a tent,' she added.

'Have you spoken to the children?' he asked impatiently.

She was taken aback by his curt demeanor. 'I've spoken briefly to Daniel,' she said, recalling the horrified look on his face before he bolted out the door.

A disgusted looked crossed his face. 'You need to remove that red gunk off your lips. You look ridiculous.'

She felt her face flush with embarrassment, wishing she hadn't rouged her cheeks. 'Yes, yes, of course,' she said, running the back of her hand across her mouth.

His face soured. 'Now look, it's all over the back of your hand, not to mention smudged around your mouth. You look like a silly clown. Go wash your face for god's sake; make yourself presentable.'

Katie fought back tears lathering soap in her hands, scrubbing her face vigorously, removing any trace of lipstick and rouge. She rinsed her face with cold water again and again, burying her face in a clean white soft towel. Staring at her mirrored image, she felt much older than her 38 years; she sighed recalling her first encounter with Perry Fleming.

She had been researching her thesis in the library at the University of Oxford in England when suddenly a young, handsome, charismatic man occupied the seat across from her, wasting no time introducing himself. Together, they discussed their studies, aspirations and hopes, all with a common thread. Time passed by so quickly, their lunch break had come and gone, zeroing in on suppertime. Perry, not wanting their time to end, invited her to join him for a meal. From that moment on, they became inseparable, furthering their studies together.

Shortly after graduation, Perry asked for her hand in marriage. The proposal came with the proposition of a new life across the ocean in Canada. It didn't take much convincing, she was not only madly in love with this handsome man, but truly fascinated by his superior take charge attitude.

The young couple settled in a two bedroom flat in downtown Toronto; soon after, Katie revealed she was pregnant. Nine months later, they welcomed Daniel. After the birth of their second child, Dana, the apartment was much too cramped for their growing family. Perry, taking it upon himself, purchased an attractive three bedroom grey brick bungalow on a quiet suburban crescent to raise their children.

In the beginning, they worked together creating a cozy home life for their family. Perry would go to work each day, returning home promptly at five for supper with his family. He was dedicated to his family; fiercely committed to bettering his career. It wasn't long before he ascended the corporate ladder securing a position with top management. But unfortunately, the promotion entailed many hours of travel to cities around the world, keeping him away for extended periods, leaving Katie to raise their children.

Hugging the towel to her chest, tears ran softly down her cheeks. *Perry, my one and only...*

Annoyed with her tardiness, Perry called from the bottom of the stairs. 'Katie, are you finished up there?' He was getting anxious to get this wrapped up.

Hastily, she dabbed her puffy eyes with a tissue.

Daniel kept running until he couldn't take another step. Gasping for breath, he sat down on the curb across from his house, eyeing his father's car. Drawing deep breaths, he lowered his head into his folded arms.

Katie and Perry stood face to face. 'Have you contacted the real estate, like I asked?' he said firmly.

She lowered her head, speaking to the floor. 'I wanted to be sure it is what you want,' she said meekly, fighting tears.

Perry hated weakness. Placing his forefinger under her chin, he jerked her head up. 'Of course it's what I want. I wouldn't have asked you to complete the task otherwise.' There was no remorse whatsoever on his part. 'Now, the sooner we get the house on the market, the sooner we can move on with our separate lives. I spoke with my lawyer yesterday and he's preparing the divorce papers...'

'Jesus Christ. It's true then,' Daniel said, slamming the door behind him. 'You're divorcing Mom. Are you divorcing your kids too?'

Perry faced his son, standing a head taller. 'Don't be ridiculous. I would never leave my kids. I have already made arrangements for you and Dana to live with me; we can be a real family.'

Katie's head spun with the news. He was leaving her and, taking the children.

Daniel had never been a violent person, choosing to run off his anger and frustrations, but standing mere inches from his father, he had to fight the urge to clock him. For some time now, he had sensed something was amiss with his father's extended absences, especially during the last few years. During his infrequent visits home, he was like a stranger, tense and aloof to everyone, especially his mother, continually criticising her weight, mannish hair style and lack of housekeeping skills. He accused her of being lazy and self-absorbed, which couldn't have been further from the truth. She was an excellent housekeeper and wonderful mother, fully committed to her children's well-being. Daniel shook his head, 'A *real* family. I thought that's what I had all these years.'

Calmly, Perry recited his well planned speech. 'Over the years, your mother and I have grown apart. Now it's time to move on and go our separate ways. I have made arrangements to ensure she will be well taken care of, affording her a very comfortable lifestyle.' He continued talking as if Katie was no longer present. 'Perhaps in time, she will meet someone...'

'I don't want to meet someone else,' she interrupted, staring intently at her soon to be ex-husband. 'It's you I love,' she said admiringly, her mouth quivering with each word. 'There could never be another love for me.'

Perry dismissed her feelings. 'As usual, Katie, you are being over emotional. You *will* get over this and move on.'

Daniel said defiantly, 'I want to stay here with Mom. I definitely don't want to live with you.'

A devious smirk crossed his father's face. 'I'm afraid you don't have a choice. I've enrolled you and your sister in one of the best private schools in Vermont. Both of you will begin your studies at the end of this month.'

Daniel felt his whole body tense. 'Are you crazy? I don't want to go to Vermont. I want to stay here with what's left of my family. You can't make me go,' he said stubbornly.

'Son, you have just turned fifteen. Therefore, I am still your legal guardian. In other words, you aren't capable or mature enough to make your own decisions,' he added smugly. 'Now, as soon as Dana comes home, I will tell her...'

'Tell me what?' Dana said, stepping inside.

Barry had tried in vain to keep up with Daniel but knew his attempt was futile. Daniel, the school's top long distance runner, held the title for the past five years. Breathlessly, he rounded the corner spotting Mr. Fleming's car parked in the driveway, deterring him for now. He walked toward home waving at the kids standing on McConnel's front lawn, calling out to Tommy.

Absently, Tommy waved back. 'Okay, in two weeks we're off to the CNE. We've collected all the Tely Fun Checks. Now all we need is a nice sunny day,' he said, gazing skyward.

Barry approached from behind. 'Is this a private meeting or can anyone join in?'

Janice said, 'We're just finalizing our plans for the CNE.'

Barry looked surprised. 'You're all going to the Ex?'

'Opening day,' Theresa smiled. 'I can hardly wait. It's the first year I'm allowed to go parent-less.'

Barry said sarcastically, 'I thought you had to be thirteen.'

'Next Monday, all gifts and cards would be graciously accepted,' she smiled happily.

Barry wanted to go with them, but they unanimously vetoed the request. The three had worked hard collecting newspapers and organizing their big day. As he walked away, he was convinced they knew nothing about his liaison with his sister.

Tammy ran home as quickly as her skinny, sun tanned legs would go. Pulling the screen door open she yelled for her sister.

Mom moved quickly toward the door. 'What's this all about? The whole bloody neighbourhood can hear you.'

Tammy gulped air. 'How come you can use swear words and I can't?'

'Tamara, I know I shouldn't swear, but at times, you are enough to make a saint swear. Now go wash up for lunch.'

'I really need to find Theresa. Do you have any idea where she is?'

Mom glanced at her watch. 'It's almost lunchtime; she should be home any minute. In the meantime, wash your hands ready for lunch. Then young lady, you can collect the peas you left to dry out on the stairs and put them in the garbage.'

Tammy quickly washed her hands then quietly snuck out the front door, tearing across Smythe's lawn coming to an abrupt halt.

A friendly smile crossed Barry's face moving toward Smythe's front door. 'Hi Tam. Where are you off to in such a hurry?'

Her eyes widened. 'Don't you talk to me!' she said, running off.

Theresa furrowed her brow listening to Tammy call out to her. It was obvious, by the petrified look on her face, something was up.

Tommy said, 'You look like you've just seen a monster or something, Tam.'

'You are not going to believe what George told me this morning,' she said breathlessly.

Barry moved quickly into Smythe's backyard, hiding behind a row of unkempt bushes growing wildly along the chain link fence.

Dana dropped her small red suitcase, running toward her father's open arms. 'Daddy, I've missed you so much!' she said, hugging him tightly. 'What do you want to tell me?' she said, eyeing the forlorn look on her mother's red face and Daniel's bowed head. 'Is something wrong?'

Dad reached for her hand, leading the way into the bright, sunny living room. 'Sit down here with me, little Pumpkin,' he said, patting the chesterfield. He had called her little Pumpkin for as long as she could remember.

Dana turned expecting her mother and Daniel to follow, but when they didn't she asked him again what was going on.

He spoke candidly about their beautiful new home in Vermont and the private school she would be attending at the end of the month.

Dana was confused. She turned toward her mom sensing she had been crying, something she had been doing a lot lately. 'Mommy, do you not want to move to Vermont?'

Her mother clamped her hands over her mouth trying to halt the sudden sobs racking her body; Daniel rushed to her side.

Perry drew a deep breath. 'Your mother won't be joining us, Pumpkin. It's just you, me and...'

'What do you mean Mommy isn't coming with us?' she interrupted.

Perry, hoping for a smooth transition said bluntly, 'Your mother and I are divorcing.'

Dana felt the walls collapsing around her crushing her beneath the rubble, gasping for breath. She thought of Gloria and how much her life had changed; now her life was about to change forever too. Not only would she never see her best friend again, but the one person Dana had always depended on would no longer be a part of her life. 'No,' she cried. 'I'm not leaving my mommy ever.'

Perry stood. 'Like your brother, you have no choice.'

In less than ten minutes, the world she had known for twelve years was changing forever. 'I hate you. I will never go with you,' she hissed, running toward the door.

'Pumpkin stop!' he demanded.

'I'm not your pumpkin anymore,' she screamed, running out the door.

The incessant ringing of the telephone shattered the sudden quiet. After numerous rings, Daniel picked it up, listening to the hesitant pause on the other end. 'It's for you, Perry,' he said disgustedly.

Perry grabbed the receiver. 'Yes,' he said tersely, holding it tightly. 'I gave you strict instructions not to contact me unless it was urgent. Now, please wait for my call.' He slammed down the phone. 'It was my secretary reminding me of an urgent meeting I must attend. I will be back.'

Daniel watched his father's hasty exit. In the last few years, his arrival home meant frequent calls from women claiming to be his secretary. *I have an urgent meeting I must attend;* his standard reply, believing his family oblivious to his charade. He often wondered if his mother knew about Perry's liaisons, choosing instead to bury her head in the sand.

He sat down beside her on the stairs. 'Mom, Dana and I will not be going to Vermont, you have my word.'

She turned to him pleading, 'You must go find your sister.'

He stared at her bloodshot eyes, hesitant to leave her. 'Will you be okay?'

'Yes, yes, I'm fine. Please find Dana.'

Reluctantly, he left her sitting on the stairs with her face buried in her hands.

Perry parked his Austin Mini between a shiny, bright red Ferrari and a beige Cadillac. He straightened his tie, briefly running a hand through his wavy blond hair, moving toward the entrance.

The doorman swung the door wide with a friendly greeting. 'Good day, Mr. Fleming; always a pleasure to see you.'

Perry nodded, pressing a bill in his hand.

'Have a good day,' he said, watching him walk briskly across the lobby. He smiled pocketing the cash. *Always a great day when he's in town.*

The young, attractive desk clerk watched Perry approach, greeting him with her best smile. 'Your suite has been prepared, Mr. Fleming. The way you like it,' she added in a low sensual voice, watching him sign the paperwork. 'Thank you Mr. Fleming. If I can be of further assistance, please do not hesitate to contact me,' she said, handing him the key. A knowing smile crossed his face in the exchange.

'Enjoy your stay,' she gushed as he disappeared into the elevator. Without counting her tip, she stuffed the bills in her bra, savouring the warmth.

Perry was used to women swooning over him; there was a time he would indulge their fantasies. He walked briskly down the hall, inhaled deeply unlocking the door, vowing it would be different this time.

The door closed silently behind him. Soft jazz music wafted from hidden speakers strategically placed throughout the suite, the lights dim, inviting. He loosened his navy silk tie moving toward the sparkling glass table. Reaching for the crystal glass, he inhaled the rich fragrant contents; one shot of Dalmore Scotch poured over two crystal clear ice cubes. Like the scent of a woman, he knew it well. He sipped the liquid gold, removed his tie, folding it neatly.

'I was beginning to wonder.'

He swirled the melting cubes once around the glass; the drink now past its prime. He took one last sip, placing it on the table beside the tie. 'You know I had to take care of things at home,' he said tersely, turning toward the voice. He felt his pulse quicken watching her saunter closer.

'You should never keep me waiting,' she said, running a finger over his lip, reaching for the tie.

His body filled with an urgency he never tired of. *I was a fool to keep you waiting.*

She read his mind. 'You know I don't like to be kept waiting,' she whispered, wrapping the tie around his neck, minimizing the gap.

With mere inches between them, his arms ached to draw her near. 'Forgive me, my love.'

She yanked the tie, kissing him passionately, stepping back as he reached for her.

His head spun. 'Oh god,' he whimpered.

Slowly she undid the sash of her emerald green robe, slipping it smoothly off her shoulders.

The sight of her soft white shoulders drove him mad with passion. 'Please don't make me beg.' Once again, he despised himself for being so weak.

She smiled confidently releasing the robe; a puddle of green settled on her manicured feet. Ever so slowly, she inched her hands toward her ample breasts, fingering the nipples. 'Tell me how much you want me,' she whispered, reaching for the solid gold comb, releasing an avalanche of long auburn hair.

Katie sat on the stairs hugging her knees, trying to recall the last time she had been intimate with her husband. During their university days when love was brand new, they had spent their time studying their notes or each other. Their love making changed when they arrived in Canada, especially after the birth of their children. But the most dramatic change occurred with Perry's determination to climb the corporate ladder. At the time, she watched with admiration all his hard work and dedication come to fruition, in turn, dedicating herself completely to the well-being of their children. His success came with a price, more frequent travel taking him away for weeks at a time. In the beginning, though she missed him terribly, she coped by keeping herself busy with the children and household chores; but weeks turned into months and Perry was seldom home. When he was home for short interludes, he made it very clear he didn't want to be, criticizing the way she looked, what she wore, her mannish hair style, even the way she spoke. It seemed there was no pleasing him and after all these years, he wanted to end their union. But Katie, ever hopeful, devised a plan, patiently awaiting his return.

Though it was close to 85 degrees, Barry broke out in a cold sweat scurrying home; the television blared throughout the house. Feverously, he wiped his clammy palms on his shirt moving up the stairs, opening Gloria's door, eyeing his siblings huddled together in the corner. 'What the hell are you doing?'

Gloria screamed.

Ben eagerly climbed into the car, anticipating the remaining leg of his journey that would place him in his driveway by four at the latest. He was anxious to get home to his family, especially Gloria; her moroseness the day he left had haunted him throughout the trip. Lately, he'd been contemplating a desk job; though it meant a cut in salary, the trade-off would be more family time, something he truly missed.

Garnet, her face distorted with anger, flung the bedroom door wide striking the wall behind. For a scrawny woman she was quite strong. 'What is going on?' she hissed. 'The whole damn neighbourhood can hear the ruckus.'

On shaky legs, Gloria moved past Barry toward her mother, stopping mere inches from her face. 'There's something going on that you need to tend to, now.'

Ben felt the tension in his neck and shoulders ease turning onto the Crescent. Though the drive had been uneventful, it seemed to take much longer. He was anxious to see his family, waving at some kids playing at the side of the road, disappointed his kids weren't among the group; assuming they were all at home anticipating his arrival.

He parked the old Ford Falcon just outside the carport, exiting the car for a good old homecoming stretch in the warm sunshine, hankering the vodka martini he would enjoy catching up with family stuff. He greeted Anne Smythe, yanking his suitcase out of the trunk, watching curiously as she bolted toward the front door, quickly shutting it behind her. He shrugged deciding she must be having another bad day. She was the talk of the neighbourhood; he was well aware of the mental issues she suffered. He felt sorry for her husband, Robert, coming home from his business trips only to be greeted by a drug dependent wife.

Walking toward the screen door, he pondered the quiet inside; for once the television wasn't blaring throughout.

Tammy stared at the shrivelled pork chop, lumpy mashed potatoes and overcooked Brussels sprouts while Dad patiently encouraged her to eat. It was apparent something, other than her disliking pork chops, was troubling her, but he decided to wait until after supper to broach the subject. He loathed upsets at dinnertime.

Tammy purposely slammed her fork down. 'I can't get this out of my mind and it's making me feel sick to my stomach,' she moaned, covering her face with her hands.

Theresa glanced at Dad. 'Tam, It's okay, we'll talk about it after...'

'No! I have to talk about it now. I want Mom and Dad to know what that creep Barry Murray has been doing to his sister.' And with that, she relayed George's verbatim word for word at the swings this morning.

Dad, his face flushed with embarrassment said, 'you can excuse yourself and go to your room.'

Tammy pushed her chair up against the wall, quickly exiting the kitchen in tears.

Dad turned to Theresa. 'Is there any truth to what she's saying?' he asked skeptically.

'I don't know what to believe. May I be excused?'

Gregory said, 'I'm sure it's not true. I've known Bar for years.'

Ken looked across the table at his wife. 'I'm not sure where Tammy comes up with this...'

Bea raised a hand in protest, 'It's all over the neighbourhood, dear. Anne made one of her rare appearances outdoors this afternoon, filling me in on all the details while I was tending to the laundry.'

Garnet's chair was turned toward three morose kids sitting on the dark rust coloured chesterfield. It was certainly not the welcoming Ben had anticipated, noting the petrified look on his daughter's face, running toward him. 'I'm so scared,' she cried.

'Sit back down, you little slut!' Garnet bellowed. 'You are a disgrace to this family.'

Gloria sobbing hysterically, latched on tightly to her father.

With absolutely no warning, Ben had just walked in to the worst nightmare of his life. 'It's okay,' his voice trembled. But it was far from okay as his demented wife tried to yank Gloria's arms away from him.

'You have disgraced the family you disgusting little slut,' her eyes wide with fury; nostrils flared, 'I hate...'

'That's enough!' Ben yelled, pressing Gloria's head tightly to his chest. 'Get away from her!'

Garnet stepped back wiping saliva from the side of her mouth with the back of her hand, briefly glancing at her husband, turning her attention back to her daughter. 'I'm not finished with you, slut.'

Ben fought back tears watching her ascend the stairs. 'Jesus Christ, what the hell is going on?'

Garnet slammed the bedroom door; sitting down hard on the bed, yanking the bedside table drawer open spilling the contents onto the floor. Her hands trembled tossing aside pamphlets on *How to grow a better garden; How to make better meat loaf; How to knit; How to be a better parent*, squares of fabric, a package of unopened condoms, finally locating a small package of Du Maurier cigarettes. She inhaled the acrid smoke deeply, focusing on the smoky image in the mirror above the dresser staring back at her; a voice unlike hers permeated the space between. Frantically she waved at the smoke. *You are a disgusting little slut, Garnet. You have disgraced the family.* Garnet felt the hair on the back of her neck rise. 'No Mother. It was not like that at all. I am not a slut. Brian raped me. He raped me while you chose to turn a blind eye to his advances, encouraging his visits. The day you left us alone to go shopping, he raped me. He told me this is what good girls do. He thinks I'm beautiful, Mother. *I don't believe you, Garnet. Brian is such a nice boy. He would never do anything like that. The rumours are true. You led him on, like a slut.*

Garnet felt the cigarette burn the tip of her fingers. Chucking it into the ashtray, she tucked a strand of lose hair behind her ear. 'Brian doesn't think I'm a slut, you stupid bitch. He thinks I'm beautiful.'

Ben turned his attention to his sons sitting motionless on the chesterfield. Barry, his arms resting on top of his legs, head bowed, stared at the floor. George, his face streaked with tears stared straight ahead. He could only imagine what his sons felt witnessing their mother's insane outburst. His throat felt parched, in need of water; the martini a long gone craving. With the front of his shirt soaked with Gloria's tears, he remained paralyzed, afraid to move.

Theresa sat down on the edge of Tammy's bed. 'Tam, you mustn't let what happened to Gloria upset you.'

She rolled over, sitting up quickly. 'I have an imagination, you know. I'm not stupid when it comes to sex. I keep picturing what Barry was doing to his sister, even when I don't want to. George told me everything. I told him Barry was raping her. He didn't know what that meant,' she added. 'Well I do. My best friend, Lois, said that if a woman doesn't want a man to do things to her private parts, it's called rape. If I was Gloria, I would have stabbed him with a kitchen knife or something sharp when he was asleep. I wish Barry was dead, the fucking creep. And to make matters even worse, George was so upset I had to hug him while he cried on my shoulder. Can you imagine hugging George, the retard?' she shuddered. 'But I had to; he was so upset he didn't know what to do. When he finally stopped crying, I told him he had to tell his mom immediately what a monster his brother is.'

Theresa sighed, 'You have done all you can, Tam. Hopefully, his mother will get to the bottom of it.'

Tammy shook her head. 'I'm not sure his mom can handle it. She suffers from some mental condition. That's probably why George isn't all there,' she added. 'I think she's kinda like the fucking whacko next door only she doesn't take pills. She just sits and smokes watching television all day. That's why he may not tell her. If he does, she could go off the deep end. And, I don't give a shit if you tell Mom about my swearing. This is enough to make a saint swear.'

Theresa reassured her she had no intention of snitching. For a brief moment she thought of the pervert at the pool, surmising everyone reacts differently under duress. 'Mr Murray drove by us this afternoon. I'm sure he can handle it.'

Ben drew a deep breath, 'I'm so sorry you had to witness your mother's outburst. I have no idea why…'

'It's rape!' George yelled. 'Barry's been raping my twin sister! It's not Gloria's fault. She's not a slut,' he cried, burying his face into the back of the couch.

Ben felt a punch to his head so severe he blanked out, legs buckling he collapsed to the floor. Gloria cried out, pulling his arm trying to stop the fall. In a dizzy haze he moved to his hands and knees. *This can't be true. Not my son.* Tears stung his eyes looking toward his eldest, his voice barely audible. 'Son?'

Barry, sweating profusely focused on a cigarette burn in the middle of Mom's coveted Persian rug.

'Answer me, damn it!' he said, rising on shaky legs. But he already knew the answer; his head snapped back with a grotesque, guttural noise emanating from deep inside his shattered soul, desperately willing the obtrusive crack in the ceiling to open up and swallow him whole. Hysterically, he clung tightly to Gloria, his only lifeline preventing him from crumbling further into the depths of hell. 'This can't be. Not my son,' he repeated dejectedly.

Barry cried into his hands. 'I didn't mean to. I swear.'

Ben looked at him in horror. 'My god, she's your sister.'

He uncovered his face. 'It just happened, Dad.'

Ben wasn't sure if it was his complacent tone or the look on his face, but every muscle in his body tensed. He had never been a violent man, but for an insane moment he wanted to punch the shit out of his eldest son.

'Daddy,' Gloria said through her tears. 'I'm so scared.'

Tears flowed down Ben's face with the reality; the family life he coveted so dearly was gone forever. He hugged his daughter protectively. 'You have my word. He will never touch you again.'

Guilt consumed Ben trying to comprehend the magnitude of what transpired during his absences; only to discover the warning signs had all been there. *Gloria's insistence he take her with him, her persistent crying; Garnet's flippant assurances it was just a phase Gloria was going through; Barry's reclusiveness, they rarely spoke when he was home; George's morose silence.* He sobbed hysterically knowing he had no one to blame but himself.

Daniel ran toward the creek hoping to find his sister. Recently, she had mentioned her secret discovery of a bend in the creek where the water flows over large rocks, creating a peaceful waterfall. She had spent hours imagining a mini version of herself wearing a yellow polka dot raincoat with matching umbrella, navigating the slippery rocks, the water cascading above.

Daniel quietly sat down beside her. 'Did you manage to stay dry?'

She continued staring at the foamy water at the base of the falls. 'No, I slipped off the rocks so many times.'

He said patiently, 'Yes, but did you climb back up to safety?'

Dana sighed, 'Yeah, but I wish I had drowned. Then it would take away all the pain.'

Daniel put his arm around her shoulder. 'Lately, it's been a hell of a time of it for you; first your best friend, Gloria, and now Mom and Dad are divorcing. But we still have each other, little sister; together we'll get through all this.' He thought of his mom at home alone. 'But right now, we really need to be there for Mom.'

Dana started crying. 'Why? This is all her fault...'

'No Dana, it isn't her fault; you mustn't think that.' *It's our fucking father's fault.* 'Mom is as much a victim as we are, maybe more. Now more than ever, it's crucial all three of us stick together. We are going to live together, on the Crescent, as a family.' He yanked her to her feet. 'And that's a promise.'

Bright morning sunshine filtered in through the partially drawn royal blue, velvet, floor to ceiling drapes. Cynthia gently slid her hand across Perry's flat stomach stopping at a patch of golden hair just below his navel. Circling her fingers through the welcome mat, as she so fondly referred to it, she moved toward his erection, stirring him out of a deep sleep. Moving deftly onto her knees, she circled the tip of his penis with her tongue; down the shaft, moving ever so slowly back up to the tip. As Perry's moaning intensified she flashed a knowing smile, mounting his ample member, manipulating it deep inside her vagina; gently massaging his testicles with agile fingers. His hands reached for her ample firm derrière spreading it wide, tightening his grip on her tiny waist with a final thrust.

Perry relaxed and satiated lost track of time. 'Damn, I'm supposed to meet with the real estate this morning,' he said, throwing back the sheet. It seemed lately whenever he was with her it was easy to lose track of time; something he wasn't used to. He had always prided himself on being punctual, but lately he was often late for important meetings.

She tossed the sheet aside, following him into the bathroom.

Perry had difficultly focusing on the real estate agent's verbatim, his mind still in the shower with the love of his life; it had been like that since his first meeting with Cynthia Bradshaw.

They met at a conference halfway around the world. Ironically, he had had little interest in attending this particular symposium, but shortly before the scheduled event he was summoned to head office and asked to fill-in for a colleague. As fate would have it, Cynthia was also filling in for a co-worker. It was during the 'meet and greet' portion he spotted a beautiful, young woman chatting with a client he had known for years. Determined to meet the sweet, young thing, he introduced himself to a life he had only longed for.

Perry watched the real estate agent hammer a wooden stake in the centre of his dried up lawn. 'Rumor has it you are Royal LePage's top agent.'

Steven Langdon smiled confidently. He began a career with Royal LePage ten years earlier. The dedicated agent worked long hours, sacrificing time with family and friends, garnering top honors in sales for the past six years.

Perry had great respect for those that worked hard. 'So I can expect immediate results.'

Steven mounted the sign on the post. He had encountered many clients with high expectations. 'Total satisfaction, is my motto. I can assure you I will do my utmost to sell your home in a timely manner, with a tidy profit I might add. I have just completed the quick sale of no. 45.' He didn't bother mentioning the list he had tucked in his shirt pocket of interested families anxious to purchase a home on the Crescent.

Perry's demeanor turned serious like it always did when he wanted positive results. 'I can confidently assume that the sale of my house is your top priority; if so, you will be justly rewarded.'

Steven smiled inwardly. 'Mr. Fleming, I will sell your home as expediently as possible.' After shaking hands, he watched Perry drive out of sight.

'Mister, please don't sell my house.'

He turned toward a young girl with long blond hair, hugging her chest in the carport. Dana choked back the tears. 'I don't want to move. I want to stay here with my mom and my brother.'

Steven sensed after his first meeting with Mr. Fleming there was another side to his controlling demeanor; there usually is. During his career, he had witnessed this scenario too many times and felt sorry for those caught up in the upheaval. But his job was to sell homes, not judge the clientele; he wouldn't have gotten this far being a sympathizer. Without looking back, he loaded the trunk and drove off.

Ronald walked toward Daniel's house for the last time. It was moving day, complete with the promise of a new start in a brand new house with his father and his new bride. He was dreading the move taking them halfway across Ontario. He wondered if he'd ever see his best friend again, spotting the for sale sign on the lawn. *What the heck?*

Dana answered the door, her eyes swollen from crying.

'Is your brother home?' Ronald said, hoping she wouldn't start crying.

Daniel appeared protectively by her side. 'Go sit with Mom. I'll be right back.'

The two friends sat down in unison at the wooden picnic table. The marked old relic had withstood nature's elements year after year, playing host to birthday parties, secret meetings, friendly chats, school projects and today, partings.

Ronald could tell by the forlorn look on his best friend's face something bad was happening. 'Why didn't you tell me you were moving?'

Daniel looked him in the eye. 'I hate my fucking father.'

Ronald's eyes widened at his tone, more so by his admission. He had never known Daniel to say a bad word about anyone, especially his dad.

'The bastard is breaking up our family. Christ, I can't believe he'd do this.' He paused remembering how close he had once been to his father. 'He was always so dedicated to us,' he said, looking his best friend in the eye. 'This is like living the worst nightmare you've ever had, but you never wake up because it's really happening.' His voice cracked with the weight of his words. 'I feel sorry for my sister,' he said, unable to hold back tears. 'When she's not crying, she sits staring off into space somewhere far away.' He shook his head despondently. 'And my mom thinks my father doesn't love her because she's too fat and not pretty anymore.' Forcefully he wiped tears off his face. 'It isn't their fault, it's his, damn it.'

Ronald, at a loss for words, believed Daniel had one of the best families and was always envious. He wanted to comfort him but suppressed the urge; real men don't hug each other, it isn't manly. He glanced at his watch. It was well past the deadline his father had stipulated he be home by, but his best friend was more important than moving day. 'We can still see each other…'

Daniel's head sprung up like a spitting cobra ready to spew its venom. 'My fucking old man is moving us to Vermont, damn him; I'll never see you again.'

Ronald threw back his head. Not only was Vermont far away but it also meant his best friend would become an American citizen, something his father detested. *Canadians are far more superior than those damn Yankees.* He pulled a neatly folded piece of paper from his pocket placing it near the dent he had meticulously carved out long ago. 'Daniel, I have to go now. This is my new address. Please write when you get settled. You are my best friend and you always will be,' he said, swinging his legs over the bench. 'I'm really going to miss you,' he sobbed, slamming the gate behind him.

Charles Donaldson, Charlie to his army buddies, paced the stark wooden living room floor, his army boots echoing the emptiness. Though short in stature, he was built like a brick shithouse thanks to a three year stint in the army after graduating high school. It was during this time he met and married Kathleen. Shortly after their union, he was hired by CNR, transporting freight back and forth across Canada.

After the birth of their two sons, Ronald and Timothy, life was on track, as they say, until Kathleen was diagnosed with inoperable breast cancer; not long after her diagnosis, the horrid disease sent her to her Maker. Devastated with the loss of his wife, coupled with the task of raising two young lads on his own, Charles did what he always did, tightened the boot straps; after all he was a survivor. But he had discovered early on, parenting and his job, taking him away for extended periods, challenging to say the least. He needed a wife/mother for his kids and as luck would have it, during a stopover in Edmonton, he met his soon to be second wife, Enid. After a brief six month courtship, he convinced her to join him at the altar.

Anxious to begin his new life, Charles stood at the window watching Ronald trod slowly up the driveway; turning on his heel, he marched toward the front door. 'I ordered you to be home by ten, it's now 10:45,' he said, staring intently at his son's face. 'Have you been crying?'

Knowing he would get no sympathy, Ronald quickly wiped his cheeks with the back of his hand. 'No sir, I haven't been crying.'

'Tears are for sissies,' Charles spewed. 'Real men don't cry. You should be thrilled and thankful the good Lord has provided a new family life for all of us.'

Ronald didn't share his father's sentiments sitting forlornly in the back seat of their station wagon, side-glancing Daniel's house one last time as they drove by.

Their new stepmom was okay, but she could never take the place of their mother.

He stared at the back of his father's head with a sense of dread.

Timothy, sitting close to Ronald, struck up a tune he had heard recently on television, in an effort to cheer him up. 'I'm a Yankee doodle dandy, a Yankee...'

Charles hit the brakes startling everyone. 'Timothy, stop singing immediately. I will have none of that American propaganda in this car or in our new home. We are truly Canadians, and never forget it,' he said adamantly.

Timothy's ears turned scarlet, a physical flaw occurring whenever he was stressed, confused or tired. 'I heard the song on television last week, Father,' he said innocently, justifying his motive.

His father's tone only intensified, 'I don't care where you heard it. You are not to sing it. Have I made myself clear?'

Timothy lowered his head, 'yes sir.'

Enid smiled warmly at her wonderful husband. She admired his patriotism but most of all, a man who knows how to take control of any situation and remedy it.

Ronald, eyes fixed on the back of his father's head, choked back tears, driving off the Crescent to begin his new life. *Real men don't cry.*

Daniel sat idly at the picnic table contemplating the disaster his life had become. The last thing he wanted was to move to Vermont with his father and his latest bimbo. He picked up Ronald's neatly folded note, chucking it to the ground, tightening his running shoes before running off.

Cynthia entered the brightly lit white marble bathroom, dismissing the maid summoned to fill the claw foot tub with her favourite aromatic oils; a combination of coconut, sandalwood and vanilla filled the temperate room. Undoing the satin kimono, a coveted gift from Perry purchased during their recent trip to the Orient, she casually let it drop to the floor revealing her svelte figure, mirrored throughout the room at different angles. At twenty-one, her ample breasts were firm and pointy, the way Perry liked them. She smiled wickedly caressing the nipples yearning for his insatiable mouth. She parted the cheeks of her ample derrière bending slightly, eyeing the tight honey pot he had become obsessed with of late; circling her tiny waist with her hands, making sure the tips of her fingers met; sliding her hands across her flat belly toward the triangular patch of auburn hair. She parted the lips of her vagina, admiring her hardened state; placing a long shapely leg on the edge of the tub, climaxed.

When she was first introduced to Perry Fleming, hooking up with him was the furthest thing from her mind; she had her sights set on William Declan, though 35 years her senior, he was filthy rich. As luck would have it, Willy was in dire need of a private secretary, available immediately, to accompany him at conferences around the world. Cynthia was more than qualified; shortly after hiring, she moved from the office to the bedroom. It was the perfect setup, until Perry appeared at her side. After introductions, William excused himself to meet with a foreign client; his first passion was making money. In the meantime, Perry wasted no time getting to know her, suggesting they continue conversing over dinner. By the time dessert was served, Perry had propositioned her with an opportunity to travel the world, coupled with a six figure salary as his personal assistant. Definitely a no brainer; not only was Perry very handsome, charismatic, younger and filthy rich, he was her answer to all things sexual. She wasted no time handing old Willy her resignation, much to his chagrin. In short time, Perry introduced her to a world of luxury, travel and fantasy fulfilling sex beyond her wildest dreams. He was always eager to have *her beautiful long legs* wrapped around him.

Cynthia secured her long auburn tresses with a solid gold comb, lowering herself gently into the warm scented water, resting her back on the soft white satin pillow secured to the tub. Feeling relaxed and satiated, she contemplated her future with Perry. She loved Perry, but not as much as the pampered life. She studied the white gold twenty carat flawless diamond solitaire he placed on her finger last night. As was his style, sparing no detail, he had ushered them by limo to their favourite restaurant for an intimate dinner, complete with string quartet and impeccably dressed wait staff catering to their every whim. He had paid handsomely to have the restaurant off limits to other patrons. She slowly moved her hand watching the light reflect off the sparkling beauty he had had specifically designed for *the love of my life*. With it came the promise of a life she would never want for anything, sealing her commitment to him. He presented her with photos of their custom built ten bedroom mansion, complete with maid and butler quarters, situated on fifteen acres of prime Vermont real estate.

She sighed contentedly, admiring her naked image in the ceiling mirror. Not bad for a high school dropout who was told again and again by her dear departed father, Clive, she would never amount to anything. *Rest in peace, old man,* she smiled smugly.

She reached for the luxurious white bath towel thinking of the only drawback to this wonderful life, Perry's kids. On numerous occasions, she tried convincing him they would be better off with their mother, but he insisted their mother was too incompetent, ending any further discussion. Still, the thought of them living together as a family under the same mansion roof turned her stomach.

Garnet inhaled and exhaled her cigarette pacing back and forth in the bedroom like a caged tiger through swirling smoke, stopping abruptly in front of the mirror to study the grainy image. She swung wildly to clear the air, leaning closer. 'Oh my god. I thought you were dead.' *No Garnet, I am alive and well. I see you are still smoking those disgusting things. It's no surprise. Most sluts take up the filthy habit.* 'At one time you smoked too, Mother.' *Foolish of me, but I was never a slut.* Garnet dragged heavily. 'Neither was I, Mother.' A peculiar calmness enveloped her. 'I never was. It was you who chose not to believe your own daughter when I told you Brian raped me.' She put out her cigarette, staring into the mirror. 'I want to reaffirm what happened that day, knowing you probably won't remember. You've always had a *selective* memory, Mother, choosing to believe only what you want. It happened when you left us alone to go grocery shopping. Brian wasted no time telling me how beautiful I was, his ticket to touch my privates. I have to admit, Mother, it felt really good. But I knew it was wrong so I begged him to stop. Instead he convinced me *it's what good girls do*. He took advantage of my innocence, Mother. I'm not a slut.' *Damn it, Garnet, you are a slut. That's why Brian did those things to you because he knew you were easy.* 'No Mother. I asked him to stop but he wouldn't. He kept repeating *good girls do this all the time*. It's all your fault. You are a very bad mother choosing to turn the other cheek on your own daughter.'

Garnet felt every emotion she had kept bottled up for years rise in anger. 'You were supposed to protect me. Instead *you* let it happen.' *Slut! Slut! Slut!* 'I hate you! I hate you!' she yelled, smashing her fists into the mirror.

Benjamin Murray felt the hair on the back of his neck stand with the sound of breaking glass; his wife's agonizing screams.

Garnet said calmly as the door flew open, 'I killed my mother. She deserved to die,' she added vehemently, oblivious of the blood running down her arms. 'She called me a slut. I tried to convince her Brian raped me, but like before, she wouldn't listen so I fixed her.' She smiled wickedly, 'That stupid bitch will never haunt me again.' Garnet turned to face her husband. 'I'm not a slut, am I?'

Theresa and Daniel sat wordlessly on the curb in front of her house. In less than an hour he would be heading to the airport to begin a new life in Vermont with his sister and father.

'This is isn't what I want at all,' he said, breaking the silence. 'My sister and I are supposed to be staying here with our mother, not moving away with him.' He fought tears thinking of how his mother had waited patiently for the son of a bitch to return; her hysterical aftermath. *It's all my fault. I let myself go. But I'm going to change. I'll grow my hair long like it was when your father and I met. He begged me not to cut it and I should have listened. I'll go*

126

on a diet to get my figure back. Then he will want to stay with me. He would never forget the look on his Mom's face when he tried to convince her that her beloved Perry was never coming back and that she would have to begin a new life on her own.

Daniel turned abruptly, 'I hate my fucking father.'

Theresa was taken aback by his admission. She had never heard Daniel talk like this. 'Maybe your house won't sell.'

'Ah T, always the optimist,' he said, fiercely pitching a stone. 'The damn thing sold this morning.'

She watched it ricochet wildly in the middle of the road taking it airborne, landing with a loud click beside his shoe. 'Well done,' she half-smiled.

He kicked the stone back into the middle of the road. 'Look, there's something I want you to know before I leave for Vermont. God, I can't believe I just said that.' He shook his head wondering if he would ever get used to the idea. 'I really like you, T; I always have. I think you're a really neat person.' He was going to miss her more than he would admit. 'When I get settled, can I write you?' He shrugged, 'more so, will you write me back?'

Theresa liked him, as a friend, not in the way he was insinuating. Daniel was Greg's age; she had always regarded him as her brother's friend. She focused briefly on the kiss in the tent last summer and how unpleasant it had been. 'If we stay in touch, I can keep Greg up to date too.'

He made one last attempt to kiss her but she turned, settling with a peck on the cheek.

Theresa watched him disappear around the corner. She felt sorry for Daniel and Dana having to begin a new life with his father and the young woman he fancied. *She's my father's former secretary and she's only six fucking years older than me. She will never replace my mother.*

She sat quietly thinking of all the changes that had taken place on the Crescent recently. Ronald and Timothy had moved to eastern Ontario and now Daniel and Dana were moving to Vermont. Her good friend, Karen, recently moved to Don Mills so her dad could be closer to his job. Their house was purchased by a young couple, the Billings, with their two year old son, Mark. Mrs. Billings was pregnant with a second child due anytime. The Murray's house was listed for sale shortly after Mrs. Murray's nervous breakdown. Surprisingly it hadn't sold, in that; the Murrays vacated the premises very quickly, which came as no surprise to the neighbours.

Tammy sat down beside her. 'Why are you sitting here all alone?'

She looked skyward. 'I just said good-bye to Daniel.'

'Are you upset? He's got a huge crush on you, you know.'

'A little, more so with all the changes that happened lately in the neighbourhood. Daniel's just a friend.' *And that's all he'll ever be.*

'Yeah, but that can change. I'm surprised I miss George, not that I have a crush on him or anything stupid like that. Yuk! He was my go to friend when no one else was around, that's all,' she said adamantly. 'He moved away with his sister and his dad to an apartment somewhere. He wasn't allowed to tell me where because it's a secret. Knowing the way George is, he probably has no idea anyway. He told me Barry wasn't coming to live with them. He was really sad about that, but he knows Barry has to be punished for what he did to Gloria. His sister has to see a shrink because she can't stop crying. Even after all that Barry did to her, she misses him. Can you imagine? I don't know if Mr. Murray misses him; probably not. He made the police come and arrest him for what he did.' Tammy's eyes widened. 'Can you imagine calling the cops on your own kid?'

Theresa inquired about Barry's whereabouts.

'He's in a corrections institution somewhere; serves him right. I hate his guts and I think Gloria should too.' Tammy paused momentarily collecting her thoughts. 'And, according to Mrs. Billings, Mrs. Murray was taken away by ambulance to a mental hospital where she will be staying, probably forever. Apparently, she put her fists through the bedroom mirror, cutting her hands all to rat shit. I wish I had been around for that. I'm not sure where I was,' she pondered. 'Probably at Jenny's house, she's my new best friend. Oh yeah, I almost forgot this part. Something weird happened to George's mom when she was the same age as Gloria. Supposedly, she was raped by some guy named Brian. When she tried to tell *her* mother what happened, her mother called her a slut, whatever that is. Her mother wouldn't believe her no matter how hard she tried to convince her it was the guy's doing. Mr. Murray thinks that's the reason Mrs. Murray didn't do anything to stop what was going on with Gloria.'

Theresa scrunched her face. 'She knew what Barry was doing?'

Tammy shrugged. 'No one can be sure because of her mental condition, whatever that is.'

Once again, Theresa was astounded by how her sister managed to get this information so readily. 'Did George tell you all this?'

She looked at her sister indignantly. 'Of course, even I don't have the imagination to make up a story like this one. George volunteered most of it; I have to admit with more coaxing I got the whole nine yards, as Greg would say. Like Daniel has a crush on you, likewise George on me. Claims I'm the best friend he's ever had. He even tried to kiss me good-bye. But I told him he would never see me again if he didn't kibosh that idea. Talk about a walking cootie. Yuk!'

Theresa shook her head. 'Sometimes it's best not to know what's going on in other people's lives.' She couldn't begin to fathom what the Murray's were going through, nor did she want to.

'Are you kidding? This is some of the best juice I've heard in a long time,' Tammy said enthusiastically. 'You know what the real hoot is, George is supposedly the retard of the neighbourhood and he's the only one doing okay.'

Theresa stared at her wide-eyed, hyped up sister; *some people just can't be changed.*

Tammy said, 'I almost forgot. Mom asked me to ask you what kind of cake you want for your birthday.'

Theresa hadn't given much thought to her approaching birthday. She discovered early in life that being born in the middle of summer meant no birthday parties; invariably most of her friends were away on holiday. 'A golden cake with chocolate icing, my usual,' she smiled.

'Yuk! I hate golden cake. Chocolate cake with creamy chocolate icing is my favourite.'

'Well you'll have to wait until your birthday in May.' She thought of her imminent birthday dinner and how Mom was surprised she had chosen spareribs, not her usual request. *I thought hot dogs were your favourite.* At the time, she had contemplated telling her why she never wanted to eat hot dogs again, instead insisted her taste buds were changing now she was turning thirteen.

On the day of her birthday, Mom served back ribs, green beans and baked potatoes. After dinner Mom lit thirteen candles, placing a chocolate cake with chocolate icing in front of Theresa. She thanked her mom who again questioned her choice. 'Change is good,' she shrugged, eyeing her sister.

'I just love birthdays,' Tammy smiled. I'll have a big piece please.'

Chapter Ten

DISTANT THUNDER RUMBLED in the early morning dawn. Theresa thought she was dreaming until the next clap of thunder, followed by a heavy downpour, proved otherwise.

Tammy rolled onto her side. 'Well it looks like the CNE is out for you today,' she said, pulling the covers over her head; she hated thunderstorms.

Theresa, the optimist, thought, *it's only six o'clock. A lot can happen in the next couple of hours*.

Bea opened the girls' door shortly after eight. 'Theresa, aren't you going to the Ex today?' she whispered. 'The sun is shining; the storm has moved on. My head is clear again.' Bea, a walking barometer, seemed to possess the uncanny talent of predicting storms. When the barometer falls, a cluster headache brewed over her left eye, across her forehead and down the back of her neck. She often predicted approaching storms while skies were relatively clear, much to everyone's astonishment.

Therese threw back the covers. 'What time is it?'

She glanced at her watch. 'Going on 8:30.' She offered to get her breakfast ready, closing the door quietly, hoping not to disturb her slumbering sister.

'Are you sure you have everything?' Mom said, handing her money for bus fare.

Theresa was surprised by the gesture. 'Thanks Mom,' she smiled. 'Yes, I made sure I had everything ready last night. Gotta run or they might leave without me. Thanks again for the bus money.' She pecked her mom's soft cheek, closing the door behind her.

Bea felt a sense of melancholy, pouring her tea, reminiscing about the times spent traipsing around the fairgrounds with three young children in tow. It was usually unbearably hot, humid, noisy and crowded. The Midway, where the kids wanted to spend most of their time, stunk to high heaven of hot dogs, burgers, corn on the cob and cotton candy, invariably turning her stomach. She never allowed them to eat Midway food, arguing *one has no idea how long it's been sitting around.* Between the racket of the rides, vendors yelling at the top of their lungs, hoping to coax them to play their ruddy games (that no one ever wins), she wondered how she managed to stay sane. Thankfully, this year, Gregory wasn't interested and Tammy was going with her best friend's parents next week. She glanced at the wall clock hoping the kids caught the bus on time.

Of the three kids, Theresa was the most level headed and sensible. She was kind and considerate; traits that would take her far in this life. She had a witty sense of humor; always quick with a smile or laugh. An average student, she concentrated more on sports, music and art rather than academics. Bea believed if she applied herself she could do much better. She wanted to be a teacher, but unless she started concentrating more on academics, such a career choice would remain elusive. Ken was especially adamant she study harder, often hounding her to do so.

At the bus stop, Tommy, Janice and Theresa waited excitedly for a CNE bus to take them directly to their destination. CNE buses were recognizable by a bright yellow flag, with CNE printed in bright red letters, mounted just above the door at the front of the bus. They watched a bus approaching but it was flagless; stepping back, signalling the driver they weren't boarding. Ten long minutes later a CNE bus appeared; the yellow flag flapping in the wind. Theresa read the display sign above the windshield, 'EXHIBITION'.

The trio deposited the fifteen cent fare, moving quickly to the long vacant backseat. There were only six other passengers; that would change as they made their way toward the Exhibition grounds. They chatted quietly singling out different points of inter-

132

est along the route. Theresa, felt an incredible sense of freedom sitting beside the open window; the warm breeze on her face.

Janice nudged her for a tissue. 'I forgot to bring some.'

Theresa unzipped her purse eyeing the envelope on top of her Tely Fun Checks. She handed Janice a couple of tissues, opening the envelope.

Dear T, Sorry I melted your transistor radio last month. I know you always take such good care of your stuff so I felt really bad. I'm glad Dad gave you his little green Sony. At least you have a radio now; I promise I won't touch it.

Also, I'm sorry I told Mom your favourite cake is chocolate with chocolate icing. I know it's not, so when my birthday comes I'll ask Mom to bake your favourite golden cake with chocolate icing. On second thought, I need to re-think that. Ha! Ha!

I hope you can use the dollar to win some prizes at the games tomorrow. Or buy some chocolate bars from the Food building.

Your loving sister, Tammy.

PS If you win a stuffed animal, think of your wonderful sister because that means it's a lucky buck and I should probably have it. If not, I'll settle for a couple of chocolate bars.

Theresa tucked the rolled up dollar into the back of her wallet, thinking about her coveted turquoise transistor radio. Last Christmas, they received identical radios; Tammy's being soft pink to differentiate the two; both encased in dark brown leather cases. She was so excited when she opened it Christmas morning. But their excitement was short-lived when Tammy's radio fell into the bathtub. (Numerous times she had been warned not to leave it on the side of the tub, but she insisted on having it with her at all times.) Theresa, not wanting the same fate for her radio, hid it at the back of her drawer; a good idea until her snooping sister found it. Unwittingly, Tammy placed it on the hot barbeque hood, transforming her coveted radio into a puddle of melted turquoise.

After what seemed like forever, the bus, with Tommy, Janice and Theresa sitting on the edge of their seat, approached the entrance to the CNE.

Tommy said. 'I can hardly wait to go on the Flyer.'

'Me too,' Janice smiled. 'What about you, Theresa?'

'Just being here sans parents is fine with me,' she smiled happily.

It was no surprise they were first off the bus, running eagerly toward the gate. They handed the attendant their free passes (courtesy of the Board of Education) and ran straight to the Midway, a colourful smorgasbord of sights and sounds. It was still early, enabling them to move unencumbered; the crowds would grow as the day progressed. The CNE marks the end of summer, for many, it's the highlight of the season.

'There's the Tely Fun Check booth,' Janice said, pointing to a small red and white wooden structure. Their hard work collecting newspapers paid off enabling them to purchase enough tickets to ride all the rides more than once.

Tommy pointed to a tall wooden structure rising high above the Midway. 'Flyer time!'

There was no lineup, making their way up the creaky wooden ramp. The two girls sat together in the middle of the train; Tommy scooped the front seat.

'Your brother is braver than me,' Theresa said, holding on tightly as the roller coaster rolled away from the loading dock.

Janice shook her head. 'At times, Tommy likes to live on the edge.'

Theresa had ridden the Flyer many times throughout the years, but still each time always felt like the first.

'This is it!' Janice said excitedly. The coaster paused briefly, providing a panoramic view of the exhibition grounds before descending the highest hill. Petrified screams filled the air flying down the hill, round a sharp bend at breakneck speed; you literally had to hold on for dear life.

When they returned to the loading dock Tommy tried to coax them into going on again.

'I'll wait here,' Theresa said, walking on wobbly legs down the ramp.

'Me too,' Janice said, tying back her long brown hair with a blue ribbon.

Tommy waved merrily from the front car. When the fast ride was done, he walked toward them smiling broadly, 'Amazing ride.'

They continued down the midway. 'Win a stuffed animal! Prize every time! Come on, you can do it!' yelled the crooked toothed vendor. There was no shortage of games to play and colourful stuffed animals to be won, should luck prevail.

'Dad said all the games are rigged so people never win,' Janice commented, watching some poor kid try to score a basket for the third time. 'See what I mean.' Downtrodden, the young lad finally gave up.

Tommy smiled, 'I bet I can do it. Basketball is my forte.' The greasy man holding the basketball explained the rules of the game, tossing the ball to him.

Tommy drew the ball close to his face, focusing on the hoop less than five feet away. Taking aim he tossed a perfect shot that should have dropped into the net rather than bounce off to the side.

'Rim shot!' the guy said confidently, quickly retrieving the ball, shoving it in his face. 'Beginners luck, son. Try again. You can do it this time,' he winked.

'I'm not your son,' Tommy said, examining the ball; a tad too inflated. 'I'll bet this ball doesn't even fit through the hoop.'

The man chuckled. 'Sure it does,' he said, grabbing the ball out of his hands and sinking it from the side. 'See. If I can do it, a young strapping boy like you should be able to. Come on, try again,' he said, shoving it in Tommy's face.

Tommy contemplated another attempt, but in the end waved off the notion. 'Come on,' he said. 'I don't feel like contributing to this crook's dental rehabilitation, not that he'd use the money for such measures. There's no doubt the game's rigged. The hoop is warped at the front, which makes sense; that's where everyone shoots at.' He was totally convinced the ball should have been in.

Walking past the Shell tower, the highest free-standing structure visible from anywhere on the grounds, they agreed to meet here should anyone get lost in the thickening crowds, making their way toward the Food Building.

'You can have a whole meal just eating free samples,' Janice said, breathing in the enticing scents. They continued following the meandering crowds moving past the vendors only to discover few were offering free samples. Tommy settled on a foot long hotdog with onions, mustard, relish, ketchup and cheese. The girls purchased a large cardboard container of spaghetti with meat sauce and a carton of chocolate milk.

The trio managed to find an area of well-trodden grass under a towering oak; a challenge with others vying for a place to sit too.

Tommy took a huge bite of his red hot. 'After lunch I think we should investigate the freak shows.' He wiped a line of ketchup at the corner of his mouth.

Theresa had been anticipating Tommy's suggestion; always a keen learner, he continually searched out mental stimulation, in any form. She, on the other hand, had no interest; her father had warned her to stay away from the side shows. *These sick individuals exploit others less fortunate, often suffering from various states of deformity, for profit.* She stared down at her half eaten pasta. 'I don't think we should.'

'Why? I think it would be really neat,' Janice said, swirling spaghetti onto her plastic fork. 'There's elephant man, the bearded lady, the two-headed Siamese twins…'

Theresa furrowed her brow interrupting, 'Do you really want to see things like that?'

Tommy shoved the last of his hot dog into his mouth. 'I certainly do.'

'It's unanimous,' Janice smiled, finishing off the last mouthful.

Theresa set her unfinished pasta down on the grass trying to think of a way to convince them it wasn't a good idea.

They sat quietly watching crowds of people milling about in all directions, most with small children in tow.

Tommy pointed to a little boy screaming at the top of his lungs in a struggle with his father for ice cream. 'That kid needs a good spanking,' he said authoritatively.

The father swept the child into his arms holding him close, but the determined child continued to protest. 'That's enough,' he said. The child squirmed in his arms. Frustrated, he stood him on the ground, stooping down, holding his little hands. 'If you don't stop crying, Derek, we will have to go home.'

'But I really want some ice cream,' the teary eyed child whined. The father gently wiped his face with a tissue. 'We can have some ice cream after we eat lunch,' he said soothingly.

'Okay,' the young lad smiled, hugging his father tightly as the spectators applauded.

Tommy shook his head proudly, 'Just another crisis solved by the ingenious male species.'

Janice rolled her eyes. 'It's the male species always causing trouble in the first place.'

Theresa couldn't agree more.

Tommy led them toward, what Theresa referred to as the seedy part of the CNE. They stopped in front of a man in a faded top hat, equally faded grubby red topcoat and tails, pitching his case on a well-worn wooden stage.

'Ladies and gentlemen, boys and girls, this event is not for the squeamish or the faint of heart. You are about to witness things you have never seen before. You will see the tallest man in the world. That's right folks. The tallest man in the world is here today behind those curtains,' he said, pointing over his shoulder toward the faded black rubber curtains billowing toward him. 'And he wants to meet you,' he said, pointing at a lady in a red hat. She blushed, smiling demurely.

'And in contrast,' he continued, 'the shortest little lady in the world will be standing right beside him. Also, you don't want to miss the one and only elephant man, my friends, or the baby with two heads.' He paused in anticipation of an expected collective gasp from the audience.

'Folks, you can see it all here. There's so much to see my friends; you don't want to miss a single minute. Just one little dollar for adults and fifty cents for children; babies are free, of course,' he added like it was a big deal. 'This is a one of a kind show my friends. And you don't want to miss it.'

He continued his spiel hoping to coax the people with enough sense to keep on walking by. 'The line-up forms to the right folks,' he said, pointing to the side of the stage.

Tommy said, 'Let's go.'

Reluctantly, Theresa took her place behind him and his sister; her father's voice inside her head. *Whatever you do, don't go see the sideshows. It's very upsetting to see people who aren't normal, suffering in silence, while people gawk at them.*

'Come on folks! Don't be afraid! Step right up! This is the chance of lifetime!' the pitchman yelled.

Waiting in line, Theresa scanned the large, once colourful murals, boldly depicting what was on the other side. *The Fiji Mermaid; No Middle Myrtle; Magical Fire Eater; Electric Chair Lady; Snake Man; El Otis the Frog Boy; The Dancing Bear; Tattoo Man; Sam the Sword Swallower...*

'Come on,' Janice said, nudging her. Reluctantly, Theresa followed her friends into the huge, dimly lit circus tent with an odour reminiscent of her grandfather's stinky breath; not that she ever got that close; one didn't have to. Percy's halitosis preceded him, along with his critical, judgemental sky blue eyes that looked right through you, waiting for you to screw up. *Well Grandfather, you'll be happy to know I'm screwing up once again being in this damn freak show tent.* To which he would reply with a big toothless know-it-all grin, *I told you so. At times, that one hasn't a lick of sense.*

'Welcome.' Everyone turned toward a petite woman with bleached blond hair piled high on her head, wearing a long, formal, low cut faded red sequined dress; her thin arms partially covered with dingy white gloves stopping short of protruding elbows. Curious males moved closer, gawking freely at her more than ample bosom spilling over the top of the dress. Like a trained thoroughbred, she recited in a soft, hypnotic tone, an oft repeated intro inviting those wanting a guided tour to follow her.

'What do you think?' Tommy said, watching the men move closer still.

I think we should get out of here Theresa thought, shrugging her shoulders.

Janice frowned. 'Do you guys want to see everything?'

Theresa said meekly, 'Not particularly.'

'Well, there are a few things I'd like to see,' Tommy said, leading them in the opposite direction. 'My bet is, this is phony as hell,' he said over his shoulder, traipsing across the dirt floor toward a dimly lit stall housing Otis the Frog Boy.

They peered over the faded divider surrounding him, observing wide-eyed, a man with the body of a four year old and a normal sized head sporting green frog legs, roll, light and smoke a cigarette using only his lips. Once lit, he stared blankly ahead, inhaling smoke, contemplating life.

'Well done,' Tommy smirked. 'But it's gotta be fake,' he said, moving to the next stall.

Curiously, they peered over the divider at a two-headed baby sharing one body dressed in a light pink grubby dress and matching booties.

'Oh my god. That's so sad,' Janice said, cupping her mouth.

The girls walked quickly toward Tommy stationed beside the Gentle Giant, standing over seven feet tall.

'Would you like to have your picture taken with me?' the huge specimen said. 'Only twenty-five cents,' he said, pointing to a man with a camera standing close by.

Shaking his head, Tommy mumbled, 'I don't think so.'

The Gentle Giant remained hopeful. 'Then maybe you would like a picture with my wife.' Without taking his eyes off Tommy, he pointed toward the stall beside him where a miniature three foot woman stood on a stool smiling pleasantly. 'Please take a picture with me,' she said, in a soft, childlike voice.

Theresa felt physically ill when the tiny woman with pleading brown eyes focused on her. She turned toward Tommy and whispered, 'Can we please get out of here?'

'In a minute,' he said, moving toward the elephant man stall. He was finding the whole experience oddly interesting, if not educating.

Theresa walked slowly behind contemplating the next horror and wasn't disappointed. A large topless man sat on an old wooden chair staring blankly ahead; the skin on his arms resembled that of an elephant; his chest, back and bald head wrinkly like elephant hide with patches of fine hair sprouting here and there. Sickened by what she saw she turned and walked quickly toward the exit.

Theresa gulped hot, humid air holding back the nausea, sitting down on a vacant bench across from the stage.

Tommy and Janice exited the tent chatting amicably, waving at Theresa sitting on the bench.

'Jan, did you see the number of tattoos that guy had? His whole body was covered with eagles, naked ladies, snakes, words and some really freaky stuff. He even had tattoos between his toes for crying out loud,' he said, sitting down beside Theresa.

'He's supposed to have over 2000,' Janice said, in a questioning tone.

Tommy rolled his eyes. 'He's claims to be the most tattooed person in the world. Like, who's going to count? T, you should have seen him.'

'I saw more than enough, thank you very much,' she said disgustedly. 'It's time to go on some rides.' She stood, joining the throngs of people milling by.

Tommy went after her. 'I take it you didn't like any of the acts.'

She stopped abruptly. 'Actually Tommy, I hated all the acts. I think it's disgusting that these poor, deformed individuals are put on show and labelled entertainment for fools like us who are gullible enough to pay good money to gawk at them.'

Tommy shook his head. 'Good old kind-hearted Theresa. You tend to take these things to heart when it's only…'

'Those people are deformed, freaks, whatever you want to label them. It's so damn sad to see these poor people, shunned by society but not by those making a living exploiting them. Then there are assholes who feel the need to quench their morbid curiosity paying to see them. It makes me sick to my stomach.'

He had never seen her so agitated; surprisingly, it really upset him to see her reaction. 'T, it's okay,' he said, in an effort to calm her down. (Like the little boy demanding ice cream earlier in the day, her ranting drew a curious crowd.) 'Come on,' he said, taking her hand, scattering the inquisitive.

'I promise not to say another word about any of it,' he said, letting go of her hand, placing them on her shoulders grimacing. (He had hoped to surprise her with the photo he had taken with the Gentle Giant when it arrived by post.) 'I'm really sorry,' he said sincerely. 'We shouldn't have gone in there. But you know me, Mr. Curious.'

Janice agreed. 'It wasn't the best experience for me either.'

The illuminated clock on the Shell Tower beamed 6:10. They navigated the crowds moving toward the food building, hoping more free samples would be offered during the dinner hour.

With two dollars left, Theresa lined up at the Shopsy's booth offering free corned beef on a slice of bread. Munching on the delicious sandwich, she stood in line for a free cup of Coke. Dessert was easy. The Tiny Tom bits booth was handing out free samples of sugar coated donut centers. 'Get in line,' she encouraged her friends. 'Second time around,' she smiled, wiping the corners of her mouth with a napkin.

'These are delicious; so fresh. I'm going to buy a dozen to take home,' Janice said, licking the sugar off her fingers.

After filling up on samples they gravitated toward the Neilson's booth. For fifty cents, you could fill a bag with six chocolate bars. Theresa bought a selection for herself, one for Tammy and a bag of Greg's favourites. Moving to the Double Bubble stand, she purchased packages of gum for fifty cents.

'Get your chocolate bars! Only ninety cents for twelve bars,' a young man called, holding up Lowney bags.

Theresa watched Tommy and Janice run toward him wishing she hadn't spent all her money, and then remembered Tammy's contribution.

The young man examined the tightly rolled bill. 'Someone must have been busy,' he said, handing her the bag and change.

'A gift from my sister,' she smiled, glancing in the bag.

Rather than unfolding it, he tucked it in his apron. 'Get your chocolate bars. Ninety cents for twelve,' he said, raising the bags above his head.

Daylight was fading as they walked toward the Midway with its flashing neon lights and loud noises. It was much busier finding their way through the slow moving crowds, stopping periodically to watch rides being loaded and unloaded with happy patrons looking for a cheap thrill.

'Come on folks! Win a poodle!' Theresa slowed in front of a very brightly lit booth listening to a man standing behind a two foot wooden counter encouraging people to take a chance and win a puppy. He turned his attention on her. 'Hey little lady, for just a dime, you can win a cute, cuddly little poodle,' he said, swinging his arm up toward the row of cages mounted on the wall. 'Aren't they just the cutest thing,' he smiled, revealing a mouthful of stained teeth.

Theresa counted five black pups, some sleeping, others whining softly circling its small cage. She couldn't help but smile at one tightly curled ball of fur staring back at her with big dark eyes.

'They are so cute!' Janice smiled. 'Tommy, look at these guys.'

He stood on the other side of Theresa. 'Yeah, they're cute. I doubt Woody would appreciate the competition if we brought one home.'

Janice nodded. 'Yeah he's getting on in years. In dog years he's 98 next month.'

They all reminisced about the time fourteen years ago Mac brought the pure bred, ten week old Water Spaniel home with him after a business trip. The brown and white puppy was an instant hit with the family; a loyal companion to anyone entering their home.

Tommy added, 'no one ever wins this stuff.'

'Now don't be too hasty, son,' the attendant said. 'Why just yesterday someone won one of these little babies. There's the empty cage to prove it,' he said, pointing toward the back exit.

He turned his attention back to Theresa. 'Aw, look at that. Buttons has taken a liking to you, little girly.'

Theresa smiled feeling an instant bond with the pup.

'Isn't he just the cutest thing? We named him Buttons because his fur is so tightly curled; looks like hundreds of tiny black buttons now don't it.'

For a brief moment, Theresa imagined what it would be like to have Buttons, but Bea would never let her keep it. Just last night she had warned her about these animals. *The poor little flea-infested dogs are full of worms and demented from sitting in a cage day and night, travelling from carnival to carnival.*

'Just ten cents on any plate and you can take home the puppy of your choice,' he encouraged.

143

'Look at all the dimes people have chucked and obviously lost,' Tommy said matter-of-factly. 'No one ever wins this foolish game.'

Theresa had been holding onto the dime change since they left the Food Building. She stood in front of the rows of shiny plates, closed her eyes and tossed the warm coin. The dime bounced from one plate to another spinning rapidly in the middle of its final destination; a crowd had gathered in anticipation.

Janice, known for being quiet and laid back couldn't contain her excitement. 'Holy mackerel! I can't believe this is happening!'

'Folks, I've never seen anything like this,' the attendant said, scratching his head, watching the dime spin at breakneck speed.

Suddenly it stopped, falling sideways in the center of a shiny pink plate.

The attendant's eyes bulged, shouting wildly to anyone who would listen. 'We've got ourselves a winner! Another winner!' he yelled, walking toward Theresa. 'This is the lucky lady, my friends!' he said, pointing a cigarette stained index finger mere inches from her face. 'She gets to take home the puppy of her choice!'

Frozen in the moment, Theresa stared at the stationary dime.

'Wow! Nice going, T!' Tommy said proudly, patting her on the back.

'You are amazing!' Janice congratulated her, smiling broadly. 'She's our best friend,' she said, acknowledging the swelling crowd.

Theresa half smiled. 'This is all well and dandy, but I can't take the puppy,' she said, trying to hide her disappointment. She looked directly at the attendant. 'Please give it to someone who can give it a good home.' She turned, disappearing into the crowd.

The stunned look on the attendant's face said it all. 'Well, now I've seen everything,' he said, shaking his head. In his twenty years working the carnival, no one lucky enough to win a puppy had ever walked away without it.

Tommy and Janice caught up with her. 'T, what are you do-ing? You won a puppy fair and square,' Tommy said encouragingly.

Theresa stopped. 'My mom forbade me to bring a wormy, flea-infested, demented animal home from the CNE.' She looked him in the eye. 'It's like somehow she knew I'd win.'

Tommy scratched his head, 'Now that's uncanny.'

Chapter Eleven

TAMMY SAT ACROSS from Theresa watching her eat breakfast. 'So, how was the Ex?'

Theresa continued fishing out pieces of Sugar Crisp floating in her bowl. 'It was okay.'

'Just okay? You were miles away from Mom and Dad. I would have gone nuts with such freedom. In fact, I have just over two years then I'm outta here with my friends.' She questioned the dollar she had tucked in her sister's purse, hoping to reap the benefits of her kind gesture. 'Did you happen to bring me anything?'

'As a matter of fact...'

'Oh boy! What?'

Theresa reached for the Neilson's chocolate bars beside her chair. 'Your favourite,' she smiled, handing her the loot.

'Wow! Thanks. Actually, I noticed the bag when I sat down, hoping it was for me,' she smiled, gazing inside. Her mouth watered in anticipation flipping through the chocolate bars trying to decide which one to consume after breakfast. She pulled out the cardboard Neilson's logo hat, folding it neatly along the indentations. 'Did you play any games?'

Theresa chuckled at her goofy sister. 'I played one game.'

'Obviously, you didn't win anything,' she said, pulling the hat down over her eyes. 'And I know you're making fun of me.'

Even blindfolded, nothing escapes this kid. 'Actually, I did win something.'

Tammy quickly pushed up the hat. 'What? Where's the prize? It must be something small,' she concluded, glancing under the kitchen table.

Theresa felt goose bumps once again thinking of her score. She still couldn't believe she had won it. 'As a matter of fact, it was small, in the shape of a poodle puppy.'

Tammy furrowed her brow. 'A *real* poodle puppy?'

Theresa nodded.

'Yeah right. How did you win it?'

Theresa pictured the bright lights reflecting off the pink, blue, green and white shiny plates. 'The toss a dime onto a plate game.'

'So where is it? Tommy's? Why didn't you bring it home?'

'I wanted to, but Mom didn't want one in the house.'

Tammy threw her head back in angst. 'We could have had a dog. All my life I've wanted one,' she whined, for her mother's benefit. 'Did you know Theresa won a puppy yesterday at the CNE?'

Mom continued filling the kettle. 'Yes love, she told me last night and made the right decision not to bring it home. Those poor creatures are usually full of worms, malnourished and neglected. Day after day they're cooped up in a cage. If they aren't sick physically, they're probably half-crazed from being caged up all the time.'

Tammy pushed her bowl into the middle of the table. 'I still want a dog, Mom. How did you manage to win it, only to forfeit it?' she said disappointedly.

'Ironically, I used a dime from the dollar you gave me.'

'That was two week's allowance, you know,' she said, holding up two fingers.

Theresa proceeded to tell her what happened. 'After I purchased the Lowney bars, the guy gave me back a dime. For whatever reason, I held onto it until I played my one and only game. Maybe the coin was a tad damp from holding on to it or just a stroke of luck. At any rate, when I saw Buttons, I figured what the heck and tossed it toward the plates. Never for one second did I think I'd win. The poodle was the cutest little thing with tufted fur resembling little buttons. Leaving it was one of the hardest things I've had to do.'

Tammy opened a Jersey nut chocolate bar, biting into it. 'Did you go to the freak shows? That would be really neat.'

The knock on the front door couldn't have happened at a better time. The last thing she wanted to do was quench Tammy's morbid curiosity.

Tammy led Debbie into the kitchen. 'T was just telling us about the Ex. She won a poodle. Can you imagine? But she couldn't bring it home because it's all wormy.'

Theresa sighed, exiting the kitchen, leading Deb away from her nosey sister. ''Long time no see,' she said, sitting down on her bed. 'Don't know about you but I've been busy.'

Deb sat down beside her. 'Me too; I've been away at camp for the last three weeks. Anyway, I've been meaning to invite you to our cottage. I promised back in May,' she said, rolling her eyes. 'We haven't been up much because Dad's been back and forth out west on business.'

Theresa smiled excitedly, 'I'd love to, thanks. I have to ask Mom, but I don't see why not.'

Tammy sat forlornly on the edge of her bed watching her sister pack. 'I don't know why they invited you and not me. Mrs. Phillips looked after me when Mom worked at Reitmans. She even made my Halloween costume four years ago. Remember when I was an adorable little Indian?'

Tammy always managed to pull at her heart strings. 'Maybe one day they will invite you. In the meantime, Deb and I have been friends since we moved here. And, we can entertain ourselves,' she said, without looking up from her packing.

'I don't have to be entertained, I can entertain myself,' she said indignantly. 'On second thought, I don't really care. I have some unfinished business to take care of around here.'

Theresa looked up from her packing to ask what, but decided to remain tight lipped. Knowing her sister, she was probably up to something that she really didn't care to know about.

Tammy smiled broadly, 'Since you're going to be away, would you like me to give Greg his bag of chocolate bars?'

'I would appreciate that; I'll be gone for a few days.' *Hopefully it will bring my warring siblings closer.*

Tammy scooped the bag, gazed inside and tucked it under the desk.

Theresa kissed her mom good-bye; Tammy followed close behind.

Mr. Phillips waited in the carport. 'Anyone need to use the bathroom? It's a three hour drive and I don't want to stop along the way.'

Janet sat in the front with her parents; Theresa, Debbie and her older sister, Jean, occupied the backseat of the four-door, two-toned grey 1960 Chrysler Imperial.

A dewy-eyed, always hopeful Tammy stood forlornly waving them off. *I can't BELIEVE they didn't take me too; especially since Mrs. Phillip's thinks I'm the best kid in the world. But, I don't really care; I've got better things to do.*

The drive north was very pleasant. Theresa sat by the window watching scenery change from houses and open fields to huge rock formations, dense forests of ancient pine and deciduous trees lining both sides of the highway. She was totally mesmerized by the rustic beauty she had only witnessed in pictures.

On the last leg of the journey, the paved road turned into a bumpy, dirt road; a dense cloud of brown dust tailgated the car as Mr. Phillips navigated the single-lane twisting, turning road toward a clearing at the water's edge. 'Phillip's cottage, here we come,' he smiled, turning off the ignition.

He was first out of the car stretching every which way; everyone exited, following suit. 'Okay, first things first,' he said, walking his suitcase down to the docks.

Theresa grabbed her case from the backseat, following Deb's lead.

'You all know the routine. Food and water in the boat first, followed by the tool box and suitcases. Mom, Jean and I will go first then I'll be back for the rest of you,' he said, loading up the front end of the grimy 16 foot fibreglass red and white Larson with its foggy windshield.

'I didn't realize you had to travel by boat to your cottage,' Theresa said, watching the boat move away from the dock, hoping there were lifejackets on board.

'It's the only way to get back and forth,' Janet said, running her tongue across her teeth. She turned and walked toward others loading their boat at the docks.

Deb smiled, 'They're the Wilsons. The young guy standing beside his dad is Edson, cute eh?'

Theresa nodded, watching him move deftly from the car to the boat with their belongings.

Deb said, 'He's almost sixteen; really nice guy.' Her face turned suddenly serious. 'Unfortunately, he was born with juvenile diabetes. That's why he's a little on the skinny side, but he's definitely got the good looks going on.'

Theresa, being on the thin side said, 'He looks toned from my perspective.'

Deb studied his physique. 'He does seem to have more muscle on his bones. I usually hang around with him whenever they come up to their cottage, which just happens to be beside ours.'

Deb returned Edson's friendly wave. 'He's an early riser. We'll probably see him first thing tomorrow morning before everyone else gets up. He likes to whip up his famous fresh blueberry pancakes. Take it from me; they are so delicious, you'll eat them until you burst.'

Edson spoke briefly to his father, running toward them. 'Hi Deb,' he smiled, hugging her briefly. 'Who's your friend?' he smiled, jutting out his hand.

'Theresa,' she said, watching them shake hands.

A white toothy smile crossed Edson's face. 'Well, any friend of Deb's is a friend of mine.'

Theresa couldn't help but notice his vibrant azure eyes. He let go of her hand, running it through his disheveled, sun bleached, wavy blond hair. 'Ready to pick blueberries tomorrow on Hope Island?' he asked, placing his hands on his lean hips, gazing back and forth between them.

'We'll be there.'

Theresa nodded feeling her heart skip watching him run back toward the dock. 'He really is good looking.'

'Yeah, he's a good kisser too.'

Theresa's eyes widened, 'you've kissed him?'

'Quite a while ago. We're just good buddies; he's my cottage brother.' Deb made a face. 'Surely you've kissed a boy before.'

Theresa thought of the kiss Daniel planted on her lips and how repulsed she had felt. 'Hasn't everybody?' she shrugged.

Deb whispered, 'No, not everybody. I'm pretty sure my sister, Janet, hasn't kissed a guy yet.'

Janet sat on the dock next to the suitcases with her nose in a book. She was tall, on the plump side, with straight, dark brown shoulder length hair, flipping around her face in the warm breeze; her soft green eyes kept hidden behind thick, black horn-rimmed glasses. Her slightly bucked front teeth were a dull yellow; she had a compulsive habit of running her tongue across them, more so whenever she was reading. At the tender age of sixteen, the consummate bookworm found solace in the written word.

Theresa said reassuringly, 'She'll have a boyfriend one day,' wondering what it would be like to have one. Though Daniel briefly crossed her mind; he could never be anything more than a friend.

Deb said, 'My older sister recently broke up with her boyfriend; Jean's been miserable ever since. All she wants to do is talk on the phone with her best friend, Elizabeth. That's why Dad decided a trip to the cottage might help her get over Clayton. She wanted to bring Elizabeth, but Dad kyboshed that idea. All they would do is talk about her break-up, which usually ends with her bawling her eyes out. She does that a lot lately.'

Theresa sat at the back of the boat observing the beautiful, peaceful scenery. She had never seen so much rocky shoreline, coupled with dense forests. Most of the shoreline was unpopulated; the odd wooden dock bobbing in the water suggested inhabitants, but the forests were so dense it was difficult to see where, if any, building was situated. She focused on a bald eagle riding wind currents in the cloudless sky while Mr. Phillips steered the boat toward a wooden dock, exactly twenty-five minutes later.

Janet closed her book, reaching for the rusted ring mounted on the side of the dock. She hopped out securing the rope tightly, running her tongue across her teeth. 'Thank goodness we're here,' she said, reaching for her suitcase, walking briskly up a narrow worn pathway toward the cottage. She was always in a rush to get unpacked and stick her nose in a book. She had picked up *Breakfast at Tiffany's* from the library, anxious to read it.

Deb climbed out of the boat; Theresa followed breathing in the pine scented warm air. ''Wow! You are so lucky to have all this,' she said enthusiastically.

'Yeah, it is nice to have a place to go to that's completely different from the city.'

Theresa thought of the creek running behind the school; her getaway place that didn't even come close to this heavenly piece of paradise; silently wishing she could stay here forever.

The cottage was a sturdy wooden structure painted dark grey with a screened-in wooden porch across the front. 'On hot nights we get to sleep out here,' Deb said, pointing toward two oversized pull-out couches. Theresa smiled hoping it would get really hot.

The squeaky hinges on the wooden screen door announced their arrival, slamming shut behind them. The cottage had a musty, pine, old wood smell, typical of seasonal dwellings tucked away in the forest. The knotty pine walls displayed various sized black and white photos of family and friend's memorable moments over the years. Theresa quickly glanced over the collection hoping to find a picture of Edson.

'This is the washroom,' Deb said, pulling her away from the photo gallery. 'We had a flush toilet and sink installed last year, thank goodness. It beats using Johnny,' she said, pointing to a small wooden structure farther up the hill. 'It's a pain in the ass at night, especially when it's rainy or cold. My dad still uses it all the time. He likes to sit with the door open and nature staring back at him while he takes a crap.'

Theresa breathed a sigh of relief. Outhouses were definitely not her forte. There were many occasions she would hold it to avoid using the outhouse at her grandparent's house. Not only did it stink to high heavens, but the thought of sitting over someone else's crap literally made her feel ill.

'And, if you want to bathe, jump in the lake,' Deb said, leading the way down a small hallway.

'This is where we sleep,' she said, pointing to two metal frame beds sporting six-inch well-worn mattresses; a small night table with a reading lamp separated the two.

'Take your pick,' Deb said, sitting down on the bed closest to the window.

Theresa placed her suitcase beside the remaining bed wondering what they used for bedding.

'Here,' Jean said unsmilingly, tossing sleeping bags on the beds. 'How do you like the place so far, Theresa?'

'Love it,' she smiled.

After Jean left, Deb said, 'She's having a rough time of it since her breakup with Clay. That's why I don't want a boy-friend...'

'Is that so?' Edson interrupted, walking into the room. 'It sounds like you haven't found the right guy, yet.'

Theresa, caught totally off-guard, hadn't heard the knock at the screen door and quickly assumed everyone must come and go as they pleased. She was even more surprised when he sat down beside her, leaning forward, resting his arms on his legs instantly bonding their thighs.

Deb rolled her eyes, 'I suppose you're an expert on matters of the heart.'

He shrugged, 'I know a thing or two.'

Deb thought of her older sister. 'With what Jean has been going through, it's just not worth the heartache. She was convinced Clay was going to ask her to marry him after they finished high school. Instead, he broke up with her.'

'Ah, the elusive Clay,' Edson smiled, leaning back stretching his arms toward the ceiling. 'It just means they weren't right for each other. It's better to discover that now than after the ring is on her finger.'

Theresa felt the coolness on her thigh as he stood. From the corner of her eye she studied his slim, deeply tanned physique; his tight, light blue denim shorts, resting just below his navel. His legs and arms, though slender, were quite muscular, professing an active life.

'Well you two, I just came over to invite you to my annual wiener slash marshmallow roast happening promptly at dusk,' he smiled, exposing perfectly straight white teeth.

'Of course we'll be there.'

Theresa felt a rush of excitement listening to Deb confirm their intention.

'See you then,' he said, turning on his bare heel, moving quickly out the room.

'Eddy is such a fun guy. It's too bad we weren't a match, but you pretty much know after that first kiss whether or not it's meant to be.'

Theresa wanted to ask her what it was like, but decided they weren't close enough. They were friends, but not best friends like she was with Judy. Their friendship was more of a convenience, in that they rarely hung around together, especially this summer. It seemed when she had time, Deb was off elsewhere or across the street at Beverly's house.

Beverly Carmichael, the youngest of four, was born with a silver spoon in her mouth. With three, much older, very protective brothers, she was the apple of her father, Richard's, eye. Like the rest of her family, she preferred the quieter, introverted life, rarely leaving the closed curtained house. When she did make an appearance, she was always made up to look several years older than her biological age of thirteen, she even accentuated her buxom figure with tight sweaters.

She never participated in any of the neighbourhood games, *too childish* in her heavily made up eyes. At school, she was top of her class, in turn, given special permission to spend recess in the library furthering her studies.

In her father's eyes, she could do no wrong; often turning a blind eye when Bev and her mother, Hazel, the disciplinarian, locked horns. *Richard, she's thirteen going on eighteen.* He would accuse his wife of overacting, stating some girls mature faster than others and to let his little *girly* be. Frustrated Hazel would find solace drinking endless cups of hot tea or tending her garden.

Theresa wondered how chummy Deb was with Beverly. 'Has Bev ever been to your cottage?'

Debbie threw her head back. 'Are you kidding? Bev doesn't like the outdoors; *the sun is really bad for your skin and causes wrinkles.* Have you seen her lately? She's like this grown woman. I spent some time with her this summer, but we really don't have much in common. She's really changed.'

Theresa, for whatever reason, felt a sense of relief that Beverly had absolutely no interest in cottage life. She had spoken to her a couple of weeks ago, their brief chat unnerving in that, Bev looked unrecognizable. Her long, mousy brown hair was now radiant blond. She wore a tight hot pink sweater, accentuating her grapefruit size breasts that seemed to have sprouted overnight. Her blue eyes were heavily made up; the shade of lipstick a perfect match with her sweater. The pair soon realized they had absolutely nothing in common.

Debbie continued, 'Not only that, Bev likes all the modern conveniences within reach. She's either bathing or standing in front of her mirror watching her tits grow. She continually plasters 2nd Debut all over her face; absolutely paranoid about getting wrinkles. Can you keep a secret? Bev hangs out at the plaza with older guys. Actually, she's seeing a guy she's crazy about. He's twenty years old! Can you imagine,' she said, widening her hazel eyes. 'He has a motorcycle and takes her for rides all over the place. Her mom has no idea and would have a fit if she knew.'

Erin crushed out his cigarette with the heel of his beat up huarache sandal. 'Hey, get a load of that.'

The guys turned in unison eyeing a young lady with bleached blond hair piled on top of her head, sporting a tight yellow turtleneck and tight blue jeans walk seductively through the parking lot. Her sophisticated look, far beyond her actual age, intrigued them. Sensing she had an audience, she lifted her chest, flashing a hot pink smile, disappearing out of view.

'Jesus Christ. Who the fuck was that? Did you see the tits on her? Not to mention that perfect tight ass I wouldn't mind getting a hold of,' Norm said, cupping his hands.

'Norman, you're such a fucking pig, you'd grab a rhino's ass given half the chance,' Erin said, lighting a cigarette, inhaling deeply.

'So I'm not picky,' he shrugged. 'Still, I wouldn't mind a run at that piece of work,' he smiled wickedly, flipping his dark brown hair to the side.

Greg pondered where he'd seen her before. 'Shit, I know who that is,' he said, dragging heavily on his smoke.

'Jesus Christ, Gregor, don't hold back,' Norm said impatiently.

'I'm almost positive it's one of my sister's friends. Guys, she's only thirteen.'

'Yeah right,' Erin said. 'Your sister may be the same age, but she sure as hell doesn't look like that. I'd like to take a run at that myself.'

The group stood agape watching the young vixen reappear on cue, when a muscular guy with blond wavy hair in a worn black leather jacket and tight jeans riding a motorcycle entered the parking lot, driving toward his target. He shut off the machine, sitting back leisurely on the bike. Few words were spoken; she cupped his face kissing him passionately, climbing on behind him. The guys watched her press her ample breasts firmly against his back, and wrap her arms tightly around his waist; cementing the bond. With a smirk on his face, he revved the powerful machine, steering it toward the exit where the guys stood. The attractive bombshell flashed a toothy white smile, winking a heavily made-up eye.

'Oh my god!' Norm said. 'That frickin' lucky guy is Gary Robinson, aka dropout; quit school halfway through grade ten, basically disappeared,' he said, watching the duo speed off. 'A friend of mine said he'd joined the army; I guess he's back. That same friend mentioned Gary had hooked up with some stacked bimbo; must be her. I wonder if he's fucking her.'

Greg stomped out his cig.

Tammy dumped her purse full of coloured poker chips onto Theresa's bed, pulling a chocolate bar out of Greg's bag. *He won't miss it. There's still seven left.* She stacked the chips by colour on her desk. *But I bet he'd miss these.*

Walking home quickly, the slutty image of Beverly Carmichael filled Greg's mind. She had grown up overnight; the comparison between her and his sister was unparalleled. He remembered when they first moved to the Crescent, the two young girls were the best of friends. A few weeks ago, he had seen them chatting and wondered if they had rekindled the friendship, but rationalized Theresa was more of a tomboy, doubting she'd have anything to do with that little piece of work.

'Hi Mom,' Greg yelled, opening the door. 'Any idea where Theresa is?' He kicked off his old runners, tossing them in the hall cupboard.

'Mom's across the street at Renee's having coffee. Why do you want to know?' Tammy asked curiously.

'Get lost,' he said, shutting the bedroom door in her face.

'We need to have a talk, bro,' she said, leaning into the door. 'If I were you, I'd let me in.'

He swung the door open, throwing her off balance. 'This had better be good.'

She shut the door behind her. 'First, push your glasses up off your nose. You look like a dork.'

At the tender age of three, Greg had been prescribed glasses to correct a lazy eye. After numerous failed surgeries, wearing glasses for the rest of his life was the only option; without the specs, his left eye turned inward permanently. His most recent pair of glasses, identical to Buddy Holly's, would hopefully be a hit with the girls he'd date. 'You're not my mother,' he said, shoving them up.

'Thank goodness for that. You're too much trouble, and, you reek of cigarette smoke.'

Greg rolled his eyes. 'What do you want, pain in the ass?'

'Watch your mouth or I'll tell Mom you've been swearing, and smoking. You need to know what happened yesterday, but first.'

He watched her run out of the room returning quickly with a bag that she tossed toward him. He was surprised to see the poker chips. 'I've been looking all over for them.'

'Thought so,' she said confidently.

He looked at her accusingly, 'How long have you had them?'

'Long enough to know you would be looking for them. We need to have a serious talk. But before we do, the chocolate bars are from Theresa, I'll have one please.'

He placed the bag of chips on the desk. 'I don't think so,' he said, eyeing the selection.

'Suit yourself. I'll have a talk with Mom instead.'

Reluctantly, he handed over the bag.

'Thanks,' she said, opening a crispy crunch, filling the room with its delicious aroma. 'Make sure you thank Theresa,' she said, savoring the mouthful.

'You've got the bars, now get out.'

She crumbled the empty wrapper tossing it into the garbage can. 'Not so fast. I still haven't told you what happened to me.'

He sat back hard in his chair.

She looked him in the eye, watching closely for a reaction. 'I was at the plaza yesterday and went into Lou's for some candy. While I was trying to make up my mind, a girl from school entered the store. She calls me by my last name, which is why I hate her guts.'

'For Christ sake, get on with it.'

'Another profane word,' she said emphatically. 'I just learned the *profane* word yesterday,' she added. 'Anyway, I hear *Rowan, what are you doing here?*'

Greg hugged his head wondering what the hell he did to deserve such a pain in the ass sister. 'Get to the damn point.'

'I am,' she huffed. 'You must learn to be more patient. Anyway, I told her to go jump in the lake, of course. Right after she left the store, Lou asked if I was your sister. When I told him I was, he gave me a message to pass along to you. *You have until the end of the week. He'll know what I'm talking about.* She could tell by the guilty look on his face he was probably gambling again. 'You owe him money, don't you?'

Bastard. 'I owe him a few bucks. I'm going to settle it tomorrow.'

Tammy smiled, 'I'll go with...'

'Like hell you will,' he said adamantly.

'Suit yourself. It's that or I tell...'

He lifted his hands, silencing her. 'Fine, but you keep your goddamn mouth shut or I'll punch your stupid little head in, got it.'

'Is that any way to talk to your little sister who's trying to help you?'

Forcefully, he opened the bedroom door. 'I don't need your fucking help. Get out.'

'Swear word! What time do you want me to be ready?' she said, tearing down the hall with the chocolate bars bouncing wildly in the bag.

It was a warm, calm perfect evening for a bonfire; the crackling fire spit hot embers into the night sky. Edson placed a thick birch log in the center of the flames before distributing long sticks he had whittled to fine points earlier on.

Theresa was surprised when he sat down next to her. 'You first little lady,' he smiled, handing her a pierced wiener. He watched it disappear into the flames. 'It will be cooked in no time,' he smiled, placing his hand on hers, gently pulling the blackened specimen out of the fire.

She didn't bother mentioning this was her first bonfire or her limited experience in the art of wiener roasting; hot barbeque briquettes in the back yard sufficed, until now.

He let go of her hand. 'Now you've got the hang of it.'

Theresa, feeling euphoric, wished she didn't have the knack, relishing the warmth of his hand. She wondered if anyone else noticed the interaction.

Theresa gazed up at the stars wishing the night would never end.

'Quite impressive, eh,' Edson said, gently pulling her hand back again. 'Your wiener was on fire,' he chuckled, tossing the charred doggie into the flames.

She smiled, 'I guess I should be concentrating more on the task at hand, it's just that I've never seen so many stars, and so clearly. Can you imagine how vast the universe is?'

He had wondered about it many times. He pierced a new wiener with the stick, handing it back to her.

With absolutely no intention of eating the damn red hot, she held it over the hot coals thinking about Edson. Not only was he good looking, but kind and considerate, not quick to pass judgement with a sarcastic remark if she screwed up.

'It looks like your wiener is done perfectly.' He removed it from the stick and placed it in a bun. 'So you won't burn your fingers,' he smiled, handing it to her.

She felt obliged to bite into it and closed her eyes, opening them in disbelief. 'Oh my goodness, this is the best hot dog I've *ever* tasted!'

Edson beamed, roasting marshmallows over the hot fire. He had never met such a sincere, enthusiastic girl. 'Your dessert, pretty girl. It's really hot, but that's when they taste best,' he said, handing her a napkin.

'Aren't you having any marshmallows?' she said, biting into the charred surface. No one had ever said she was pretty until now. She had flaws, number one, being blessed with more than her share of body hair, not to mention a dark line of it above her lip that Tammy was always quick to point out, usually in front of others. She had spoken to her mom about her excess hair, but Bea fluffed it off suggesting more time in the sun to bleach it out.

Edson gave her a light nudge. 'You seem to be far away,' he said, offering more marshmallows.

'No, thank you,' she said, turning so he couldn't see her face. She was high on his compliment, wanting this amazing feeling to last.

He placed his hand on her arm, rubbing gently. 'Are you sure you're okay?'

She looked skyward, 'yes. I'm great, thanks. Just enjoying the scenery, the fire and the company,' she smiled, turning briefly toward him.

'You have a beautiful smile,' he said. *Guys are going to be beating down your door.*

She was tempted to mention her surgical procedure at age six. She had been born with a piece of skin, commonly known as a *duck's foot*, separating her two front teeth. After a trip to the dentist, he recommended the procedure, without delay; otherwise there would be a permanent gap between the two front teeth. Today, she was more than thankful her parents went ahead with his recommendation.

For the remainder of the evening, Theresa and Edson chatted about their interests, school, friends and family until the fire burned down to embers.

'We have so much in common,' he said, reaching for her hands, pulling her up to her feet. For a brief moment, she thought he was going to kiss her, but they had an audience.

'I had a great time,' she smiled, heading back down the hill with Deb.

Theresa lay on the creaky old cot listening to the crickets, thinking of her stupid vow to never eat hot dogs again. *Finally, the past is in the past.* Focused on the present, she fell asleep dreaming of Edson.

Just before dawn, a light tapping noise awoke her. Theresa rolled over in the sleeping bag, smiling broadly at Edson waving outside the window. With a quickened heart, she slipped quietly out of bed, tiptoeing past her slumbering friend.

'Time's a wasting,' he whispered. 'You don't want to miss a single minute of cottage life. I've got pancakes and fresh blueberries waiting to be cooked up.'

Suddenly, Deb bolted upright. 'Go away and let us get dressed. Edson's pancakes are the best.'

For a brief moment, he placed his hand against Theresa's on the screen then ran toward the deck.

The threesome followed a narrow path lined with dead pine needles; the air warmly scented with pine.

'Where's Mom and Dad?' Deb asked. They were all one big happy family.

'Sleeping. They sat up with your folks until the wee hours and will probably spend the morning in bed.'

Theresa's eyes widened at his casualness mentioning his parents slept in the nude, passing by their open bedroom door. To her knowledge, her parents always wore pajamas; skimpy as her Mom's baby dolls were, at least it was something.

The girls sat down at an old knotty wood pine table with mismatched high back chairs, chatting amicably while Edson whipped up his famous, fluffy blueberry pancakes. It didn't take long for the rustic cottage to fill with the rich, buttery aroma, enticing their empty stomachs.

'For you, pretty girl,' he smiled, topping off the fluffy stack with a heaping spoonful of fresh blueberries. Theresa, feeling on top of the world, breathed in the heady aroma.

'Dig in,' he said, pouring batter onto the hot skillet. 'Pancakes are best when they're hot.'

Theresa cut into them, 'Oh my goodness! These *are* the best I've ever tasted!'

He smiled confidently handing Deb a serving. She breathed deeply. 'They smell delicious, as usual.'

With full stomachs, they sat back in their creaky chairs mapping out the remainder of the day.

'We have to replenish the blueberries,' Edson said, collecting the plates, moving swiftly toward the tarnished metal sink, filling it with water.

Deb said, 'That means a trip to the island.' She turned toward Theresa. 'Do we swim or take the boat?'

Theresa wondered about the distance, hesitating to ask questions. She was an average swimmer, but to the island?

'I'm up for the swim,' Edson said, patting his washboard stomach. 'I need to work off the pancakes.'

Deb volunteered to see what her sisters had planned, exiting the kitchen.

Theresa remained seated, offering to dry the dishes.

'Around here, we just let them air dry and pull 'em off the rack as needed,' he smiled, sporting dimples on each side of his face. Till now, she hadn't noticed how pronounced they were; the more sincere his smile, the deeper the dimples.

Edson, Debbie and last but not least, Theresa, jumped off the dock into the tea coloured water to begin the thirty-five minute swim to Hope Island. The mandatory lifejackets were cumbersome, but Theresa was more than happy with the steadfast rule, *life jacket or you're in the boat.* There was no way she could swim to the island; something she didn't want to admit to her friends.

Janet, poised as spotter at the front of the sixteen foot aluminum boat, looked up periodically from her novel; Jean steered the six horsepower motor toward the island, a task she had performed many times.

Zeroing in on the point, she cut the motor, coasting toward the rocky shoreline. The swimmers emerged on shaky legs, watching Janet toss plastic containers ashore.

Edson said, 'We have to pick lots of berries. I'd like to show Theresa the island. See you in a couple of hours.'

Amused, Jean shook her head. 'It used to take you less than thirty minutes,' she smiled wickedly. 'At the very least, try to get some berries,' she added, feeling an emotional tug at her heart. She had hoped to bring Clayton to the island one day to do more than pick berries.

Edson said, 'I just want Theresa to enjoy the whole experience.'

'See you at three,' Jean said, pulling hard on the cord, frantically waving to disperse the thick blue smoke encircling her.

Theresa removed her life jacket, opening it wide on the sun drenched rocks to dry. She had found the swim invigorating, feeling a sense of inner pride with her accomplishment. Until now, she would never have thought herself capable, but with Edson's encouragement it wasn't daunting at all; thoroughly enjoying the experience.

Deb arranged the lifejackets. 'Do you mind if I stay here and catch up on my tan. It's starting to fade and I want to look good when I go back to school.'

Edson chuckled. 'My guess is it has something to do with Freddy.' It was no secret she had a mad crush on him and that they'd be classmates when school commenced in September.

She flicked her hand, 'Just go pick berries.'

It was a perfect summer day filled with the warmth of the sun shining in a clear blue sky. Edson reached for Theresa's hand; silently they walked a rocky trail toward a patch of short dense bushes. She couldn't help believing this was the closest to heaven one could get and Edson was the angel sent to guide her. She glanced down at her hand entwined in his, wishing the moment would last forever. They moved carefully through speckled blue bushes harbouring luscious ripe blueberries waiting to be picked, but surprisingly didn't stop.

They continued walking toward a stand of huge, ancient white pine trees gently swaying in the warm summer breeze. On the other side of the forest, Edson stopped, focusing intently on the tea coloured water gently lapping the shoreline. He gripped her hand tightly. 'This is my favourite place in the world. It's a place so sacred and untouched it brings tears to my eyes.' Gently, he tugged her hand, encouraging her to sit beside him on a large, lichen dotted grey rock. Quietly, they sat gazing out over the lake; the continuous lapping of the waves on shore soothing, yet invigorating; a united entity on top of the world. Theresa had never felt such peace and contentment.

She turned toward him, 'I can see why you love this place so much.' A strand of blond hair draped across his right eye; she was tempted to move it, turning her attention back to the lake.

Edson encouraged her to take deep pine scented breaths. Giving her hand a loving squeeze, he reached into the pocket of his swim trunks. 'This is my other favourite go to.' He smiled, watching Theresa's eyes widen.

Greg, ever thankful his buddies weren't hanging out at the plaza, moved quickly through the parking lot; as instructed, Tammy followed a few yards back. The last person he wanted to be seen with was his pain in the butt sister.

Tammy watched him enter the store, running toward it.

'What's with the kid?' Lou mumbled disgustedly, as the door flew open.

Tammy wasted no time introducing herself, breaking into her best smile, hoping to score a chocolate bar or at the very least a piece of gum.

Greg said, 'Pretend she isn't here. We've got some unfinished business to take care of.'

Tammy watched them sink below the counter, positioning themselves on three-legged wooden stools, the top of their heads level with the counter.

'Never been opened,' Greg said, producing a new box of cards, pointing toward the seal.

Lou raised an eyebrow. 'You aren't accusing me of cheating just because I totally wiped your ass last time, are you?'

Greg dealt the cards. 'No doubt in my mind, Lou. You're an honest crook.'

Lou smirked, nodding appreciatively.

Tammy inched closer to see what they were up to; the aroma of chocolate, candy and gum packed tightly on the shelves below distracted her. She ran her fingers along a Cadbury Rum and Butter bar; mouth watering, she fingered the indentations. She peered over the counter convincing herself Lou and Greg were preoccupied with their card game, stuffing it, a Crispy Crunch bar and a package of Juicy Fruit gum, her sister's favourite, in her underwear quietly announcing her departure.

She walked quickly toward the back of the plaza, breaking into a sprint toward two large green metal garbage containers; glancing over her shoulder to make sure she hadn't been followed.

Sitting on the curb behind the bins anticipating her first mouthful of Cadbury's Rum and Butter chocolate, she tore off the wrapper, shoving a row in her mouth; the buttery goo dribbling onto her chin. She devoured the rest like a deprived animal, tearing at the Crispy Crunch wrapper; biting a mouthful, combining rum and butter with peanut buttery crunch; *pure heaven*. Licking each finger, she hid the gum behind the waste receptacle.

Edson opened the bright yellow package of Juicy Fruit gum.

'I don't believe it,' she smiled, peeling off the wrapper. 'This just happens to be my most favourite gum in the world.'

His dimpled smile broadened. 'Great minds think alike. This is just another thing we have in common,' he said, putting his arm around her shoulder, drawing her closer. Savouring the taste and sweetness of the gum, they looked out over the lake wishing for eternity.

Tammy quietly slipped through the glass door, tiptoeing to the counter. Focusing on the top of Lou's balding head, she reached for a package of spearmint candies, but decided the crinkly package was too noisy; not wanting to announce her presence. Quickly she gathered her favourite peppermint chocolate bar, a box of Macintosh toffee and two Neilson's milk chocolate bars, stuffing them into her underwear.

'Where's Lou? ' a gruff voice said.

Instantly Lou appeared. 'Who wants to know?'

The man motioned with his thumb toward Tammy, 'You gotta customer.'

Lou ignoring his motion half-smiled, 'What can I do for you, Eddie?'

Tammy, holding her breath, tried not to choke on the candy she had popped in her mouth mere seconds before his arrival.

'I need some smokes,' he said, reaching into the pocket of his grubby pants watching Tammy move silently toward the door. 'Hey! Where are you going?'

Tammy stopped, her heart beating so rapidly she thought she'd pass out.

'You were here first, kid. Lou, look after the little lady.'

Lou ignored him, reaching for a package of Export A king size.

'It's okay, I was just looking,' Tammy said, sliding out the door; on trembling legs, she ran behind the plaza.

Edson turned to Theresa. 'I guess we should pick blue berries before they come back for us.' She had almost forgotten the reason for visiting the island, reluctantly nodding.

He stood reaching for her outstretched hands, pulling her into his welcoming arms. Embracing her tightly he kissed her gently. She felt a tidal wave course through her, sliding his tongue between her lips. Holding on tightly, he kissed her with a passion she had no idea existed; coupled with the scent of Juicy Fruit gum, she felt heady, alive, wanting this moment to last forever.

Reluctantly, he pulled back. 'You're amazing,' he said, staring languorously into her beautiful black-brown eyes. 'I have a feeling you'll be breaking young men's hearts in the not too distant future. You are a wonderful, fun, inquisitive, kind, loving girl. I have never met anyone like you and I love you for this,' he said, holding on for dear life. *Thank you so much, Theresa.* Gently he kissed her lips. 'Let's pick some berries.'

Theresa followed his lead, eyeing him out the corner of her eye. He had become distant, quiet, ignoring any attempts to converse, moving quickly through the task.

He picked up the containers. 'That's enough for today.'

She followed suit moving close behind, wishing she could hold his hand.

Back at shore, Edson handed the containers to Janet then tossed his lifejacket toward the center of the boat.

'Edson, aren't you swimming back?' Deb said, handing Theresa her lifejacket.

'You're usually first in the water.'

Stealthy, he moved toward the middle seat. 'I'm taking the easy way back.'

Deb turned to Theresa. 'Do you want to swim back?'

Theresa shrugged, 'Sure,' secretly wishing she could sit beside Edson.

Deb and Theresa climbed onto the large sheet of smooth rock beside the dock, removing their saturated lifejackets.

'That was fun,' Theresa said breathlessly. But her accomplishment was marred by Edson's quick exit, watching him disappear into the woods. She picked up Edson's containers, following the path, periodically glancing toward his cottage hoping he'd be back.

It was shortly after six when they gathered at the table in the screened in porch for supper. Theresa sat at the end of the bench facing Edson's cottage hoping to see him running the path. But dinner came and went without a trace.

'I think we will head home tomorrow,' Mr. Phillips said, aiming the last mouthful of fresh baked blueberry pie toward his open mouth.

Theresa's heart raced counting the hours left to spend with Edson. Though Edson hadn't suggested a bonfire, she wondered if it was just an oversight, enquiring about the possibility.

Mr. Phillips smiled. 'You really enjoyed last night's fire,' he winked, 'but unfortunately, mother nature's predicting rain.' As if on cue, a flash of lightning followed by the distant thunder echoed across the lake. 'Looks like sooner than not.'

Tammy, chin resting on her hand, continued to rearrange supper on her plate. 'When is Theresa coming home?'

Mom looked up from her dinner. 'I have no idea when they're coming back,' she said, placing a piece of chicken and potato on her fork.

Tammy said accusingly, 'You have no idea when you own daughter's coming home? Some mother,' she said, stacking beans and carrots.

Mom ignored the comment, placing her utensils neatly on the side of her plate. 'Why do you want to know? I would think you'd enjoy having the bedroom all to yourself.'

'I just miss her. May I be excused, please?'

Tammy rolled her eyes watching Mom's weird chewing motion start up; an annoying unconscious habit she performed when she wasn't impressed. 'You may, but scrape your plate into the garbage.'

She cleaned it off quickly to avoid the stupid lecture about cooking good food only to toss in the garbage. (Mom had no idea her lack of hunger was from eating too much candy, not to mention the close call of getting caught stealing it.)

Tammy sat on her bed thinking about George's run in with the cops for stealing perfume. *It's just not worth it. I'll never steal again.* She tossed the unopened package of Juicy Fruit gum onto her sister's bed.

Theresa sat forlornly in the backseat, staring aimlessly out the window. The scenery she had so thoroughly enjoyed on the drive up was just a blur.

Everything had seemed so right from the moment she felt Edson's warm handshake, followed by the invitation to the bonfire with his thigh touching hers sitting side by side on the bed. The warmth of his hand guiding hers at the bonfire. The delicious blueberry pancakes he prepared next morning. Swimming over to the island with Edson alongside, keeping a watchful eye, encouraging her all the way.

Their time on the island, an experience she would never have dreamt of. Edson holding her hand; sitting side by side on a rock they fondly named *forever;* gazing out over the water, the warm summer breeze caressing them, their mutual wish this moment would last forever. Theresa felt tears sting her eyes reliving the warmth of his embrace; the kiss, igniting feelings within she had never experienced before. *This must be what falling in love means.* Everything had been so perfect until berry picking. For whatever reason, Edson became aloof, quiet and indifferent; choosing to ride back in the boat, something he had never done before. At first she believed, or rather hoped, his mood change was the result of neither of them wanting to leave their newfound paradise. But it was obvious when they docked, he was anxious to get away, running off to his cottage without a word.

Jean leaned forward in the seat. 'Oh my god! I need to hear that song, turn up the radio,' she said, throwing her head back, covering her face with her hands.

Reluctantly, her father cranked up *The end of the world.*

Theresa, her head against the window, listened intently to the lyrics. *Why does the sun go on shining? Why does the sea rush to shore? Don't they know it's the end of the world 'cause you don't love me anymore…*

At the end of the song, Jean wiped her eyes with a tissue. 'Oh my god, Skeeter Davis nailed it,' she said, thinking of her lost love, Clayton. 'All guys do is break hearts. They're all the same.'

Deb nudged Theresa, 'Not all guys, right, T?'

Fighting back tears she shrugged, turning back to the window, reliving her last day at the cottage.

In dawn's early light, she slipped out of the cottage, running the path to Edson's only to discover the cottage locked up tightly; the boat no longer bobbing beside the dock. Stuffing the piece of paper with her phone number into the pocket of her shorts, she ascended the hill to the fire pit, locating the stick Edson had meticulously carved, feeling the warmth of his hand on hers.

Deb interrupted her thoughts. 'You're so quiet, T. I've got just the thing,' she said, reaching into her pocket.

A horrified look crossed Theresa's face. 'Where did you get that?' She stared wide-eyed at the opened package of Juicy Fruit gum.

Deb was taken aback by her unexpected response. 'Juicy Fruit is your all-time fave so I brought some from home,' she said, opening a piece.

The pungent smell turned Theresa's stomach; declining politely she turned back to the window.

When Mr. Phillips pulled into the carport, Theresa was first out.

'Someone must be glad we're home,' he said, moving toward the trunk, watching her retrieve her suitcase.

'Not really, Mr. Phillips. It's just that I have to use the bathroom. I had a wonderful time, thank you very much for having me. I'll call you later, Deb.' Without looking back she scurried home.

'I'm pretty sure it has something to do with Edson leaving without saying good-bye,' Deb sighed.

'Ah, young love,' Dad said, reaching for a suitcase.

Bea called out from the kitchen when the door opened. 'Is that you, Theresa?'

On the verge of tears, she had hoped to seek solace in her room. With a fixed smile, hoping to dupe her mother (Bea seemed to have a sixth sense about these things) she entered the kitchen.

'Well dear daughter, how was your time at the cottage?' she said, continuing to stuff a chicken for supper.

Thinking of Edson, swallowing back tears, she was grateful her mom was preoccupied. 'I had a nice time, thank you. Do you happen to know where Tammy is?'

'She was out in the yard earlier on,' Mom said, turning briefly. 'Look at you, all brown as a berry. You must have had good weather.'

She sighed, 'we did. I'd better go unpack.'

Mom raised a brow. 'Are you okay?'

'Yes,' she said, a little too emphatically, turning on her heel.

Gingerly, she opened the bedroom door praying her little brat of sister was still outside.

'Boo!' Tammy said, jumping out from behind the door.

'You little jerk! You scared the shit out of me.'

Tammy's eyes widened. 'I see you've learned a new swear word while on vacation,' she said, jumping on Theresa's bed, continuing on to hers.

Theresa dropped the case on the bed. 'Don't you have any friends? Why aren't you outside?'

'I missed you too, sis. Hate to tell you, but this is my room too.'

Theresa emptied her case onto the bed, sorting through her clothes. 'What the hell?'

Tammy stopped jumping. 'It's your favourite, Juicy Fruit gum. I'm giving it to you because I missed you, believe it or not.'

Theresa pitched the gum with such force it bounced off the wall, narrowly missing Tammy's head. 'Get out of this goddamn room!'

Grabbing the gum, she ran full tilt out of the room. 'What the hell is wrong with Theresa?' she said, running through the kitchen.

'I've asked you a million times not to use foul language in this house,' Mom cringed as the door slammed shut. *Little bugger.*

Chapter Twelve

ANNE SMYTHE WAS vaguely aware of the commotion outside her bedroom door, rolling over and focusing sleepy-eyed toward the ceiling; her eyes followed a cobweb anchored to the white bug-filled ceiling fixture, ending on the dusty curtain rod. Spellbound, she watched the dust-coated specimen sway back and forth like a hammock coaxed by a summer breeze. For a brief moment, she wondered how she had missed it; cursing herself for not noticing it sooner. Standing on shaky legs, she swung wildly; but her 5'2" bulky frame was no match for the distance between. She needed a stepladder which in turn meant moving the bed, definitely too involved. *It's a man's job* she decided making a mental note to get Robert to take care of it when he returned. Her job was looking after the kids.

She reached for her housecoat at the end of the bed, side-glancing her image in the mirror. Her hair, a dishevelled black rat's nest, she piled on her head, anchoring it with a large brown clip, rather than brushing through the wiry mass. Surprisingly, she mimicked the new beehive style she saw recently in a magazine, smiling smugly at her image.

She searched for her slippers under the bed and assumed one of the youngsters had taken them. Gingerly, she opened the bedroom door, scanning the hallway, moving quietly to the bathroom. She tried the doorknob. 'Who's in there? I've got to pee.' A trickle of warm urine christened her doughy thigh. She ran a barefoot over the floor absorbing the evidence.

Sherry rolled her eyes. 'I'm brushing my teeth,' a white stream of toothpaste spilled out her mouth. She quickly wiped the trail with the dirty towel hanging by the sink.

'I have to pee!' Anne yelled, crossing her legs tightly.

The door flew open. Sherry slid between her mother and the door jam. 'See you at lunch,' she said.

Anne plopped herself on the toilet seat, breaking wind a few times, accompanying the flow of urine, easing the tightness in her gut. 'Where are you going?'

Sherry closed her eyes. *Why can't I have a normal Mother like my best friend, Betsy?* Her mom does everything for her and her two brothers, including getting up early and cooking a wholesome breakfast every day. Their dad was always home for supper, every night. On weekends, they did everything together, as a family. Today, she felt much older than her ten years. 'I have to go to school,' she yelled, moving hurriedly toward the dented aluminum screen door, feeling the freedom she felt every morning leaving this godforsaken house.

Anne hastily got off the toilet. 'School? Where's your sisters and brothers?' Hearing no reply, she anxiously pulled up her underwear running to the kitchen, breathing a sigh of relief watching Glenn feed Rose her breakfast.

'Mama,' Rose said, pointing her little finger.

Katherine sat in the green highchair beside her sister, shoving fistfuls of Frosted Flakes in her mouth; tiny bits settled in her tight blond curls.

'You must be saving these for later,' Glenn smiled, meticulously pulling the bits out. He glanced at the wall clock. 'I've got to run.'

Anne stood in the entrance watching him kiss the top of their heads. 'Morning, Mom. Jimmy left thirty minutes ago and Sherry just left,' he said, kissing her flushed cheek. 'I won't be home at lunch. There's a game of touch football at noon.'

A sense of dread crossed Anne's face watching him scoop his lunch bag off the table; rapidly turning to anxiety when the screen door closed behind him. She detested the beginning of school, more so watching the girls bang their empty bowls on the wooden trays. During the summer months, she was totally dependent on the older kids to look after these two youngsters; the shift in responsibility overwhelmed her and she reached into the pocket of her housecoat. Shakily, she popped the lid off the pill bottle, tossing two tablets in her mouth, chasing them down with Katherine's orange juice.

'Mine!' Katherine said determinedly, grabbing the empty red plastic cup. 'Bad girl!'

Anne walked toward the kitchen counter. 'You, young lady, need a lesson in sharing. It's important to share with Mommy.'

Katherine tipped it over; watching the last few drops drip onto the tray. 'All gone,' she said, throwing the cup on the floor. 'Me want down,' she said, raising her arms, kicking her feet.

Rose, mimicking her sister, raised her arms.

Anne ignored the pair, filling the coffee percolator, measuring six heaping spoons full of Maxwell House into the metal basket and plugging it into the food splattered outlet.

'Down!' Katherine said, banging both hands on the wooden tray. 'Down, down, down,' she chanted.

Little Rose joined the chorus, but the impact on the wood stung her little fingers setting off the waterworks.

Anne glanced over her shoulder at the two standing on the seat of their highchairs. 'What are you doing?' she yelled, moving toward them.

Katherine watched Mommy grab Rose's tiny arm, stopping her from tumbling sideways. 'Bad girl!' she said, whacking her bottom. 'You're a very bad girl!' She whacked her hard once more. 'How many times have I told you not to stand up in your highchair?' she scolded, placing the hysterical child on the floor.

She turned her attention to Katherine crouched down in her chair, hoping to avoid her mother's wrath. 'And you, you little brat for showing your sister how to be bad.' She hauled her out of the chair whacking her bottom and sitting her beside her bawling sister. 'Now don't either of you cry babies move. You need to grow up and stop all this silliness,' she said, reaching for her *Best Mom Ever* mug. With a trembling hand she poured the steamy brown liquid, reaching into her pocket.

Bea looked up from her novel, *Gone with the Wind,* conscious of the unsettling racket emanating from next door. She had no sympathy for Anne, *the pathetic woman next door,* and thoroughly believed her exasperating situation was self-created with no one to blame but herself. Sadly, Anne preferred to keep herself doped up rather than deal with her responsibilities, especially when it came to motherhood.

In the beginning, Bea had felt sorry for her next door neighbour, making a concerted effort, on numerous occasions, to help her get on track, but she soon realized Anne was not the least bit interested in helping herself. Bea had no tolerance for lazy individuals who won't, at the very least, make an effort.

As the noise intensified, Bea closed the windows and side door, on such a lovely day too, but it was better than listening to the seemingly endless Smythe ruckus.

Anne dragged the two girls kicking and screaming into the living room, sitting them down in the middle of a well-worn Armenian rug. 'Now sit there and don't move,' she said angrily, turning on the television, upping the volume. She picked up the large bright red plastic barrel of toys, dumping it upside down beside them. 'Now sit and play quietly,' she said, plopping herself down on the brown swivel chair, wiping perspiration above her brow with her housecoat sleeve.

Like a miracle, the two girls stopped crying when the familiar intro to *The Andy Griffith Show* filled the room. Anne used a moment's peace to sneak into the kitchen in search of something to eat. Quietly, she opened the refrigerator, reaching for one of the two sugar-coated donuts she had hidden in the corner on the bottom shelf, her mouth salivating, biting into it.

'Share,' Katherine said, holding out her hand.

Anne jumped, dropping it on the floor. 'Get back in the living room!' she said, her mouth full of donut. 'I told you to stay put,' she yelled, chasing her out of the kitchen. Katherine loved a game of chase, tearing off to the second entrance with her younger sister joining in the fun.

'Got you!' Anne hissed, grabbing their arms, dragging them back into the living room. 'Now sit and stay put!' she said, shoving two plastic telephones into their laps.

Katherine picked up the receiver. 'Hello, no one there,' she said, hitting Rose's head, pushing her backward. Rose's head hit the threadbare rug with a loud thud.

Rose screamed as Anne shoved the last piece of donut into her mouth. 'What happened?'

Rose lying spread-eagle on the floor, screamed at the top of her lungs while Anne yanked Katherine to her feet, whacking her hard on the bottom. 'Get to your room, you bad girl!'

Katherine tore off down the hall to avoid a further spanking, slamming the bedroom door behind her.

Anne pulled Rose's tiny arm. 'Get up now,' she said, yanking her to her feet. 'That's enough now,' she said, wiping tears with the palm of her chubby hand. 'You're okay. Just sit and play,' she said, reaching into the pocket of her housecoat.

For the first time in her life, Theresa was happy it was the first day of school, a welcome reprieve from the miserable days spent over-thinking her time at the cottage with Edson. When the recess bell sounded, she was first out of the classroom, walking quickly across the field toward the creek. She sat down on a large rock, listening to the water caress the rocks; a reminder of the gentle waves lapping the shoreline on Hope Island. She had never felt so connected to anyone and wondered if she ever would again.

The tone of Edson's voice was gentle, kind, convincing. *You are an amazing girl. I have a feeling in a couple of years you'll be a real heartbreaker, not that you aren't now. You are fun, inquisi-*

tive, patient, kind and just a totally great girl, and I love you for this. I've never known anyone like you. She relived their first kiss, as she had again and again, sealing their love; the recess bell sounded, saving her from tears.

Tammy ran quickly toward her sister on the way home at lunch. 'Wait! Wait!' she yelled, hoping Theresa would hear her. When she didn't stop, she ran faster still, catching up with her. 'Didn't you hear me calling you?'

Theresa picked up her pace. The last thing she needed was her bratty sister bugging her.

Tammy, struggling to catch her breath, grabbed her sister's arm. 'What's wrong with you? You've been acting so strange ever since you got back from Debbie's cottage.'

Theresa jerked her arm away. 'I just want to be left alone.'

'Was it the Juicy Fruit gum I gave you? I thought you loved it. I still have it if you want it.' Tammy stood dumbfounded watching her run off.

Mere minutes separated Jimmy and Sherry's arrival home for lunch. Once again, Sherry had been reluctant to come home knowing Glenn was staying at school for lunch today. Enviously, she had watched her friends leave the school grounds in a rush to get home, knowing their mothers had prepared lunch.

Other than noise from the TV, the house was quiet. Rose was asleep on the floor with her toys and Mom was lying on her bed. Jimmy found Katherine sitting on her bed sucking her thumb, turning the pages of a dog-eared book of nursery rhymes, tossing it aside when she saw her brother. 'No Mommy, no Mommy,' she cried, shaking her head from side to side.

'What's this all about?' he said, picking her up, her wet diaper making an impression on his light blue shirt.

Sherry tiptoed past her sleeping sister, discovering once again, no lunch sitting on the kitchen table. She rubbed her face in frustration, the motion momentarily abating her hunger. On the verge of tears, she swung the fridge door wide. Blinking her blue eyes in rapid succession, she focused in disbelief, on the illuminated top shelf housing a large plate of neatly cut triangle sandwiches. 'Finally, Mom did it!' she said, on the verge of hysterics, placing the weighted plate on the table.

'Did what?' Jimmy said, placing Katherine in her high chair.

'She made sandwiches.' She took a bite of a salami, mustard and relish triangle. 'So delicious.'

Early this morning, Jimmy had witnessed Glenn patiently preparing the selection; deciding to keep tight-lipped, he placed a cheese sandwich on Katherine's tray as Rose wandered into the kitchen.

'Up,' Rose said, lifting her arms up to Sherry.

'Mommy made us lunch,' she smiled, sitting her in the highchair, handing her a cheese sandwich.

Anne woke herself up with a loud snore. She rubbed her temples trying to decide what to wear, only to discover she was already dressed. She popped two pills in her mouth sauntering down the hall.

Sherry greeted her as she entered the kitchen. 'Thank you so much for the delicious sandwiches,' she said, jumping up and hugging her waist, trying to remember the last time she embraced her mother.

Anne awkwardly returned the hug. 'What sandwiches?'

Sherry furrowed her brow looking up at her. 'The sandwiches you made us for lunch.'

She chuckled, 'I didn't make any sandwiches. It must have been Jimmy.'

Sherry turned stone-faced, listening to Jimmy profess how Glenn got up early to make them knowing he wouldn't be home for lunch.

Anne smiled proudly. 'I knew I could count on my eldest son. He's so dependable.'

Sherry backed away from her mother. 'Yeah, it's really lucky for us kids or we'd probably starve to death.'

'That's not true at all,' Anne said indignantly, resenting the insinuation.

Sherry retorted, 'Yes it is! You should feel really bad about yourself. If it wasn't for my brothers, nothing would get done around here. All you do is lie in bed and take stupid pills, instead of being a real mother,' she said, running out the front door.

Anne rubbed her temples trying to ward off another tension headache.

Being the second oldest, Jimmy felt more empathy toward her. 'It's okay Mom...'

'No, it's not okay,' she interrupted. 'Sherry is right. I have a wonderful family I love with all my heart,' she said convincingly. 'It's just that I have all these issues to contend with and at times, I just don't know how to cope,' she sighed deeply. 'But starting now, I'm going to be the best mom ever.'

Jimmy smiled, 'I know you can do it, Mom.' He kissed her warm, flushed cheek.

Anxiously, Anne watched her second eldest run out the door, dragging her self-confidence with him.

Theresa spent most of her time doing school work to keep her mind off Edson. Though several weeks had passed, the pain still felt like it did yesterday; if possible intensifying as she watched Deb and her family pack the car for one last trip to the cottage. She had made a concerted effort to avoid Deb, a constant reminder of her time with Edson, since school began. With it being Thanksgiving weekend, she assumed Edson and his family would be closing up their cottage for the season too. *Lucky Deb* she thought, wondering if he would even bother asking after her. In the meantime, all she wanted was to be left alone with her misery. Even annoying Tammy kept her distance and gave up trying to figure out what was wrong.

Early Saturday morning, there was a light tap on her door.

'Theresa,' Greg whispered, leaning into it.

She opened her eyes to darkness, answering groggily.

'Get dressed and meet me at the front door.'

A few minutes later, she was standing at the door with her brother. 'What's going on, Greg? The sun isn't even up yet.'

He quietly unlocked the front door. 'Follow me.'

She fastened her jacket. 'This better be good.'

It was a grey, misty, cool fall morning crossing the street toward Carmichaels' heavily dewed front lawn.

'What are we doing?' she said impatiently in the eerie silence.

'Just wait a sec, will you.'

'I feel like a total jerk standing in the middle of, of all the places you had to choose, Bev Carmichael's front lawn.' She glanced toward the house, the drapes drawn tightly.

Greg scanned the area for early risers, unzipping his old blue ski jacket. '*SURFIN' SAFARI* by the Beach Boys,' he said, removing the 45rpm from its sleeve.

Theresa's stomach soured. She had no idea what he had in mind, but her gut was saying it may not be a good idea. Greg was full of what he considered *good ideas*, which invariably were anything but.

He surveyed the neighbourhood one last time drawing a deep breath, moving his right arm to shoulder level. 'Keep your eye on the first ever Beach Boy's flying saucer,' he said, flicking his wrist orbiting the record.

Theresa stood in stunned silence watching the speeding record move rapidly toward its destination, which unfortunately happened to be Smythe's dining room window, smashing cleanly through the double six foot panes of glass. The sound of shattering glass, coupled with screaming children could be heard clearly from their vantage point.

'Jesus Christ! That wasn't supposed to happen.' Greg took off running with Theresa close behind. Reaching for the doorknob he directed her to get into bed and pretend nothing happened.

'Are you crazy? Something did happen!'

'Just go back to bed and don't say a fucking word to anyone.'

Theresa began a tug of war with her dew soaked boots at the front door.

'Just leave them on,' he hissed, disappearing into his room.

She finally managed to yank them off in her room, climbing into bed with her coat on; an accessory to Greg's stupid experiment, she lay very still trying to calm her racing heart. Fortunately, Smythe's dining room drapes had been closed. She prayed it was enough to prevent broken glass from travelling too far, injuring the children. Either way, they were in deep trouble.

Robert, hearing the girls' screams threw back the covers. He arrived home late last night; with only a few hours sleep he wondered if he'd dreamt it, the banging on the bedroom door confirmed his fear. He grabbed his housecoat from the bottom of the bed watching Anne sleep soundly. He swore she would sleep through the coming of Christ; opening the door the girls charged toward him.

'We were just colouring at the dining table when something hit the window and broke it into pieces. It scared the wits out of us,' Sherry said, holding onto her father for dear life.

Katherine and Rose held onto his legs.

He led the girls down the hallway into the dining room, eyeing the drapes moving slightly.

'All of you stay put.' Gingerly he pulled back the curtain, revealing a gaping hole in the middle of the window. Studying the pieces of broken glass, he was thankful the full-length beige drapes contained the fragments; it could have been much worse. It was obvious someone threw something against the window; whatever was used remained a mystery. He looked at his eldest daughter. 'Tell me again what happened, sweetheart.'

She explained how her sisters woke up early and wanted to colour. 'I brought them to the dining room table and then all of a sudden there was a huge crashing noise of breaking glass.'

He examined his daughters for injuries. 'Did you hear anything hit the window?'

Sherry shook her head, 'It happened so fast, there was just the crashing noise.'

Robert sighed, 'Fortunately, everyone is alright. I want you to take the girls to the bedroom and stay there.'

Sherry watched him pull his dark brown cardigan from the hall cupboard. 'Dad, are you going outside in your pajamas?'

He shrugged, 'Hopefully, no one is up.'

Buttoning his sweater on the go, he walked around the corner of the house toward the broken window, studying the jagged entry point. *What could possibly*...he stopped mid-thought, staring into the window well.

Tammy rolled over, stretching leisurely. 'T, you awake?'

Therese pretended to be asleep as Tammy threw back her covers.

'What are your boots doing in here?' she said, picking up the wet rubbers. 'Mom is going to...'

Theresa sat up. 'Give me them,' she hissed, snatching the pair.

Tammy shook her head. 'Lately, you've become such a...' she stopped mid-sentence listening intently to the banging on the front door. 'Now, who the hell could that be?' Anxious to find out, she tore off down the hall. She was surprised to find the door unlocked; opening it a crack, she was even more surprised to see Mr. Smythe, in his pyjamas, on the other side of it. She eyed him cautiously.

'Good morning, Tamara,' he said, pushing his glasses toward the bridge of his nose. 'Sorry to bother you this early. Is Mom or Dad up?'

She hated being called Tamara; it usually meant she was in some sort of trouble. Though it was eight o'clock, not necessarily considered early by some, her parents bowled last night then partied with friends afterward; it was very early by their standards. 'My parents are both sleeping. Is there anything I can help you with,' she said, eyeing the record in his left hand.

Mr. Smythe, a man used to getting immediate results, asked when they would be available.

Focusing on the record, she pointed, 'Where did you get that?'

Mr. Smythe held it up long enough for Tammy to read the label. 'Please, just tell your mom or dad I need to talk to one of them as soon as possible.'

Tammy ran back to her bedroom. 'Well that was strange. You're never going to guess who was at the front door. Mr. Smythe, in his pyjamas no less, holding a record that looked very familiar,' she said smugly.

Theresa, lying on her back with her eyes closed, knew Greg was in deep trouble; she the innocent accomplice.

Bea awoke to the incessant knocking on the bedroom door.

'You need to get up, Mom,' Tammy said, from the other side.

Bea slipped out of bed quietly, donning her cotton housecoat.

Greg lay in bed listening to Tammy follow Mom down the hall. He had heard bits of conversation, surmising there was no way he could be involved in the unfortunate incident. *Lots of kids have 45 rpms*. He knew he could count on Theresa not to say anything, unlike blabber mouth Tammy who would have told half the neighbourhood by now. His stomach grumbled with hunger but he stayed put.

Bea filled the kettle with cold water. She needed a hot cup of steeped *Earl Gray*, especially after a night out partying with friends.

'Mom, don't you want to know what happened this morning?'

Bea warmed the teapot, filling the strainer with tea leaves. 'You know I don't deal with anything until I've had my cup of tea,' she said tersely. When the tea was steeped she poured it into her finest china. After her first sip, she asked what could possibly be so urgent this early in the day.

Tammy glanced at the clock. 'This isn't really early...'

'Get on with it,' she said impatiently. Last night's partying was coming back to haunt her.

'Well, there was a knock at the door; I answered it, of course, because no one else...'

'Will you get to the point,' she said, reaching for her cigarettes.

Tammy stared indignantly at her mother. 'I am. Anyway, Mr. Smythe was standing there in his *pyjamas*. He had on this raggedy, old, dark brown sweater and some old beige...' stopping in mid-sentence, watching Bea shake her head. 'What?'

It never failed to amaze her how observant her youngest daughter was. 'Carry on.'

'Anyway, he had a 45 record in his hand.'

Bea thought of the 45rpm, *The Twist,* Armand had borrowed from his son for the party last night. They all had a great time learning the latest dance craze. 'So?'

'It's Greg's *SURFIN' SAFARI* record, I'm sure of it.'

Bea put out her cigarette, emptying her cup with one gulp. 'How do you know it's his? Lots of kids have records nowadays.'

Tammy said, 'Don't you think it's a little strange when your next door neighbour, dressed in pyjamas no less, comes knocking on *your* door early in the morning wanting to see you as soon as possible?'

Bea refilled her cup, her mouth in cud-chewing mode. She was convinced that the family next door were all going daft trying to endure life with a spaced out poor excuse of a woman who spent the better part of her life in bed. 'Not particularly,' she said, lighting a cigarette.

She shrugged. 'Anyway, the message from Mr. Smythe is, he wants to speak to you or Dad as soon as you get up.'

Tammy walked toward her bedroom to confront her sister lying in bed, with her boots nearby. She was totally convinced it was Greg's record. *Where there's trouble, he's usually involved. I'm glad I'm not like that* she thought confidently, swinging open the bedroom door. 'Well big sister, you might as well tell me what happened.' When she got no response, she moved toward her bed, sitting on the edge, crossing her arms over her chest. 'On second thought, I'm a patient person; I'll find out sooner or later.'

Bea dragged heavily on her smoke, butting it out. She stared pensively at the kitchen window contemplating a visit to the madhouse next door.

'Good morning, my sweetie,' Ken said, tucking his shirt into his beige trousers. He smiled broadly as she moved toward him kissing his lips. 'Now this is what I call a really good morning,' he said, hugging her tightly.

Reluctantly she pulled away, reaching for her black slacks folded neatly on the dresser. 'I'm afraid now isn't the time, love. I have to go next door, hopefully for just a few minutes.'

Ken watched her dress. 'What does Audrey want to chat about this early in the morning?'

Bea motioned with her head, 'other side.' She buttoned her white blouse, filling him in on the latest from Tammy.

Ken tensed. 'Do you think there's any merit to what she's saying? After all, Tammy's the messenger,' he whispered, rolling his eyes.

She leaned into the mirror applying a thin coat of red lipstick to her parched lips. 'I won't know until I speak with Robert.'

A puzzled look crossed his face. 'Have you spoken to Greg?'

She dabbed her lips with a tissue. 'He's still in bed and will probably be there till noon.'

'There's your answer,' he smiled confidently.

Bea stood outside Smythe's backdoor listening to the ruckus beyond. Knocking loudly, she had forgotten what it was like to have little ones. *Thank goodness* she sighed, knocking louder; a sullen faced Sherry answered.

'Good morning, love,' Bea smiled, shifting on the wobbly step. 'Is your father...?'

'Dad! Mrs. Rowan's here.' Sherry stared at her as if she had just landed from another planet.

Insolent little bugger Bea thought dryly.

187

Robert finally appeared, ushering her inside. 'Sorry, I was busy cleaning up the mess.'

Bea followed him into the chaotic living room; the television blared so loudly she fought the urge to cover her ears.

'Sorry about the mess,' he said apologetically. The place looked like a cyclone had gone through. Over the intolerable noise he instructed Sherry to turn off the television and take the young ones to the bedroom.

Sherry was having no part of it. 'I want to stay,' she said, focusing on Bea.

Rather than be the target of this child's misguided anger, Bea turned her attention to the jagged edges of broken glass surrounding a gaping hole.

Apologetically, Robert repeated his instructions; Bea accredited his patience to the fact he was seldom home. *No bloody wonder* she thought watching the little bugger march off with the younger ones in tow. She had already decided their mother was still in bed.

Robert could add mind-reading to his credentials. 'Anne retreated to her bed earlier on. I'm afraid this morning's commotion was just too much for her.'

Bea smiled lamely, feeling no sympathy.

He motioned her toward the toy strewn worn chesterfield, tossing toys and books onto the floor, exposing the stained cushions. She found it challenging to find a small clean section to sit down on.

'Can I get you a cup of coffee? I did manage to put a pot on.'

Bea, hoping for a quick exit out of this hell hole, declined. 'I'd like to get on with it,' she said, glancing at a perfect set of handprints on the dining room wall christened with crayon and who knows what else.

'Then I'll get right to the point,' he said, sitting in the swivel chair.

Bea listened intently before asking how he came to the conclusion Greg was involved. 'He's been in bed asleep all morning,' she said conclusively.

Robert excused himself and began rifling through the cluttered dining room table, handing over the record.

Bea was getting anxious to leave. 'Many kids have records,' she said, in an irritated tone, handing him the record.

'Other side,' he said patiently.

Bea flipped it over, *Greg Rowan* written in his uneven script. Greg's penmanship was unique; the result of numerous unsuccessful eye surgeries to correct a lazy eye as a toddler. She was convinced the botched attempts permanently altered his eye hand coordination; he had spent many hours practicing his penmanship to no avail.

'Are you positive this is the record that broke the window?'

He nodded, 'I found it in the window well directly beneath the window.'

She stood poised, speaking with intent. 'I can only apologize from the bottom of my heart. I give you my word the window will be replaced immediately, and my son will suffer the consequence of his actions.'

Bea, trembling with anger, opted to use the front door as opposed to the back, attempting to ease the tension, but it did little. Without removing her shoes, her steadfast rule for anyone entering the house, she marched down to Greg's room. 'Gregory Albert Rowan, you have exactly two minutes to get yourself out of bed and into the living room.'

Ken came up from the basement in time to hear her yelling. He could tell by her fiery brown eyes she was livid.

'That son of ours...' She stopped mid-sentence to compose herself.

Ken's heart beat double time. 'Is there anything I can do?'

'Yes, put the bloody kettle on for tea,' she said, reaching for her cigarettes.

Greg whipped back the covers knowing he was in deep trouble whenever Mom used his full name. *The shit's going hit the fan* he sighed, pulling on his dark brown pants.

Tammy sat on the edge of her bed listening to the commotion. Mom's angry voice could be heard three blocks away. 'Ha ha. Greg's in shit and I bet I know why.'

Theresa felt sick to her stomach knowing all too well the predicament her brother was in.

Greg remained tight-lipped moving toward the turquoise swivel chair; Mom's angry voice stopped him.

Bea said through gritted teeth, 'I want you in this chair.' She pointed to the dining room chair stationed in front of where she sat on the chesterfield.

Focusing on his face she said, 'Now, I'm going to ask you one question. Did you break Smythe's dining room window?'

Tammy opened her door slightly, allowing a clear view of Mom sitting on the edge of the chesterfield, arms resting on her legs, leaning toward Greg sitting directly in front of her, but it was difficult to hear what was being said.

Greg tried not to swallow before speaking. He had heard on one of the detective shows it was an admission of guilt. 'I'm not sure what you're talking about,' he said, pushing his glasses up where they belong.

Bea, knowing her fifteen year old son very well, expected an evasive reply, guilt written all over his face. 'You know damn well what I'm talking about,' she said, sitting back on the couch. 'Tammy, get back in your room.'

'I have to pee, Mom.'

'Make it quick.' She turned back to Greg. 'At some point very early this morning, someone shattered Smythe's picture window. The impact sent broken glass into the dining room where the kids sat colouring at the table.' She paused, breathing deeply. 'Thank goodness the drapes contained the glass, but needless to say, it was very distressing for the youngsters, as you can well imagine.'

He remembered feeling ill listening to their terrified screams. 'Are the kids alright?'

Bea reaffirmed they were shook up but uninjured.

'Did someone throw a rock or something?'

Bea felt the hair on the back of her neck stand. 'You know bloody well what was thrown.'

'No Mom. I'm afraid I don't,' he said, sitting back in the chair, sensing she wasn't positive of his involvement.

'You lying bugger!' she said through clenched teeth. 'How do you explain this?' she said, handing him the record.

He shrugged. 'Could be anyone's.'

'Flip it over. It's got *your* bloody name on it.'

Tammy ran back to her room. 'I was right! I knew Greg had something to do with it. The stupid idiot signed the record. He'll probably say it was an accident or something dumb like that.'

Theresa said, 'Actually, it was an accident.'

Tammy's eyes widened. 'How do you know?'

Theresa stared straight ahead. 'I was there when it happened.'

Fingering the evidence, Greg spoke, 'It was an experiment that turned into an accident. I wanted to see if the record would fly, you know, like a flying saucer. I have to admit, when I fired it off I had absolutely no idea it would go that far, not to mention take a window out. I was petrified and didn't know what to do so we ran...'

'We,' Mom interrupted.

'Theresa was with me, but she had nothing to do with my stupid idea. I asked her to accompany me; very reluctantly she agreed.' He focused on the record. 'I just thought it would be really neat to launch a record into space. Are you sure the kids are alright?' he asked remorsefully. Mom looked him in the eye. 'You can thank your lucky stars the curtains held back the flying glass. Now, what are you going to do to about it?'

Theresa confirmed Greg's admission. 'To be honest, Mom, I had no idea what he had planned. Just the same, I had a lousy feeling just walking toward Carmichaels. I regret not stopping him, but when Greg's mind is set, I knew it would be futile trying to change it. I never imagined the record would travel so far, so quickly and do so much damage.'

Mom raised her brow, 'Were you going to talk to me about this?' Lately, she suspected, by her daughter's moodiness, she was holding back some things.

Though she didn't like ratting on her brother, Theresa knew she would eventually talk to her about it at some point; her conscience, as usual, would get the better of her.

Mom made her promise to come to her anytime she felt something was amiss. 'I'm always there for you, love.'

For a brief moment, Theresa thought of the pervert, promising half-heartedly.

Greg surmised it would take all his savings to replace the glass. He waited until the repairman finished installing the new glass then went next door to apologize.

Speaking candidly with Mr. Smythe about the unfortunate incident, expressing true remorse for his actions; Mr. Smythe was so moved by his heartfelt admission he offered to pay half of the $250.00 price tag.

Greg was astounded and thanked him profusely for his generous offer; relieved he wouldn't be destitute, walking away with most of his savings intact. 'I must admit, Mr. Smythe, it would have been a struggle to come up with the total cost.' Again, he apologized for the trauma he had put the family through.

Greg decided to remain tight-lipped about Mr. Smythe's generous offer. He had taken his cue from his favourite character, Eddie Haskell, master brown-noser on Leave it to Beaver. *Thanks Eddie for showing me how it's done.*

Thanksgiving dinner at the Rowan's was always a family affair. Year after year, Bea prepared a delicious turkey dinner with all the fixings and everyone would marvel at how she completed the arduous task so effortlessly. Today was no different; Bea was busy in the kitchen; the relatives were in the living room drinking, smoking, nibbling on mini sausage rolls, mushroom tarts, nuts and bolts and ruffled potato chips and onion dip.

Uncle Joseph, or Uncle Joey, as the kids fondly referred to him, was married to Ken's youngest sister, Eleanor, a quiet, judgemental, serious woman; quite the opposite of her outspoken, loud, often humorous, obnoxious husband. He loved the kids, especially Tammy, who seemed to morph into more of a brat the moment he walked in the door. She would sit beside him or in his lap for most of the visit, much to Aunt Eleanor's objection. Most family photos taken on these occasions portrayed the inseparable duo hamming it up in front of the camera.

Uncle Joe lit a cigarette, inhaling deeply. 'So what's dis, Theresa?' he said, in his thick Dutch accent. 'Next year you'll be in high school. Gotta a boyfriend yet?' A wide toothy grin, reminiscent of a piano keyboard, crossed his rectangular face. He had a large dimple in the middle of his chin of such depth it would be difficult to keep hair free.

Theresa, in spite of herself, felt her face glow immediately thinking of Edson; hoping her antagonistic uncle didn't notice.

Tammy rolled her hazel eyes, adding her two cents. 'The way T's been acting lately...'

'What's dis?' Joe interrupted, sensing Theresa was holding back something. He gulped two mouthfuls of beer. 'You gotta boyfriend and you're not tellin' your Uncle Joey all about him?' He nudged Tammy sitting with her arm around his shoulder; he was by far her favourite uncle.

Eleanor crossed her arms over her ample chest. 'Joseph, that's enough.' He could be so annoying at times, especially when he had an audience.

He turned to Tammy. 'Do *you* know about your sister's boyfriend?' He tickled her side trying to get the answer, sending her into shrieks of denial.

Theresa, thankful for the reprieve, slipped into the kitchen, offering to help her mother.

Bea sipped a scotch and water. 'No thanks, love. Everything is done. The turkey's cooking nicely and the vegetables are all prepared.' She glanced at the kitchen clock. 'It'll be at least another hour before supper.'

Theresa retreated to her bedroom hoping she wouldn't be missed. She could hear Uncle Joe trying to converse with Aunt Harriet, the oldest of the three siblings. Unlike her husband, Harry, who enjoyed a good debate, Harriet tended to be on the quiet side. Sandra, their daughter, loved a good jarring session, like her father. Whereas Sandra's husband, Alex, was content to sit and munch on rippled potato chips and onion dip that he rarely ate at home.

Ken smiled contentedly sitting in his brown swivel chair, puffing a cigar, sipping a rye and ginger ale. He thoroughly enjoyed the holidays; a time to reconnect with his sisters. Normally, he wouldn't drink on a Sunday, but long weekends and good company equalled an opportunity to sit back and enjoy a few snifters. During the week, he adhered to his steadfast rule of no alcohol, fearing it would affect his work ethic. Smiling contentedly, he sat back, enjoying the banter.

Theresa thought of her grandparents spending the holiday alone. This morning, during a rare visit, she had tried coaxing them to join the family for a delicious turkey dinner. She was not surprised by her grandfather's refusal or condescending look quelling any further discussion.

Periodically, she had witnessed the same patronizing look on her dad's face. *Like father, like son.* It had taken years of self-doubt to finally realize her grandfather and father had issues going on inside that had nothing to do with her.

When the dinner bell sounded, the family gathered around the table. Uncle Joe wasted no time targeting Greg, passing the white china turkey platter to him. 'So I hear records make great flyin' saucers, is not.'

Greg shot a daggered look at Tammy over his glasses. 'What?' she said innocently. 'Mom would eventually tell Aunt Eleanor, who would then tell Uncle Joe, so I decided to tell him first,' she smiled, shoving a forkful of turkey in her mouth.

Uncle Joe chuckled. 'I bet that set you back a few bucks.'

Greg remained focused on his dinner. 'I've taken care of it, Uncle Joe.'

'Vell, you vill never do that again, is not,' he smiled, nudging Tammy.

As usual, Tammy took the bait. 'Even Greg's not stupid enough to try that again,' she said, rolling her eyes. She had spent most of yesterday trying to figure out how much the window had set him back him, but mostly where he'd gotten the money to pay for it.

For dessert, Bea placed a large platter of homemade cookies and tarts, offering to make coffee and tea.

After dinner the women moved into the kitchen to start the arduous task of tackling the dishes. Clean up was always more of a good time than laborious, tonight was no exception. Eleanor picked up a tea towel singing, 'Cruising down the river on a Sunday afternoon...' Needless to say, it didn't take long for others to join the chorus.

Monday morning Theresa got up early. The house was quiet; a far cry from yesterday's gathering of the clan. Family celebrations were interesting, at times challenging, but invariably everyone enjoyed themselves.

Uncle Joe's questions about her love life stayed with her, like a nagging toothache. She wanted to tell him she had met this really neat guy at her friend's cottage. But it was proving to be nothing more than a fantasy. She had not heard from him since; drawing the conclusion, he probably thinks she's too skinny, hairy or just not good enough.

After lunch, Mom, Dad and a reluctant Tammy, decided to deliver turkey leftovers to her grandparents.

'I want to stay home with Theresa,' she whined.

'Get your coat, you're coming with us and that's final,' Mom said, reaching for her beige car coat.

Dad tried bribing her with Grandma's sugar cookies.

'It's Theresa who likes them, not me.'

'Well then, you can be a good sister and bring some home for her,' Dad smiled.

Tammy rolled her eyes, slamming the door behind her.

Theresa finished her math homework. At times, she often found it difficult to concentrate; thoughts of Edson would often supersede assignments. She pushed her history textbook aside. It was rare that everyone was out, even more rare having the luxury of watching TV all by herself. She switched on the television and the most amazing music she had ever heard sent chills through her. Totally enthralled with the melody, she turned up the volume, settling on the floor less than two feet away from the screen. She was so enthralled with the movie; she didn't hear her family return.

'I thought you had lots of homework to do?' Mom said dryly, hanging up her jacket.

Theresa smiled broadly. 'It's so rare having the television all to myself I decided to take a break. Luckily I did. The movie I've just watched was absolutely amazing.'

Dad hung up his jacket inquiring about it.

'*A Summer Place*; I absolutely *love* the music.' She felt euphoric thinking of the melody, not to mention, the young couple's love and dedication.

Dad was surprised. He was familiar with Percy Faith's composition, *Theme from a Summer Place,* least expecting his diehard rock and roll daughter to be so enthralled. He had to admit, it was a beautiful instrumental.

Theresa wanted to spend the remainder of the day alone, without her annoying sister hanging around. 'Where's Tam?'

'She decided to stay outside. It seems she's had enough of old people for one day.'

Tammy stood outside Smythe's new window contemplating the cost of replacement. *It must have set Greg back at least a hundred bucks.* She figured his excessive gambling habit squandered most of his money; why else would he have sold his baseball glove? She walked along the walkway dividing the two houses, spotting Jimmy in his backyard.

Jimmy lost in his own world, watched Tammy open the gate.

'I haven't seen you for a while,' she smiled sweetly. He was two years older than her, a couple of inches taller and they rarely spoke.

'You've gotten way taller,' Tammy said, watching his emerald green eyes momentarily light up. She could tell by his sullen face he probably wanted to be left alone, but she needed some answers and had a gut feeling Jimmy was her ticket. Breaking the silence, she asked about his teacher.

He shrugged. 'She's okay. Miss Campbell was my brother's teacher a couple of years ago; said she's pretty strict, but so far she's okay.'

He turned on his heel; Tammy reached for his arm. 'I'm really sorry about what happened, you know, the broken window stuff. It must have been very frightening.'

He pulled his arm away. 'I was still in bed, but it was really scary for my sisters. That was a really stupid thing your brother did, but my dad did an even stupider thing by paying for half of it.'

Tammy's eyes widened. 'Your dad paid half? Wow, what a nice man!' She really wanted to know the total amount of replacement. 'How much did it cost?'

His face turned crimson. 'Your stupid brother throws a goddamn record through our dining room window, scares the shit out of my sisters and my brainless Dad takes pity on him paying half of the 250 bucks to replace it. In my opinion, your asshole brother should have paid for it all. Lucky for Greg my dad's a nice guy.'

She couldn't agree more.

Tammy found her dad exercising in the basement. 'I need to ask you a question,' she said, watching him run on the spot. 'What's half of 250?'

Breathlessly he queried, 'haven't you studied fractions in school yet?'

Tammy rolled her eyes, 'No Dad. Can you just tell me, please?'

He bent over, breathing deeply. '125. You're welcome,' he gasped, as she tore upstairs.

Tammy spotted the note written in Mom's distinct scribble and cash sitting on the kitchen table.

Dear Greg:

Though you made a very bad decision Saturday morning, we are proud of the way you took responsibility for your foolhardy action.

We realize the cost of replacing the window would drain most, if not all, of your hard earned savings you've accumulated delivering newspapers. (Your dedication to your paper route, in all kinds of weather, is admirable).

Therefore, Dad and I decided to contribute $25 toward the cost.

Love Mom and Dad.

Tammy dropped the letter onto the table. *That son-of-a-gun always manages to come up smelling like a rose.*

Greg jumped when his bedroom door flew open. 'Do you mind?' he said angrily. 'I could be dressing, you little twerp.'

Tammy waved a hand, 'I've seen you in your underwear before. You're a little scrawny, but you'll fill out.'

'Look who's talking, bone rack. What do you want?'

She moved quickly to his bed and sat down. 'You may think you're clever, pulling the wool over everyone's eyes, but I've just heard from a little bird, not mentioning any names, you only paid for half of the window; Old man Smythe paid the other half. It seems some stupid people took pity on poor Gregory, including Mom and Dad.'

Unaware of his parent's contribution, he shrugged, encouraging her to carry on.

'Now, I could tell Mom and Dad that their *responsible* son isn't as responsible as they think. Or, we can make a deal, and I'll keep my mouth shut.' She sat back anticipating an argument.

'What's the deal?' he smiled.

She was taken aback by his response. 'Are you feeling okay?'

'Very well, thanks.'

His cooperation really baffled her. 'Okay, here's the deal. When you go to Lou's, I go with you. Whenever I want,' she added, waiting for him to balk. But again he agreed. 'Are you sure you're okay?' she said, scrunching up her face.

He chuckled, 'I'm fine. In fact, I'm off to Lou's Saturday after breakfast.'

Tammy's face lit up.

During recess Tuesday morning, Theresa finally came to the realization she had wasted enough time pining over Edson. She would always be thankful for the time they shared but it was time to move on. *Life is like that,* she sighed, walking toward a group of friends rounding up players for a game of handball.

'There you are,' Deb said breathlessly. 'I've been looking all over for you. Usually I can find you moping down by the creek,' she chuckled, handing her an envelope.

Theresa felt the pulse beating in her head, studying her name printed neatly on the front of it.

'I wanted to give it to you last night, but we didn't get home from the cottage until really late. It's from Edson. Aren't you anxious to open it?'

Theresa gripped it tightly. 'I think I'll wait.'

Theresa watched Deb disappear behind the school then ran toward the creek. Apprehensively she opened the envelope; her hands trembled extracting a letter wrapped around a package of Juicy Fruit gum.

> *Dear Theresa,*
>
> *I hope you are doing well.*
>
> *Please accept my apologies for not getting back to you sooner.*
>
> *During our time together, I neglected to tell you, or rather didn't want to, that I have juvenile diabetes, a chronic disease where my body doesn't produce enough insulin that I must live with every day.*
>
> *On the day we went to Hope Island, my blood sugar dropped dangerously low, hence my hasty retreat on arrival back at the dock. This was my fault entirely; I have to be vigilant of my insulin levels at all times, but I enjoyed our time together so much, I literally lost track. I have no regrets. Meeting you has been one of the biggest highlights of my life.*
>
> *When it was time to leave the island, I knew there was no way I could make the swim; it was all I could do to get back to my cottage after we docked. I left hurriedly to avoid alarming anyone, especially you. After that, I was confined to my bed until my departure very early next morning.*
>
> *I am determined to get past this. In the meantime, I want you to know I meant everything I said to you that day on the island. You are an amazing girl.*
>
> *Keep smiling that beautiful smile of yours.*
>
> *All my love, Edson*
>
> *PS The gum is a reminder of our time together sitting on the rock we named forever. I will always cherish the memories. I hope you will too.*

Theresa inhaled the open package they shared during their time on the island. Feeling a sense of relief, knowing he really did care, filled her with a contented joy she hadn't felt in weeks. She opened a stick of gum thinking of their first kiss, his warm embrace, turning toward the empty school yard.

When the lunch bell sounded, Theresa was the first out of the classroom after enduring the longest hour and fifteen minutes ever. She searched frantically for Deb in the crowd of hungry kids. 'Deb,' she called out breathlessly.

Deb waited for her to catch up. 'Did you read Edson's letter yet.'

Without revealing too much, Theresa asked about his diabetes.

Deb sighed, 'unfortunately, some kids are born with it. Edson happens to be one of them.'

Enviously, she asked if she had hung out with him on the Thanksgiving weekend.

Deb picked up her pace. 'No. He wasn't at the cottage. His mom gave me the letter to pass on to you; he composed it shortly after Hope Island.'

Theresa was confused. 'His mother was at the cottage, but Edson wasn't.'

'His parents were only at the cottage long enough to close it up for the winter then hurried back to the city.'

She sensed something wasn't right. 'Is there something you aren't telling me, Deb?'

She suddenly stopped, sighing deeply, 'Edson is in the hospital.'

Tammy opened the screen door yelling at the top of her lungs. 'Theresa's crying her head off,' she said, catching her breath.

Mom walked toward her, 'Is she hurt?'

'I don't think so. She's standing with Deb at the side of the road just bawling to beat the band.'

A worried look crossed her face. Bea had noticed changes in her eldest daughter for quite some time now, chalking it up to changing hormones.

Theresa hid the letter under a stack of towels in the linen closet, away from Tammy's prying eyes. Her eyes were noticeably puffy, sitting down silently at the table, biting into a grilled cheese sandwich, hoping to ease the knot in her stomach.

It was no surprise Tammy was dying to know why she had been so upset. 'I saw you talking to Deb on my way home from school,' she smiled, dipping the corner of her sandwich into a blob of ketchup. 'Is everything okay?'

Fighting back tears, Theresa chewed the mouthful into mere mush. 'I don't want to talk about it.'

Tammy persisted, 'Why are your eyes all red? I couldn't help noticing you were bawling your eyes out. Did Deb say something to upset you?'

Theresa quickly washed the mush down with a mouthful of milk and ran out the door.

'Boy, something's really bothering her,' Tammy said. 'T's been acting really weird ever since she got back from Phillip's cottage. I knew they should have invited me instead.'

Bea sighed, 'Finish your lunch, it's getting late.'

Ken arrived home from work early.

'Well, this is a nice surprise,' Bea said, as he wrapped his arms around her waist. 'You're home early.'

The traffic was light and he was thankful he didn't have to drive his co-worker home.

In a weak moment, feeling it was the honorable thing to do, he had offered to drive Barbara Adams back and forth to work, rather than her take the transit. Unfortunately, his kind gesture tacked more travel time to an already tedious commute.

After inquiring about her day he asked after Theresa.

'I think she's in her room,' Bea said, pecking his lips. 'She was upset about something at lunch, but I haven't had a chance to talk with her. When she came home from school, she went straight to her room.'

'She has been a lot quieter lately, but this should perk her up.' Ken smiled, waving a white plastic bag.

Theresa stuffed the letter under her pillow when she heard the knock on the door.

Dad poked his head in, 'Just me. How are you doing?'

'I'm okay,' she said, glancing at her watch. 'Aren't you home a little early?'

'Traffic was light,' he said, handing her the bag with *Sam the Record Man* printed in bold red letters across the front.

Excitement mixed with melancholy brought tears to her eyes. The *Theme from a Summer Place*. She looked up at her dad, smiling through her tears. 'I absolutely love it. Thank you so much.'

Saturday morning, Tammy stretched languidly in bed. *I've got a hankering for chocolate, lots of chocolate.*

After breakfast, she followed Greg to the store; holding the door ajar, he ushered her inside. 'Lou, ready for a rubber?' he called out like he owned the joint.

Lou's slick eyes moved from Tammy to Greg, nodding once toward the counter.

Tammy watched them disappear behind the counter. Her mouth watered trying to decide whether she wanted a Cadbury's Rum and Butter or a Neilson's Fudge Bar. Unable to make a decision, she stuffed both down her top, quietly exiting the store, running full tilt to the garbage bins at the back of the plaza. Sitting down on the curb, she was about to take a bite of the Fudge bar when a flash of pink caught her eye. *Shit!* She rolled behind the obnoxious smelling garbage bin, hoping she hadn't been seen. She bit into the bar watching a girl preen herself in a shiny gold compact, contemplating where she had seen her before. The sudden roar of a motorcycle scared the wits out of her, diving back behind the bin, quietly choking on her mouthful of chocolate. Remaining hidden, she could hear chatting turn into silence. Shoving the remainder of the Fudge bar into her mouth she peaked around the corner. The young couple, unaware of the audience, held each other tightly and kissed with more passion than any movie she had ever seen. Keenly, she kept her eyes riveted on the exuberant pair, oblivious to the steady stream of chocolate drooling down her chin, settling on her new jacket. Without taking her eyes off of them, she tore open the partially melted Rum and Butter bar, shoving half in her mouth and almost choking when the guy lifted the front of the sweater, grasping her large grapefruit size breasts and sucked them. The contorted-faced female whipped her head back, vigorously massaging his blond head. Suddenly, he yanked the sweater down; a secret message passed between them. Quickly he started up the motorcycle; she hopped on wrapping her hot pink arms tightly around his waist, resting her hot pink face contentedly on his back.

Tammy, now positive the motorcycle mama was none other than Theresa's friend, Bev Carmichael, stood awe-struck watching the pair disappear around the corner. She could hardly wait to tell her best friend, Lois, about the encounter. *I bet she's never seen sex before.*

Quietly Tammy entered Lou's eyeing the top of her brother's head. She tiptoed to the counter, reaching for another Rum and Butter bar (the previous one melted in all the excitement), a Jersey Milk bar, a box of Macintosh Toffee, a Pep bar and a package of Bazooka Bubble Gum for recess on Monday, tucking them all safely down her top. *And maybe another Fudge bar*...a firm hand gripped her shoulder.

Bea closed her novel enquiring about the scrambled eggs she had prepared for Theresa. 'To your liking this morning, dear daughter?' she smiled.

She nodded appreciatively. Mom always made the best scrambled eggs.

Bea poured a cup of tea waiting for Theresa to finish eating. She couldn't remember the last time the two had spent time together chatting; with the house empty she took advantage of the quiet.

'It's just the two of us, love,' she said, lighting a cigarette. 'Is there anything on your mind you would like to talk about?'

Theresa put her plate on the counter; sitting back down across from her mother. It was nice to spend time alone without Tammy hovering close by. 'As a matter of fact, there is. How did you know Dad was the right man for you?'

Bea smiled warmly thinking of the first time she had met Ken. 'I just knew.'

'But how does a person know if they're in love?'

Mom smiled confidently. 'Believe me, you will know.' She proceeded to tell her how she had met her future husband while attending a small gathering at a local pub, The Lion Cat. Her face grew pensive. 'It was one of a few pubs that hadn't been blown to smithereens during the air raids in London.'

Theresa couldn't even begin to fathom what her mother had endured during World War II. Bea had only been a few years older than her when it started. 'It must have been a horrible time for you.'

Bea butted her cigarette with a little more force than intended. 'It was hell. Your grandmother was killed during an air raid hanging laundry, my brother died of malaria and my youngest sister was shipped out every day by train never knowing from one day to the next if she'd return. My other three sisters spent their days doing various jobs, contributing to the war effort. I really don't like to talk about this time in my life; the memories are still very raw. Meeting your father was the only good thing.'

She lit another cigarette before continuing. 'A group from work, in a show of solidarity against the bloody war, frequently met at the pub for drinks. One never knew if they would live to see the next day,' she added sadly. 'On this particular evening, your father and six other air force personnel arrived at the Lion. It didn't take long for the groups to mingle.' She smiled reminiscing about their first introduction. 'Your father was quite shy, more observer than converser. He was very handsome, with wavy brown hair, hazel eyes and a slim build. He preferred remaining in the back-ground watching the others socialize. It wasn't until they were about to leave he finally got up the nerve to approach me. Appar-ently, your father had had his eye on me right from the start.' She chuckled, 'of all things, he offered to buy me a glass of lemonade. In those days, your father didn't drink. I suggested a scotch and water. I'll never forget the look on his face, but, obligingly he went to the bar returning with a scotch for me and a lemonade for him-self. We sipped our drinks and chatted, your father was very soft spoken. Then he thanked me for my time and returned to the base.'

Theresa's eyes widened. 'Didn't he want to see you again?'

Bea shrugged, 'apparently not. He made no suggestion of such and to be honest, I was okay with that. I was engaged to someone else.'

A shocked looked crossed Theresa's face.

'I was engaged to Todd, an Aussie. We worked together in the same office. We were quite fond of each other. Just before he left for his tour of duty, he proposed. I was only seventeen, but I fig-ured what the hell, I may never see him again. Not everyone was on board with our engagement. My father was very cross, begging me to come to my senses. I was much too young for marriage.'

'Your father and his comrades remained stationed in London and when off-duty frequented the pub. At long last he finally asked me for a date. In the beginning, our time together was rather awk-ward; your father being quite reserved, whereas, I was much more outgoing. But after a few dates, we became inseparable.' Bea paused, 'Your father was also engaged, to a Canadian, Helen. Ap-parently, during his weekly correspondence to his mother, he had mentioned meeting a pretty, feisty, brunette British gal. Needless to say, your grandmother wasted no time reminding him of his en-gagement, subtly suggesting he curtail, or rather cease, spending time with me.' Bea smiled triumphantly. 'Well we all know the outcome of that directive. Your father and I were married in Lon-don shortly after the war ended.'

Theresa said, 'so obviously, your feelings for Dad were much more intense than for Todd.'

Bea flipped her hand, smiling confidently. 'Night and day; there was absolutely no doubt I loved your father, still do, will all my heart, and wanted to spend the rest of my life with him.'

Theresa had felt the same about Edson that day on Hope Island. 'Is there a certain age one has to be to fall in love?'

Bea smiled confidently. Her intuition that her eldest daughter had met somebody explained her mood swings of late. She leaned toward her. 'My dear, love appears when we least expect it.'

The grip on Tammy's shoulder tightened sending a wave of fear through her core. The threat of up-chucking the evidence became all too real; her stomach churned with confiscated chocolate. She stood motionless swallowing three times; her best friend, Julie, claims it settles the stomach. Well her best friend was full of shit. She turned her head slightly, staring wide-eyed at the tall, black-eyed police officer with a vice-like grip locked on her shoulder. His tanned face, though clean shaven bore the shadow of a beard permanently etched. His bushy eyebrows ran undivided above the nose. It was a face she would not soon forget.

Easing his grip, he spoke in a rich, deep baritone voice sending shivers through her. 'I was called to the store to investigate a possible theft. Have you stolen anything young lady?' he questioned authoritatively.

Tammy's skinny legs trembled with fear thinking of George's perfume heist and how he must have felt when the policeman arrived. He had told the truth immediately, but chocolate bars aren't as expensive as perfume she reasoned. 'Who wants to know?' she said meekly.

They turned in unison as Lou and her brother stood up behind the counter. The officer tightened his grip. 'Just answer the question. Have you stolen anything from the store?'

Tears spilled down her cheeks. 'I didn't mean to,' she cried. 'It was only a chocolate bar and I'm putting it back,' she said, reaching down her shirt, replacing it on the shelf.

The officer's face hardened. 'I'm afraid you are going to have to come with me to the station. But first we need to call your parents.'

Images of Mom's angry, disappointed face filled her head and she latched on tightly to his arm. 'No! Please officer! You can't tell my parents! Please, please,' she cried, burying her face in the sleeve of his uniform.

Greg and Lou moved from behind the counter. 'Officer, I'm her brother. I will take full responsibility for her actions.'

Tammy sobbed uncontrollably running toward Greg, hugging him tightly around the waist.

The officer spoke to Lou. 'As owner of the establishment, do you want to press charges?'

Lou, his jaw squared, spoke disgustedly. 'No.'

The officer said, 'Well young lady, it seems you are in the clear, this time. But for the records, I will need your name and address.'

Tammy felt her gut wrench. 'Why?'

The officer's face hardened. 'Young lady, stealing is a crime, punishable by the full force of the law. Had the owner pressed charges, you would have been escorted to the station, fingerprinted and charged with theft.'

'It was only a chocolate bar,' she said innocently, glimpsing at Lou's angry face. 'Or two,' she added, wondering how he knew; he was so wrapped up in the card game with her brother.

The officer said firmly, 'Let me explain something to you young lady. It doesn't matter if it's a piece of gum or a book. A theft occurs when *any* unpaid item is removed from a store. Do you understand?'

Tammy swallowed. 'Yes officer.'

He extracted a notepad and pen from his shirt pocket. 'Please print your name, address and phone number neatly.' He looked her in the eye. 'I want you to remember, if this ever happens again, your name will be on file, therefore, you will be arrested and charged with theft. Do I make myself clear?'

'Yes,' she said between sobs. Crying softly she printed the requested information, promising never to steal again.

The officer glanced over the paper, handing it to Greg for verification.

Tammy said indignantly. 'Do you think I would lie or something?'

'I hope not, young lady. Lying is right up there with theft,' he said, folding the piece of paper, tucking it in his shirt pocket. He reminded Greg about his responsibility for his sister's actions.

'Yes, Officer…'

'Giovanni,' he said, tipping his hat.

The three watched the officer exit. 'I'll leave you two alone,' Lou said, walking to the back of the store.

Tammy focused on the green tiled floor, avoiding eye contact with her brother. She still couldn't figure out how she had gotten caught. *I was so careful.* 'How did he know I stole something?' she asked, raising her head.

Greg pointed toward the 18" circular security mirror mounted in the corner of the store. 'No matter where Lou is, he can see everything.'

Tammy's eyes bulged. *He must have seen everything I took.* She quickly realized she would be in even bigger trouble if Mom ever found out, begging Greg not to squeal.

'Only if you promise *never* to steal anything ever again; you were very foolish to believe you could get away with it.'

Tammy soon morphed into her defiant self. 'What about all the gambling you do with Lou. I've *seen* you in action,' she said belligerently, crossing her arms across her chest. 'If you open your mouth, I'll tell Mom about your gambling habits here at the store.'

Greg shook his head. 'For your information, I haven't gambled for weeks.'

Tammy flung her head back. 'Who are you trying to kid? You were behind the counter with Lou just a few minutes ago, Gregory. What were you doing, holding hands?'

Lou appeared and stood beside Greg. 'Actually young lady, we were only pretending to play cards, watching you steal candy. Your brother is telling the truth. He hasn't gambled for weeks.'

Greg said, 'Tammy, I want you to apologize to Lou, and promise him it will never happen again.'

Red faced, she shifted her gaze back and forth. 'I apologize.'

'And,' Greg said forcefully.

'And, I promise never to do it again. Can I please go now?'

Lou said, 'After you put back the candy stuffed down your shirt.'

Officer Giovanni climbed into his vehicle. After re-reading Tammy's note, he pulled the wad of gum out of his mouth, stuck it in the middle and tossed it on the floor.

Theresa reached for the tissue box sitting on top of the fridge, wiping her eyes. Though she felt better telling her mom about Edson, she was worried sick about his health. 'Deb said he's in hospital and not doing well.' Tears stung her eyes. 'I'm beginning to wonder if I'll ever see him again.'

Mom poured another cup of tea. 'Well, dear daughter, all you can do is take one day at a time.' She sipped her hot tea, remembering the booklet she wanted to give to her.

'While I've got you here, I've been meaning to give this to you,' she said, handing her a booklet. 'Now that you're becoming a young lady, you need to know about all the changes that will happen to your body. I've glanced through it and found it quite informative.'

Theresa read the title *Growing up and liking it.* 'What's it about, Mom?'

'Just have a good read, love,' she said, exiting the kitchen.

Chapter Thirteen

LAST NIGHT'S RAIN cut the real estate agent's hammering time in half. He attached the for sale sign to the wooden post, picked up his tools and walked toward his car.

'Hey! What do you think you're doing?'

He turned, watching a scrawny girl struggling with her coat run toward him.

'What do you think you're doing? The people that live here aren't moving. You've got the wrong house so pull out your dumb sign.'

Throughout his ten year career, Steven Langdon had thought he had seen and heard it all, until now. 'I'm afraid that's not going to happen,' he said patiently. 'Your next door neighbours have commissioned me to sell their home. Now if you'll excuse me, I have more signs to post.'

Tammy watched him drive out of sight.

Edson slid in out of a coma vaguely aware of the people in his sterile hospital room. He slid his bandaged hand along the blanket, opening his eyes briefly listening to hushed voices emanating from somewhere in the room.

'I'm sorry Mrs. Wilson. The test results confirm your son's kidneys are no longer functioning…' they both turned when Edson mumbled, his mom moved quickly to his side.

Dr. Jansen had seen this all too many times, hopeful parents clinging to the odds their child will recover. He quietly left the room.

Mr. Phillips turned away from the picture window. 'Didn't our real estate agent call this morning to say the "for sale" sign had been posted on our lawn?'

Audrey lit another cigarette, inhaling deeply, joining him at the window. 'That's strange. It was there this morning. I saw it with my own eyes. I'll call and see what the hell's going on.'

John Brown raised his left bushy eyebrow, standing behind the floor to ceiling white living room sheers wondering which little bugger from the street erected a Royal LePage for sale sign in the middle of his front lawn. It was bad enough the kids called him *Crabby Appleton*, but this latest insult was inexcusable. He picked up the phone, dialing the number listed on the sign.

'Good morning. You have reached Royal LePage. If you've got a house you want sold, we will sell it in no time,' the cheery voice sang.

Tammy ran her sleeve across her face, excusing herself from the table; her infuriating motion hadn't gone unnoticed.

Mom said, 'How many times have I asked you not to wipe your face on your sleeve? I will never make a lady out of you.'

The furthest thing from Tammy's mind was being a lady; vaguely promising not to do it again. Thankfully, there was a knock on the door avoiding further lecturing. She ran out of the kitchen. 'I'm getting it,' she said, opening and shutting the door. 'No one there,' she called out, running full tilt toward the bedroom.

Theresa watched Tammy jump into bed, yanking the covers up over her head. 'You are such a twerp,' she sighed, placing the needle at the beginning of the record. For the umpteenth time, the music of *A Summer Place* filled the room.

Bea looked up from her novel; the persistent knocking grew louder. *Bloody hell* she mumbled. She was sure Tammy said no one was there.

Opening the door, Bea met up with three stern faces staring back at her, recognizing Lorne Phillips only.

'Good morning, Bea. Sorry to bother you,' Lorne said. 'There's a mystery unfolding as to why the for sale sign erected on my lawn this morning by my agent, Mr. Langdon, ended up in the middle of Mr. Brown's front lawn.'

As if on cue, John Brown raised the sign.

A perturbed look crossed Bea's face wondering why these three were here in the first place. 'Well, you've got the sign back now. So what's the issue?'

Lorne half smiled. 'Bea, the agent has a gut feeling it was your youngest daughter, who pulled the sign shortly after he drove off, in turn, erecting it in the middle of John's lawn.'

Bea said emphatically, 'don't be ridiculous, Lorne. Why is it whenever anything goes wrong in this bloody neighbourhood my kids are at fault? Tammy has just finished her breakfast and she's in her room. It's not possible she was involved.'

'Excuse me,' the agent said, introducing himself. 'Is it possible to speak with your daughter? I'm sure a brief conversation with her will clear this up in no time.'

Bea left the trio standing at the door. 'Don't you ever get sick of that bloody song?' she said to Theresa, opening the bedroom door.

Reluctantly, Theresa turned off the record player, watching the turntable spin to a stop.

Mom walked over to Tammy's bed, asking suspiciously why she was back in it.

Tammy remained stationary. 'I'm sleeping.'

Bea asked if she was feeling alright.

Tammy faked a yawn, starting up Bea's perturbed chewing motion. 'I just want to sleep some more, Mom. That's all.'

'You wouldn't happen to know anything about a for sale sign mysteriously disappearing off Phillip's lawn this morning and ending up in the middle of Mr. Brown's, would you?'

Theresa said, 'There's a for sale sign on Phillip's lawn?'

Tammy bolted upright, 'not anymore! I mean, it was there this morning when I got up. They must have changed their mind or something.'

Deb never mentioned anything about moving when she spoke to her a couple of days ago. 'It can't be.'

'Tamara, you little bugger, you've got your bloody clothes on. Get out of bed and come with me.'

Tears stung Theresa's eyes tucking *A Summer Place* into its sleeve. Deb was her only hope of reconnecting with Edson.

Tammy confessed she had confiscated the sign. 'I did it because I don't want you to move, Mr. Phillips. Mrs. Phillips is like a mother to me, and I really love her,' she said, wiping her eyes on her sleeve. 'When Mommy went back to work, she looked after me when I came home from school. Mrs. Phillips would always have some cookies and milk for me. She even made my Halloween costume two years ago. Remember when I was an Indian princess? It's my most favourite costume in the world.'

Mr. Phillips smiled awkwardly. 'Why did you remove it?'

Tammy wiped her nose on her sleeve. 'I thought if I took it away, you would forget about moving. I don't want you to move. You are the bestest neighbours ever.'

Mr. Brown, still holding the sign said matter-of-factly, 'But you want me to move.'

Tammy glared at John Brown aka Crabby Appleton. 'No comment.'

Bea shook her head. 'Tamara, I believe an apology is in order.'

'I'm not sorry for what I did. I did it because I don't want them to move away.' She ran sobbing down the hall.

Bea, not one to admit defeat, reluctantly apologized for her daughter's actions. 'Tammy tends to do things on the spur of the moment with little thought of consequence. But I believe her heart was in the right place. We're all surprised by your sudden move, Lorne.'

Tammy smiled broadly closing the bedroom door. 'I bet you're wondering what I did to get out of trouble and, because you are my bestest sister in the world, my only sister that is, I'm letting you know my secret.'

Theresa placed the record on the turntable, ignoring her jabber.

'I turned on the waterworks,' she said.

Theresa increased the volume, hugging her knees to her chest.

'Works every time!' Tammy yelled, running out of the room with her hands over her ears.

A sallow faced Audrey Phillips hung up the phone. Lighting a cigarette with a trembling hand, she inhaled the acrid smoke deeply, tucking the gold lighter into the empty side of package. She dragged heavily, summoning her youngest daughter.

Deb sat across from her mother at the kitchen table. She could tell by the look on her face something was wrong, assuming she may be having second thoughts about moving to Vancouver; the drastic move out west caught the girls by surprise.

Her mom dragged heavily on the cigarette. 'There is no easy to say this so I'll get right to the point. Edson died in hospital this morning.'

Tammy ran past the three Phillip's girls hugging in the carport, stopping abruptly on the road.

Deb wailed, ''I can't believe Edson is dead!'

Janet and Jean cried alongside of her.

Jean hugged her sisters closer. 'We all loved Edson so much.'

Mom looked up from her novel as Tammy walked in the front door. 'I wanted to have a word with you, young lady, *before* you went outside.'

Tammy rolled her eyes. 'I already apologized and promised not to do it again.'

Bea lit a cigarette inhaling deeply. There were times she could shake the living daylights out of her youngest. 'First of all, you had no right pulling the sign out of Phillips' lawn, and then have the nerve to hammer it into Mr. Brown's lawn.'

Tammy said conclusively, 'Crabby Appleton is a jerk and the whole neighbourhood wishes he *would* move.'

Bea shook her head in frustration. 'Do you understand you can't take the law into your own hands just because you don't agree with something?'

She nodded, trying to ease the sudden kink in her neck. 'Yes Mother. I told you I will never do it again.'

Bea sent her off to her room to think about it. 'Will you please tell your sister I'd like a word with her?' She had to do something about that infernal record being played over and over again.

Tammy marched down the hall, yelling over the music. 'Mom wants to talk to you. Be ready, she's in one of her yappy moods.'

Theresa turned off the record player.

'Oh, and there's one more thing, T. After your chat with Mom, you may want to go see Deb. She's in the carport bawling her eyes out and her sisters are all sobbing too.' She screwed up her nose. 'I think I heard someone say Edson, or something like that.' She shrugged, 'yea, I'm pretty sure that was the name they were tossing around. Anyway, he died.'

Theresa's legs buckled, the high pitch scream sent Tammy tumbling off her bed smashing her arm into the dresser, crying out in agony.

Bea felt the hair on the back of her neck stand on end. 'Jesus Christ!' With a racing heart, she moved quickly down the hall.

Deb sat stone-faced on the chesterfield; her sisters on either side, holding her hands. 'I have to tell Theresa, but I can't. Edson really liked her,' she sobbed.

As Bea approached the bedroom door, Theresa bolted past her. 'What the hell is...' she watched her disappear out the front door. 'Bloody hell,' she muttered, moving toward Tammy. 'What happened?'

Tammy rubbed her elbow. 'I tripped and fell against the dresser. I really hurt my arm,' she cried.

Bea didn't believe her for a second. 'I bet you were jumping on your ruddy bed again,' she said, examining the arm. 'Nothing is broken, thank goodness; you'll have a dandy bruise. Now, I shall ask again, what happened?'

Tammy sat on the edge of her bed, rubbing her sore arm. 'I told Theresa you wanted to see her. Then I mentioned Deb and her sisters were in their carport crying because someone named Edson died.'

Deb and her sisters watched Theresa run out of sight around the corner.

Janet wondered if she knew about Edson.

Jean said, 'That's impossible. We just found out. She's obviously upset about something. She looked like she'd just seen a ghost.'

Breathlessly, Theresa jumped high onto the washed out silver chain link fence, scaling it like a caged monkey. Straddling the top, she lost her balance, realizing too late she was still in slippers, toppling sideways to avoid the jagged top she gripped the other side. With her shirt sleeve reddening from the cut on her arm, she jumped to the ground, burying her tear stained face into her sore hands.

Walking toward Phillip's carport, Bea tried to recall the name Theresa had mentioned when they had their chat a few weeks ago.

'Mrs. Rowan!' Deb cried, hugging her tightly. 'This is so sad,' she said, sobbing on Bea's shoulder.

Janet relayed the grim news, confirming Bea's suspicions; Edson was the young fellow Theresa was smitten with. Knowing her sensitive daughter would be devastated, she was anxious to know her whereabouts. It was starting to get dark.

Jean pointed down the road. 'She ran by here about twenty minutes ago heading that way.'

Theresa sat beside the creek hugging her knees. 'Edson, I miss you so much. I can't believe you're gone. You are the best thing that's ever happened to me.' She was on the verge of hysterics. 'We were going to be together. Oh god, I miss you so much.'

'I miss him too.'

Theresa turned. 'Deb!' she cried, hugging her tightly.

That night, dinner at the Rowan house was a solemn affair. Tammy stared at Theresa's empty chair. She felt sorry for her sister. She now knew Edson was the reason she hadn't been herself since visiting Phillips' cottage. She hoped Theresa would be back to her old self again real soon. She missed her big sister, more than she would ever admit.

Deb and Theresa sat on the edge of Deb's bed consoling each other. 'He was such a great guy,' Deb said, wiping her red eyes. 'I can't believe I have any tears left I've cried so much.'

Theresa nodded. 'I love him,' she sighed, fighting back tears. 'I had hoped we could be together when he was better.'

Deb said, 'He loved you too. While he was in hospital, he kept mumbling your name; his mother finally figured out it was you.'

Theresa turned to face her. 'Why didn't you tell me?'

'I just found out. Mrs. Wilson asked my mom to pass it on to you.'

It was little consolation, but Theresa felt a brief moment of elation knowing Edson loved her. She would always cherish the love they shared that day on Hope Island.

It was no surprise Phillips' house sold quickly. Tammy watched the movers load the huge truck with all their belongings, transporting them to a new life in British Columbia. She was still angry at Mr. Phillips for accepting the job transfer, in turn, taking Mrs. Phillips, her other mother, away forever.

Strangely, Theresa felt differently about the move. Though she would miss Deb, she was a constant reminder of Edson. The two promised to write; possibly visit one day. Tearfully, they said good-bye, promising to stay in touch.

The movers locked up the truck. Tammy clung tightly to Mrs. Phillips crying. 'I love you like a mother,' she said. 'Don't tell my mom, but even more better, sometimes.'

Mrs. Phillips broke into a tearful smile. 'And I love you like a daughter. I'm really going to miss you. I promise to write and you can write to me.'

Tearfully, Tammy waved from the curb watching the Phillips' car drive out of sight.

Chapter Fourteen

MAC MCCONNEL RETURNED home in mid-December on a welcomed three week hiatus to spend Christmas with his family before returning to the Amazon at the beginning of January; he couldn't be happier. Due to conflicting schedules with project managers and foreign engineers, the birth of his son, Ernest Adam, came and went, making this homecoming even more significant. He could hardly wait to see the latest member of the McConnel clan; he hoisted his suitcase out of the trunk, handing the cab driver some cash.

'Merry Christmas,' the Polish man said, stuffing the wad in his pocket. He drove out of sight before counting his loot. 'Fifty bucks, biggest tip ever! It's going to be a Merry Christmas after all,' he smiled. 'Deck the halls with boughs of holly…'

Mac strolled up the driveway focusing on the chaotic scene in the carport; a wide assortment of bikes missing fenders, handle bars and seats all awaiting repair, were haphazardly piled in a heap. One would be hard pressed to find at least one bike intact. He spotted his red tool box, tools strewn nearby; someone's half-hearted attempt to repair a bike he supposed. But it was the dark navy blue pram missing its back wheel, tossed carelessly inside, that tugged at the old heart strings. Each of his children had spent their infancy in this regal carriage.

Danny stood at the base of the ladder watching his father scale the roof clutching a mahogany wooden speaker to chest. He lost his footing on a small patch of ice sliding out of control, stopping just shy of the carport edge. 'I'm okay Danny, my boy.' He held up the speaker. 'I still have a hold of it,' he smiled proudly.

Endre Herczeg, a tall, muscular, handsome, dedicated family man with a full head of wavy brown hair and devilish green eyes, was always more than willing to tackle any job big or small. Confidently, he moved surefooted toward the chimney, successfully mounting the speaker. 'Danny, my boy, go get your mom.'

Eleven year old Danny was fiercely proud of his father. He too had been blessed with the Herczeg good looks, a younger version of his father with the same determination. When his dad was out of town, he quietly filled his father's shoes as man of the house.

Betty was less enthused about the speaker being mounted on the side of the chimney. In order to appease the men in her life, she yanked her old black coat out of the hall cupboard; placing it over her shoulders, struggling to pull on her well-worn black boots. With the passage of time, bending was no longer a feasible option; motherhood had planted a permanent cushion of fat where a slim waist once was. Wrestling with her boots, she vowed, once again, to lose the extra baby weight she still carried after the birth of their third child, Charlie, four years ago. With her chubby feet booted; her pock-marked face crimson with effort, she ran a hand through her short black hair making herself somewhat presentable.

She took her place beside her son watching Endre adjust the speaker.

'Rozsa, my love, what do you think?' he called down.

Betty still came all over alike whenever he used this term of endearment. *Rozsa,* Hungarian for rose was the only Hungarian word permitted in the house. Right from the start, she wanted their three children growing up in an English speaking environment; her native Italian took a backseat also. Lately, for whatever reason, Endre was much more attentive whenever he was home, which wasn't often.

The Herczeg Moving Company he started up with his brother, Etika, had grown well beyond their expectations. Fifteen years ago, they had one truck and two able bodied brothers determined to make a go of it. Their slogan: *We always put family first and guar-*

antee a safe, worry-free move, coupled with hard work and determination grew the company into a fleet of 75 trucks and 300 employees. Betty often wondered why Endre continued to drive the long hauls, taking him across the country for multiple days, while his brother, Etika, residing down the street with his wife and four kids, refused to drive anywhere; he was always home for dinner. When she questioned Endre, he claimed it was in his blood, something he just had to do.

She looked up toward his tall frame leaning casually on the chimney where the speaker was mounted. 'It looks fine,' she said indifferently, turning to go back inside.

'Danny, now that we have Mom's approval, go inside and crank up the Herczeg's annual Christmas music presentation for 1963,' he said proudly.

With Christmas two weeks away, Endre assigned his family the task of making sure Christmas music wafted throughout the neighbourhood during daylight hours and early evenings, especially on weekends.

Christmas songs filled the house. With a trembling hand, Betty filled the tarnished coffee pot. She definitely had to work on her Christmas spirit, especially for Charlie's sake; this year it was a struggle. She could hear Endre and the kids in the living room singing joyfully and contemplated joining them, reaching for the Aspirin bottle sitting on the window sill.

'Deck the halls with boughs of holly,' Endre sang, stacking Christmas albums neatly beside the stereo. ''Tis the season to be jolly. Come on everyone; let's have an old fashioned Christmas sing along. Rozsa, come,' he beckoned, encouraging the kids to sing louder.

Betty retrieved her coat from the hall cupboard, slipping quietly out the door.

Mac wheeled the repaired pram toward the front door. 'Merry Christmas!' he said, when the door opened.

A look of skepticism crossed his daughter Rebecca's face. Condescendingly, she said, 'It's not Christmas yet,' stepping aside.

Mac, surprised by her greeting, or lack of, steered the pram into the entryway. 'Correct me if I'm wrong, but aren't you the McConnel kid who can't wait for Santa's arrival, chaffing at the bit to bake cookies, decorate the house long before the official start of the season?'

Rebecca huffed, crossing her arms across her chest. 'That was before,' she said. 'Things have changed.'

Mac raised his eyebrows in surprise. 'They have?'

'Yup.'

'Why, pray tell?'

She leaned in closer. 'There is no Santa.'

Mac's face turned serious. 'Really. And just who told you that?'

Rebecca didn't want to name any of her older siblings. 'Let's just say, there's a rumour going around this establishment that there is no Santa; you and Mom bring us our presents. And furthermore, I have outside confirmation backing this theory.' She waved him down to her level, whispering in his ear, 'Some of the older kids on the street have said that Santa is just a figment of the adult imagination.'

Mac smiled, admiring her intensity. Of all the children, ten-year-old Rebecca was the most sincere and dedicated to the cause, whatever that may be. Today, it was Santa, tomorrow the children starving in Africa. Her big, almost black, brown eyes searched his for answers. She was definitely a younger version of her mother, and just as determined. 'Well, we will just have to get to the bottom of this,' he said, tucking a strand of dark brown hair behind her ear.

'When?'

He also admired her persistence. 'I will call a special Santa Claus meeting with the family very soon.'

'That's fine and dandy, but what about the neighbourhood kids out spreading the *no Santa* propaganda? That's what Derek, my classmate, calls all this rubbish.'

'Hmm. That calls for an all-encompassing meeting; we'll invite them too. And, because it's Christmas, we better ask Mom to make plenty of her best hot chocolate.'

Though Rebecca was fiercely independent and liked to solve problems on her own, she knew Mac had a better handle on these things. He was much more capable at solving dilemmas, once and for all. He seemed to have a way of making even the worst crisis solvable.

Rebecca smiled. 'Thanks, Dad. We can have some of Mom's special homemade Christmas cookies that I helped bake,' she said proudly.

Betty hadn't noticed she was still in her pink stained slippers until she was halfway up her brother-in-law's driveway. She had no idea what she'd say dropping in uninvited like this.

Allison opened the door wide, giving her the once over, focusing on her slippers. 'Hello Aunt Betty,' she said dryly.

Betty folded her coat tightly across her chest as if concealing something; feeling more like an intruder than a relative. 'Hi Honey,' she said cheerfully, hoping to hide her awkwardness. 'Is your mom around?'

Allison, Joyce and Etika's eldest daughter, was a tall, blond, blue-eyed beauty reeking of self-confidence. At sixteen, she was smart, athletic, confident, but most of all poised; attributes Betty sorely lacked, and had most of her life. 'Mom, there's someone here to see you.'

Betty stood in the carport watching Allison disappear into the living room. Located at the other end of the Crescent, the layout of their house was identical to hers and though close in proximity, they rarely visited one another.

Joyce rounded the living room corner. 'Oh for goodness sake, Al. Why didn't you ask your aunt to come inside?' she said accusingly, swinging the door open. 'Betty, please, in the future, just walk in. After all, you're family, you don't have to knock, my goodness gracious.'

Betty hung her coat on the rack by the door, following her sister-in-law into the immaculate kitchen. She sat down at the polished oak oblong table with matching press back chairs, consciously searching for similarities between the two homes. The aroma of traditional Hungarian goulash simmering on the stove filled the kitchen. Fresh herbs planted in clay pots formed a perfectly straight line across the windowsill above the sink. The black and white checked linoleum floor was spotless; the appliances shiny and clean like new, virtually free of fingerprints. She couldn't remember the last time she gave the fridge and stove a good cleaning.

'Coffee?' Joyce said, interrupting her visual tour.

'Yes, please.' She watched her sister-in-law fill the shiny metal coffee pot. Feeling rather anxious, Betty ran her hand through her hair hoping to look more presentable, only to discover it too was in need of a damn good wash; whereas Joyce's perfect updo reflected a woman with a weekly hairdresser's appointment. For a brief moment, sitting up straighter in her chair, she contemplated growing her short pixie cut out. 'So, how have you been, Joyce? I haven't seen you for ages.' For the life of her, she couldn't remember the last time they had gotten together.

Joyce's beautifully manicured hand placed a cup of steaming hot coffee in front of her, followed by a small delicately flowered China cream and sugar set. 'It was last year at Easter, as a matter of fact, when you invited us for supper; that was the last time we spoke.'

Betty poured a shot of cream into her coffee, followed by two lumps of sugar. 'Has it really been that long? Time just seems to fly by.' She had no recollection of what she had served for dinner;

assuming it was probably a Hungarian dish of some sort. She sipped her coffee. 'Is Etika here?'

'He went out with Billy to buy cigarettes. They should be back soon,' she said, reaching for the coffee pot.

At the mention of cigarettes, Betty felt an instant craving. She had quit smoking years ago, around the time the weight began piling on. She admired her sister-in-law's svelte figure, saying enviously, 'How do you manage to stay so thin?' Joyce sucked in what little tummy she had. 'I work at keeping myself in the best shape possible,' she said, in a hinting tone. 'Etika insists that I always look my best for him. Keeps him at home, where he belongs,' she smiled confidently.

Nonchalantly, Betty glanced down at her ever expanding belly. At times like this, there was no denying just how fat and out of shape she was. But Endre didn't seem to mind, she hoped.

Joyce, anxious to get on with her day, asked what brought her down to this end of the street? Her sister-in-law's impromptu visit was highly unusual, piquing her curiosity; the two had never been close.

Betty decided to get right to the point, placing her cup on the red and green festive place mat. 'Does Etika ever drive truck on any of the out of town moves?'

Joyce whipped her neatly coiffured head back, 'Are you kidding? I would kill him. He would be gone for days on end, not to mention the mischief he could get into. You know what they say *while the cat's away, the cat will play*,' she said, purposely changing the caption. 'The moving company is notorious for breaking up even the best of marriages.' She could tell by Betty's stunned look she had divulged too much information. 'But most of the men don't mess around,' she added confidently. 'My Etika stays put, managing the company as he has for years. Coffee?' she said, reaching for the pot.

Betty felt her face burn with the realization of how out of touch she had been with her husband's company. She was the boss's wife with absolutely no idea what transpired during the day when he left for work, often times for days on end. They lived by the code; the man goes to work and the wife tends the home. Feeling sheepish, she declined more coffee.

The sky, a typical mid-December dull grey, offered up the odd snowflake as Betty traipsed home slowly, focusing on the previous years, trying to calculate the number of cross country moves Endre had driven. Her head spun with the effort, coupled with the blaring Christmas music, she felt the onset of a migraine as she ascended her driveway.

Charlie greeted her at the door. 'Mommy, you got your slippers on. You are not suppose to wear your slippers outside,' he scolded. 'Come Mommy. We singin' Christmas carls. Beck the dolls with bows and dolly.'

Betty kissed his flushed chubby cheek; hanging up her coat she watched him run back into the living room. Quietly, she moved upstairs, closing the bedroom door behind her.

With a glint in her eye, Joyce watched Etika place two large packages of du Maurier king size cigarettes on the table. She was anxious to tell him about her visit with Betty, but Billy, the second oldest and spitting image of his father, stood close by.

'You seem eager about something,' Etika said, reading her like a book. He lit a cigarette, passing it to her.

'I'm fine,' she said, watching him light another.

Billy began frantically waving his arms. 'The smoke is disgusting. You two need to quit,' he said, exiting the kitchen.

Paying no heed to his outburst, Joyce leaned closer to her husband. 'You are never going to guess who paid me a visit today, in her pink stained slippers.'

Etika Herczeg was tall and muscular; a physique he acquired long ago during his moving days, and maintained daily lifting weights in his finished basement. Other than a full head of wavy brown hair, he had little resemblance to his brother, Endre. His perceptive blue eyes missed nothing. He was a happily married, devoted straight forward no bullshit guy with zero tolerance for assholes and no patience for silly games, encouraging his wife to get to the point.

Joyce's eyes widened. 'Betty, in her slippers for goodness sake.'

Etika shrugged. 'So? What is the point of all this?'

Joyce, a petite woman standing less than five feet, hazel eyes and dark brown hair, piled on her head most of the time, had the uncanny resemblance to Annette Funicello. Like her husband, she was totally devoted to their marriage and family. Knowing Etika very well after twenty years of marriage, she sensed his distress; keeping a discerning eye on his tense shoulders casually commented, 'I didn't realize Endre still drives the out of town moves.'

Etika lit another cigarette dragging heavily.

Joyce persisted. 'Is there a reason why the owner of the company should have to do this? I thought those days were long gone, for both of you.'

Etika shrugged nonchalantly knowing she saw right through him; the only person capable of such a feat. 'He likes to do them, it's in his blood.' He stared down at the table avoiding her penetrating eyes.

Joyce leaned toward him. 'My ass! There's more to this, and you know it.'

Etika stood up. 'It's his life.'

She dragged heavily on her smoke watching him exit the kitchen.

Heavy snow fell overnight, continuing next day. Mac, cradling Ernest sleeping peacefully in his arms, stared out the living room window, relishing the winter scene. The snow was beginning to mount and he couldn't be happier. The McConnel family was in for yet another surprise.

The kids watched a large, grimy white delivery truck come to a stop out front, each trying to guess its contents.

Rebecca said, 'It's probably this year's Christmas tree.'

'Doubt it,' Tommy said conclusively. 'It wouldn't take a truck like that to deliver a tree.' He noticed the forlorn look on his sister's face. 'Maybe it's two Christmas trees, Becca,' he smiled encouragingly.

Sandra, the oldest, was getting impatient; anxious to get back on the phone to chat with her best friend, Valerie. She had just turned seventeen and boys were much more interesting than a truck's cargo.

They watched their father disappear into the back of the truck, descending the metal ramp on a bright yellow machine encased in a thick cloud of blue smoke; its roaring engine loud enough to drown out Herczeg's Yule music.

'What the heck?' they all said in unison.

'By crikey, it's a Ski-doo!' Tommy flung his arms up toward the ceiling. 'Yeah Dad!'

The girls didn't share their brother's enthusiasm watching Mac drive like a maniac up and down the street, parking it in the driveway behind their 1963 dark green Chevy Impala station wagon.

'Well, what do you think?' Dad smiled mischievously.

The kids, other than Sandra, were anxious to have a ride on it; Dad had a plan. 'Round up your friends and have everybody meet here at three for a special meeting. 'Mom and Rebecca, we are going to need lots of hot chocolate and those special cookies you've been baking.'

Sandra rolled her brown eyes. 'Do I have to attend this meeting?'

He smiled pleasantly. 'Absolutely.'

At three, the neighbourhood kids filed through McConnel's backdoor and into the basement. Everyone excitedly chatted about the newly fallen snow.

Mac raised his hand asking for quiet. 'It's so nice of you all to join us here today,' he smiled. 'I have called this meeting to set a century old record straight.'

The younger kids had no idea what he was talking about but the older kids had an inclination where this was going.

Mac continued. 'I have heard, most recently, from a very reliable source, that rumors are circulating in this house and the neighborhood, regarding Santa's impending visit on Christmas Eve.' Some of older kids giggled in the background. 'Today, I'm setting the record straight. I want everyone to remember this, no Santa, no presents,' he said smugly. 'Santa *will* arrive on December 24th like he has every Christmas Eve, for over 100 years. In the meantime, the older kids can share their stories about past Christmases with the younger ones. There are some delicious homemade cookies to nibble on,' he added, biting into the Santa shaped shortbread. 'And, for anyone interested in having a ride on the McConnel's snowmobile come back at seven sharp. Please bring a toboggan if you have one.'

Shortly after seven, kids and toboggans, gathered around the Ski-doo. Mac was surprised by the numbers. There were far too many for individual rides so he tied a toboggan to the back of the Ski-doo, lining up the remaining two and securing them tightly to one another. The two smallest kids were seated on the black padded ski-doo seat in front of him; the remaining crew excitedly hopped on the toboggans.

Mac started the machine encircling them in a thick cloud of blue smoke. The noise of the engine was deafening as Mac navigated the side streets but the kids didn't mind, each holding on tightly to the person in front. He stopped at the corner, making sure everyone was accounted for before manoeuvring the machine across bare pavement toward the traffic lights at a busy intersection. He stopped, waiting for traffic in all directions to come to a standstill. Only Mac McConnel could get away with such a stunt. In awe, people watched a wild man driving a ski-doo, sparks flying, as metal scraped the bare pavement, towing three toboggans of screaming kids quickly through the intersection.

Moments later, they were speeding across the snow covered boulevard toward the entrance to Addison Park. With the full moon illuminating the way, Mac navigated the stark white fields toward a narrow bridge spanning the creek. Crossing the bridge he turned sharply, unwittingly dumping the occupants on the last toboggan over the edge.

Tommy, Theresa, Tammy and Sarah laughed hysterically landing on the soft snow, that is, until Sarah's mitten felt too soggy for just plain snow.

'The creek's not frozen!' she yelled, scurrying quickly up the bank with the others close behind.

In the bright moonlight, they watched the shallow creek swallow the last of their indentations.

'Wow! That was a little too close,' Tammy said.

They all nodded in agreement watching a noisy, single bright light move quickly toward them.

Mac hopped off the ski-doo, making sure they were all okay. The kids were happy to report it was the best part of their adventure.

Mrs. McConnel had prepared a huge batch of her delicious hot chocolate for their arrival. The kids excitedly rehashed how much fun their first ski-doo trip had been, especially being dumped into the creek. Unanimously, they agreed it was the best time ever.

Relishing the moment, Mac, smiling broadly, raised his cup of hot chocolate, 'Cheers.'

For some time now, Betty had sensed something was amiss but had chosen to ignore her gut feelings. That all changed after her impromptu visit with sister-in-law, Joyce. Again, she had confronted Endre, packing his suitcase for yet another cross country move. *Rozsa, stop meddling in my business and just take care of the kids and the house.* She became obsessed with trying to find out why

Endre continued the out of town runs, frantically searching the house for clues; coming up empty.

She loaded the washing machine and shut the lid. Walking toward the stairs, she stooped to pick up a pen with the company logo printed in gold lying in the entrance to the recreation room. Flicking on the light switch, illuminating the cold, bleak room, she scanned the finished room, rarely used by the family, and rightly so, the room was anything but inviting. There was an old chester-field, inherited many years ago, when one of Endre's customers begged him to keep it; a child's table and chairs covered in a thick layer of dust; a wooden rocking horse missing a rocker; two dust covered brown leather swivel chairs that Endre just had to have and boxes of unused toys. She focused on Endre's desk tucked away in the far corner where he spent many hours working on his paper-work; a practice he had deemed necessary to compensate for all his time away; his strict *do not disturb me under any circumstance* or-der. Up until then, their lives had been an open book.

Betty sat on the accommodating dust-free black leather swivel chair; leaning into the large solid oak desk, her heart beat erratical-ly, from untrusting guilt or what she might discover. Either way, with the kids at school and Endre on a long distance move until Christmas, it was an opportunity she couldn't afford to miss. She breathed deeply scanning the top of the desk, void of anything oth-er than a monogrammed *E* cup housing multi-coloured pens sitting on the corner of the desk pad; a few textbooks piled neatly on one side. The initial cup was as unfamiliar as the desk; she assumed an employee had given it to him as a gift.

Her hands perspired profusely, though it was as least ten de-grees cooler than upstairs. She rubbed them briskly, tugging the handle on the top drawer, locked up tightly. She tried the remaining locked drawers then sat back heavily in the chair spotting a black telephone she didn't know existed, deftly camouflaged in the shelf's shadow. With no clue as to how long it had been there she picked up the receiver, listening to the dial tone. She wondered why she had never heard it ring; tipping it over the ringer had been turned completely down. She chastised herself for not being more vigilant but the only time she ever came down to the basement was to do laundry, a room in itself, by-passing this area of basement. She remembered vividly the day Endre volunteered to maintain the room. At the time, she thought he was being kind and considerate. After all, there weren't many men anxious to come home from a hard day's work to do housework. *It's my room; the least I can do is keep it clean.*

Betty tapped her fingers on the desk contemplating where the key to open the desk might be; concluding he probably carried it with him on his key chain.

Resting her head on the back of the chair, she studied the nude portrait of herself mounted above the desk; Endre had painted it shortly after they wed. *I want to capture your beauty forever on my canvas.* At first, she had been reluctant and shy to bare all, but her shyness quickly turned into a need to be captured in this euphoric moment. She smiled reliving feelings of enlightenment, sensuality; traits she would never have believed she possessed until Endre. Slowly her eyes scanned an image portraying sensual emerald green eyes, contoured lips parted in an erotic smile; firm breasts, tiny waist and flat stomach, the black triangle at the top of her shapely legs. Her eyes misted remembering how happy they had been during this wonderful time in their marriage. Endre would paint a few strokes, steal a kiss, caress her body; culminating with amazing sex. There was a time they couldn't keep their hands off each other.

She dabbed her eyes with her sweater sleeve feeling like a traitor, betraying her husband's trust and love. *I have to stop this obsessive behaviour immediately or I'll destroy my perfectly good marriage.*

Momentarily, she stood in front of the shelving that housed some family portraits strategically arranged on the dust coated shelf. There was a photo of Endre and Etika, arms resting on the other's shoulder, grinning broadly; a picture of Endre's parents, void of any expression, staring into space; a black and white 8x10 of Grandma Herczeg, aka Cecilia, portraying a handsome, proud woman with spirited eyes and an uncanny resemblance to her grandson, Endre. So much so, one could say he was the male version of this very attractive woman. Her hair fell in great waves beyond her shoulders and her smile, unheard of in portraits of this era, reeked of self-confidence.

Betty remembered the enthusiasm on Endre's face, proudly relaying his dear departed grandmother's virtues.

Cecilia Herczeg, the youngest of five siblings, had a mind of her own from a very young age. She was not content to settle down; raise a family (expected in those days), instead she yearned to see the world. At age fifteen, she left home to work as a maid for a well-to-do family in the south of Italy, but after a brief affair with the master of the house, was forced to move on. Not one to be discouraged, she travelled throughout Europe working odd jobs before returning to Hungary, her birthplace, and working in a local pub to support herself. It was during this time she met her future husband, Viktor. After a brief courtship, the two married.

Feisty like her grandson Betty chuckled reaching for the heavy framed photo, stopping abruptly. Tipping her head to one side, the ceiling light reflected off the heavily fingerprinted glass. Further observation revealed the other framed photos seemed anchored in the thick layer of dust, except Cecilia's.

Christmas morning Charlie ran into his parents' bedroom dragging a long, red and white striped stocking behind him. 'Merry Quismus!' he said, lifting the bulging stocking. The hall light shone brightly behind him creating an angelic image. Betty squinted at the clock. It was just after six. She had had a restless night awaiting Endre's arrival and must have fallen asleep. The first clue she had he was home was him jumping out of bed to greet their youngest.

'Merry Christmas!' Endre said, scooping him up in his arms. 'Did Santa come? Let's go wake up Sharon and Danny.' He glanced toward Betty lying still on her side. 'Hurry Mommy or you'll miss all the fun.'

Betty's trembling hand poured hot coffee into the two ornamental mugs she had purchased for their first Christmas. She felt void of any festive spirit after spending Christmas Eve wrapping presents until after midnight, at which time she climbed into bed, crying herself to sleep. She had no idea what time Endre had arrived home.

Sitting on the living room floor with the kids waiting to open gifts, Endre was getting impatient. 'Rozsa, what are you doing? We want to open presents.'

She leaned into the counter trying to speak but nothing came out.

Mac sipped a cup of hot coffee watching the sun rise over the house across the road, shining brightly on newly fallen snow. *The magic of Christmas has begun* he smiled, summoning the family into the living room.

It didn't take long for a colourful mountain of discarded wrapping paper to form in the middle of the living room floor. While the kids admired each other's gifts, Rebecca sat quietly on the couch watching Tommy examine the Nikkorex Zoom 35 camera. 'This is fantastic! I've wanted this for so long. Thanks so much Mom and Dad.'

Rebecca spoke emphatically. 'Santa brought it, *not* Mom and Dad. All our gifts were delivered by Santa.'

Tommy looked toward Dad.

'You are correct, Rebecca. Santa arrived last night just like I said he would.'

Janice rolled her eyes, 'Dad…'

He raised his hand, 'I have proof Santa was here.' He glanced at his watch. 'It's 11:30. I imagine most of your friends would be free for a few minutes to see firsthand, what happened last night,' he smiled, encouraging them to make some phone calls. 'Meet me outside by the chimney.'

Excitedly, the neighbourhood kids gathered at the side of McConnel's house; Mac greeted them with candy canes. 'Merry Christmas everyone! Guess who was on my roof last night?'

One of the younger kids wrestling with the cellophane yelled, 'Santa!'

'That's right! And all his reindeer!'

'Sure,' one of the older kids said defiantly.

Mac walked over to Kevin, placing his hand on his shoulder. 'Kevin, you can be first up the ladder. But first, kick the snow off your boots. I don't want you slipping on the rungs.'

Kevin scaled the ladder like a seasoned roofer. His eyes widened at the scene that greeted him. In total awe, he climbed back down, his face red with excitement. 'You are not going to believe what I saw. There are sleigh tracks, reindeer footprints, and Santa's boot prints near the chimney.' He began helping the young ones up the ladder, encouraging everyone to climb up to experience the magic.

When all was said and done, the children headed home to spread the word that Santa had indeed arrived on McConnel's rooftop on Christmas Eve.

Once inside the house, Rebecca hung up her coat smiling contentedly, 'This is the best Christmas ever.'

Betty sat quietly on the beige cushioned chair watching the kids tear open their gifts.

Endre, a big kid himself, didn't hold back his excitement sitting beside them on the floor. 'Rozsa, why so glum on this happy day? Come down here and join the family,' he said, patting the floor beside him. 'We have so much to be thankful for.'

Awkwardly, she moved to the floor sitting down beside him.

'Merry Christmas, my love,' he said, placing his arm on her shoulder, pecking her flushed cheek.

The Rowans waited for Ken to return home from church before opening their gifts. Tammy greeted him at the door. 'You aren't going to believe what I just saw, Dad.'

He tilted his head to one side. 'Santa?'

Tammy's eyes widened. 'How did you know? I didn't really see him, but I saw where he had been last night. There were all kinds of reindeer tracks and sleigh marks on McConnel's roof; not to mention Santa's footprints around the chimney. Maybe we should get the ladder and check our roof,' she suggested. 'I was really surprised because I stopped believing there was a Santa Claus when I was eight.'

Ken kissed Bea's cheek. 'Sounds like Mac's been up to something once again. It really smells good in here, sweetie.'

Bea was busy cutting up vegetables for tonight's big feast. She had been up since five stuffing the turkey and accomplishing as much as possible before company arrived at two. 'Mac is a big kid himself,' she smiled, cutting up the last of the potatoes. 'He really likes to go all out where the kids are concerned; very admirable. He may be away most of the time, but he always makes a concerted effort to compensate when he's home.' She dried her hands, pecking his lips. 'Merry Christmas, love,' she smiled, leading him into the living room.

Theresa decided shortly after Deb moved out west not to correspond. The memories of Edson, her first love, were still too raw. She had hoped Deb would follow suit, but a parcel arrived a few days ago.

Tammy shook the small package wrapped in royal blue paper before handing it to her sister. 'Open your gift from Deb,' Tammy encouraged, shaking a neatly wrapped gift from Mrs. Phillips. 'I bet this is some sort of clothing,' she said disappointedly, tearing the wrapping off. 'Just as I thought.' She held up a red knit sweater with a big white heart on the front and read the note tucked inside. *'To dear, sweet Tammy.* That's me,' she smiled. *'This sweater is made with love from your other mother. I really miss your smiling face. Love Mrs. Phillips xo.* Well, at least she misses me' she said, stuffing it back in the box. She watched Theresa gingerly unwrap her gift. 'A ring! I wish I had gotten that instead of a silly sweater I'll never wear.'

Theresa sat quietly reading the enclosed note. *Dear Theresa, I hope you like this ring. It's very special; there are two small hearts carved into the silver band. When I saw it, I thought of you and Edson, two hearts joined together forever. I hope you like it. If you get a moment, please write. I miss you. Love Deb.*

'What does the note say?' Tammy said.

'Merry Christmas, love Deb,' Theresa said, folding it neatly.

The ring fit perfectly on her middle finger. Initially, she had thought the gift would be too upsetting, but was encouraged by Deb's thoughtfulness. *I shall write her and thank her very much.*

'Do you like it?' Tammy said, hoping she didn't and the ring would come her way.

Theresa's smile widened. 'Absolutely love it.'

Betty felt her shoulders tense when she heard the heavy knock on the front door.

'Merry Christmas,' Etika said, stepping inside with Joyce and the kids following close behind.

Joyce waited while the kids handed her their coats; running excitedly into the living room to join their cousins around the Christmas tree.

Endre moved quickly down the stairs. 'Merry Christmas!' he smiled, moving toward his sister-in-law hugging her tightly. 'Merry Christmas, Joyce. You seem to get more beautiful with each passing day.'

Her face turned crimson breaking into a warm smile; holding her head that much higher she adjusted her snow white mohair sweater. 'Oh Endre, you do say the sweetest things,' she gushed. 'Where's Betty?'

He raised his hands, 'in the kitchen, of course, a woman's place, right Etika?' he said, slapping him on the back, hugging him tightly. 'Merry Christmas to the best brother in the world.'

Etika reluctantly returned the gesture then followed Joyce into the kitchen.

Betty stood at the stove basting the turkey, perspiring profusely. A blast of hot air greeted her opening the oven door as she placed it on the bottom rack... 'Merry Christmas to both of you,' she smiled, shutting the door. 'The turkey is cooking nicely,' she said, placing the oven mitts on the counter.

'Merry Christmas, Betty,' Etika said, hugging her warmly.

Joyce hugged her briefly, 'Merry Christmas.'

The sympathetic look in her sister-in-law's heavily made-up eyes turned her attention back to the stove. 'So, how was your morning? Did the kids get everything they wanted?' Betty said jovially, moving pots of vegetables onto the burners.

Joyce, her arm around her husband's waist, could barely contain her excitement. 'Etika spoils us, especially me,' she gushed, shoving her diamond clad skinny wrist under her nose.

Betty's eyes widened. 'Wow. That's the most beautiful diamond bracelet I have ever seen. You are a very lucky gal.'

Joyce smiled demurely, 'I'm sure Endre spoiled you too.'

Betty thought of the fifty dollars he had given a few weeks ago. *I've got a couple of big moving jobs and won't have time to shop. Get yourself something special for Christmas and wrap it.* She had used the money to buy extra gifts for the children. 'Of course,' she said, turning back to the stove. 'Can I get you anything? Coffee, tea?'

Endre greeted his nephew and nieces warmly; moving casually toward the makeshift bar at the end of the counter he said, 'Joyce doesn't want a coffee for crying out loud. She wants a gin martini, with two sweet onions. After all, it's Christmas.'

Joyce was flattered he remembered. 'But only one, Endre. The last time I had two, I couldn't eat my supper, remember Etika? Speaking of which, dinner smells delicious.'

Endre expertly mixed the martini. 'That's my Betty, best cook any man could ask for. When she cooks, that is,' he winked, handing Joyce the chilled martini glass.

Betty felt her neck tensing. Excusing herself she walked toward the bathroom, locking the door behind her. Leaning into the sink for support, she studied her flushed reflection in the mirror. Flecks of grey throughout her short black hair seemed to have popped up overnight. She tucked the sides behind her ears hoping the grey strands would be less noticeable. She searched her tattered make-up bag for the only tube of lipstick she owned. Shakily, she ran the bright red crayon back and forth across her thin lips. Reaching for some green eye shadow she heard Endre paging her at the bottom of the stairs. She ran a hand through her hair scurrying out the bathroom.

After what seemed like a very long day, the kids were finally in bed and the house was quiet. Betty sat on the chesterfield, feet resting on the coffee table; Endre's head in her lap. Another Herczeg Christmas had come and gone. Everyone raved about the delicious turkey dinner. At first, she had felt guilty breaking protocol shying away, much to Endre's chagrin, from the traditional Hungarian dishes she usually prepared. It was much easier to cook a turkey, with all the fixings, than spending the days leading up to and including Christmas, cooking over a hot stove.

She stared at Endre sleeping peacefully in her lap. Time had been kind to him, or good genes; there seemed to be no sign of aging. If anything, he was even more handsome and charismatic. His body was still muscular and toned compared to the cushy stomach he slept on.

Gently, she stroked his forehead, unable to hold back tears sliding silently down her cheeks.

Chapter Fifteen

FOR THE SECOND year, Maxine Carlson spent Christmas Day moping around her apartment imagining what it would be like to spend her favourite festive day of the year with the man of her dreams, vowing next Christmas would be different.

Betty's mother and father picked the children up early on Boxing Day extending their Christmas celebrations; the children were elated at the prospect of spending time with their grandparents; more gifts and goodies were sure to come their way.

'I want you to be good for Grandma and Grandpa,' Endre said, doing up Charlie's winter coat. 'I will be home in a few days.'

He saw them all off with a kiss, shutting the door behind them. 'Rozsa, why so glum? You should have joined them.'

It was the first time she felt nothing hearing his endearment. 'I don't understand why you have to work on Boxing Day...'

Endre raised a hand in protest. 'I told you before, this move is exceptional. I have personally promised my clients to deliver their cherished belongings in time for New Year's Eve. I volunteered for the job so my staff could enjoy the holidays with their families.'

Though she found the gesture noble, she wondered who would be working with him, reiterating Etika no longer drives truck anymore.

'For the last time, Etika is the businessman, I am the muscle man. Now I must go,' he said haughtily. 'I will see you in a week's time, if everything goes as scheduled.' He pecked her cheek, slamming the door behind him.

She stared at the back of the wooden door, chipped paint and all, trying to remember the last time they made love. There was a time he would make love to her before any moving jobs, especially the longer hauls taking him away for days on end.

Boxing Day, Maxine rose early and spent the better part of the morning sweating over a hot stove cooking Bajai fish soup, stuffed cabbage, and bejgli for dessert. The cooking had taken much longer than expected, moving hurriedly to the tiny bathroom for a much needed shower.

Stepping out of the shower, she wrapped a hot pink luxurious housecoat around her. Reaching for the gold comb on top of her head, she released her thick, blond tresses, settling strategically across her chest. She coloured her lips bright red, smiling wickedly hearing the key in the door.

'Merry Christmas, *Kis szepseg*. I have come bearing gifts.'

Maxine ran toward Endre's open arms, almost tripping over the gifts at his feet.

'My *Kis szepseg*. How I have missed you,' he gushed, hugging her tightly, helping himself to the belt on her housecoat. 'Such obstacles,' he said impatiently, slipping it off her shoulders. 'Ah my *Kis szepseg*. You are even more beautiful than the last time we met.'

Maxine giggled. 'We were together on Christmas Eve.'

'Ah, but it seems so long ago,' he said, reaching for her large firm breasts. 'I have missed you so,' he said, burying his face in her chest. 'I need you so badly,' he whispered, lifting her effortlessly, moving toward the bedroom.

Maxine pulled away from Endre's loving embrace. 'My soup!' she cried, throwing back the pink satin sheet.

Endre chuckled tucking his hands behind his head, focusing lustfully on her perfect bare ass running out of the room. 'It smells delicious. You are finding the way to a Hungarian man's heart, *Kis szepseg*.' He felt himself harden watching her saunter slowly toward the bed.

She pulled the sheet up, settling in beside him. 'What does it mean?'

'What does what mean, my *Kis szepseg?*'

'That,' she said, trying to pronounce it his way.

'That is Hungarian for *little beauty.*'

'I see,' she said disappointedly.

He rolled toward her gazing into her sky blue eyes. 'What's this? Such a sad look on such a beautiful face.' He reached under the sheet, tweaking her nipples.

For a brief moment she wanted to shove his needy hands away. 'I thought maybe it meant, my love, my sweetheart,' she pouted.

'That too!' he said, rolling on top, spreading her legs wide.

If it hadn't been for the thick layer of dust, dotted with oily fingerprints, Betty would never have stumbled across the key to Endre's desk. She had made the discovery a few days before Christmas, but the arrival of the kids after school sent her heart racing with guilt, and had her moving quickly up the stairs. Today, with the children away and Endre on assignment, she was finally able to investigate undisturbed.

Her hand trembled slightly reaching for Cecilia's picture. Gingerly, she flipped it, removing the back; a small key twanged onto the desk. Judging by its size, she determined it wouldn't open a desk drawer, but the larger key tucked in the bottom right corner might. She returned the smaller key, securing the thick black cardboard backing, placing it back on the shelf.

Sitting down heavily on the chair, she sensed Cecilia's intense dark eyes staring back at her. Feeling her spine tingle, she turned the picture around, pulling her thick sweater tighter, warding off the sudden chill.

She inserted the key; hearing it click she pulled open the top drawer. She tried the remaining drawers, opening with ease. The top drawer housed a stapler, pencils, pens, envelopes and some writing pads. The remaining drawers contained files, phone books and manuals pertaining to the company. She was relieved to find the desk full of company stuff; respecting Endre's need to work undisturbed.

Content nothing was amiss; she attempted to lock it, but the bottom right drawer was slightly ajar. She tried to close it sitting in the chair before getting down on her knees and pushing it with two hands. When it still wouldn't shut, she yanked the drawer, noticeably shorter than the others, out. Peering inside the darkened space her eyes widened.

Carefully she manoeuvred a wooden box out of the space. The dark brown pine box was locked up tightly. Gently she shook it, focusing on its contents. Studying the tiny lock she reached for Cecilia's picture, retrieving the small key. Her hand trembled so much; she had difficulty inserting it into the lock. Her heartbeat echoed in her head; she clicked it open. Her whole body was aflame; engulfed in her own fire she anxiously tugged at the sleeves of her sweater, chucking it to the floor. With her hands resting on either side of the box, she gulped cool air to calm her nerves, trying to convince herself the box contained a few mementos; her gut protested otherwise.

Staring at the contents, she thought it was Endre's bible. A wave of relief washed over her; short-lived when she discovered a thick leather *1962* diary zipped up tightly. She had absolutely no clue of her husband's inclination to pen his inner thoughts, anxiously unzipping it.

Monday, January 8: A beautiful angel from heaven, Maxine Carlson, sauntered into Herczeg looking for a job. I felt my heart race when she seated herself on the worn cracked black vinyl chair, wishing I had replaced the damn old relic. She removed her pure white coat, revealing broad shoulders encased in a soft, red mohair sweater accentuating her large, firm ample breasts and tiny waist. Slowly, she crossed her long shapely legs, offering a glimpse of hot pink panties. Her sparkling blue eyes creased charmingly when she smiled; tiny dimples appeared on her soft cheeks. Her teeth were straight and whiter than new fallen snow. She spoke softly, articulating each word, stating why she wanted to work for my company. I've always wanted my own private secretary. I hired her on the spot.

Tuesday, January 9: I couldn't wait to get to work knowing Maxine would be sitting at the desk I had installed directly outside my office. She smiled demurely when I greeted her; my heart raced with joy. I was about to offer her a coffee when Etika pulled me into the office, closing the door behind him. 'What the hell do you think you are doing?' His face reddened, his eyes were that of a deranged, rabid animal. I quietly explained how I needed a secretary to take care of my paperwork so I could spend more time with my family. Maxine had the qualifications. (What she lacked in brains, the curvy twenty-one year old aced in body). Needless to say, I ignored his unwarranted protests, ordering him the hell out of my office. It hurt me to talk this way to my brother, but I'm the boss around here.

Betty focused on yesterday's Christmas celebrations. The relationship between the two brothers did seem strained at times.

Thursday, April 19: It's been a while since I've written. So much has happened and I want to remember this for the rest of my life. Tomorrow is Good Friday. I sent everyone home early today to begin their celebrations. Maxine, bless her heart, volunteered to stay to answer the phones while I did some paperwork. Earlier, she wrapped a black E mug filled with chocolate Easter eggs and left it on my desk. She thinks of everything, almost.

She had been flirting with me for several weeks, but this is the first time we were all alone. I'm anxious to see if Maxine will back up her flirting. I need her to change my boring life more than a mug of chocolates.

Betty eyed the E mug, trying to recall this period of time. Endre wasn't his usual loving self. He seemed tense, critical, more on edge. At the time, she had no idea why. It was like he didn't want to be home, making it well known, constantly complaining about everything she did. Sex, though frequent, was urgent. She'd come away feeling unfulfilled, used and unloved. They hadn't been intimate since.

Maxine didn't disappoint. She blew my fucking mind! She sauntered into my office; the heat from her luscious body filled the office. She walked toward my desk with a manila folder. Placing it on the desk, she opened it, leaning forward. Hungrily, I witnessed her firm ample breasts unite in her V-neck sweater; my mind blurred, her soft voice broke the spell. I inhaled her intoxicating fragrance as she pointed a long, slender, manicured red lacquered fingernail at a discrepancy on an invoice. Her big tits retreated when she straightened up. Seductively she placed her slender hands on her curvy hips, accusing me of not paying attention. I felt no shame confessing to this beautiful goddess I was much more in-terested in the deep cut of her sweater, or rather, what was under it. She smiled tantalizingly reaching for the ribbed edge; gyrating slowly, seductively, stripping off the sweater, tossing it over her shoulder. The meat between my legs throbbed watching her lei-surely unhook her red lace bra releasing the most beautiful big tits I'd ever seen. She played with her silver dollar beige nipples mov-ing slowly toward me. 'Suck 'em' she commanded thwarting the hardened nipples in my face.

Betty felt the bile rise, cupping her hands over her face breath-ing deeply. The penmanship was Endre's, but the man writing such filth was not the man she had married twenty-three years ago. She shut the diary, picked up her sweater and trudged up the basement stairs; warming this morning's coffee, briefly thinking about something to eat, but food was the last thing she wanted. Waiting for the coffee to heat, she sat down at the kitchen table skimming the diary; stopping at the mention of her name.

Thursday, May 9: Betty arrived at the office, unannounced, even though I had given her explicit instructions not to just drop in at her leisure. Once again, I reminded her, I'm a very busy man.

Betty felt her face burn recalling the humiliation she had felt. It explained his very harsh reaction to her impromptu visit; the condescending tone of the young woman sitting outside his office.

She was about to introduce herself when Endre grabbed her arm, ushering her quickly into his office, slamming the door behind him. She was flabbergasted by the look on his face, interrogating her like she was some kind of criminal. *What is the purpose of your visit? How many times have I told you never to just drop in when you feel like it?* Though he had spoken harshly, Betty explained she wanted to surprise him and take him out to lunch. *Joyce surprises Etika with invitations to lunch; I thought I'd do the same.* But he had made it very clear he wanted no part of her scheme, escorting her out of his office as quickly as he had dragged her in.

Scheme Betty sighed, reaching for the coffee. She sipped it recalling the smug look on the young woman's face after her mêlée with Endre.

Maxine sat at her desk sizing Betty up, watching her leave with her tail between her legs. *He's all mine now fat, ugly cow.* She watched his wife exit through the glass doors. Confidently, she pasted on her best smile, sauntering into Endre's office.

Betty was barely out the front door when Maxine came into my office, smiling like the cat that swallowed the canary. She asked me why Betty came to visit. I told her I had absolutely no idea. That should have been the end of it but foolishly Maxine made the mistake of questioning me further. I immediately stopped the discussion; my home life is none of her business and she's to keep it that way.

Betty continued skimming the diary documenting his sexual encounters with a secretary she had no idea he had hired; finding some consolation, in that, it was just sex. She had read about married men going through mid-life crisis, often reaching out to other women to satisfy some inner macho need. Invariably, they would settle back down again. Under no circumstance was she content with Endre's escapade, but there was still a chance he'd come to his senses.

Tuesday, June 19: I handed Maxine the keys to an apartment, pocketing one for myself, allowing me to come and go as I please. She loved the new leather furniture I had purchased, especially the bedroom suite. I decided after six months of paying for hotels, an apartment would be cheaper and much more accessible; nooners are now the norm. I also insisted she give up her job; (Etika was ecstatic), rumours were making the rounds at my company. At first she balked, but as usual saw things my way. I told her she didn't have to work, I would pay the bills. I want her available anytime day or night.

This last excerpt changed everything. Betty covered her face with her hands weeping loudly in the empty house, Endre's house. Her husband was living a double life with a woman half his age and there wasn't a damn thing she could do about it.

Her head pounded and her back ached from sitting all day. With great effort, she climbed the stairs falling fully clothed onto the bed and just when she thought there couldn't possibly be any tears left, cried herself to sleep.

Maxine and Endre lay in bed quietly caressing each other with feathery strokes. 'Your cooking smells delicious, *Kis szepseg.*'

She sighed, 'I hope it's not overcooked. We really should think about eating,' she said, watching him suck her breast. 'Seriously Endre, I've worked so hard preparing your favourite dishes. I really don't want them to go to waste. And, I want to see what's in all those beautifully wrapped gifts my Santa delivered. I have a special gift for you too, Santa,' she smiled radiantly.

'You are my special gift,' he said. 'You bring me such joy,' he smiled warmly, kissing her lips gently.

She was taken aback by his words. It was the first time he had spoken so lovingly to her. 'I love you, Endre.'

'Let's eat. I'm famished,' he said, throwing back the sheet, running his hands through his hair.

The meal was delicious. Endre was very proud of her cooking expertise. 'You have captured the Hungarian secret to a man's heart, his stomach,' he smiled, reaching for the bottle of palinka and pouring them each a glass. He held his glass high, 'To *Kis szepeg*, my wonderful Hungarian cook.'

Maxine, hiding her disappointment, had hoped for a more endearing toast. For the past two years, she spent most of her time imagining what it would be like to live with him permanently. Though there was a twenty year age gap, Endre was very handsome, fit, hard-working and a dedicated family man; a virtue she admired most. There was no doubt Endre was perfect husband material; her destiny. 'I love you my handsome Hungarian,' she said, raising her glass.

He smiled contentedly. 'Present time,' he said, distributing all the brightly wrapped packages.

Endre spoiled Maxine with gifts of perfume, lingerie, sweaters, three low cut dresses, a leather coat and thigh high black leather boots. When she finished opening all her gifts, he reached behind his back, handing her a small box wrapped in silver paper.

Half smiling, she determined the box was too big to be the diamond ring she longed for. Quickly removing the wrapping, she lifted the lid of the royal blue velvet jewel box, gasping loudly. 'Oh

Endre, it's beautiful,' she said, staring wide-eyed at the diamond solitaire necklace. 'I bet it cost a pretty penny,' she said, thrusting the necklace toward him.

'It's an 18K solitaire on an 18K gold chain. Nothing but the best for my girl,' he said, fastening it around her neck. 'It looks beautiful on you, *Kis szepseg*,' he said confidently.

She gently moved her finger across the diamond pendant feeling the love and thoughtfulness. *He truly loves me.* 'I have one more gift for my wonderful man,' she said, reaching under the chesterfield for a small neatly wrapped package.

'My Kis szepeg, you have spoiled me enough with all these wonderful gifts,' he smiled warmly, gesturing toward the open packages. He sighed contentedly, 'You are by far, my most precious gift.' A self-satisfied, content feeling engulfed him removing the wrapping.

Endre felt the colour draining from his face extracting a tiny pair of white leather shoes. 'Is this some kind of a joke?' he half-smiled, turning toward her.

Maxine smiled warmly, 'Merry Christmas, Daddy.'

Endre's black Cadillac turned white overnight. He had been sitting in it long enough to sense daybreak, but too numb to care about his Caddy's new facade. Feeling chilled to the bone, he zipped his coat moving quickly in an effort to preserve his new Italian loafers through deep snow to the side entrance, cursing himself for not grabbing his boots in his haste to get the hell out of the apartment.

Once inside the warm building, he tore off his coat, flinging it toward his intended target, missing it by a long shot. He sat down heavily at his desk. He was thankful for the quiet of an extended holiday for his employees; he had planned on spending it in bed with Maxine. He ran his hands through his damp hair. Their arrangement had been perfect, until she ruined it. The last thing he needed was another fucking kid. He questioned her about the paternity of the child.

You bastard. How can you even ask me if it's your child. Of course it's your baby. I have been true to you since the first day you hired me.

She cried hysterically when he insisted she abort it; all expenses paid.

I will never have an abortion. I want our baby, Endre.

The house was quiet when Betty woke up at dawn. Surprisingly, she had slept through the night. In need of a nice hot shower, she stripped off her dirty clothes.

Feeling refreshed, she donned her good black slacks and ivory gold flecked cashmere sweater. Searching her wooden jewel box for the gold locket Endre had given her their first Christmas, she opened the heart shaped pendant eyeing the smiling portraits of her and Endre, squeezing it shut to block out the memories. *There will be no more tears. Tears are self pity. Today is the beginning of my life.* She dropped the pendant into the jewel box slamming it shut.

The kids arrived home shortly after lunch. Betty had never been happier to see them. They were loud and off the wall from an overdose of sweets at Grandma's but she enjoyed every second of their excitement. So much so, when they decided to go outside to play in the snow, she donned her coat and boots and joined them.

Together they worked as a team building a huge snowman in the middle of the front lawn. Charlie wanted a Daddy snowman, whereas, Sharon insisted it's a Mommy. They turned in unison toward Danny for the tie breaker.

'Definitely a Dad snowman,' he said authoritatively.

Betty handed the kids a long, lumpy carrot, two large black buttons and a collection of smaller buttons for the mouth. From her pocket, she pulled an unworn black silk scarf she had given Endre last Christmas; he abhorred the damn thing insisting scarves were for sissies, tying it tightly around the neck, short of decapitating the huge white specimen. 'Yup, looks just like your father,' she smiled, admiring the masterpiece.

Betty and the children tackled the driveway even though Endre insisted he wouldn't be back any sooner than New Year's Day. It didn't take long for the complaints about how heavy the snow was and how tired they were. Sensing they'd had enough, she sent them inside to watch television.

It felt good to be outside in the fresh air, boosting her self-esteem, something she hadn't felt for months. She flung the last bit of snow at the snowman, hitting it on the side of the head. *There is going to be major*...She moved quickly inside, locking the door.

Tammy, looking for a distraction from snow shovelling, leaned on her shovel. 'Hello Mr. H!' she yelled. 'I really miss your Christmas music.'

Endre walked hurriedly toward the door.

'On second thought, I'm glad it's over for another year,' she yelled, tossing a shovelful of snow over her shoulder.

Betty leaned against the kitchen counter trying to calm her racing heart, listening to Endre hastily greet the kids, ordering them to stay put.

'Hello Betty.'

She was so nervous she felt dizzy, turning to face him. 'Well this is a surprise. I wasn't expecting you...'

'I need to speak to you immediately,' he said, ushering her upstairs, shutting the door behind him. He sat down on the edge of the bed. 'We need to talk.'

She leaned against the dresser for support watching him run his hands through his hair then his unshaven face. He was grubby and dishevelled, like he hadn't slept all night, sitting hunched over staring at his clasped hands. 'I don't know where to begin.'

Betty's palms began to perspire, wiping them slowly on her slacks. 'Why not start at the beginning.' Her voice was much calm-er than she expected.

He stood quickly, facing her. 'I've been having an affair.'

Like a sharp slap to the face it stung at first; an infidelity confession spewed across their maternal bed by the man she thought she knew. Surprisingly, she felt a sense of calm after spending yesterday scanning his diary.

He stared in disbelief. 'Betty, I have just confessed…'

She raised her hand, 'I know all about your other life with the bimbo you hired.'

For a brief moment, he wondered how she might know. He was totally taken aback by her lack of hysterics, unlike Maxine who completely lost it. 'There's more. She's pregnant. I don't know what to do,' he said, stuffing his trembling hands into his pockets.

Betty felt her insides cave, finding it difficult to speak. 'Your baby.' The struggle to say these two words was lost on him.

'She says its mine.' His tone was sarcastic and doubtful.

Betty stared at him in disbelief trying to find her voice. 'You and your ex-secretary are having a baby and you don't know if it was your seed that impregnated her?' Under different circumstances, she would have burst out laughing at his feeble attempt at being naive. She crossed her arms across her chest. 'Let me get this straight. You were fucking, and probably still are, this bimbo, and you didn't bother to think about the possible consequences of your illicit behaviour.' Placing her index finger on her chin, their eyes met, 'Until now, I would never have described you as a stupid man, Endre.'

He was shocked by her foul language, more so by her insinuation he was stupid. He had always prided himself in being a very smart man. In all their years of marriage, she had never spoken to him like this. 'She told me she was on the pill, I just assumed…' he stopped mid-sentence. 'I don't know what to do,' he shrugged.

Betty felt no sympathy for the pathetic man she once called husband. The situation was much more complex than a midlife fling; Endre and his mistress conceived a child, his child, changing all of their lives forever.

She opened her drawer, reaching for her old red Christmas sweater and turned to face the pathetic man on the other side of the bed. 'I will make it easier for you to decide what to do. I want a divorce.'

His faced turned ashen. 'But…'

With trembling hands she tore away the sweater, pitching his diary across the room, striking her intended target in the side of the head.

'You'll need that to write the next chapter.'

Chapter Sixteen

KEN DREW BACK the beige and turquoise patterned, floor to ceiling drapes, curiously watching a woman in a black coat walk quickly out of sight. He turned to Bea, 'I'd swear that was Betty hightailing it down the road.'

Bea looked up from her novel. 'Probably; she's been out walking every day. I haven't seen Endre's caddy parked in the driveway since we rang in the new year. Something isn't...' the loud voice emanating from the kitchen stopped her mid-sentence.

'He's flown the coop!' Tammy yelled, hoisting her bowl, slurping back the milk. She closed the box of Sugar Crisp; running into the living room she sat down hard on the couch beside her mom. 'Mr. H is shacked up with some bimbo half his age.'

Ken furrowed his brow. 'Tam, that's no way to talk.'

She squished her face. 'Why? It's true. Mrs. H kicked him out.'

Bea placed the open novel on the table. 'How do you know all this?'

Tammy flashed a big smile. 'Kid's talk, especially Sharon. She's really upset her mom gave him the boot. Can I go over to Alice's house?'

Bea sighed heavily. 'Yes, be home for lunch.'

Ken stood at the window watching her run down the driveway. 'Do you believe what she just said?'

Bea smacked her lips. 'I don't know what to believe, nor do I care,' she said, reaching for her novel.

Endre stared at the brown watermarked ceiling above the bed, trying to block out Maxine's dry heaves in the bathroom. Since moving in six weeks ago, his life had been anything but blissful. The great sex they once shared was now a quick hand job if she wasn't too nauseated or too tired. Maxine, three and half months pregnant, griped constantly about how lousy she felt; cursing the pregnancy wreaking havoc on her once beautiful svelte figure. She made it very clear her massive tender breasts were off limits also.

He reflected on how much his life had changed since the beginning of 1964. His once friendly employees were barely cordial and his dear brother, Etika, went out of his way to avoid him at all cost. All they shared now was the business, briefly as needed. But the hardest part was his kids not wanting anything to do with him or his now ex-wife, Betty. After she kicked him out, she didn't care where he ended up. She demanded he pay all family living expenses, but most of all to stay the hell away.

Maxine looked as if she had been hit by a Mack truck, climbing into bed beside him. There were dark circles under her eyes and her once smooth long blond hair was a disheveled mass of tangled rats' tails. He rolled over onto his side, gently caressing her luscious tits hoping to get laid.

'Stop it Endre. My breasts are so sore,' she whined, turning away. 'All you ever think about is yourself.'

He threw back the covers.

'What are you doing?' she said, sitting up in bed, watching him dress.

He pulled a sweater over his head. 'I need to get out of here.'

'You don't understand what being pregnant is like,' she whined. 'I feel like crap all of the time carrying your kid.'

His eyes bore into her. 'You chose to have it. I wanted you to have a fucking abortion.'

She cried hysterically as the door slammed shut.

Betty undid the buttons of her black coat, walking swiftly toward the empty schoolyard track. For the first time in years, she was twenty pounds lighter and felt better both inside and out. She had been carrying too much weight, physically and mentally, for far too long. She thoroughly enjoyed her new life without Endre. She applied for a receptionist job at a local doctor's office and was anxious to begin her new career tomorrow. She draped her coat on the back of the bench; jogging around the track feeling exhilarated and free.

Endre drove by the house four times, parking within sight of it. He leaned back in the seat, hoping to get a glimpse of his children. Even Danny, his most staunch supporter, wouldn't take his calls.

Betty walked quickly toward home, spotting Endre's black Caddy parked on the street in front of the Jackson's house. He sat up with a start when she knocked firmly on the window. 'You're not stalking us by any chance?' she said curtly as he rolled down the window.

He noticed her cheeks were flushed; her short black hair was glossy in the sunlight. Her skin was clear and smooth, smoother than he remembered. 'You look wonderful, Rozsa,' he said sincerely.

She ignored him. 'I suggest you get your ass out of here, otherwise I'll proceed with a restraining order.'

He swallowed hard, fighting back tears, watching her slimmer figure move quickly up the driveway.

Betty dropped her coat on the floor by the door, running upstairs to the bedroom. *Damn you Endre.*

Theresa sat down on the floor in front of the television to watch *The Ed Sullivan Show,* a family favourite, airing Sunday nights at eight. Her best friend, Janet, had called a few minutes earlier reminding her not to miss tonight's special episode. A new group, *The Beatles*, from Liverpool, England would be performing. She had no idea what to expect until Ed Sullivan introduced the group. The audience went berserk, screaming loudly as four young, good looking, long haired lads wearing dark suits, white shirts and black ties started singing. The screaming continued on and off while they performed three amazing songs.

'That was fantastic!' Theresa said, anticipating their final performance near the end of the show.

The other acts were mediocre in comparison until finally Ed introduced the Beatles once again, sending the audience into even more of a frenzy.

Theresa was over the top with excitement and could hardly wait to call Janet. 'The Beatles are absolutely the best!'

Bea looked up from her novel. 'It sounded like a bloody load of crap to me.'

'Oh Mom, they're from over 'ome,' she smiled, mimicking a British accent.

'I don't care where they're from. A bloody lot of racket is all I heard.'

Theresa's heart pounded waiting for Janet to answer the phone. 'Oh my god! Do you believe it! The Beatles are amazing!' The two chatted animatedly until Bea had heard enough. 'I have to go now. Be at school by 8:30.'

Groggily, Anne Smythe turned over with no concept of time or day.

Glenn stood at her bedroom door. 'Mom, it's time to get up now.' He was fed up being her alarm clock, not to mention fill-in parent and cook. 'Jimmy and Sherry left for school earlier. I have to get going or I'll be late again.' His stomach flinched, watching her place two tablets on her white coated tongue.

'Just give me a minute,' she pleaded, rubbing her face vigorously.

'I can't, Mom, I'm late now. Rose and Katherine are in their room.'

She waved a backhand. 'Go, I'm getting up.' She listened for the door to close, laying back down waiting for the pills to do their magic.

School was buzzing with Beatlemania, the newest craze, especially popular with the older kids. It seemed everyone tuned in to the Ed Sullivan Show last night. Even the principal was on board, mentioning the fab four during morning announcements, with an added assertion, it was time to buckle down and pay attention to today's lessons.

When the recess bell sounded, no one needed coaxing out of the building. Theresa met Janet, Marcie, Linda, Barbara, Julie and Cathy at the side door. The girls chatted animatedly about John, Ringo, George and Paul. In the end, it was unanimous; Paul McCartney was the cutest Beatle.

'I am going to buy all their records!' Linda said excitedly. 'My parents already said they would give me the money.'

The others agreed that they too would get their parents to buy the records as soon as they were in the stores.

Theresa wondered if her dad would surprise her with a Beatle record as he had with *Theme from a Summer Place.* If not, she had some savings to purchase one.

'What about you, Theresa?' Marcie queried sarcastically.

Marcie Armstrong didn't want for anything; an only child, she asked and she received. Born in Ottawa, she was an accomplished pianist and honor student, spending her previous school years attending the best private schools the Capital had to offer until her father's recent transfer to Scarborough. It was no surprise she felt superior to the rest of the group and everyone knew it, especially Theresa. Shortly after they were introduced, Marcie, in subtle ways, made it very clear she wanted nothing to do with her and seemed determined to undermine her friendship with Janet.

Marcie stood beside Janet announcing she was having an amazing Beatlemania party at the end of the month and everyone was welcome 'but you must bring a Beatle record to attend.' Confident Theresa wouldn't be attending she didn't acknowledge her.

Katherine sat on her bed calling for her mother before setting out to find her. 'Mommy sleeping,' she whispered. She reached out to touch her mother's peaceful face eyeing the pill bottle sitting on the bedside table. Grabbing the bottle, she ran merrily down the hall. When she decided Mommy didn't want to chase her, she sat behind the swivel chair, shaking it vigorously.

Anne woke with a start. She rubbed her blurry eyes until the ceiling above came into focus, listening for the kids. Her mouth was parched; her tongue felt thick and awkward. She reached sideways for her water glass and the pill bottle beside it. Bolting upright, she was positive it had been there earlier on.

Getting on her hands and achy knees she searched the floor and under the bed, discovering some used tissues imbedded in the thick layer of dust. After a futile search, she attempted to stand but her right knee caught the hem of her cotton nightgown. She cursed pulling the excess fabric out from under her fat knee; perspiration formed above her lip, sitting down on the edge of the bed in desperate need of her pills. Positive her meds were beside the glass earlier on, she pulled her long black mop back, securing it with an elastic band. Reaching for her housecoat, she checked the pockets for the pills moving quickly toward the bathroom with the sudden urge to pee. From her vantage point, the girls' bedroom door was shut. She washed her face patting it dry with the dirty green towel hanging beside the sink.

Quietly, she opened the bedroom door. Rose slept soundly in the corner of her crib; Katherine's bed was full of toys. She quietly shut the door calling for her young daughter, walking toward the kitchen. She waited for a response; other than the hum of the refrigerator, the house was quiet. 'Katherine! Where are you?' She waited for a reply. 'Stop playing your silly hiding games or Mommy will have to spank you.'

Bea walked into the clean living room with a cup of tea, cigarettes and her book. After seeing the kids off to school, she worked feverishly doing laundry and cleaning the house, rewarding herself with a hot cup of tea to enjoy finishing off the last chapter of her book. The pounding on the backdoor and accompanying horrendous screams sent streams of hot tea cascading down her hand. 'Jesus Christ!' she cursed, setting the cup down, wiping her hand on a tissue. Her heartbeat quickened as the piercing screams grew more urgent, moving quickly toward the side door. 'What the hell is going on,' she said, reaching for the doorknob.

The police and ambulance arrived shortly after Bea placed the distressed call. She held Rose tightly to her chest unable to hold back tears watching the ambulance attendants try desperately to persuade Anne, firm in the belief Katherine was just sleeping, to relinquish the child's lifeless body.

Glenn rounded the corner, spotting the police car and ambulance parked in front of the house. His head filled with anxious thoughts running full tilt toward home. His head pounded swinging the door open, focusing on the attendants crouched down on the floor behind the brown swivel chair. Crying out in angst he collapsed to the floor beside Katherine.

Sitting crossed leg on the floor, Anne, unable to comprehend all the fuss said, 'Katherine is just sleeping. She'll wake up soon.'

The funeral for Katherine Irene Smythe was held five days later. When the church service ended, friends, family and neighbours stood mournfully beside a black hearse watching Glenn and Jimmy gently place the tiny white coffin laden with a garland of baby's breath, white carnations and tiny white roses in the back. Robert, overcome with grief, held on tightly to his youngest daughter, Rose.

Forlornly, Sherry stood stoned faced holding Bea's hand eyeing the funeral attendant. 'Don't shut the door!' she cried, moving toward the casket. 'I want my sister back!'

Robert moved quickly, gently placing a hand on her shoulder. 'Sherry...'

'Don't touch me!' she cried, pulling his hand away. 'It's all your fault. If you hadn't given Mom all those bad pills Katherine would be alive today. We would have had a good mother like all my friends. Now Katherine is dead and never coming back,' she cried hysterically, running into Glenn's open arms.

Bea stood sombrely at the living room window watching the real estate agent hammer the wooden for sale sign into Smythe's front lawn. Three weeks had passed since little Katherine's untimely death; those closest to the family were still reeling, especially Bea. She had witnessed death and carnage many times living in London during World War 2, but the image of Anne holding Katherine's lifeless body was permanently ingrained in her mind.

Anne was committed, indefinitely, to an insane asylum after a botched drug overdose the day after Katherine's death. Sherry was under psychiatric care and living in northern Ontario with Robert's older sister and her family. Little Rose was staying with Robert's younger brother and his wife indefinitely. Glenn and Jimmy, too distraught to return to school remained with their father at the house. Robert was on a leave of absence until he could make suitable arrangements for the kids. He had come too far in his career to relinquish the job he truly loved.

Betty's new job at the doctor's office was busier than she had anticipated but she proved herself to be a keen, fast learner. Her significant weight loss prompted a complete wardrobe change that enhanced her new svelte figure; rather than burying herself in the ill-fitting, baggy outfits she had lived in for years. (Confident she'd maintain her remarkable weight loss; she bagged all her big clothes and personally delivered them to Goodwill). It was the first time in years she felt great, and looked good too.

Surprisingly, the children adapted very quickly to life without their father. They willingly helped out at home all the while maintaining good marks at school. Ironically, no one seemed to miss

Endre, especially Betty, feeling totally liberated not having to answer to him.

Endre sat in his leather chair staring glumly out of his office at Maxine's unoccupied desk. His life, once full of promise, had spiralled out of control. She was pregnant with his unwanted child; his wife and kids wanted nothing to do with him. Etika, barely civil, spoke to him about business matters only; his respectful employees who used to come willingly to him now sought Etika's expertise. It was like he didn't exist. But on the bright side, the business he had built continued to flourish. The last thing he needed was a lack of funds enabling him to live comfortably, not to mention the added costs of Betty's monthly expenses. He signed her cheque just as the phone sounded. 'Yes,' he said gruffly, the receiver planted on his shoulder.

Maxine's childlike voice on the other end made the hair on the back of his neck rise. 'When are you coming home? You've been gone for hours.'

His chair squawked loudly, leaning back heavily. He had to work at keeping his tone even. 'I had to catch up on the paperwork piling up on my desk. I do have to work.'

She spoke softly, 'my feet are swollen, honey. Remember what the doctor said, I have to take it easy, so I need you to come home and make me and our baby some supper,' she smiled, patting her swollen belly.

'I'll be there as soon as I can,' he said, eyeing her empty desk.

'When?' she asked impatiently.

He massaged the tension building in the back of his neck. 'I still have some work to…'

She interrupted with her pouty tone that drove him half mad. 'But I'm getting hungry, Endre. The doctor said I'm supposed to eat when I'm hungry so the baby gets its nutrients; I'm still experiencing morning sickness, remember. We want our baby to be healthy, don't we?' She rubbed her expanding girth.

He pictured her pouty face, a face that once turned him on. 'I'll be home shortly.'

He hung up, buzzing Doug in receiving. 'I want the desk outside my office removed immediately.'

Endre parked his Caddy in front of the house anticipating Betty's arrival. When she pulled into the driveway, he marvelled at how quickly and easy she slid out of the car seat. There was a time it was such an effort getting in and out.

'Betty,' he said, moving quickly up the driveway, eyeing the navy dress she wore, flattering her slim figure perfectly. Her shiny black hair, styled differently, accented her flawless complexion with only a hint of makeup. He felt his pulse quicken.

'You're staring,' she said accusingly, meeting his gaze.

Endre, blushing with Hungarian charm smiled. 'I guess I am. And why shouldn't I feast my eyes on such a beautiful woman.' Ironically, he remembered feeling the same when they first met.

He had just returned from Hungary suffering from jet lag, when his best friend, Wally, insisted he attend a family reunion that evening. Ironically, Betty, a friend of Wally's sister, Kristie, had been invited too. Shortly after they were introduced, he knew he was staring into emerald green eyes of his future wife. They were married a year later.

He fumbled with the envelope. 'I was just in the neighbourhood so thought I would drop off your cheque,' he smiled, not bothering to mention he had been sitting in his car for over an hour anticipating her arrival.

Betty plucked it from his hand. 'Next time, drop it in the mail.'

In stunned silence, he watched her move quickly toward the front door, swiftly closing it behind her.

The apartment elevator creaked and moaned coming to a jarring halt on the sixth floor. Endre wondered if he would ever get used to the nausea he felt every time the lethargic dented doors opened, ushering in a variety of disgusting cooking odours.

He hated coming home to such cramped quarters, tossing his keys on the small oak telephone table beside the door. The apartment was quiet. Assuming Maxine was resting, he moved silently into the compact kitchen to mix a much needed drink.

Maxine appeared in the doorway, hands on her hips. 'Where have you been?'

He continued mixing a gin martini, ignoring her indignant tone.

'Endre, where were you?' she questioned demandingly.

Obviously, she needed a lesson on how not to question him. He raised the glass to his nose, swirling the clear liquid and took a sip, feeling the cool blend slide easily down his throat. 'I told you I had lots of work to do.'

Frustrated, Maxine sighed deeply watching her handsome man enjoy his drink. His dimpled smile momentarily dissipated the anger she felt. 'I called the office. Your brother didn't hesitate to inform me you were on your way to Betty's house.' She watched closely for his reaction. 'Did she invite you in for coffee? A piece of ass? After all, this is out of bounds,' she said, pointing at her vagina.

Endre had spoken briefly to Etika about a pending moving contract before mentioning he had to go over to Betty's house. He sipped his drink wondering if there was an ulterior motive. Needless to say, he was pissed, vowing to be less transparent with him. 'I was in the area and dropped off a cheque.' He didn't bother to mention Betty made it very clear she wants nothing more than his monetary support.

'What cheque?' she said vehemently.

He stared at her once angelic face, distorted with authority. In all his encounters with the opposite sex, Maxine was the only woman ever to question him.

Sternly, he looked her in the eye. 'We need to get something straight right now. What I do with my family is my business,' he said, swigging the last of his martini.

Cursing in his native tongue, he mixed another.

Chapter Seventeen

THERESA SAT AT her desk trying to concentrate. 'I'm trying to do homework, do you mind?'

Tammy serenaded a moment longer. 'As a matter-of-fact I do. This is my room just as much as yours and if I choose to sing, I'll sing,' she said, lying down on her bed. 'You are my sunshine, my only sunshine…'

Swiftly, Theresa gathered up her books.

'Don't you like my singing?'

She shoved the chair under the desk. 'You are the most annoying little bugger on the face of the Earth.'

Tammy's eyes widened. 'I'm telling Mom. You know how she feels about foul language in this house. You'll be in so much trouble.'

Theresa reached for the doorknob. 'Do you really think I give a shit? You're enough to make a saint swear.'

Tammy's face turned sullen. 'Ever since you started hanging around with Janet you've changed. You aren't the nice person you used to be.'

Theresa's face reddened. 'Leave my friends out of this. I'm like this because I have to share my room with a goddamn brat who never knows when to shut the hell up.'

'Wow! I'm going to pretend this didn't happen. I won't tell Mom, this time. But if you swear at me once more, I'll have no choice,' she said, cringing as the door slammed shut.

Tammy yelled, 'You're just jealous because I'm a better singer than you are. You are my sunshine, my only sunshine; you make me happy when skies are grey; you'll never know dear how much I love you; please don't take my sunshine away.' She sat up wondering what to do next.

When school started last September, Janet Levinson was assigned to the empty desk next to Theresa's. As soon as she sat down, the pair became fast friends.

Janet's family settled in Scarborough after Mr. Levinson's company transferred him from North Bay. This was their third move in seven years, but the nomadic family was resilient settling in quickly. Mrs. Levinson, a registered nurse, preferred the nightshift at the local hospital. Janet and Helen, her younger sister, had strict instructions to come straight home from school to tend to Andy and Derek, the youngest siblings.

On most days, Theresa would accompany Janet home after school. Unfortunately, once Marcie befriended Janet, she would join them; forcing Theresa to make a concerted effort to be friendly, but their only commonality was Janet.

Marcie bragged about her Beatlemania party; the place to be for everyone other than Theresa. (She had purchased a Beatle record intending to go but decided last minute it was the last place she wanted to be).

But her absence didn't go unnoticed. The next day, Marcie wasted no time rubbing it in her face in front of all the girls about the fabulous time she had missed by not attending. 'And, Janet spent the night. My mom let us stay up all night listening to Beatle's music, stuffing our faces with chocolate.'

Lately, Marcie seemed to influence everything Janet did; right down to the makeup she began wearing. She would apply makeup at school, removing it before going home, contrary to her mother's stipulation she had to wait until high school. *There's lots of time to apply all that goop on your face.*

Theresa was astounded by all the makeup Janet had stashed in her drawer, but more so, how she could afford it. Janet just shrugged, passing a devilish look to Marcie, suggesting her involvement somehow.

Theresa heard the phone ring, sitting at Greg's desk finishing up the last of her homework.

'It's for you, T. It's your best friend, Janet.' Tammy held the receiver against her chest as she approached. 'Say please.'

She was in no mood for her sister's shenanigans. 'Give me the phone.'

Tammy moved her head slowly from side to side.

Theresa rolled her eyes, 'please.'

'That's better,' she smiled, sitting down on the cushioned seat attached to the telephone table.

Theresa tilted her head. 'Do you mind?'

She crossed her arms over her chest. 'I need the phone…'

'Mom, *please* tell her to buzz off.'

Tammy pounded her feet into the living room, sitting down heavily at the end of the chesterfield to wait her turn. 'I need to use the phone too,' she mumbled.

Mom ordered her to sit quietly and wait her turn.

Theresa hung up the phone. 'I'm going to Towers with Janet and Marcie.'

Mom glanced at the wall clock. 'Dinner's at 5:30.'

'You can have the phone now, Tam.'

'On second thought, I don't need it. You are my sunshine, my only sunshine,' she sang, tearing off down the hall, shutting the bedroom door behind her.

The three girls entered the department store, walking straight toward the cosmetic counter. Janet and Marcie were very familiar with the layout, seamlessly navigating the area.

Theresa stood back watching Janet try to decide whether she wanted Yardley's hot pink lipstick and matching soft pink blush or the new coral shade.

Marcie said, 'I really love this new shade. Do you think it would suit me?'

Janet smiled. 'Anything looks good on you, Mars.'

'What about you, T?' Marcie said, sampling the lipstick.

Theresa was surprised she called her T, a name reserved for family and close friends, something Marcie would never be. 'I don't have enough money.' She caught the mischievous look passing between Janet and Marcie. 'Last night I babysat for the couple next door but Mrs. Thurston didn't have enough money to pay me.'

Janet said, 'Are they living in the house where the little girl died? I couldn't even go in there.'

Theresa admitted at first she wasn't keen, but the new people are really nice and have the cutest little one year old daughter, Kelly.

Marcie added her two cents. 'Well, that would give me the creeps. This is the new mod look,' she smiled, studying a doe-eyed poster model wearing green eye shadow, thick black eyeliner and false eyelashes. 'I really love this look.'

Janet considered the compact housing five different shades of green eye shadow, readily agreeing with her friend.

Theresa wondered what all the fuss was about. She had never given makeup much thought; she wouldn't be allowed to wear it anyway. She assumed it was for older girls or Bev Carmichael; she began wearing heavy eye makeup and lipstick in grade seven.

'I really want this colour,' Janet said, picking up a tube of lipstick. 'And I'll get the eye shadow the model is wearing to go with my green eyes,' she said, batting her long eyelashes.

Theresa volunteered to go stand in line at the cash, knowing this would probably take a while. 'Hi Mrs. Gardiner,' she smiled, standing behind her neighbour.

'Oh, hi there, Theresa. I haven't seen you for a while. You are getting so tall. Either that or I'm shrinking,' she chuckled, unloading her cart.

Theresa felt ridiculous standing in line with nothing to purchase. 'I'm just waiting for my friends,' she shrugged, craning her neck. Marcie had mentioned picking up the latest issue of *Glamour*.

Theresa caught up with them cutting across the hydro field. 'Where were you?' she said breathlessly. 'You could have told me you were leaving. My neighbour must have thought I was nuts standing in line, buying nothing. Where did you pay?'

Marcie looked at Janet, bursting out laughing. 'Cosmetics,' Marcie said condescendingly.

Janet emptied her large brown leather shoulder bag onto the bed, rifling through her purchases for a particular lipstick. 'I love this shade of pink,' she said, opening the seal. 'I couldn't decide which shade I like better so I got them both,' she smiled, comparing the two. 'I love the matching pink blush too.' She skimmed her finger along the cream, dabbing it on her flushed cheeks.

Marcie flipped through the Glamour magazine searching for the Jean Shrimpton advertisement. 'I hope this is the same eye shadow,' she said, comparing her new compact with the ad. 'Thank Christ it is. I didn't want to go back to the store on my way home.' She opened it, encouraging Theresa to try it on.

'My mother would kill me,' she sighed.

'You can wash it off before you go home,' she said pointedly.

Janet smeared black eyeliner under her bottom lashes. 'Just don't tell her, silly. My mom would crap if she knew I was putting on this stuff.'

Theresa thought it a total waste of time getting all made up only to turn around and wash it all off. 'Besides, I can't begin to afford all the makeup you two have,' she said, eyeing the absurd collection.

After dinner, Theresa sat at her desk thinking about her friend's shopping spree this afternoon. She was certain there was no cash register in cosmetics, contrary to Marcie's claim. But then again, she was unfamiliar with the department store.

Greg looked up from his homework when he heard the knock on his door. 'If it's Tammy, go away. Anyone else, enter.'

Theresa smiled, stepping into his room. 'Don't blame you, Gregor.'

'What's up?' he said, tossing his red pen onto his notebook.

'Do you ever shop at Towers?'

He looked at her strangely. 'Sometimes, why?'

'I need to know if there's a cash register in the cosmetic counter.'

Greg eyed her curiously. 'To my knowledge, there are only three, located at the front of the store. A friend of mine works there part time. He said that having the cashiers at the front of the store makes it easier to keep tabs on shoplifters, supposedly.'

The next day when Janet invited Theresa over, Marcie, sporting a new Beatle haircut, heavily green shadowed eyes and false eyelashes, answered the door. 'You're just in time, everyone's out and we're celebrating with a makeup party.'

The transformation of Janet's desktop neatly divided into groups of lipsticks, eye shadows, foundation, blush, eye pencils, nail polish and cologne was astounding.

'That shade of lipstick looks horrible on you,' Janet said, handing Marcie a tissue.

'You think so.' She rubbed her lips vigorously making her way to the bathroom to wash it off.

Janet said, 'T, since you're my best friend, I'll let you try on this brand new, never been opened Yardley pale pink lipstick, but I want it back because it's my fave.'

Theresa studied the sealed tube. 'Where did you get it from?'

Janet screwed up her face. 'You were there, silly, from the store.'

'Did you pay for it?'

Janet rolled her heavily made-up eyes. 'As a matter of fact...'

'What?' Marcie interrupted, walking back into the bedroom tossing a tissue into the wastebasket.

Theresa held up the sealed tube. 'Pay for this.'

'What about this?' Marcie said, mimicking her, holding up a bottle of nail polish. 'And these?' She picked up a couple of the eye shadow compacts, waving them mid-air.

Janet said proudly. 'Gees Mars. There's a lot of stuff I didn't pay for.'

'I guess that makes you a thief,' Theresa said, abruptly ending their silly game.

Marcie's heavily made-up eyes bulged. 'Holy shit! Nothing like being in the same room as your fucking conscience.'

Theresa's heart pounded heavily. 'Obviously, something neither of you have.'

Marcie had been biding her time just waiting for a moment like this. From the second they met she wanted nothing to do with her. 'You fucking goodie two shoes. I bet you've never stolen anything in your life. Everybody steals for Christ sake.'

Theresa stood her ground. 'No, not everybody.'

'You're the only person I know who doesn't. Get with it for Christ sakes. It's the only way to get the things you want.'

'What about paying for it?' Theresa said sensibly.

'If I waited until I had the money, I'd never have anything.'

Theresa was surprised by her admission. Marcie always dressed in the current styles with the best clothes, shoes, purses and makeup. She couldn't possibly have stolen it all. 'Don't you get an allowance?' she queried, thinking of her own meager three dollars a week.

Marcie retorted, 'I get 40 bucks a week; it's not enough. Plus, I get a thrill out of stealing *and* getting away with it,' she said arrogantly.

Janet nodded in agreement; foolishly believing stealing was the way to always get what you want.

'Neither of you has a conscience…'

Marcie interrupted, 'you pompous asshole. You sit there judging us, your friends, because you don't happen to steal. Just who the hell do you think you are?'

Theresa's face reddened. She really had no right sticking her nose in their affairs and apologized. 'It's none of my business what either of you do.'

'That's better,' Marcie smiled. 'T, you need to get with it and steal something.'

That evening, Theresa sat at her desk breaking the cellophane seal on the tube of Yardley pale pink lipstick, running it smoothly across her lips. Tucking it at the back of her drawer, she admired her mirrored image. *It's my fave now.*

Chapter Eighteen

MAXINE LAY RIGID on the bed too frightened to move. She tightened her grip on the satin sheet as another contraction sent a wave of pain through her bloated body. Beads of sweat covered her anguished brow; her disheveled blond hair wrapped tightly around her neck, she screamed in agony.

Endre finished washing the dishes. With a list of tasks to complete before noon, he vacuumed the recently installed dark beige wall to wall broadloom.

Reluctantly, Betty had agreed to Endre's latest proposal, enabling him to spend Monday to Friday, during the day, with the kids. Wanting nothing to do with him, he entered the house after her departure for work at 7:45. Daily, he would park out front waiting for her to drive off then run inside to get the kids ready for school. The kids were content with this arrangement, in that, they had missed their dad.

The arrangement worked extremely well for Betty. Early morning hassles were now a thing of the past, handing over the responsibility of getting them up, fed and out the door for the nine o'clock school bell was Endre's responsibility. The added bonus, no more lunch bags to fill the night before. Endre made lunch and had supper in the oven or on the stove; all she had to do was dish it out.

Betty chuckled watching him scurry up the driveway as she drove off contemplating an invitation to join them for supper.

Endre turned off the vacuum when he heard the phone ring; secretly hoping it was Betty when he answered.

Etika said gruffly, 'What are you doing? I've been trying to get a hold of you.'

Endre questioned how he knew where he was.

'You're rarely in the office,' he said decisively. 'And I know you're not at the apartment.'

Endre encouraged him to get to the point.

'Maxine's in the hospital having your baby.'

The news hit Endre like a ton of bricks; the baby wasn't due for two and a half weeks.

'Did she call you?' He hadn't bothered mentioning his arrangement with Betty; Maxine readily assumed he was at the office every day.

'No. Some guy called the office looking for you. He asked me to try and find you. Also while I've got you on the phone, I'm not your damn secretary,' Etika said, slamming down the receiver. Lately the brother he had always admired, often emulated, did nothing but piss him off; his steadfast rock, had let him down miserably. Endre's latest endeavour of scaling back his work schedule to accommodate his children left him angry and frustrated.

'Harry, cover for me,' Etika said, walking briskly toward the side door.

Mumbling Hungarian profanity, Endre glanced at the wall clock. It was 9:30 and the kids wouldn't be home until noon.

The doctor coached Maxine to push one more time; a few moments later a baby's cry filled the delivery room.

'Congratulations Maxine, you have a beautiful baby boy.'

Maxine's eyes filled with tears, listening to her baby wail.

'He's a healthy 7lb 14oz feisty little boy,' he said, handing the newborn to the nurse.

After a few moments that seemed like an eternity to Maxine, the nurse placed the swaddled baby on her chest. 'He's so beautiful. Your daddy's going to be so proud and happy.'

Endre exited the elevator, running a hand through his hair approaching the nurses' station. The young nurse looked up from her desk, appreciatively admiring the handsome man standing in front of her. 'Can I help you?'

Oblivious of her flirty tone, he inquired about Maxine.

The nurse pointed to a young doctor reading a chart close by. 'She would be Dr. Gibson's patient.' She waited until he finished writing on the chart. 'Dr. Gibson, Maxine's husband has just arrived.'

'Congratulations on the birth of your son,' he said, shaking his hand. 'He's a feisty little guy.'

Endre felt his insides mesh, tears welled in eyes. 'Can I see her?'

'She should be in her room by now,' he said, moving quickly toward the elevator.

The nurse smiled warmly, 'That would be room 412.' She watched him walk proudly down the hall. *Some women have all the luck.*

There were four beds in the room, each encompassed with dull beige curtains swaying back and forth. Walking toward Maxine's bed by the window, he could hear a dull monotone voice. Pulling back the curtain, he eyed Frank Armstrong leaning casually against the window sill. He had introduced himself to Endre recently exiting the elevator at the apartment. *I'm Maxine's neighbour. I'm three doors down the hall.*

Frank stood tall; a congratulatory smile crossed his face, reaching out his hand.

Endre ignored the gesture, planting a lingering kiss on Maxine's lips.

Frank moved toward the end of the bed. 'I should be on…'

'No!' Maxine said, breaking away from the kiss. He had come to her rescue this morning.

Endre caught her needy tone.

'Just grab a bite to eat and come back,' she said pleasantly.

Frank caught the stern look on Endre's face. 'Are you sure?'

She nodded briefly.

'I'll be back then,' he smiled, vanishing behind the curtain.

Endre asked if Frank placed the call to the office.

Maxine thought of her predicament when labour began unexpectedly. 'I didn't know what to do. The baby wasn't due for over two weeks, but when it started coming, I was so frightened, Endre. I tried to reach you at work, but you weren't there. I didn't know what to do so I called Frank.'

He said suspiciously, 'You have Frank's number?'

She nodded, 'he gave me his phone number a long time ago. I first met him in the laundry room. The washing machine I was using broke down mid-cycle, of course. That's usually when these things happen. Frank kindly offered to help me transfer all my sopping wet laundry to another machine. We've been friends ever since and still laugh about it. Then and there, he made it very clear if I ever needed his assistance with anything to call him.' She reiterated about not being able to get a hold of Endre. 'Bless his heart, Frank arrived immediately. It made me wonder if my guardian angel was just outside the door waiting he arrived so quickly, calming all my fears; assuring me everything was going to be alright. The kind soul even packed my suitcase for me then drove me to the hospital,' she sighed gratefully.

Gingerly, Maxine got out of bed, leading Endre to the nursery. Together they watched the nurse navigate three rows of plastic bassinets, stopping in the middle of the second row. She picked up the sleeping bundle and met them at the window; gently pushing back the receiving blanket to reveal a full head of thick blond hair.

'Oh my god, look at all the hair,' Endre said proudly. He felt tears sting his eyes watching the baby stir, briefly opening his eyes. 'Look at that! He's looking right at me,' he said excitedly.

Maxine smiled joyfully. 'He's our son, Endre Jr., named after his wonderful daddy. His second name is Christopher, named after my daddy. Endre Jr. Christopher Herczeg,' she smiled, placing her hand on the glass separating them.

Renee Johnson stopped ironing her husband's white shirt, walking quickly toward the black and white RCA television, turning it down. She was positive she could hear someone banging something, but in the quiet of the house, all she heard was the hum of the refrigerator emanating from the kitchen.

Charlie's empty stomach grumbled miserably. His chubby hand reached for the doorknob, trying to turn it. 'Daddy! Daddy!' he yelled, kicking the black wooden door. 'Open the door!' he yelled, pounding his fists against it. He pounded his fists so hard they ached more than his tummy, setting off the tears.

Renee found a tearful Charlie in a crumpled heap by the door. The youngest of the three Herczeg kids was by far her favourite. The five year old had been blessed with thick, wavy, blond hair, sky blue eyes and the cutest dimpled smile. He was short, stocky, and cuddly. Often he would visit her for a chat. His parent's separation had been very difficult for all three kids, especially little Charlie.

When he heard Renee's voice he stopped crying, wiping his dirty tear stained face with his chubby hands.

'Do you know where your dad has gone, angel?'

Charlie shook his head. 'He's suppose to be home making lunch for me and I don't know where he is,' he cried, falling into Renee's welcoming arms.

'It's okay. You can come over to my house and have lunch with me,' she said, taking his hand.

Danny and Sharon ran toward them. 'Where's Dad?' Danny said breathlessly, noting the Cadillac was not parked out front.

Renee said, 'I'm not sure where he is. The car was there earlier this morning. I'll call your mom at work, maybe she'll know. In the meantime, I'll make some lunch.'

Betty was taken aback hearing Renee's voice on the phone; even more stunned to learn Endre wasn't at the house.

Renee assured her the children were fine and she would make them lunch.

Betty was upset she couldn't leave the office to attend to her kids. *Thank goodness Renee lives next door.* She couldn't ask for a better neighbour. After the separation, she had kindly volunteered to keep an eye on the kids for her.

She wondered what could possibly make Endre disappear without calling her. It was totally out of character for him to leave the kids stranded. Vowing it would never happen again, she tried to concentrate on her work.

Endre stopped talking when Frank took his place on the other side of Maxine at the nursery window. 'That was a fast bite,' he commented sarcastically.

'It was sufficient,' Frank replied, fixing his eyes on Maxine's beautiful smile. 'How's our new Momma?'

'I'm a little sore, if you know what I mean. But otherwise, I feel wonderful.'

A wary look crossed Endre's brow. 'Don't you think that's too much personal information to relay to a stranger?'

Maxine chuckled. 'Frank's not a stranger, he's my friend. A good friend who is always there for me,' she said, slipping her arm through Frank's. 'I don't know what I would have done today if he hadn't come to my rescue.' She turned to Endre. 'Remember, *he* drove me to the hospital.'

Endre was about to make a snide remark; the time on the wall clock above Frank's head curtailed it. 'I have to go,' he said, hastily kissing her cheek.

Maxine's heart sank watching Endre disappear into the elevator. Unable to hold back her tears, she fell into Frank's accommodating arms.

The traffic on the road outside the hospital was bumper to bumper. Throngs of students from a nearby high school, making their way home, moved slowly across the hospital's only exit. After what seemed like an eternity, Endre edged out onto the congested road, but a two car crash blocking a main intersection two blocks away had brought traffic to a standstill. He shut off the caddy, leaning back heavily in the seat.

Betty left work early, driving straight to the school to pick up the kids. They were surprised to see her and not their father, bombarding her with questions. She explained she had absolutely no idea where he was and by the time she turned into the driveway her headache had morphed into a full blown migraine, something she hadn't experienced in months.

She unlocked the door insisting the children go to their rooms and do homework while she prepared supper. Surprisingly, the kitchen was clean and tidy with the table set for lunch; four cheese, ham and lettuce sandwiches wrapped in wax paper sat on the top shelf in the refrigerator. The vacuum stood plugged in awaiting its turn.

By the time traffic started moving again, Endre debated whether to go back to the hospital or face Betty. He arrived at the house shortly after 5:30, knocking heavily on the front door.

'Daddy!' Charlie said, his happiness dissipating into a pout. 'Where were you at lunch? You were a post to be here.'

'I think you mean *supposed* to be here,' he smiled. He was such a cute kid; he loved him more than words could express. 'Can I talk to Mommy, please?'

Stepping out into the carport, closing the door behind her, Betty demanded an explanation.

Endre said sheepishly, 'Maxine had the baby this morning. I had to leave in a hurry, I'm so sorry. I have another son,' he added, trying not to sound too proud.

The words cut through Betty's core; her head pounded with each heartbeat. Though she knew his mistress was pregnant with his child, the news of its birth dashed any hope she may have garnered of a possible future with this man she once called husband; the newborn baby boy, a lasting reminder of his infidelity.

'Your new family needs you now,' she said dejectedly, locking the door behind her.

Chapter Nineteen

THE LAWYER FIRMLY shook Etika's outstretched hand. 'Have a seat Mr. Herczeg,' he said, pointing to the chair in front his desk. He opened the red folder on his desk. 'After examining all the evidence you have provided, you do have a solid case against your brother. If you would like me to proceed, I will have the necessary paperwork prepared immediately.'

Etika nodded. 'Definitely.'

The lawyer stood extending his hand. 'Mr. Herczeg, I will contact you in a few days.'

Etika felt elated leaving the lawyer's office, after all, he was getting exactly what he wanted; total control of the company he and his brother Endre worked so hard to build into the reputable family business it is today. *In a matter of time, the company will be all mine,* he smiled cockily, unlocking the car door. *It will be my responsibility alone to keep the business up to its valued standard.*

He leaned into the steering wheel and cried.

Endre leaned over the white wicker bassinet, picking up the crying baby. 'There, there. Life can't be too hard for you little guy. All you have to do is eat and sleep and cry, which you do very well,' he said, patting his tiny back. ''You've never had it so good. One day you will have to go to work, like me, maybe follow in my footsteps, running the moving company I built from the ground up. Yes, it takes a lot of sacrifice and hard work but I did it just like you will one day.' He smiled contentedly watching Endre Jr.'s eyes gently close.

'Is he asleep?' Maxine said, entering the bedroom, towelling her wet hair.

'Out like a light.'

Maxine leaned over the bassinet, her housecoat opening slightly with the effort.

Endre felt himself harden, eyeing her full breasts. *The beauty of youth* he thought moving toward her. 'Ah my *kis szepseg*,' he said, wrapping his arms around her waist from behind. Inhaling her perfumed hair, he slid his hands along her body, gently massaging her full breasts.

Maxine stood rigid. 'Endre, you know what the doctor said. No sex for six weeks.'

He ignored her, continuing to caress her breasts. 'It has been six weeks since the baby was born.'

'Not quite,' she said, pulling his hands away, tightening the belt of her housecoat. 'There are three more days still until I see the doctor for my checkup.'

'Oh for Christ's sake. What's a day or two?'

'Endre! Don't swear in front of our son,' she said in a hushed tone.

'Jesus Christ, I need to get laid,' he said, startling the baby awake.

'Now look what you've done. You've woken him with your selfishness. Sex is all you ever think about.'

Endre, mumbling in Hungarian, left the room.

'Where are you going?' she said, cuddling the crying baby.

'The office. I'll be home late.'

She held the baby tightly, shielding him from the slamming door.

There was a spring in Endre's step walking toward the side entrance of the building. He had been housebound far too long. Today he felt like a caged animal being released back into the wild, reaching for the doorknob. *What the hell?* He thought it strange it would be locked in the middle of the day. He knocked loudly; mumbling in Hungarian, he tried inserting his key.

It had been weeks since he'd been to the office or for that matter spoken to Etika. He tried the front entrance, locked up tighter than a drum. Pounding his fist on the glass door he yelled, 'I'll break this fucking door down.' He searched the area for a small rock.

Etika held the door ajar. 'That won't be necessary, Endre.'

Endre moved toward his brother. 'What the hell is going on? This door should always be open for all of our employees, not to mention customers walking in off the street.'

'Follow me,' he said calmly.

Walking by his office, Endre spotted Danny Everett sitting at his desk. 'What the hell do you think you're doing, Danny my boy? Trying to make your way to the top by stealing the boss's seat?'

Danny's non-expressive face reddened; ignoring him he continued working.

Etika shut the office door, pointing to the chair in front of his desk.

Endre sat, running a hand through his dishevelled hair. 'Little brother, what's with all this? New locks, Danny sitting at my desk, new furniture,' he said, sliding his hand along the new leather chair, stretching his legs out casually. 'I hope all these changes aren't running over budget.'

Etika clasped his hands, placing them on the desk in front of him. 'You are no longer part of my company.'

Endre straightened. 'What do you mean *my* company?'

He squeezed his clasped hands. 'I am now sole owner of Etika's Friendly Movers. I guarantee a safe, trouble-free move every time; my company's new slogan.'

Endre smiled broadly, turning his gaze toward the floor. 'Ah little brother. It seems I have been away far too long.' He leaned forward, looking him in the eye. 'In my absence, you have had plenty of opportunity to concoct some very foolish thoughts in that thick skull of yours. I must say, this one tops them all. So let's stop with the child's play...'

'It's not child's play!' Etika said, slamming his fist on the desk. His expression turned vile. 'Your selfishness has been going on far too long. You are a disgrace to the company, not to mention the family. You have become a self-centered, immoral, unreliable, antisocial...'

Endre raised his hand, halting the verbal assault. He was taken aback by his brother's outspokenness; unlike himself, Etika had never been an assertive individual. Yet sadly, most of the accusations were true; his life, outside the company was a shambles, but that was his problem and had nothing to do with the business he built from the ground up. 'I assume you are in the process of having me removed, little brother. But let me remind you, I was the one who started the company. You only came on board...'

Etika interrupted. 'With little encouragement from you, I might add. Right from the beginning, I did my share of the work and sacrifice, working very hard alongside of you.'

Endre said confidently, 'Yes of course, but the fact is, it is my company too and you can't make *any* changes whatsoever without my consent.'

Etika sat back in his new reclining leather chair, relishing the moment. 'That is where you are wrong, Endre. There's a clause in our original signed agreement that states, *'should one brother default in the smooth, ongoing operation of this company for longer than 60 days, without mutual agreement, the person not at fault has the option of becoming sole administrator and owner of The Herczeg Moving Company.'* A satisfied smile blossomed watching his brother squirm.

At the time, Endre had dismissed the lawyer's suggestion of adding this ridiculous clause to their agreement. *It's totally unnecessary. Nothing will ever come between us. We are brothers for life, through thick and thin. We will always work hard together.*

Etika wanted nothing more than to end the meeting. 'This has been going on for over two years. And during that time, I turned the other cheek running my end and your end of the business while you were out sowing your wild oats, in turn, making a total mess of your life. Well I decided not long ago, I have had enough. Now, do us both a favour and get out.'

Endre's heart pounded heavily, leaning over the desk, his face mere inches from Etika's. 'No one will ever take me down, including you, you son of a bitch.'

Endre moved quickly toward the entrance of the Best Buck Tavern. It was almost noon; the lunchtime patrons had yet to arrive. He sat down heavily on a bar stool. The bartender appeared instantly, taking his order of a double vodka martini; his first customer of the day. 'And hold the fucking olive,' he said, resting his elbows on the bar, cupping his face in his hands, thinking about his brother's takeover of the company he established. He needed a drink, and a lawyer.

Antal Biro, a brilliant lawyer with the reputation of being the best at settling business disputes, came to mind. He had heard about Antal through a friend needing counselling during a foreign takeover bid of the company he had started solely. The end result was very favourable. Not only did his friend maintain all assets, but the foreign company had to pay millions in restitution. Endre sipped the martini, downing the remainder. 'Another,' he said gruffly, sliding the glass forward.

The bartender adeptly mixed another martini. Throughout his 26 years tending bar, he had witnessed the good and bad times with his patrons, firm in the belief a few drinks would absolve their issues; but invariably they would end up with a hefty bar bill and a dandy hangover instead. He also knew which customers needed a shoulder to cry on and those who wanted to be left alone. Silently he placed the martini on the coaster, disappearing out back.

Endre fumbled with his key in the lock.

'Where the hell have you been?' Maxine said, opening the door wide.

A confrontation with her, or anyone for that matter, was the last thing he wanted. He had consumed any number of martinis before switching to scotch, closed the bar and fell asleep in his car. His head pounded and his stomach felt like it had been hit by a cannonball aimed less than a foot away. He was hot and sweaty; his mouth akin to an old suede jacket.

'Where have you been? I have called everywhere looking for you. I thought you were in an accident so I called all the hospitals.' She paused giving him the once over. 'Have you been in a fight or something?' She moved closer. 'You smell like a goddamn booze can, probably out hustling women,' she said accusingly.

Endre felt his anger rise. 'The last thing I would ever do is hustle a goddamn woman. Look what it got me, a bimbo, a kid and loss of my company. Do you really think I would be that stupid again?'

The word bimbo resonated throughout the room. 'You think I'm a bimbo? Is that what you really think of me?' she said, holding her head high. 'I am the mother of your son,' she hissed.

At the bar sipping martinis, he had given considerable thought regarding this Frank guy, the convenient, always present neighbour. 'I don't believe it's my kid.'

Maxine's eyes widened. 'He sure as hell is.'

'What about this Frank guy?'

'You leave Frankie out of this,' she said defensively.

'Frankie? Little pet name for your lover?'

'Frank is just a friend, a good friend.'

He tossed his keys onto the telephone table. 'Good enough to hop into bed with and knock you up. There were many times we were apart.'

Maxine half smiled. 'Now wouldn't that be a perfect scenario for you if Frank was the father, absolving you of any responsibility where *our* baby is concerned. But here's a little secret. I was already pregnant when I met Frank in the laundry room. The baby is all yours, Daddy,' she said, pecking his unshaven cheek.

Chapter Twenty

MONDAY MORNING TOMMY sat down sombrely at his desk.

Side-glancing the clock, Mr. Coulter stopped talking. 'You're late Mr. McConnel and you've disrupted the lesson.'

Tommy, never one to draw attention, reddened in the face. On the way to school, he hastily decided to search out some of his favourite haunts, losing track of time. 'I'm very sorry, sir. I promise it won't happen again.'

Tommy was one of the brightest students in the class and the teacher quickly decided this was an isolated incident, any discipline for his tardiness unnecessary. 'I will hold you to that,' Mr. Coulter said, turning back to the blackboard.

Theresa tried to get Tommy's attention. She could tell by the look on his face he was upset about something, yet totally absorbed in the minerals of the Earth lesson. He had decided to follow in his father's engineering footsteps.

Mr. Coulter said, 'Is aluminum a mineral, Lynda?'

All eyes turned toward the back of the classroom watching a tall, plain, self-conscious girl tug at her tight green skirt, moulded permanently to her thick thighs, stand up beside her desk.

Theresa used the moment to get Tommy's attention; after several attempts succeeding. 'What's wrong with you?'

'We're moving,' he whispered.

Theresa gasped just as Lynda pronounced aluminum, *al- u- min- i- um*. She knew immediately she was in deep trouble when Mr. Coulter, glaring ominously, turned in her direction, his eyes penetrating to the core.

'It seems Theresa doesn't agree with Lynda's pronunciation of the word. Now that you have everyone's attention, it's your opportunity to tell us the correct one.'

Theresa stuttered, 'I, I…'

'Stand up.'

Feeling an explosion of heat throughout, she swallowed back breakfast standing on shaky legs, her heart pounding double time.

Again, he asked for the correct pronunciation.

She was in such a state; she couldn't even remember what the word was. On the verge of tears she said meekly, 'I don't even know what the word was.'

Mr. Coulter casually sat down on the corner of his desk. 'That's interesting. Usually when someone disrupts a class, it leads me to believe that person is very knowledgeable.' He gestured with his hand, 'you've got the floor and it's your opportunity to share your knowledge.'

It was all she could do to hold back tears. 'I have no idea, sir.'

The silence in the room was deafening as Mr. Coulter walked down the aisle. Standing mere inches from her he said, 'You are going to know how to pronounce the word and by the time you write *aluminum al-u-min-i-um*' and its' meaning 100 times you will not only be able to pronounce it, but you will know exactly what the word means, no matter how it's pronounced. You will then present this knowledge to the class. Do you understand?'

'Yes sir.' Thankfully the recess bell sounded. Rather than sitting back down at her desk, she walked hastily out of the classroom with her head downcast.

It was sunny and quite warm for mid-April. Theresa located Tommy talking to Billy and John.

Billy said, 'Boy! Old man Coulter really came down hard on you.'

Theresa shrugged, 'I deserved it.'

'Wow! You're taking it well,' John said. 'I don't know what I would have done, being centered out like that in front of the whole class.'

Without disclosing the embarrassment she had felt, at the hand of her favourite teacher, she replied, 'I shouldn't have done it. Tommy, can I talk to you for a moment please?'

Walking toward the field Theresa said, 'I hope I didn't hear you correctly this morning. Tell me you aren't moving.'

His face confirmed her worst fears. 'Yeah, we're moving. Mac said we need a bigger house.' His referral to Mac instead of dad happened when he wasn't pleased with one of his dad's ideas.

The reality of him moving away hit her like a ton of bricks. 'Is it for sure,' she said, scrunching her face. 'Sometimes parents talk out loud, but it doesn't happen.'

He kicked a stone. 'It's for sure. Not only that, our new home is in Edmonton.' He started to walk away then walked back. 'T, I think you're the bravest, coolest, best, fun girl I know and I like you.'

Theresa watched him walk toward the school. They had been friends and classmates since her family moved to the Crescent. She had never thought of him as anything more than a friend, until now. Unable to hold back tears, she walked slowly in the opposite direction.

With only a two day grace period, Theresa wrote out *aluminum al-u-min-i-um* and the meaning 100 times in her best penmanship. By the time she had written the last word, her hand ached, but not as much as her self-esteem. She was already one of the lower achievers in the class, better known as class clown and now class jerk.

The next day she arrived earlier than her classmates to speak with Mr. Coulter. The scent of stale cigarettes greeted her entering the classroom. She moved toward the blackboard where he stood drawing a graph.

'Good morning Mr. Coulter. I have completed the assignment, as requested,' she said, jutting the sheets of paper toward him.

Mr. Coulter rubbed white chalk off his nicotine stained fingers. 'This is by far some of your best penmanship,' he said encouragingly. 'Very impressive indeed, Theresa,' he said, flipping through the pages.

Shortly before recess, Mr. Coulter addressed the class. 'One of our students has requested an opportunity to speak candidly to us,' he said, sitting down on the edge of his desk, keeping the students in suspense.

Without introduction, Theresa stood. 'Thank you Mr. Coulter, and fellow classmates, for giving me the opportunity to apologize for my rude outburst a couple of days ago, both untimely and inappropriate. I especially want to apologize to Lynda,' she said, turning in her direction. 'There *are* two ways to pronounce aluminium, I know this for a fact,' she smiled modestly. 'Writing a word and its meaning 100 times cements it here,' she said, pointing to her head. 'Once again, my sincere apologies to you, Lynda, my classmates and last but not least, Mr. Coulter.'

A pleasant round of applause erupted as she sat back down.

When the recess bell sounded, Mr. Coulter gently pulled Theresa aside. 'I'm very proud you,' he smiled.

She returned his smile. 'Thank you, sir,' she said, trying to recall the last time she had felt this assured.

Tommy watched Theresa out of the corner of his eye, half listening to Larry and Jamie talking animatedly about last night's baseball game. He had thought of her as a friend throughout the years, a fill-in if they were short baseball players, but lately his feelings toward her were changing. 'Hey T,' he called out, running up behind her. She was surprised to see him. 'I just want you to know it took a lot of guts to stand up in front of the class like you did and apologize. Not many people would be as brave. Including me,' he added as an afterthought.

Theresa just wanted to put the whole episode behind her. 'I did what I thought was right. It shouldn't have happened in the first place.'

'But it did and you handled yourself splendidly,' he smiled.

She chuckled at his use of words. Tommy was always one to come out with the unexpected, especially in vocabulary, just like his dad. 'Thanks.' He remained at her side, gently kicking at the ground, a habit of his when he wanted to say something, but wasn't sure how to go about it. 'Is there something else you'd like to talk about? ' she said, after a lengthy pause.

Tommy had created a small hole with the end of his shoe. 'Actually, there is. Remember a few days ago when I told you I liked you?' He swallowed. 'Well I do, a lot. And I'm really going to miss you,' he added.

Theresa's heart beat a little faster. 'I like you too,' she said, smiling at the sudden spring in his step as he walked away.

Saturday morning, Endre sat on the chesterfield contemplating the future. He had taken the necessary steps to regain control of his company when he met with Toronto's most competent criminal lawyer; over a couple of martinis they toasted a pending victory. *I, Antal Brio, guarantee you will be back at the helm of Herczeg Moving Company very soon. Together, we will kick Etika's butt to the curb.*

Endre, content knowing this aspect of his life was taken care of, focused on the shambles his domestic life had become. He knew he couldn't survive much longer in the apartment with Maxine and the baby. He missed his kids horribly, spending most of his time yearning for his old life. Recently, he had finally convinced Betty it would be for the betterment of their children if he was there during the day while she was at work. Very reluctantly, she had agreed to their former arrangement, but remained apprehensive and cautious about his real motive. He, on the other hand, was confident and hopeful, that over time he could convince her of his sincerity, eventually moving back in. Now all he had to do was figure out what to do about Maxine and the baby.

Endre stood at the window watching Maxine navigate the white and navy pram toward the entrance of the apartment, stopping suddenly to watch Frank, waving frantically, run toward her. She hugged him warmly, steering the pram back toward the sidewalk, disappearing around the corner. *What a handsome couple they make.*

Theresa sat at her desk trying to concentrate on speech writing, but all she could think about was Tommy. *T and T* he had said walking home from school this afternoon. He had reached for her hand and held it most of the way home, talking animatedly about the past and present, avoiding the inevitable future. The McConnel house had sold last week; they were moving to Edmonton after graduation at the end of June.

The students had been given two weeks to prepare a speech and present it to the class. The student with the best speech would go on to compete in the Scarborough speech finals, a yearly contest with entries from all Scarborough grade eight classes. The theme this year must begin with *my life as*. Mr. Coulter had given some suggestions; *a book, worm, tree, radish, lettuce; any non-human genre.*

Theresa sat back in her chair trying to think of something novel. Having absolutely no idea, she remembered the *Oh Henry* chocolate bar hidden in her drawer. She felt the sleeve of her dark green cardigan, hoping Tammy hadn't discovered it first. Her mouth watered opening the yellow wrapper, biting into a mouthful of delicious milk chocolate, fudge, caramel and peanuts. Savouring the fudge, she decided it was the crunchy peanuts that took it up a notch. She studied the half eaten bar, folded down the wrapper and picked up her pen.

Endre stood at the kitchen counter cutting ham and cheese sandwiches into little triangles, placing them neatly on the plates, anticipating the kid's arrival at lunch and he couldn't be happier. At long last, he had severed his relationship with Maxine; the parting had been hell.

Maxine guided the pram into the apartment, ignoring Endre's brooding face greeting her at the door.

He watched her check on the baby sleeping soundly in the pram. I see you had a nice walk with your good friend Frank.

Lately, he sounded like a broken record where Frank was concerned and she was getting tired of it. No need to worry, Endre. Frank is just a friend who enjoys spending time with Endre Jr.

And you, he said pointedly.

She turned away from the sleeping baby. You're not jealous, are you? She smiled confidently.

Endre chuckled. On the contrary, my dear, I'm happy he enjoys your son, but a man would have to be totally blind not to see he enjoys you even more.

Our son, she corrected.

Endre, once again, questioned the paternity of the child.

Though time and time again, she was adamant the child was his, it made no difference, he wanted out. Maxine, I cannot live like this anymore. I have tried, but my heart lives on the Crescent with my family.

Maxine placed her hands on her ample hips. Does your wife feel the same? She already knew the answer, smiling smugly. Maybe, just maybe, she doesn't want you back.

As I have said before, my home life is none of your business.

Oh but it is, she said, sauntering toward him. Your family life is here with me and Endre Jr. Together, we can buy a house and fill it with our kids, starting now, she said, yanking off her sweater.

Hungrily he buried his face in her ample bosom caressing and sucking her breasts. She smiled contentedly, tilting her head toward the ceiling, feeling him pull away. I can't do this, he said, running a hand through his disheveled hair, ordering her to put the sweater back on.

Maxine quickly complied, pulling it down hastily. What the hell is going on? You wanted me as much as I wanted you. Do you have any feelings for me at all? I love you with all my heart, Endre, and I truly believe over time, you will grow to love me too, she said, gently placing her hands on his shoulders. I want to be your wife and have your babies.

This was not going the way he wanted. Forcefully, he pulled her hands off his shoulders. I already have a wife, and children. I realize now, our affair should never have happened, or your selfish decision to get knocked-up and surprise me with your pregnancy, knowing full well I did not want more kids. You are a very foolish woman to believe such practices steer a man down the aisle. The truth is, I have never loved you Maxine, and I never will.

He walked toward the window, speaking to the glass. Besides, I'm not even sure the kid's mine. How the hell do I know what you do when I'm away from here? Maybe I should ask your friend Frank, he's always hanging around.

Tears slid down her flushed cheeks. I'll tell you what goes on whenever we are apart. I pine for you, anxiously awaiting your return, because I love you so much. And whether or not you choose to believe me, Endre Jr. is your son. You are the only man who has ever bedded me. I was a virgin when we met.

Endre turned to face her. I want out and that's final. I will issue a handsome cheque to cover the child's expenses...

She moved toward him. Do you think you can just pay me off and that's the end of it? Well there's no bloody way.

Standing mere inches from her face, he spoke clearly and concisely, you would be wise to accept my offer and stay the hell out of my life.

Tall, blue eyed, brown haired Frank Armstrong was a meticulous, kind, easy-going, God fearing man who had spent the previous year nursing his ailing mother until her demise. He preferred the simple life, working part time in the produce aisle at the local A&P, supplementing the more than sufficient estate left by his dear departed mother. With no siblings, the only family he had ever known was a smattering of cousins scattered throughout the States and an aunt and uncle living in Vancouver that he dutifully corresponded with at Christmas. He had had a few close friends but they married, had children or moved away. Other than his job to keep him busy, he devoted most of his spare time volunteering at the church. In doing so, periodically, the minister and his wife felt obligated to invite him to dinner, which he gratefully accepted. They sensed his loneliness, suggesting he start dating. *You are such a nice, handsome young man. I believe you would make some lucky woman a very good husband* the minister's wife gushed.

Shortly after, he began dating Sarah Jamison, a part time cashier he'd met recently at work. It started simple, eating lunch together in the lunchroom, gradually morphing into a few date nights. Frank enjoyed Sarah's bubbly personality, bright brown eyes and toothy grin, but when she hinted toward a more serious relationship, he kindly explained he wasn't ready to settle down. Marriage just wasn't in the cards for him he confessed one night. The following day, Sarah transferred to another store thus ending any further communication.

Frank prepared lunch feeling high on his chance encounter with Maxine and Endre Jr. He decided Endre was the luckiest man on Earth, spreading a thick layer of mustard on a piece of bread, reliving his walk earlier on with Maxine and Endre Jr. Her radiant smile had touched his inner core, filling his heart with pure joy. *What I would give to have a life*...the loud phone interrupted his thoughts; the mournful cry sent him scurrying out the door.

Chapter Twenty-one

THERESA'S STOMACH FLIPPED walking up the six steps toward the microphone stationed in the middle of the auditorium stage. She was the last competitor to take her place on stage where other finalists had stood presenting their speeches, hoping to score high marks with the judges seated in the front row. She drew a deep breath in an effort to calm herself, scanning the sea of faces waiting patiently for her presentation.

The honour had been bestowed on her shortly after placing first in the classroom speech competitions, in turn, securing an opportunity to compete against other Scarborough schools for first place. She found the experience unnerving; much more traumatic than singing the second verse of Silent Night solo during the church Christmas pageant at the tender age of seven.

Breaking out in a cold sweat, her eyes searched the audience, focusing on Mr. Coulter standing at the back of the gym. Reassuringly, he nodded, smiling confidently, an injection of courage. Taking a deep breath and focusing just above peoples' heads, as he had instructed, she began, 'Judges, parents, teachers, special guests and students. My name is Theresa Rowan. The title of my speech is *My Life as a Peanut*. I had just been picked, roasted and shipped to the market…'

When she finished reciting her speech, Tommy McConnel was first on his feet, leading the audience in a standing ovation. When the applause finally stopped, one of the judges rose from her seat, turning toward the audience to announce the winner. 'A unanimous decision has been reached by all the judges; Theresa Rowan's, *My Life as a Peanut* is the winning speech of the Scarborough Public School competition finals.' She turned toward the stage. 'Congratulations, Theresa. Your speech, and presentation, was very well done.'

The audience applauded loudly as the principal, smiling proudly, presented Theresa with the coveted Scarborough Speech Honours trophy. 'This is a great honour for our school to have one of our students, not only make it to the finals, but win first place, a feat that has never occurred until today. We are very proud of you, Theresa Rowan. Congratulations,' he smiled, handing her the trophy.

At the end of the assembly, Mr. Coulter congratulated her. 'You did it kiddo. I am very proud of you. Keep up the good work and you'll go places.'

At dinner that evening, Theresa was so excited; eating was the furthest thing from her mind. 'I can't believe I won the speech competition out of all those kids. I have to admit, I almost died when it was my turn to recite it,' she added.

'We are all very proud of you,' Mom smiled.

'Yeah, it was really the best speech by far,' Tammy concurred.

Theresa discussed the forms they were given earlier in the day regarding the high school courses they could choose from. 'I've decided to take the five year Arts and Science courses. I want to be a teacher,' she said confidently.

Dad looked up from his plate. 'Sounds a little ambitious, don't you think?'

She frowned, 'not really. I've always wanted to be a teacher ever since I can remember.' She reminded him of the area of unfinished basement she used as a makeshift classroom; on a good day she was able to coax Tammy into being her student.

Dad smiled. 'Playing school is a far cry from completing the hard work and studying it takes to become a teacher. Frankly, I don't believe you're capable.'

Theresa's heart sank. The self-assurance she had felt earlier dissipated with his lack of confidence in her. It was the second time his words cut to the core. The first occurred in grade five. For nights on end, she had worked very hard to complete a project on Canada. Her hard work and effort had paid off scoring an A- on the assignment. Her father's only comment, *why didn't you get an A+?*

She said determinedly, 'I want to become a teacher. I *will* work very hard in high school to accomplish my dream.' *I will not let you dissuade me. It's my future, not yours.*

Dad placed his knife and fork neatly on the side of the plate. 'Your marks aren't good enough; your report cards throughout the years justify this. In recent years, you've barely passed. You will need to work twice as hard, studying all time, including weekends.' His eyes met hers, 'I don't believe you are scholastically capable. My recommendation would be the four year Business and Commerce course. The secretarial field is vast with new companies starting up, increasing the need for competent employees, like I'm sure you would be. Becoming a secretary will get you out of school a year earlier. You will be able to start earning a living and get on with your life. Believe me, it goes by far too quickly.'

Theresa didn't want to be a secretary. 'I *want* to be a teacher.'

Dad spoke calmly. 'You do realize after five years of high school it's on to university, then teachers' college. And even if you were to succeed, it costs money to go to university. Money I don't have, therefore, funds you would have to come up with.'

After supper, Theresa sat at her desk re-reading the five year Arts and Science forms she had completed earlier on. Her father had dashed her dream of becoming a teacher. *He seems to know what's best for me* she sighed holding back tears, tossing the completed forms into the garbage can.

The end of the school year was quickly approaching. Graduation was less than a month away. Bea suggested a trip to the Golden Mile Plaza to shop for a new dress. Theresa's eyes widened at the prospect of being able to choose a dress. Until now, Bea, handy with a sewing machine, had always made her dresses. When she outgrew them, Tammy would wear the hand-me-downs.

Saturday morning, Bea asked Tammy to join them, but she had made other plans for the day. Theresa was more than happy with her decision.

The hot sun made for a hot walk to a variety store Tammy absolutely hated. Since Lou banned her from his store, she had to clock four extra blocks for a candy fix; she was not pleased. The plaza was always busy with a Steinberg's grocery store at one end and Woolworths at the other; Saturday was by far the busiest day.

Tammy stood at the counter contemplating the chocolate bar she wanted. She was totally annoyed with this store not having bins of one cent candies; Lou's carried an extensive selection of such. She had worked tirelessly trying to convince the Italian owner it was the way to go, if he wanted to make some real money. In response, he'd throw up his hands, mumbling irritably in his native tongue.

She looked up at the security mirror in the corner of the store, watching as a woman with a squeaky voice, similar to fingernails scraping a blackboard, entered the shop demanding the owner help her find the perfect birthday card for her two-year-old grandson. Obligingly, he led her to the card section at the back of the store.

Periodically, Tammy glanced over her shoulder, exiting the busy parking lot. She broke into a run for the first few blocks slowing long enough to open a Fudge bar. Biting off a mouthful, she walked at a leisurely pace, savouring the rich chocolate. With her free hand, she felt the chocolate bars and gum stuffed down her shirt; it was the first time she had stolen anything since being caught red-handed at Lou's. Though it was sunny and hot, she felt clammy remembering that horrible day. She had never forgotten the police officer's firm grip on her shoulder, his deep authoritative voice or his black piercing eyes. Scarred shitless, she looked over her shoulder. *One can't be too careful* she concluded, tearing open a package of gum, shoving two pieces in her mouth. *Today I got away with it AND saved all my allowance.*

Tammy ran up the neighbour's driveway listening to Greg's loud voice emanating from the backyard. *He's probably laughing at one of his stupid stories that are never funny* she decided walking toward the gate. She recognized Randy, Frank and Jimmy, but could only see the back of the other guy's head. She yelled greetings to her brother, enticing the mystery guy to turn around, briefly catching a glimpse of her worst nightmare.

With Theresa in tow, Bea, in her usual take charge manner, quickly scanned the dresses, pulling six possibilities off of the rack before proceeding to the change rooms. *So much for choosing my dress for graduation* Theresa sighed, watching her mom hang them on a hook in the change room. 'Try these on, love,' she said, drawing the curtain. 'I'll see what else I can find.'

A few moments later, a small box appeared behind the curtain. 'You'll need this too,' Bea said.

The front of the box read *Young Ladies First Bra, Size AAA.* Theresa had never thought about a bra, never had too with little to fill it. She wanted to tell her mother she was comfortable wearing undershirts but decided a confrontation with her would be futile. Once Bea's mind was made up...She quickly pulled off her top and undershirt, eyeing her basically flat chest; trying to figure the best way to put the damn thing on. She was too embarrassed to ask her mom, hooking it up front then twisting it to the back, slipping her arms into the straps.

The first two dresses, one bright yellow, the other Christmas red, had full skirts with stiff crinolines that jutted the skirt away from her skinny legs. *I look like an umbrella* she decided pulling off the dress. Next, she tried on a light blue satin short sleeved dress. The bodice was plain; diamond crystals were sewn strategically on the A-line skirt portion of the dress. It fit perfectly. She stood in front of the full length mirror admiring her reflection. Surprisingly, the padded bra created the image of small breasts, filling out the bodice nicely.

Her mom returned with two more dresses. 'You can try...Oh my, don't you look smart,' she said, drawing back the curtain. 'That dress really suits you. Do you like it?'

'Yes, very much,' she smiled, secretly hoping Tommy would too.

'Well dear, if you're satisfied with that one, I'll put these back and meet you at the cash register.'

Theresa watched Mom grab a pair of short white gloves.

'These lovely sateen gloves will finish off your outfit nicely,' she said, instructing the cashier to include them with the purchase.

Theresa wanted no part of the gloves but didn't protest. She absolutely loved her new dress.

Tammy, wishing she had stashed her candy by the door rather than feel it bouncing under her shirt, marched quickly toward the group. 'Well, if it isn't Officer Giovanni. You're not a cop. You're just one of my brother's stupid asshole friends.'

Steve glanced at Greg.

'And you!' she said, turning on her brother. 'How could you do that to your own sister? Do you have any idea how petrified I was that day in Lou's thinking this creep was a real cop?'

Greg spoke sternly. 'It was for your own good, you little jerk. It was just a matter of time before you'd get caught stealing, then you'd be in real trouble.'

Tammy raised her hands in protest, unleashing the morning's haul onto the grass. Quickly, she knelt down, stuffing the loot down her top. 'I bought these this morning,' she said defensively.

Greg watched her tuck her shirt into her shorts. 'That's a strange place to put candy. Most people ask for a bag.'

'I was in a hurry. Besides, it's none of your business what I do.'

She turned toward the cop impersonator. 'And you, you freak of nature. I hate your goddamn guts,' she said, stomping off.

Steve smirked. 'Any bets the goods were stolen?'

Tammy's heart pounded dumping the loot into her drawer. 'I've got to stop...'

'Stop what?'

She hadn't heard Theresa come into the bedroom. 'Eating junk,' she said, shoving the drawer closed, running to the bathroom, slamming the door behind her.

'Tamara quit slamming the doors,' Bea said, filling the kettle for a hot cup of tea. *Little bugger.*

Chapter Twenty-two

EACH DAY BEFORE rising, Frank Armstrong whispered a silent prayer of gratitude, thanking God for the beautiful woman sleeping peacefully beside him. It took one frantic phone call that fateful day, to change his life completely.

Running out of his apartment, he had absolutely no idea what had happened until her door flew open, hysterically falling into his open arms. *Endre has left me! He walked out on me and Endre Jr. and he's never coming back. What are we going to do?* There was nothing left to do but comfort this beautiful, broken woman.

From the moment Frank met Endre, he didn't like him. Secretly he prayed this mismatched pair would one day part. With Maxine safely in his arms, his prayers had been answered. *There is a God.*

In the beginning, he spent time running back and forth between apartments until Maxine asked him to move in permanently. In an instant, his life had changed; they became inseparable. He was crazy in love with her.

Maxine, still reeling from the loss of Endre, didn't feel the same. She cared about him very much, but Endre was her first true love and the father of her son. Frank, a patient man, prayed everyday his endless love would heal her and she'd forget that no good louse.

This morning, as Endre Jr. slept soundly in the crib, Frank caressed her soft skin. Gently kissing her full lips; the love juices flowed. He had had no sexual experience and always assumed he'd die a virgin until Maxine taught him how to kiss, caress and *fuck* like a stallion.

Slithering with his touch, she hastily pulled the sheet down exposing her ample breasts he hungrily caressed and sucked. With eyes closed, she arched her back, whispering hoarsely, 'fuck me.'

Frank, delirious with lust, climbed on top and after a few short thrusts rolled onto his back. 'You are so amazing, my beautiful angel. I love you so much,' he gasped.

Maxine quickly turned onto her side; tears spotted the pink satin sheet.

After several attempts, Endre managed to convince Betty he was finished with Maxine for good. Endre Jr. was not his child and she was happily shacked up with the child's real father. Though skeptical, Betty, once again, reneged with even stricter boundaries than before. He must sleep in the basement, do all household chores, including laundry, make sure there's always plenty of food in the fridge, prepare all the meals and take care of the children while she was at work. Should any of these obligations not be fulfilled he would be shown the door for good.

Endre willingly worked very hard to appease her, hoping one day they could all be a family again.

Though there were still issues to be settled with his moving company, Endre's lawyer had countersued his brother, Etika, for total control of the company. With a little more finagling, his lawyer had promised he would be back at the helm by the end of the month.

Endre prepared lunch for the kids then poured himself a cup of coffee. Sipping the hot brew, he contented himself with the knowledge his life had finally taken a turn for the better and no one could screw it up.

Maxine spoke gently to Endre Jr., buttoning his sweater. 'We have to go see the doctor today to make sure you are growing up big and strong,' she smiled, tying his little shoes. 'But Dr. Fitzgerald is on sick leave so we have to go see his colleague, Dr. Cassie, my little angel.' The baby cooed, smiling happily. 'I hope this doctor is a nice man,' she said, picking up the happy baby boy. 'I want nothing but the best for my little darling.' She kissed his cheek loudly, sending the child into fits of laughter. 'I love you so much, Endre Jr,' she said, cuddling him tightly.

Frank's eyes welled with tears watching Maxine bond with her baby, silently praying one day she would share the same bond with his child, their child.

Dr. Cassie's office was crowded to capacity with young and old. Frank walked Maxine to the only available black vinyl chair on the other side of the waiting room. 'Honey, you sit while I check in with the receptionist.' He waited patiently watching the woman write on a folder.

'Can I help you,' she said, placing the folder aside.

'Yes, I'm here with my wife and son, although they aren't really my wife and son,' he said jokingly. 'But I hope to change that...'

'May I have the name, please,' Betty interrupted impatiently. The office had been in total chaos when she arrived early this morning and the last thing she needed was another yappy individual droning on.

'Sorry, I do get carried away sometimes. His name is Endre Jr.,' he smiled proudly. 'Herczeg is the last name, but I'm not sure how to spell it. It should be on your list because my wife, I mean my girlfriend, booked it last month with Dr. Fitzgerald, who's away on sick leave.'

Betty didn't hear anything after Herczeg. She sat paralyzed staring at the list of patients. With the office so busy, she hadn't had a chance to read the roster the nurse had prepared. Invariably, she would have read the list upon arrival and pulled the files, but the patients were already lined up waiting at the door when she arrived. Silently, she cursed Dr. Fitzgerald.

Betty took a deep breath. 'I'm sorry, what did you say your name was?'

Frank broke into an accommodating smile. 'Oh, the appointment isn't for me, I'm Frank Armstrong. I'm just accompanying little Endre Jr., that's who the appointment's for. His mother is Maxine Carlson.' He leaned in closer. 'She chose to give Endre Jr. the last name Herczeg after his biological father, who between you and me is a nothing but a scoundrel for deserting her and his son. The cad has a whole other family; a wife and three kids. I'd sure like to meet his wife. She's a total fool for taking him back.'

Betty's face paled feeling the walls closing in around her.

'Are you okay, lady? You look like you could use a doctor yourself,' Frank said sympathetically.

She picked up the folder, fanning her face rapidly. 'Please, have a seat until the nurse calls your name.' Frantically, she waved Alice over to cover the desk.

Betty splashed cold water on her face, desperately wanting a glimpse of Endre Jr. without his mother knowing. She stuck her head out the washroom eyeing Mary, the doctor's nurse, exiting an examining room. She frantically waved her over.

Mary was more than willing to assist her good friend. 'Go wait in the supply room and I'll join you shortly.'

Maxine held the baby close to her chest, following the nurse to the examination room. 'He's still asleep,' she whispered, entering the room.

Mary was all business. 'We have to weigh him before the doctor examines him.'

Maxine protested. 'But he's asleep. It's his morning nap time,' she said, cuddling him closer.

'I promise I won't disturb him. It's actually easier to weigh and measure babies when they're asleep, less fuss for everyone,' she half smiled, extending her arms.

Reluctantly, Maxine handed over Endre Jr. 'Where are you going? Can I come too?' she said, following her to door.

'I'm afraid not,' she said, possessively holding the child. 'The scales are located in a room down the hall. Dr. Cassie likes to keep the hallway clear of patients; makes it easier to move from one examination room to another. This will only take a moment I assure you.'

Betty's nerves were so frazzled she jumped when the door opened. 'Mary, I can't thank you enough for doing...' stopping mid-sentence she stared wide-eyed at the sleeping bundle.

Mary saw the horrified look on her face. 'Christ, Betty, you look like you've just seen a ghost.'

Frantically, Betty searched her handbag for her wallet; flipping through some photos she removed one and handed it to Mary.

'Oh my god! How did you get a picture of this baby?' she whispered, studying the photo.

Betty's throat ached, her voice barely audible. 'It's a photo of my son, Charlie, when he was this age.'

Mary returned Endre Jr. to his mother. 'Your son weighs 14 pounds and is 26" long. He's such a good little baby he slept the whole time.'

Maxine beamed. 'He's a really good sleeper now,' she said, cuddling the baby tightly.

Mary smiled confidently. She knew from years of experience new moms loved to talk about their baby; Maxine was no exception. 'I can tell by how happy you are motherhood agrees with you.'

Maxine looked up from her sleeping son. 'I never thought I could love anyone as much as this little angel, other than his father, of course. But sadly, his real daddy, Endre, that's who I named Endre Jr. after, left us to fend for ourselves. Didn't he, my little pumpkin,' she said, kissing the baby's forehead. She focused on Mary. 'Can you imagine anyone abandoning their own son? I thought Endre would be the best dad in the world; he already has three children. Instead, he decided he wanted to go back to his family, even after his wife kicked him out. I assume she took him back because he hasn't even come to visit him,' she said, tearing up. 'He tried to pay me off, like I was some kind of bimbo just looking for money. He's willing to sacrifice time with his son with a monthly allowance. Can you believe a man would sink that low?' Tears streamed down her cheeks. 'But the truth is I don't want his money. I want him. I still love him with all my heart. Secretly I keep praying his wife will come to her senses and kick him out. He would come back to us, I know it. Then we can be a family, right sweetheart,' she said, watching the baby stir.

Mary found Betty sitting in the supply room. Closing the door behind her, she sat down across from her friend, reaching for her hand.

It was later than usual when Betty pulled into the driveway. She sat numbly staring at nothing. The remainder of the day had been a slow moving blur after Mary disclosed Maxine's verbatim. The temptation to drive off and not look back was overwhelming.

'Mommy! You're home! Daddy made max and cheezes,' Charlie said, running to the door, wrapping his chubby arms around her legs.

She ran her hand through his soft blond hair, holding back bitter tears. 'That's good, sweetheart. You go back to the table and finish your supper now while Mommy gets changed.'

Betty sat listlessly on the edge of the bed. The knock on the door made her jump.

'May I come in?' Endre said, hoping soon he wouldn't have to knock.

She continued staring at the floor. 'Close the door behind you,' she said tonelessly.

A concerned look crossed his face. 'Betty, what's the matter? Are you alright? Did something happen at work?'

She stood mere inches from his face. 'You lying, fucking, bastard. Yes, something happened at work. The mother of your love child arrived at the office this morning with your son, Endre Jr. Herczeg.'

He shrugged like it was an everyday occurrence. 'So?'

Betty's eyes widened at his off-handedness. 'Is that all you can say? It was your son, Endre Jr., named after his father, who just happens to be you.'

He held up his hands defensively. 'Betty, I told you before he is not my…'

'Stop! Stop right now!' she said angrily, briefly closing her eyes. 'He is your son, you lying cheat. One of my co-workers had a lengthy conversation with the child's mother and she didn't hold back anything, including how you paid her off, absolving yourself of any responsibility.' She paused, rubbing her temples in an effort to thwart a migraine. 'Ironically, even after all your mistreatment your mistress still loves you. Secretly she prays I'll come to my senses and kick your sorry ass out the door into her loving, waiting arms.'

Endre wanted desperately to hold Betty and console her. 'There's no proof that the baby is mine,' he said reassuringly.

'To hell there isn't!' Betty turned, dumping the contents of her purse onto the bed. Her hands trembled uncontrollably opening her black leather wallet. 'Your baby looks exactly like Charlie. So much so, they could pass for twins,' she said, shoving the photo in his face. 'I saw Endre Jr. with my own eyes.'

Endre felt his insides cave. Everything he had done in an effort to get his life back on track had been futile. Despondently, he handed the photo back to her.

'Take it with you.'

Chapter Twenty-Three

WITH LESS THAN three days before graduation, Theresa had mixed feelings of excitement and melancholy. She was excited about graduating into high school, melancholy she'd be leaving her teachers and friends throughout the years. But it was Tommy's impending departure to Edmonton that would be the most difficult change in her life. Over the past few months, they had become great friends spending as much time together as possible.

Tammy ran into the bedroom. 'Someone's here to see you,' she said mischievously.

Theresa wasn't in the mood for her sister's silly antics. 'Just tell me who it is,' she said, doing up her blouse.

'I'm not going to tell you, because I was told not to,' she said defensively, getting shoved out of the way.

Daniel waited in the carport in anticipation. He was up from Vermont visiting his mother and wanted to surprise Theresa.

He was finding it awkward staying at the cramped apartment; his mother, still reeling from the divorce, was much more clingy, bombarding him with questions about his home since his arrival. He had hoped she would find someone to share her life with, but foolishly she remained steadfast to the selfish prick. *I married your father for life and no one can or will ever take his place.* It was truly an old fashioned way of thinking, wasting precious time on someone who couldn't reciprocate. She was still attractive at thirty-five and young enough to find another man to treat her better.

'Daniel!' Theresa said, charging out the screen door. 'I had no idea it was you.' She ran into his open arms. He hugged her tightly, uniting the past, reluctant to let go.

'You look fabulous,' he smiled broadly. 'And taller, that's for sure,' he said, doing a quick measurement. 'But not as tall as me,' he smiled, indicating the difference with his finger and thumb.

Theresa noticed a change in him too. He seemed much more adult than awkward teenager. She led him toward the gate. 'We need to get away from prying eyes and ears,' she whispered, watching Tammy scoot away from the door.

'Yeah, I know what you mean. My little sister is always watching me. It's like having another mother at times.'

'How is your mom?' Theresa said, sitting down on a green and white striped vinyl chair.

He shrugged. 'I think she's doing okay. She's pretty lonely, but coping.' He thought of their conversation this morning before he left. *Where are you going? When will you be back? Shall I prepare lunch?* 'Ever since I arrived, she won't leave me alone,' he added.

Theresa felt sorry for her. 'I can understand that. You are her son and it must be very difficult for her with you and your sister living in the States.'

He shrugged. 'I guess. She's got a nice little apartment down in the Beaches overlooking Lake Ontario.'

She could tell by the look on his face and the tone of his voice there was something more going on. 'Is Dana visiting too?'

'No. My father won't let her visit Mom.'

Theresa's eyes widened. 'How does your mom feel about that?'

'I'm sure she hates it.'

Theresa didn't know too much about laws governing such cases but assumed it can't be right to keep a mother from her kids. 'Doesn't your mom have any legal rights in regards to seeing her own kids?'

Daniel sighed deeply. 'Probably, but you don't know my father. Hell, I don't even know the bastard. He claims my mother isn't fit mentally because she cries on the phone whenever she speaks to Dana. He doesn't want her lack of self-control rubbing off on his daughter. All Mom wants is her kids,' he said sadly. 'She's a very lonely woman who needs to find someone else.'

Theresa felt sorry for Daniel, changing the conversation. 'So, how is life in the States?'

He half smiled. 'Shitty, but I'm coping. Once I finish school, I'm going to join the army, get as far away from my asshole father and his so-called wife.'

Theresa was hoping for a more positive response. 'What is she like?' She couldn't begin to imagine another woman filling her mother's role.

Daniel shifted on the chair. 'All she's really good at is spending my father's money, which he readily gives her, I might add. I'm sure he does it to appease her and wouldn't dare stop or say anything to upset her. I believe he has this great fear she'll fly the coop, which I'm sure she will eventually.' He smiled confidently. 'She takes off whenever she pleases with girlfriends, so she says, on weekly trips. As smart as my father thinks he is, he hasn't figured out she's probably dicking around on him. If he has, he's choosing to turn the other cheek; he's crazy about the stupid bimbo.'

'Is she pretty?'

Daniel sighed, concluding it must be a girl thing. 'You sound like my mom. She's always asking me silly questions about her.'

Theresa shrugged, 'Sorry, it's a girl thing.'

Daniel said, 'Don't be. To be honest, I have never really looked at her that closely. I only talk to her when I have to and try my damnedest not to. Usually, when she's around, I take off.'

Theresa smiled earnestly. 'What else have you been up to? Have you heard from Ronald?' In all the years she had known Daniel, she had never noticed his intense emerald green eyes.

'I've been corresponding back and forth with Ronald.' He didn't mention how thankful he had been that Dana had picked up Ronald's crumpled address or he would have lost all contact with his best friend. 'He hates his new life with his stepmother. He calls her the bitch from hell. Apparently, she's his father's right arm, especially when he's away, which is most of the time. He was flunking out at school but is buckling down so he can move out after high school.'

Theresa was very perceptive where Daniel was concerned and felt he was hiding something. 'Okay, what's really going on? I bet it's got something to do with a girl.'

Half smiling, his face reddened.

'Oh my god, you've got a girlfriend! That's what this is about. Who is she?'

He had never been good at keeping anything from her. They had always been so close; he could talk to her about anything; she had the uncanny ability to see right through him at times, today was no different. He shrugged, 'just a girl.'

She gave him a friendly shove, repeating his admission. 'Should I be jealous?' On the contrary, she was very happy for him. They had always been good friends, turning to each other often.

He was flattered by her response. 'Are you kidding? No one could ever come close to you,' he said adamantly.

She asked if he had met her at his new school in Vermont.

'No. I met her here a few days ago. She's a friend's sister.'

Theresa furrowed her brow. 'You met her just recently. Is she pretty? How old is she?'

Daniel shook his head, 'All these questions. You're such a nosey parker. She's the same age as you; not as pretty, of course.'

His admission perked her curiosity. 'Does she live around here? Better yet, do I know her?'

He held up his hands, halting the onslaught of questions. 'Now it's my turn to ask questions. What's been happening since I moved away? Have you got a boyfriend?'

She glanced at the ring Debbie had given her last Christmas, briefly thinking of Edson.

'Is there some lucky guy I should know about?'

'No. Tommy and I are good friends,' she smiled.

Daniel raised a questioning brow trying to read her expression, hoping it wasn't serious. 'How close?'

She felt a brief tug at her heart thinking of Tommy's pending move at the end of June. 'We're just good friends, Daniel, nothing more.'

'So there's no need to feel jealous,' he said, glancing at his watch. 'I'm afraid I have to get going.'

Theresa smiled wickedly. 'Meeting your secret love?'

Daniel pulled her to her feet. 'As always, it was so good seeing you. I'm really glad you took the time to see me.' *You have no idea how much I've missed you.*

'Daniel, I'd always make time for you, you know that. Even if it's only a short visit,' she said, pouty faced.

The truth was he didn't want to leave her. He really enjoyed being with her; nothing had changed in all the years he'd known her. 'I have to go now, can I write you?'

Theresa smiled warmly. 'Of course,' she said, hugging him tightly. 'You are such a good friend, Daniel.'

'I love you,' he whispered before running off.

On Graduation Day, the graduating classes had the afternoon off to prepare for the ceremony and class photos, beginning at six sharp.

Bea prepared an early supper that Theresa wanted no part.

'I'm sorry, Mom. I'm just not hungry at all.' With all the excitement her stomach was in a tight knot and had been most of the day.

Bea glanced at Theresa's plateful of good food and with a brisk tut excused her from the table.

'She's just really excited, Mom. That's all,' Tammy said, coming to her defence. 'It's a big time of it for her. I'll probably feel the same way when I graduate so don't make me any supper,' she said, counting the years on her fingers.

Theresa stood in front of the full length mirror hanging on the back of the cupboard door admiring her dress. She had never dressed so stylish and truly felt on top of the world.

'Wow! Don't you look smart, Dad cooed. 'We've got a new roll of film loaded in the camera ready to go. Also, this is for you,' he said, handing her a small neatly wrapped gift. 'It's just a little something for your graduation from Mom and me.'

Theresa wasn't expecting a gift. Her parents had made it very clear her new graduation outfit set them back more than they had budgeted. She opened the package hoping for a ring, necklace or bracelet to mark the occasion; similar to grad gifts her friends had received.

Reluctantly, she pasted a smile on her face staring at the sky blue case. *Who the hell gives their kid a travelling alarm clock?* 'Thank you Mom and Dad. It was very thoughtful.'

It was a beautiful, warm evening. The students gathered on the lawn outside the school for their graduating class photos. The photographer decided to use the school's red brick wall as a backdrop, instructing shorter students to sit on the benches upfront, taller kids to stand on the benches behind. Everyone was in a jovial mood. The photo session was completed quickly without incident. The kids and parents moved inside for the graduation ceremony, followed by dancing and homemade snacks.

It was no surprise the students grew restless during the seemingly endless speeches and awards. The principal, promising to be brief, offered a few congratulatory words then concluded the ceremony. He held up his hand silencing the exuberant crowd. 'It's time for anyone *not* graduating, including me, to exit the auditorium. It seems there's going to be some serious dancing going on.'

Theresa waited until her parents left then stuffed her silly white gloves Mom insist she wear, into her beaded purse placing it on the bench beside the knitted shawl her mother had made.

Though it was a lovely gesture, she doubted she would ever use it. *It looks like something grandma would use* and contemplated giving it to her.

Rubbing her sweaty palms together, Theresa moved toward the refreshment table and filled a glass with orange punch, listening to the group of girls talking animatedly at the other end of the table. Focusing on the back of one girl standing a head taller than her adoring audience; Theresa almost choked on her punch as she turned toward the table, reaching for a chocolate brownie.

The transformation of insecure, shy, homely Lynda was nothing less than spectacular. Her rich black hair was piled high on her head, secured in place with a dark purple clip, a perfect match to her stunning velvet empire waist dress, complimenting her full figure. More like a Hollywood starlet than graduating senior, she stood regal and tall. The scant makeup she wore highlighted her high cheekbones; the eye shadow complimented her sparking green eyes; she radiated confidence and maturity, unlike the gaggle of girls surrounding her.

Elaine gushed enviously, 'Oh Lynda, you're so lucky. What's your new boyfriend's name?'

Theresa watched her bright white smile widen, relishing the moment.

'Daniel,' she sighed deeply.

Theresa jumped when she felt the gentle touch on her arm.

'T, what's up?' Tommy said, studying her face. 'Are you okay? You look like you've just seen a Martian or something.'

She forced a smile, trying desperately to hear what Lynda was saying. 'I'm fine.'

Music blared from the auditorium. 'You promised me a dance,' Tommy coaxed. He looked so handsome in his dark brown suit, beige shirt and brown striped tie.

She held up her glass, 'just having a little refreshment.'

He smiled, 'I'll wait with you.'

Damn. She had to get rid of him somehow. 'Oh look, there's Johnny trying to get your attention.' She waved in his direction. 'You go talk to him while I finish this,' she said, reaching for a chocolate wafer.

He smiled warmly. 'Don't be long, T. I really want to dance with my best girl.'

Theresa, hoping she hadn't missed too much of the conversation, nonchalantly stood behind Elaine, leaning in closer, listening to Lynda speak in hushed tones. 'We had sex.'

The girls gasped in unison, clamping their hands over their mouths. Lynda waved frantically to shush them, filling in the details of her first sexual encounter with Daniel.

Carol whispered. 'Weren't you worried about getting pregnant?'

Lynda rolled her big eyes toward the ceiling. 'Thank goodness I got my period the day after. But Daniel told me he loves me. I'm positive if I *had* gotten pregnant, he would marry me. I love him so much. I just wished he didn't live in Vermont. We could have more sex,' she smiled wickedly. 'We promised to write back and forth every week.' Lynda crossed her fingers with a dazzling smile. 'Hopefully, he'll give me a promise ring when I visit him during summer vacation. Then when I finish high school we can get married. I'll invite all of you to the wedding,' she gushed.

Theresa moved hurriedly through the group of kids standing near the exit. Met with a blast of cool air, she regretted not fetching the shawl. Even the stupid white gloves would provide some warmth. She rubbed her arms briskly walking across the grassy field; her kitten heals sinking, slowing her movement.

So Lynda is Daniel's mystery girlfriend. She was puzzled by the secrecy when she had plied him for answers during his impromptu visit. *Was it the impending sex or the need to protect Lynda's reputation?* She wondered if Daniel really loved Lynda or said so just to have sex. She had heard that guys will do that just to score. *He did whisper he loved me…*

'There you are,' Tommy said, startling her. 'I've been looking all over for you. Why pray tell are you standing out here all by yourself in the cool night air? I doubt your gorgeous blue dress offers much warmth,' he said, removing his jacket, draping it over her shoulders.

She thanked him, instantly feeling the warmth from his body, slipping her arms in the sleeves. 'I have a question. Do all guys want to have sex?'

Tommy reeled back, 'I don't know. I mean I guess so. I have to admit, I've sort of thought about it.'

She raised her left brow. 'Have you ever had sex?'

One thing about Theresa Rowan, you never knew what she's going to say next. 'T, what's gotten into you?'

She could tell by the way he scrunched his face he wasn't impressed. The truth was she was trying to justify Daniel's liaison with her fellow classmate, make it alright somehow, because this is what guys do. 'Well, have you?'

Persistence was one of the things he liked most about her. He slowly shook his head. 'I haven't.'

Oddly, she felt a sense of relief knowing Tommy hadn't gone where Daniel obviously had. The real truth was, she knew very little about sex and hoped Tommy could shed some light on the subject. 'I need you to tell me exactly what sex is?'

Tommy's eyes widened. 'Geez T, hasn't your mom ever discussed this stuff with you?'

Theresa thought of the *Growing Up and liking it* booklet her mother insisted she read about getting a period every month and which sanitary napkin is the best. 'I read a booklet my mom gave me from cover to cover about menstruation, but there was nothing in it about sex.'

By no means was he an expert on the subject. He had basic knowledge, following a discussion with Mac, regarding matters of the anatomy and what to do with it, but felt odd having this conversation with Theresa. 'T, I suggest you talk to your mom,' he said encouragingly.

She tilted her head to one side. 'If you had sex with a girl, would you tell her you love her?'

Tommy chuckled, 'If I was having sex with a girl, it would be *because* I love her. That's usually how it's done, or at least how I would go about it. It's a celebration of a couple's love for each other,' he added, remembering his dad's advice.

Theresa wrinkled her nose. 'Do some guys have sex with girls even if they don't love them?'

At times she was so naïve, something he found very attractive about her. He smiled and shrugged, 'Yeah, there are some guys who would.'

She looked him in the eye. 'Would you?'

Until now, it was something he hadn't thought about. 'Probably not.'

'Probably not,' she repeated emphatically. 'You mean there's a chance you would say you love a girl just to have sex with her?'

Tommy gently placed his hands on her shoulders. 'T, I have no idea what this is about. And I'm not sure I want to know,' he added. 'Personally, I would want to be madly in love with the girl before having sex with her.'

She pecked him on the lips, reaching for his hand. 'Come on, let's go dance.'

The dimly lit auditorium was a mass of sweaty, stale perfumed bodies swaying back and forth to the heady music until the disc jockey announced *Love Me Tender* was the last song of the night. Tommy and Theresa held each other tightly; wishing the song would never end.

That night in bed, Theresa thought of her graduation. Other than finding out, in a roundabout way, namely eavesdropping, that Daniel was Lynda's mainstay, she had enjoyed herself immensely. She decided Daniel had always been and would always be just a friend, no matter what he whispered in her ear.

Tommy on the other hand, she would miss very much. She had grown quite fond of him in recent months but knew it wasn't love. Her feelings for Tommy were nowhere near what she had felt for Edson, her first true love.

On moving day, the neighbours gathered to say good-bye to the McConnel clan. Through tears and laughter, people shared their memories while the movers filled a huge moving truck with the family's furniture and belongings. It soon became apparent; the Crescent would never be the same.

Mac, overwhelmed by such sincerity, was moved to tears as he walked around his backyard one last time. He had purposely left his navy and white striped 'margarita' canvas chair in the middle of the yard, marking the occasions he had spent hot summer evenings listening to Caribbean music and counting his blessing until dawn. He decided long ago, the symbolic chair should remain part of the landscape, making it available for anyone wanting to sit and count their blessings.

Tommy gently grabbed Theresa's arm, leading her away from the crowd to the side of the house. 'I have something for you,' he said, handing her a white envelope. 'I hope you'll see the humour in it,' he smiled, hugging her tightly, whispering in her ear. 'I will be back for you, I promise.'

Tears stung Theresa's eyes watching the McConnel station wagon drive away. Over the past year, Tommy had become a good friend; someone she could depend on, with a wicked sense of humour. She knew she would really miss him, sitting down on Mac's old canvas chair, opening the envelope. Unfolding the neatly written letter, a photo of Tommy and the Gentle Giant, standing side by side, grinning from ear to ear fell onto her lap.

Dear T,

Before you get all angry with me for having this picture taken with this amazing man, there's a reasonable explanation. (There always is).

I'm sure you recall our great time at the CNE last summer. (I still think you should have brought Buttons home with you. After all you won him fair and square. Well done, by the way).

I know you weren't keen on seeing the sideshows, and to be honest, neither was I. But, you know me. I figured what the heck and basically found the whole experience fascinating, hence this photo marking a memorable occasion.

The Gentle Giant's name is Maurice and his wife's name is Mary. (Talk about opposites attracting. He is over seven feet, eight inches tall; she a mere three foot six inches. They met for the same reasons, in that they had both been shunned from 'normal' society because of their physical appearance. Needless to say, steady employment had always been unattainable until a carnival man offered them food and shelter in return for a life on the road with the travelling fair. I was amazed at all the places they've travelled to, including most of Europe, China and Japan. T, they are really nice, happy, friendly people, not like the sad people they portray for their audiences. (Maurice confided in me, it's all an act to get people, including me, to feel sorry for them and have a picture taken. He said most people fall for it every time). The good news is all the picture proceeds go directly in Maurice and Mary's pocket.

Maurice and Mary take it all in stride; he doesn't want any sympathy, this is what he does for a living. He said if he was a comedian on stage in Vegas, people would just laugh and enjoy the show. Instead they stare out into the crowd; hopefully have a picture taken and move on. He claims there's not any difference at all; just a different career path.

In the end, I'm so glad I had a photo taken with him. T, I learned a very valuable lesson that day and wanted to share it with you, my best girl.

Love always, Tommy

PS You have to admit, we could pass for brothers.

Theresa couldn't help but smile. Through tears she whispered, *Tommy McConnel, you are a giant of a man.*

Chapter Twenty-Four

MAXINE MOVED PROMPTLY toward the door, 'what did you forget...' Her heart skipped a beat, her smile disappeared. 'What are you doing here?'

Endre continued smiling, 'It's good to see you too. Is the boyfriend here?'

She looked at him indignantly. 'His name is Frank, and no, he just left for work.'

'Good, may I come in then?'

Her first inclination to slam the door in his face morphed into curiosity. *Why after all this time?* She looked him in the eye. 'I'm surprised you didn't let yourself in. I presume you still have your key,' she said sarcastically, sauntering toward the couch.

He sat down across from her, admiring her alluring beauty and voluptuous figure. 'You look wonderful,' he said seductively.

Maxine felt her face warm. 'Endre Jr. keeps me on the go.'

'How is he?'

'I suppose you mean your son. He's fine, growing like a weed.'

'With a beautiful mother like you, it's no surprise.'

Maxine's eyes widened slightly, but she wasn't going to fall for his smooth talk, not this time. 'Endre, why are you here?' she said frostily.

He knew she was putty in his hands, always has been, always will be. Some women are just like that; Maxine was no different. He wasted no time persuading her to let him come back into their lives. 'I want to come back to you and our son. We can be a family.' He said with such sincerity she felt an instant high. For so long, she had wished and prayed for these words.

Remorsefully he continued. 'I know I haven't treated you kindly,' he said, pausing for effect. 'I want to change all that and make it up to you, and our son. All I need is a chance to make everything right. I promise you, you won't be disappointed.' He sat back watching her digest his plea, undressing her in his mind, yearning for their amazing sex life. 'So what do you say, my *kis szepseg*?'

Little beauty, she felt a warm inner glow as he flashed his sexy, dimpled smile. Feeling in control, she sat taller knowing, like old times, he was focusing on her bounty. 'Why the change of heart, Endre?'

He knew exactly how to manipulate her. Looking her in the eye he tenderly said, 'I need to be here with you, *kis szepseg*. I have missed you.' *Not to mention fucking that luscious body of yours.* He kept Betty's harsh directive to leave and never come back and the fact he had nowhere else to go under wraps; it was none of her business. *In the next few minutes I'll be getting laid* he thought wickedly, eyeing the luscious tits she casually thrust forward. He said confidently, 'I'm back to make a new life with someone who cares about me.'

Maxine knew he was putty in her hands by the hungry look on his face. *But why the sudden change of heart?* 'Did your wife kick you out again?' She truly wanted to believe his sincerity. 'How do I know you will keep your word and not run back?'

Endre chuckled. 'My dear, that won't happen.' He sighed heavily. 'I come from a family that has washed their hands of me. Now, what do you say, *kis szepseg*. Do *you* want me back?' He smiled inwardly knowing her answer.

Maxine tossing her head back, unable to contain her excitement, was finally going to have it all at last. A husband she loved with all her heart, a child and a house in the suburbs; a dream she had had all her life. 'Can we have more children?' she asked, moving toward him.

He swiftly pulled the sweater over her head, hungrily sucking and caressing her luscious breasts. 'We can have a house full,' he said, yanking her pants down.

Maxine lay back on the couch. 'You have made me the happiest woman on Earth, Endre,' she said, spreading her legs wide.

The kids had become uncooperative little brats since Betty banished Endre from their lives. Anxiously she dropped them off at school, driving quickly to the doctor's office. Today would be the fourth day in a row she'd be late for work; her tardiness hadn't gone unnoticed.

'Late again,' Doctor Cassie said curtly, watching his disheveled receptionist fling her jacket over the back of her chair, plunking herself down on it.

'Young lady, don't sit down. I need you to locate Alice Wicker's file,' he said, intentionally slamming the file cabinet drawer. 'I'm not used to retrieving the files I need,' he said sternly. 'I didn't graduate med school to become a file clerk. Have it on my desk ASAP.'

Red faced and dry mouthed Betty searched for the file. When Endre lived at the house she was never late. She would arrive early, organize patient files and enjoy a leisurely coffee long before the doctor's arrival. She made a silent vow to arrive earlier from now on, placing the requested file on his desk, quietly closing the door behind her.

Unsurprisingly, Betty's evenings weren't much better. She was thankful Renee was next door, but lately she'd began complaining it was becoming too much having the kids at her house every day after school. Supper preparation had turned into a nightmare; the kids griped constantly about whatever she put in front of them, unless it was hot dogs.

It was close to 9:30 by the time she managed to get the kitchen cleaned up, lunches made and the kids into bed. Bedtime had its share of bedlam too. It seemed everyone wanted to use the bathroom at the same time; screaming matches between the two older kids were not uncommon.

She sat down heavily on the chesterfield, massaging her temples, warding off a migraine (her headaches had returned with a vengeance since Endre's exile). She placed her head on the back of the couch; contemplating another load of laundry before a much needed shower.

Sharon moved quietly down the stairs eyeing her mother asleep with her head resting on the back of the chesterfield. Her mom looked so peaceful she debated waking her but she desperately needed to talk to her, without the others around.

'Mom,' she whispered close to her ear.

'Huh,' Betty sat upright. 'I must have fallen asleep. Is something wrong, dear?' she said apprehensively, glancing at the wall clock. 'It's 10:30. Why aren't you asleep?'

Sharon, a precocious eleven year old with brilliant green eyes and long straight black hair was a younger version of her mother.

Shortly after her sixth birthday, she developed the habit of fiercely rubbing her fingertips together mere inches from her face. Her parents were concerned and baffled by this often annoying gesture and were quick to assume their daughter was anxious or stressed. As any doting parents would do, they sought medical advice. After numerous tests it was determined Sharon was destined to use this harmless exercise to help her concentrate on what she was going to say. Tonight was no different confronting her mother. 'I need to talk to you, about Daddy.'

Betty felt the tension in her neck and head return as her daughter's hands dropped to her sides. 'Sharon, we've been down this path a few too many times. Countless times I have explained the situation, which is not going to change, to you and your brothers. Your father has a child with another woman and it's time for him to take responsibility for his actions.'

She watched Sharon's fingers get in motion. 'What about his responsibilities to this family? He has three kids here that need him.'

Betty moved her head slowly from side to side trying to get the kink out of her neck. Sharon had matured so much, more so lately it seemed. 'Your father pays the bills and that's what matters most.'

'Maybe to you, but I miss Daddy so much,' she said, rubbing with her fingers intensely. 'I want him to come home to *our* family.'

Betty massaged her temples. 'It's getting late, dear. I have to go to work tomorrow and you have school.'

Sharon flung her hands behind her back, clasping her hands. 'Are you going to ask Daddy to come back home or am I?'

Betty was taken aback by her daughter's obstinacy. 'I don't want your father back in this house, ever, and that's final.'

Sharon placed her hands on her hips. 'I think you're jealous of the other woman and that's the reason he isn't here,' she said with a confident smirk.

'That's not true at all. He fathered another child and he needs to take on the responsibility, something that you obviously don't understand.'

Sharon, unable to hold back the tears said, 'I understand that you are the one breaking up our family, not Daddy. I hate you,' she sobbed, running up the stairs.

Theresa waited until everyone was out of the house before approaching her mother.

'What is it you want to talk to me about,' Mom said, filling the kettle with cold water.

Theresa sat down at the kitchen table. 'Sex.'

Mom plugged in the kettle. 'Did you read the booklet I gave you, dear? It explains everything,' she said a little too curtly.

She had reread the book many times. It described menstruation, puberty and what size sanitary napkin to wear, but nothing about sex. She watched her mom busy herself at the sink. She was beginning to wonder if sex was a taboo subject where her mother was concerned and decided to seek advice elsewhere.

Endre wasted no time getting Maxine in the sack; fondling and kissing her, his need to make love urgent until Endre Jr. wailed. Hearing the baby's cries she moved out from under him. 'You are going to have to wait your turn,' she said, picking up the child, hugging him tightly. 'Daddy has to learn to wait, doesn't he? You're always number one,' she cooed, changing his soiled nappy.

An overpowering fecal smell permeated the bedroom. 'Jesus Christ,' he said, throwing back the sheet.

'Where are you going?' she said, watching him grab his underwear.

'I need a drink,' he said, swallowing a gag.

Frank sat alone in Ben's apartment thinking about Maxine and the baby. A few weeks ago he had been on top of the world with his new family. Today, he sat staring at the four walls of his co-worker's unit bewildered and depressed, constantly reliving the moment his life fell apart.

He had worked his lunch hour in order to leave an hour earlier to be with Maxine and Endre Jr. On the way home, he purchased a large bouquet of flowers then literally ran home to his family. As soon he entered the apartment he sensed something was amiss. Lately, she had gotten into the routine of greeting him at the door with a hug and kiss. Today, she sat on the chesterfield with the forlorn look he hadn't seen for quite some time. The flowers he had carefully chosen were more of an irritant than a thoughtful gesture, watching her place them on the table without incident.

He took a seat across from her, feeling his insides cave with every word. *I'll get right to the point. Endre came by today. He wants to come back to me and Endre Jr. so we can be a real family. I know this is hard for you Frank, but I've never stopped loving Endre. He is the father of my child and he wants to be his Daddy. I'm so sorry, Frank, but this is my dream come true. I want to begin a family life with Endre.*

Without a word, Frank packed his belongings and left her apartment with nowhere to go. (Confident their relationship would last forever; he had sublet his apartment shortly after moving in with her). Fortunately, Ben, a co-worker, had a spare room he could use until he got settled elsewhere.

Reliving that horrible day, he wished he had spoken up about Endre, the no-good cad. He was certain the bastard would leave her again. Creeps like him are takers not givers.

Just before leaving, he tucked a note in Maxine's housecoat pocket.

Endre swung the cupboard door open, reaching for the bottle of scotch where he'd left it. He was tempted to pour a good shot, but decided one drink would suffice to take off the ediness; reaching for the shot glass tucked away in the back corner. He read the note tucked inside. *My beautiful Maxine, I love you with all my heart. I will always be there for you. Call me anytime. Frank xo.* Endre studied the phone number before crumpling it into a ball.

'There's Daddy,' Maxine said, walking toward him. 'What's that?' She asked curiously, realizing too late it was the note Frank had given her. Her heart ached watching him toss it into the garbage can.

'You don't need to keep that pining asshole's number,' he said, swigging his drink. He reached for his son, but the little guy wanted no part of his dad, wailing in protest. 'What's the matter? Don't you know who I am,' Endre said, in a sarcastic tone, handing him back to his mother.

Maxine smiled warmly hugging the child, calming him immediately. 'He's been acting shy with strangers lately.'

Endre grabbed his glass off the counter. 'He'll get to know me better,' he said, moving toward the bedroom.

Maxine quickly retrieved Frank's note, stuffing it in the bottom of the diaper bag.

Betty unlocked the front door setting off a free-for-all; the boys ran into the living room fighting over which television show to watch. Sharon ran full tilt up the stairs to her bedroom, slamming the door so hard the hall mirror convulsed. She had not spoken to her mother for over a week. Needless to say, what little patience Betty had, dissipated with the slamming of the door. She placed the bags of groceries on the kitchen table, walked into the living room and turned off the television.

'From now on, when I get home from work, you are to go to your rooms and do your homework.'

Danny watched the screen blacken. 'What if we don't have any homework,' he said belligerently.

'You can read,' she said impatiently. 'Now move it.'

She followed the boys upstairs. 'And don't slam the door.'

After a quick, forceful knock, Betty swung Sharon's door open and sat down on her unmade bed. 'We need to have a talk,' she said firmly. 'This has gone on long enough.'

'I don't want to talk to you,' Sharon hissed, burying her face in the pillow.

'Fine, then listen. I have given considerable thought to your angry words and I realize you and your brothers don't like it around here since your father left...'

Sharon sat up, 'You kicked him out. I heard you send him away.'

Betty recalled that horrible night, confessing, 'I realize now I may have acted too hastily...'

Sharon's face brightened for the first time in days. 'Does that mean you are going to ask Daddy to come back home?'

Betty drew a deep breath of resignation, 'Sharon, I have given that considerable thought, but I'm just not ready…'

'Ready for what?' she interrupted. 'You still love him; I know it because he's the father of *your* kids.'

Her statement held some merit, but Betty couldn't erase the image of Endre's love child from her mind. 'It's just that…'

Sharon folded her arms across her chest. 'It's just that you are being selfish and inconsiderate to all of us because there's another woman who loves him too.'

She sighed deeply. 'No, Sharon, you don't understand.' She wanted to say, *I know that when you father was dedicated to us, everyone was happy and things ran smoothly. I didn't have to worry about anything. I know for your sake and your brothers, he should be present in your everyday lives. But unfortunately I can't trust the son of a bitch and the possibility of reconciliation is nil.*

It was a perfect summer day for sitting side by side at the picnic table in Janet's backyard flipping through Marcie's latest *Glamour* issue. Together they discussed the endless array of virtually flawless, malnourished models with heavily made up doe-eyes and pouty lips, gracing the pages.

Janet pouted her lips, pointing at a tall, lanky blond in a green pink-flowered peasant dress. 'Do you think I could be a model? I have the same dimpled cheeks and my eyes slant downward like hers.' She analysed the photo intently. 'My eyelashes are way longer,' she concluded, fluttering her big green eyes. 'In fact, I bet she's wearing false eyelashes. I can tell.'

Marcie studied her best friend. 'As far as your face is concerned, you probably could pass for a model.'

Janet's dimpled smile blossomed, her face lightly flushed. 'But your boobs are way too big. If you look closely, they're flat as a washboard. Not to mention, skinny as a bloody rail. Shit. Speaking of skinny,' Marcie said, watching Theresa waving happily, walking toward them.

Marcie said mockingly, 'Now she could be a model with those toothpick legs.'

Theresa's face reddened, sitting across from the pair. She had always been very self-conscious of her long, thin legs and tended to take an instant dislike to those commenting negatively about her long, lean gams. 'How are you doing?' she said, moving forward.

'Fine thanks, bean pole,' Marcie said. 'Ironically, we were just discussing what it takes to be a model. With your skinny legs you could be one hands down. My advice is, grow your hair long then get yourself to the nearest model agency. You really do have a pretty face.'

'I would be so jealous,' Janet swooned. 'I've *always* wanted to be a model.'

Marcie studied Theresa's chest. 'You don't have any tits either. That's a huge plus. Still wearing undershirts?' she asked sarcastically, knowing full well.

Theresa had had enough of her cheap shots. 'Do you have a problem with me or something, Marcie? Every time I see you, you start making bloody negative comments about me; always when Janet's around,' she added.

Marcie felt her face redden. 'I don't have a problem with you at all,' she shrugged.

'Then stop all your damn bullshit. I'm so fed up with people like you saying whatever they want to me. I do have feelings.'

'Wow! I'm sorry. I really wasn't trying to hurt you. I do think you would make a great model with those legs,' she said, turning her attention back to the magazine. The girls focused on the magazine, talking animatedly about clothes and make-up.

With the tension eased between the two, Theresa, hoping to find answers, asked if their moms had discussed sex or totally avoided the conversation like hers had.

Marcie smiled apologetically. 'Most parents don't like to talk to their kids about sex. I think it's because they can't imagine their kids partaking in it, if you know what I mean.'

Theresa shook her head. 'Partaking in what? That's what I don't understand.'

Though she was no expert, Marcie proceeded to explain all aspects of sex from French kissing to intercourse.

Janet piped up. 'Wow Mars! You know a hell of a lot about sex. Is that from experience?' she smiled wickedly, raising a perfectly shaped brow.

'I learned about sex at the private school I attended in Ottawa. And no, I've never done it. I'm not sure I'd want to,' she said, turning up her nose. 'Parts of it sound so yucky.'

Theresa thought of Lynda's dreamy recount of sex with Daniel and how wonderful she had portrayed their sexual tryst.

'Personally, I'd be worried about getting knocked up,' Marcie said matter-of-factly, catching the naïve look on Theresa's face. 'Knocked up means get pregnant, T.'

Theresa remembered the relieved look on Lynda's face when she announced she had gotten her period.

Janet shrugged. 'What's wrong with having a baby? I'd love to have one?'

Marcie's eyes widened. 'Are you fucking crazy? Talk about ruining your whole life. There's so much to do and see. Having a kid would kibosh any chance of doing anything. I would never want one. Before I'd even consider having a baby, I want to be well-travelled, have a good job, happily married to a man who can support my habits and living in a beautiful house.'

Theresa was shocked by Marcie's adamant stand against Janet's desire to have a baby. *Maybe she's not so bad after all* she thought smugly.

Janet said, 'What about you, T?'

'I'm with Marcie on that one. There's no way I'd want a baby at this age.'

After the sex talk with Marcie and Janet, Theresa felt she had finally come of age. So much so, when she arrived home she pitched her undershirts into the rag bag, transferring the bras her Mom had purchased to the top drawer of her dresser.

Feeling elated for the first time in many months, Endre wheeled his leather chair closer to the desk. It had been a hell of a fight but he was back at the helm and sole owner of the company, Herczeg Movers. His first order of business had been to clean shop. Loyal employees that had remained steadfast to him were kept on; those that weren't were kicked to the curb, along with his brother, Etika.

Today, with his business in order, he needed to resolve issues surrounding his home life, starting with the stuffy one-bedroom apartment. Living conditions were far too cramped, not to mention baby interruptions, usually at inappropriate times. His former children were well past this stage; he was unaccustomed to a baby's demands, annoying him immensely. Maxine had made it very clear when he moved back in she was anxious to have more children, he on the other hand, was dead against anymore offspring.

Searching the phone book for a real estate company, he was interrupted by the knock on his office door. Quickly closing the directory, he shoved it back in the drawer.

Maxine took Endre Jr. to the doctor for his monthly check up. She was thankful Dr. Fitzgerald had returned from sick leave, watching him examine the happy baby.

The doctor smiled, 'Endre Jr. is a very healthy baby boy,' he said, watching her dress the child. 'And how is Mommy doing? I can tell by his happy face, motherhood agrees with you.'

Maxine smiled, 'Mommy is doing much better since Endre's daddy came back to us.' She had mentioned during a previous visit that she was on her own, but all that was in the past now.

'Well that's good news. I am happy for all three of you. Do you have any health concerns, Maxine?'

She had been quite tired lately, assuming it was part motherhood. 'A little tired at times,' she said, buttoning the baby's sweater. 'My stomach's been a little queasy lately, but my stomach tends to act up from lack of sleep,' she added.

The doctor furrowed his brow. 'Has the baby been keeping you up at nights?'

'Oh no, he's been sleeping through the night for months, thank goodness. One morning last week, my stomach was so queasy I actually thought I was going to be sick.'

The doctor looked up from his notes. 'Maxine, when was your last period?'

She pondered the question, 'about a month ago.' She quickly realized where his line of questioning was headed. 'I know I'm not pregnant,' she said confidently, feeling her face flush. 'If I was pregnant, I'd be sick every morning like I was with this little guy. Right sweetheart,' she said, kissing his rosy cheek.

The doctor gave her a maternal smile, 'every pregnancy is different, my dear. I'll see you next month.'

Maxine hurried back to the apartment; anxiously flipping through the calendar, counting the days between her menses.

She ran to the bathroom, stripping to the waist examining her swollen breasts, eyes trained on the large, dark blue veins protruding above her nipples. *Oh my god. I'm pregnant. Endre will be so happy.*

Endre moved quickly toward his daughter with open arms. 'Sharon, my princess, my girl,' he said, lifting her into his arms, hugging her tightly. 'I have missed you so much.'

'Oh Daddy, I've missed you too.' Unable to hold back tears she cried uncontrollably.

'There, there,' he smiled. 'Daddy's here. Everything's going to be alright.'

He took her hand, leading her to the chair beside his desk; wiping her tears with a tissue. 'Is Mommy alright?'

Sharon nodded.

'Does she know you're here?'

She shook her head. 'I left school at lunch because I just couldn't eat there anymore. I hate eating lunch at school with all those bratty kids. I want to have lunch at home with you and my brothers.'

He smiled warmly, asking how she had gotten here.

'I took the bus.'

He raised his eyebrows. 'That's pretty brave, princess.'

She looked up confidently. 'I remembered how to do it from the time Mommy brought me here to see where you worked. Remember our visit?' she said, smiling for the first time since her arrival.

'That was over four years ago. You have a great memory, like your mom,' he said proudly. 'Why did you come here?'

Her face turned serious. 'Daddy, I want you to come back home to us. I hate being there without you. And I hate Mommy because she won't let you come back.' She looked hopefully at her father. 'Can I come and live with you?'

Endre thought of the already overcrowded one bedroom apartment. 'I'm in the process of looking for a house…'

'I want to come live with you today!' She cupped her face, crying into her hands.

There was a tap on the door. 'Sorry to interrupt, Endre. Line one is for you,' Carl said.

'Take a message. Can't you see I'm dealing with my…'

'It's Betty,' he interrupted, disappearing around the corner.

Endre had never witnessed Betty's hysterics before. He barely understood a word she was saying but figured the phone call was about Sharon. 'Sharon is here in my office,' he interjected, speaking calmly into the sudden quiet on the other end. 'She's safe here with me,' he said reassuringly, sitting back in his chair.

Betty's hysterics turned to anger. 'Why is she there with you? She's supposed to be at school. Did you kidnap her?'

Endre shook his head. 'No, I did not kidnap her. I will be bringing her home shortly. We need to have a long talk,' he said, replacing the receiver.

Betty was far too distraught to argue.

Maxine answered the knock on the door. 'Oh, hi, Frank,' she said, feeling her pulse quicken. 'It's not a good time. Endre will be home...'

He raised a hand in protest. 'I just dropped by to see how you and little Endre are doing,' he said, staring hopelessly into the face of the woman he loved so deeply. 'I can see by your radiant smile life must be treating you kindly.'

She relaxed, feeling at ease. Frank always made her feel good. He was patient and kind all the time. 'Actually, life is very good,' she said, thinking of the new life she and Endre had conceived.

'I'm glad,' he smiled with quivering lips. He turned, moving quickly toward the elevator, pressing the button urgently until the lazy doors parted. Once inside, he cupped his face, unabashedly bawling.

Maxine made an appointment with the doctor, anxious to verify the pregnancy before telling Endre. After completing his examination he confirmed her intuition.

'Everything looks fine. You are almost three months...'

She interrupted, 'But that can't be.' Her face flushed crimson. 'I've only missed one period.'

The doctor raised his eyebrow. 'Maxine, I have been in practice for over 25 years and I haven't been wrong yet,' he said, noting the concerned look on her face. 'Is there anything wrong?'

'No, no, Doctor Fitzgerald. It's just that I didn't think I was that far along.'

He smiled kindly. 'When I get the results of your blood tests I'll be able to give you a more definite due date.'

Back home, Maxine's heart beat double time flipping through the calendar; tossing it in the garbage she cried hysterically.

Betty sobbed uncontrollably wrapping her arms tightly around her daughter. 'I love you so much. Please don't ever scare me like that again. I don't know what I would do without you.'

Endre stood close by watching the emotional pair. After a few moments he asked Sharon to go to her room so he could talk with her mother.

'Promise me you won't leave,' she said pleadingly.

He winked assuredly. 'I promise, sweetheart.'

Betty sat on the chesterfield, her hands folded in her lap, eyes puffy and red from crying. She looked and felt like she had aged ten years since receiving the call from the school stating her daughter hadn't returned to class after lunch. In a barely audible voice she asked her ex-husband for an explanation.

Endre felt sorry for her, explaining how Sharon randomly showed up at his office. 'I could not believe my eyes when I saw her standing there. It broke my heart when she spoke of how much our separation had affected her. I wanted to shield her from all the pain, but it is not possible being estranged from you and my children. Betty, I have never stopped loving you and my kids.'

Just when she thought she couldn't cry anymore, Betty felt tears sting her eyes. Her lips quivered, 'Endre, please come back home to us.'

Maxine ran to the door when it opened, throwing her arms tightly around Endre's neck. 'I missed you so much,' she said, feeling his body tense. She stepped back from their one-sided embrace. 'Did something happen at the office?'

Without hesitation he spoke about what transpired this afternoon and his emotional meeting with Betty. 'She has asked me to come back home…'

Maxine's eyes widened in fear. 'No! Your home is here with me and Endre Jr.' she said, suddenly feeling sick to her stomach.

Endre shook his head. 'Maxine, you know my heart isn't here and it never could be. We need to end this charade once and for all. I need to go back to my family. I have to pack my clothes...'

She grabbed his arm, stopping him mid-step. 'This is not a charade,' she said adamantly. 'It never has been. I love you with all my heart and you know it. You promised you would stay this time.'

He wrestled his arm out of her tight grip. 'I'm pregnant,' she blurted, watching the colour drain from his face. 'I saw Dr. Fitzgerald today and he confirmed it.'

Endre's mind reeled with the totally unexpected news. 'How far along are you?' he asked, noting her hesitation.

Maxine's face reddened, 'just over four weeks.'

She had always been easy to read; he sensed she wasn't being forthright.

'It's your baby,' she said defensively, anticipating his next line.

Endre rubbed his forehead, mentally calculating how long he'd been living with her. He had moved in a few months ago; their sex life had been sporadic at best.

She read his mind. 'It only takes one time, Endre.'

He entered the bedroom with Maxine in tow. Her eyes widened, watching him wrestle the suitcases out from under the bed. 'What are you doing?'

'Be quiet now. You don't want to wake up junior,' he said, tossing clothes into the cases.

She stood beside him. 'This is your baby,' she whispered, pointing to her abdomen.

Snapping the cases shut, he moved hastily out of the bedroom.

Maxine, on the verge of tears, latched onto his arm. 'Where are you going? You promised me you would stay.'

He pulled his arm away, 'back to my wife and children. Your pregnancy, which I question, doesn't change a damn thing.' The phone rang loudly in his ear bending over to pick up the luggage. 'Yes,' he said gruffly into the receiver.

The man at the other end chuckled. 'This is Dr. Fitzgerald. I hope I haven't called at an inconvenient time. Is it possible to have a word with Maxine?'

Endre turned away from her, speaking calmly into the receiver. 'She's busy with Endre Jr. I'm the baby's father. Is there any message?' Maxine tried to grab the receiver but he tightened his grip on her wrist.

'Well then, I can certainly give you the message. By my calculations your little bundle of joy should be arriving just in time for Christmas,' Dr. Fitzgerald said so convincingly, Endre almost started crying. 'Maxine didn't think she was that far along, but like I said to her, I've been doing this for over twenty-five years and have never been wrong. Congratulations to you both.'

Endre felt the weight of the world roll off his shoulders, thanking the doctor profusely for making his day. 'Well my dear, it seems congratulations are in order. You and Frank will be welcoming a Christmas baby.'

'Dr. Fitzgerald is wrong. I'll get a second opinion and prove it,' she said adamantly, rubbing her wrist.

Endre shook his head. 'You are a very foolish young woman, Maxine. You knew damn well the baby wasn't mine and still you tried to pin it on me. And not that I give a shit, but what about your boyfriend, Frank? Doesn't he have a right to know you are carrying his child?'

Maxine felt tears sting her eyes. She reached for his arm, grasping it tightly. 'It's you I love, Endre and I always will. Ever since the day we met, I have wanted to be your wife and raise a family with you.'

He pulled his arm free. 'You need to make a phone call.'

Chapter Twenty-Five

JOYCE POURED HOT coffee into Etika's mug, sitting down across from him at the kitchen table. He had become a lost, depressed soul ever since the courts awarded Endre exclusive ownership of Herczeg; the verdict was taking a toll on their once rock solid marriage.

In the interim, Endre, being a good brother, offered him part time work, driving truck, which Etika vehemently refused. *I would rather shovel shit than work for that goddamn bastard.*

Joyce focused on her cup. 'You can't keep going on like this day after day.'

He looked up from his coffee. 'So what do you suggest I do?'

She met his gaze, 'I don't know, get a job.'

Etika's face burned with anger. 'I had a job. A good job I looked forward to going to every day. I had responsibilities, a reason to get up in the morning. I had a paycheque. But most of all, I had my honor.'

She shook her head. 'Etika, you can have all that again.'

'How? I don't want to go work for somebody else.' He pushed back his chair. 'I had my own company. Yes, in the beginning it was Endre who encouraged me to come to Canada to help build Herczeg. At the time, I was an awkward teenager with no future in Hungary so I jumped at the opportunity to start a new life. *Together* we made the company what it is today. Then that bastard took it all away from me. It's my company too,' he said proudly, holding back tears.

'He did offer you a job,' she said meekly.

'I'm a manager, not a fucking truck driver.' He had never felt so insulted in his life.

Joyce's eyes widened. In all their years of marriage, she had never heard him use such profanity.

'Can't you see what he's trying to do? He's trying to destroy me, his only brother.'

Joyce walked toward him, placing her perfectly manicured hands on his muscular shoulders. 'Then don't let him, Etika. You are a proud Herczeg. In our twenty years of marriage, I have never seen you falter like this. You were always willing to stand up for what you believe in, for your rights, for your family. Don't let Endre take you down to the depths of hell. Fight back, like I know you can and will. Start you own moving company. Grab hold of all the men he fired and start again. Show that creep Endre what you are made of.'

The hot summer sunshine felt good on Tammy's shoulders pumping the swing higher. It was just last week kids said their goodbyes to school chums, marking the beginning of summer vacation and she couldn't be happier. *No more getting up early; Yummy Man treats once a week after supper; playing outside until the street lights come on...*

'Hi Tammy.'

She averted her eyes from the turquoise blue sky to the deep baritone voice behind her. 'Holy shit, George! You scared the crap out of me.'

He sat down on the swing beside her. 'Sorry,' he yelled, choking on the dust created dragging her feet on the sandy dirt beneath the swing.

When the swing finally came to a halt she felt awkward sitting beside him, studying his pimply face with patches of long black hairs sprouting amongst the peach fuzz on his cheeks and chin. His mousy brown hair was long and greasy. He was at least a head taller than the last time she had seen him. 'You've sure changed,' she said, matter-of-factly. The truth was he made her skin crawl studying the juicy blackheads on his face, fighting the sudden urge to pop a few.

He focused on the ground in front of his long legs suddenly feeling very self-conscious. 'I should have washed my hair last night,' he said apologetically.

Tammy's demeanor softened, feeling sorry for him. Though they hadn't had any contact for well over a year, she still considered him a friend. She was anxious to know what had transpired after he moved away, quizzing him incessantly, overwhelming him with her queries.

He held up grubby hands protesting, 'What are you a cop or are you writing my book?' he smiled, exposing a mouthful of big yellow stained teeth. He had learned the saying a long time ago from his brother; it felt good using it on her.

Tammy ignored the remark. Turning up her nose, she backed her swing up, suspecting his breath was probably as bad as his teeth. 'You should have brushed your teeth this morning. They are so stained.'

He pulled a package of Export A cigarettes from his shirt pocket. 'It's probably because of these.'

She moved back beside him. 'You smoke?' she said accusingly, watching him light up.

He inhaled deeply. 'Yeah, I've been smoking for a while now.'

She watched the smoke come out of his mouth and nose simultaneously. 'I've never tried it before.'

He handed her the package. 'Help yourself.'

'Nah, it doesn't interest me. I'll stick to my chocolate addiction,' she said, swinging back and forth slowly. 'So George, what happened to your family? Do you see your *pig* brother?'

Her name calling stung. Usually he liked her frankness, but Barry was his brother and he still loved him. 'I don't see him, but I call him once a week at the detention center. Gloria never talks to him. She's doing better, but still suffers from nightmares. My dad works during the day and doesn't travel anymore. My mom is in an institution trying to get re-ha-bil-i-ta-ted,' he said, sounding out the word, unsure of its meaning.

Tammy had no idea what the word meant either. 'Are you allowed to see her?'

George thought back to his visit with her a couple months ago. 'Sometimes my dad takes us to see her.'

Tammy scrunched her face up. 'Does she remember you?'

George lit another cigarette. 'Yeah, of course, 'cause we're her kids.' He thought back to the most recent visit. 'My mom gets this weird look on her face though, whenever she sees my dad and calls him Brian.'

'Brian?'

'Remember when I told you about the guy that raped her? I think that's who she thinks my dad is.'

'Doesn't she scream when she sees him?'

'No. She just asks him if he thinks she's beautiful.'

'What does your dad say?'

'Yes, of course.'

Tammy thought the whole thing was weird, but then again, they were a weird family, starting with the mother. 'Is she ever going to get out of that place?'

George shrugged, 'Don't know.'

Tammy swung forward, jumping off the swing. 'I have to get going for lunch.' She could tell by the wanting look on his face he was hoping for an invite, but there was no way she could bring George home looking like that and smelling like stale cigarettes. Bea would have a fit.

George caught up with her, reaching for her hand. Standing mere inches away he smiled. 'I like you a lot,' he said, giving her a tight bear hug.

Tammy squirmed like a flipped over snake, releasing his tight hold. The feeling was definitely not mutual. 'Bye,' she said, running away as fast as her skinny legs would carry her. *Shit! I've got the cooties.*

She made it home in record time, still reeling from George's sudden burst of affection. She rubbed her body vigorously trying to erase his touch. She would have thought nothing of his gesture but she remembered what her best friend, Abigail, said recently. *When a guy hugs you, his wiener starts to grow because something happens inside of him. He can't stop it from happening, it just does. AND, if he really likes you, it grows even bigger, bursting at the seams.*

Bea heard the bathtub taps running, walking up the basement steps. 'Tamara, what are you doing?' she sighed heavily.

'Having a hot bath,' she said, checking the water temperature.

Bea rolled her eyes. 'It's the middle of the bloody day. Why on Earth do you need a bath?'

Tammy focused on the sickening image of George's pimply, hairy, smiling face after the big bear hug, thoroughly convinced his wiener must have outgrown his underwear. She made a sour face, 'Because I came in contact with some major *crap* that really needs scrubbing off.'

Bea shook her head. 'I'll never make a lady out of you,' she said, closing the door behind her.

Frank unpacked the groceries trying to decide what to cook for his supper. He was thankful Ben had let him use the spare room but it was time to find an apartment of his own. He glanced at the circled possibilities in the classifieds with regret he had given up his all too familiar unit down the hall from Maxine. But with Endre back in her life, it was just as well. Seeing the three of them together as a family would tear his heart out.

He opened a can of beans, a mainstay these days; with little appetite for anything else, dumping the contents into an aluminium pan. The wall phone sounded loudly startling him. He was even more stunned by the voice on the other end.

Frank had no idea what to expect knocking on Maxine's door and was even more baffled when she opened the door with red swollen eyes. Swallowing hard, he asked after Endre Jr.

Maxine reached for his hand, 'Endre Jr. is fine, not so his mother.' She sat on the chesterfield and spoke in a serious tone, 'I'm not sure where to begin.'

Frank, his face a gentle unsure smile said, 'My mom always used to say, it's best to start at the beginning.' He cautiously sat down beside her.

Maxine felt the tension easing. Frank was probably the best friend she had ever had. He had a knack of saying the right thing, no matter what the situation. 'Endre has left me, again. This time for good,' she added. 'It seems his wife wants him back.' She felt tears sting her eyes.

Frank felt sorry for Maxine, but relieved the poor excuse of a man had moved out.

She wiped her eyes, composing herself. 'I know I don't have any right to ask you to come back, especially after what I've put you through, but it's what I would like more than anything.'

Frank's heart beat faster kneeling on the floor in front of her. He had hoped and prayed for this very moment, but now it was here he was overwhelmed; his head spinning with uncertainty. 'Are you sure Endre is out of your life for good? Or will he come back again, like the last time. It's too difficult for me to live with that uncertainty.'

Though it hurt like hell to say the words, she convinced him she was through with Endre. 'Even if he had a change of heart, I would not let him back into our lives. Besides, he will never come back. He is out of my life for good now. I assure you, I don't want him back. I know this has been very difficult for you and I'm so sorry I've put you through all this. Yet, here I am again asking you to make a life with me and Endre Jr. You have my word, this time I'm really sure. I want us to share our lives together, like a real family.'

He took her hand in his, through tears he could no longer hold back. 'There's nothing I want more in this world than to be with you, my angel sent from heaven, and little Endre. I love you with all my heart, Maxine. I always have and I always will. I don't know if I have the right, seeing Endre Jr. has a Daddy, but I love him too, like a son.'

Maxine smiled warmly. 'I know Endre Jr. loves you too, Frank,' she smiled, wiping the tears from his face. 'There's something else you need to know.'

Apprehensively, Frank sat back on his heels.

'Nothing bad,' she said reassuringly. 'I am pregnant, with our child.'

Frank was stunned by her admission but only for a moment. 'I'm going to be a father?' he said, jumping to his feet. 'Me? I mean us?'

'Yes. Our baby will be born just in time for our first Christmas together as a family.'

Frank pinched himself to be sure it wasn't a dream, asking her to repeat the wonderful words. 'This is amazing! It's my dream come true; you, me, Endre Jr. and now our baby. I am truly blessed. Thank you God,' he said, raising his head and arms toward the ceiling.

Gingerly, he pulled her to her feet, embracing her with his love. She felt his warmth radiate through her. 'No Frank, I'm the one who's truly blessed.'

He kissed her gently on the lips. 'There is only one more wish, a wish I have had since the moment we met. He bent down on one knee. 'Would you do me the honor of becoming my beloved wife?'

Gently, she placed her hands on either side of his loving face, 'Yes.'

Chapter Twenty-Six

THERESA SPENT THE first half of summer babysitting for the next door neighbours and the O'Sullivans, a new family that moved into the McConnel's vacant residence.

Not surprisingly, Bea took an instant dislike to the O'Sullivans. At the best of time, she had little use for the Irish, more so when they took advantage of her daughter's willingness to babysit for free. Theresa had offered up the excuse that free child-care was only temporary and they promised to pay her once they got on their feet. Needless to say, Bea was having no part of an Irish man's promise. 'Nobody's that damn poor,' she concluded. She was certain this so-called promise wouldn't come into fruition anytime soon. Mr. O'Sullivan, a mere cab driver, spent most of his time smoking cigarettes, driving around looking for fares hoping to put food on the table for his wife, left alone to raise their three kids. He was also in the habit of heading to the local pub at the end of the day, tipping back a few before heading home.

The O'Sullivans, true Catholics, attended early morning mass every Sunday. (Bea claimed they went to the early service so he could dump his wife at the house then drive around in his hack all day in peace and quiet.) This Sunday was no different. Theresa ate a quick breakfast and ran over just in time for the couple to attend early mass.

She spotted Mr. O'Sullivan sitting in his cab smoking a cigarette; Mrs. O'Sullivan waited impatiently at the front door. 'I didn't get a chance to change the wee one's nappy because she's still asleep,' she said with a thick Irish accent. 'Sarah is still sleeping too…'

'Mommy, Mommy,' Michael said, running toward her trying to hug her legs.

'Michael, don't dirty my dress,' she said, holding him at arm's length. 'It's the only one I've got. You're supposed to be in bed asleep.'

'I just woke up,' he said, holding his nose. 'Colleen has done her poo poos.'

Mrs. Sullivan moved quickly down the hall with Michael in tow, returning promptly when she heard the horn beeping. 'She needs a change of diaper. I've got to run,' she said, swiftly exiting the house.

Theresa and Michael stood waving at the door; their gesture unreturned.

The smell of fecal matter permeated the hall. Theresa covered her nose in an effort to ward off the disgusting stench but it was futile; tears flowed and she gagged repeatedly into her hand. She took refuge in the bathroom gulping huge breaths of air; tears streamed endlessly down her cheeks. Grasping tightly to the edges of the sink, it took every ounce of willpower to hold down her cereal. By the time she stopped retching, her face was crimson and blood shot eyes stared back at her in the cabinet mirror. The baby's crying intensified; she splashed cold water on her face.

Theresa's stomach settled down somewhat, but the dilemma of how to handle the stinky situation overwhelmed her. If she had listened to her mom, she would still be in bed, not cleaning up a load of baby crap for free.

Counting to three, she held her breath, ran into the baby's room yanked Colleen out of the crib and ran back to the bathroom with Michael in tow. Leaving the two children sitting on the floor near the tub, she ran to the kitchen gulped air, held her breath, ran back into the bathroom, filled the tub, removed the poop filled nappy and dropped it into the toilet. She ran back to the kitchen breathing deeply returning just in time to grab Colleen's little leg, preventing her from tumbling headfirst into the water.

She placed Colleen in the tub, instructing Michael to fetch a clean diaper, washing the baby with plenty of soap.

After the bath, she reached for Colleen's clean little hand to investigate her bedroom; it was difficult to fathom the damage this little angel had done upon waking. There was shit from here to yonder. Theresa pulled the door closed.

Other than a few cans of beans and cookies, the kitchen cupboards were practically bare; with little to choose from she asked Michael what he usually eats.

'Cereal,' he smiled happily. He was a good looking little boy with expressive big blue eyes and tight curly blond hair. Colleen, a year younger, was almost identical. Because of her large size; she could easily pass as his twin.

Theresa found a box of frosted sugar flakes in the refrigerator next to half a bottle of homogenized milk. *Strange place to put cereal, but to each his own* she concluded, reaching for two bowls.

'There's a dirty diaper in the toilet so I can't pee.'

Theresa turned toward the harsh voice and was greeted with a sour-faced Sarah standing defiantly at the kitchen entrance. The surly seven-year-old, arms crossed over her chest, demanded Theresa take care of it immediately. With long, straight brown hair and emerald green eyes, there was no resemblance in looks or disposition to her younger siblings.

Theresa explained, 'I've been busy getting breakfast for Colleen and Michael.' The truth was she had forgotten about the filthy thing and the last thing she wanted was to revisit it.

While Sarah held her crotch, jumping up and down, Theresa searched the empty cupboards for a pair of rubber gloves. There was no way she was going to touch the diaper without them.

In the meantime, Sarah turned, running quickly down the hall, triumphantly returning a couple of minutes later. 'I just peed on the diaper,' she said, sitting at the table.

When Mrs. O'Sullivan returned, Theresa mentioned the dirty diaper in the toilet and that she hadn't had time to clean up

Colleen's room. Making a hasty exit, she took deep breaths of fresh air content with the knowledge that even if she had had the time, she would not have cleaned up either. This morning she had dealt with enough baby crap to last a lifetime.

Bea was sitting at the kitchen table when she arrived. 'Well, did they pay you? You've done a month of Sundays.' She couldn't help but notice her daughter's flushed cheeks, sitting down across from her asking suspiciously how the morning went.

Theresa described the scenario that confronted her shortly after the O'Sullivans left for mass. 'I had no choice but to bath little Colleen.' She didn't mention clinging to the sink beforehand trying to hold breakfast down. 'And once I dealt with that mess, there was no way I was cleaning up her bedroom. There was crap all over the walls, crib, floor, you name it.' She felt nauseated just talking about it.

It was no surprise Bea reacted vehemently. 'There's no bloody way you should have cleaned it up. And I'd bet my last buck that sneaky woman knew about the mess before she left to polish her halo. That's the end of babysitting for those Irish freeloaders,' she concluded.

Theresa voiced her disappointment; she was quite fond of little Michael.

When Mrs. O'Sullivan called the following Saturday, Bea intercepted the call stating that unless she started paying her daughter, she was to find another sitter. 'You've had a bloody good run of it,' she said, after listening to her go on about their money woes. 'Theresa has been more than generous with her time and if you aren't going to pay her, you'll have to find another sucker. Or better still; take the bloody bunch to church with you.'

Two weeks later a Royal LePage sign stood in the middle of the O'Sullivan's front lawn.

Chapter Twenty-Seven

JANET INCREASED THE volume filling her bedroom with Beatles music, uniting them in song. 'Paul McCartney is my favourite,' she said, as the song end.

Theresa thought John Lennon was the coolest, opening a tube of Yardley peach lipstick. 'I really like this colour.' The start of high school was approaching quickly and it would be nice to have a new lipstick; the pale pink lipstick she scoffed from Janet was almost gone.

Janet applied a peachy shade of lip gloss to her thin lips stating a trip to Towers was warranted. 'My make-up is so old or almost gone and I really need to replenish my stock before school starts. Not only that, I know Marcie stole my favourite Yardley pale pink lipstick, even though she swears up and down she didn't. She's a bloody lying thief.'

Theresa chuckled to herself. *Imagine a stealer accusing another stealer of stealing.* She decided not to confess she had taken it, detecting her best friend's venomous tone. *Payback for how Marcie used to treat me* she thought wickedly.

Janet admired her beige, brown and white striped purse. 'It probably holds a lot.'

Theresa handed her the purse; a birthday gift from her parents.

Janet held it up. 'If this purse had a long shoulder strap it would be so hip. Shoulder bags are all the style now,' she said, struggling to put the strap over her shoulder. 'You need to find a longer strap then this purse would be absolutely perfect.'

The department store was busy for a Tuesday morning, moving toward the handbag section. Janet rummaged through a large bin of handbags and found one with a long strap. Trying it on for size she said, 'This strap would be perfect for your handbag, same colour. Here, try it.'

Theresa tried the fit on her shoulder. 'It's good, but I already have a purse. I can't afford this bag,' she said, reading the price tag.

Janet hauled the purse off her shoulder, examined the attachment and within seconds detached the strap, tossing the strapless handbag into the bin, stuffing the strap into Theresa's purse. 'All you have to do is remove your short strap, replace it with that one and you've got a totally in style handbag,' Janet smiled proudly.

Theresa's stomach flipped. 'I can't take this. I don't have enough money to pay for it.'

'Who said anything about paying for it?' Janet said, giving her a friendly nudge toward the cosmetics counter.

Janet encouraged her to start loading up her purse. 'No one's around, hurry.'

Theresa's heart pounded walking quickly toward the eye shadow display; grabbing a compact with different tones of brown, shoving it in her purse. Watching out of the corner of her eye, she dropped three lipsticks and a bottle of *Oh! De London* cologne into her bag. Circling the counter, she stopped at the Cutex nail polish display, gently placing a bottle of white and light pink nail varnish beside the cologne. She picked up two crème blush containers, light pink and apricot, placing them in her purse before Janet pulled her toward the eye pencils and mascara.

'This stuff really makes your eyes look bigger.'

'Can I help you?' the young girl said, approaching them from behind.

Theresa thought she would die on the spot, whereas Janet turned toward the girl smiling sweetly, 'Do you happen to have this pencil in a dark green?'

She studied the label. 'I'm pretty sure we have some out back. Would you like me to get you one?'

'That would be great.' Janet grabbed Theresa's arm moving toward the exit.

They ran quickly across the hydro field toward the wooden gate into Janet's backyard, sitting down at the picnic table.

Theresa emptied the contents of her purse onto the table. 'I can't believe all this stuff.'

Janet emptied her handbag. 'I got way more stuff than you did,' she said, separating the cosmetics into piles.

Once Theresa divided her loot into categories, she was actually stunned by how much she had stolen. 'I don't remember putting all this in my bag.'

Janet chuckled, 'I kinda helped you; being a novice, I figured you needed a hand. I just knew if I liked a certain product, you would too.' She caught the forlorn look on Theresa's face. 'Don't feel bad. I'm the one who got Marcie hooked on shoplifting, even though she can afford to buy *anything* she wants. Hell, I wouldn't have any stuff if I didn't steal it. Won't be long before you're totally onboard; gets in the blood, T. I call it my cosmetic fix.'

Theresa's palms perspired profusely loading her handbag with the stolen goods. 'I have to go home for supper. I'll call you later,' she said, walking quickly toward the gate.

Bea raised her eyebrow watching her eldest daughter pick at the food on her dinner plate. 'Aren't you hungry? I've spent all afternoon cooking.'

Theresa's stomach turned, poking through the steak and kidney pie. The flakey white pastry was soggy brown and reeked of kidney. 'I guess I'm just excited about going downtown with Aunt Eleanor tomorrow.' Until now, the annual outing had been the furthest thing from her mind.

'I love it, Mom,' Tammy smiled broadly, picking up a piece of steak, shoving it in her mouth.

Theresa knew Tammy hated steak and kidney pie more than she did but felt too nauseated to call her bluff, excusing herself from the table.

'You haven't eaten a bloody thing,' Bea said indignantly.

'I'm sorry, Mom. I'm just not hungry.'

'Just leave your plate on the counter and I'll deal with it. I'm not going to throw out good food.' Living in London during the Second World War, followed by the Great Depression when food was very scarce, Bea had never forgotten what it was like to go hungry for days on end.

Theresa retrieved her purse hidden under a jacket on the cupboard shelf. She listened intently before unzipping it. (The last thing she needed was her prying sister asking questions). Gazing into the bag, her palms began to sweat; her heart pounded wildly with the reality check. This afternoon with Janet, stealing had been fun. Tonight, she felt like a common thief. *Thieves get arrested, lose their identity and end up in jail. It's all Janet's damn fault.*

Lying in bed listening to Tammy sleeping soundly, sleep evaded her; her guilty conscience had a firm grip; she had gone against her moral ethics embarking on a stealing spree with Janet.

A dim light shone in the living room, the television barely audible. Her father turned abruptly hearing the wooden floor creak. 'Theresa, what are you doing up?'

She sat down on the chesterfield. 'Can't sleep.'

He sensed something was troubling her by the look on her face. Of all the kids, Theresa had always been the easiest to read. 'I was just going to bed. Do you want me to leave the television on?'

She squeezed her hands tightly, willing herself not to cry. 'I did something really stupid today, Dad. I stole a purse strap from Towers.' *Not to mention lipsticks, blush, eye shadows, perfume and nail polishes, mascara, eye pencils.*

'I see.' He found it difficult holding back his disappointment; Theresa had always been honest and trustworthy. 'I hope you realize the consequence of your actions. If you had been caught, you would have been in trouble with the law.'

She had thought about George being caught stealing perfume and how the police showed up at his door, not to mention the embarrassment his family endured by his foolishness. 'Unfortunately, I didn't think of it at the time,' she said, breaking down.

He felt sorry for her but knew she had to deal with the consequences of her behaviour.

'What do you intend to do about it?'

She wiped her eyes. 'Take it back to the store, of course.' It was her only recourse if she wanted to free up her conscience. 'It's just a purse strap,' she added, hoping he wouldn't be too upset with her.

His voice turned stern. 'Yes, it was just a strap, but what about the purse you removed it from?'

She hadn't given any thought to the part left behind. He was right; the handbag was totally useless without the strap.

'I suggest you go to the manager and tell him what you've done.'

Theresa's eyes widened. 'He'll call the police.' Just the thought turned on the tears.

'You should have thought about that before you stole it,' he said quietly.

She wiped her eyes on her pyjama sleeve. 'I'm supposed to go downtown with Aunt Eleanor tomorrow; I really don't think I should. I know I won't have a good time.' Normally, she looked forward to this yearly tradition of lunch and a birthday gift of her own choosing, but all she wanted to do was return to the scene of the crime and make things right.

'You don't want to disappoint your aunt. My suggestion is carry on with the day. When you get back home, do the right thing, which I'm confident you will.'

After little sleep and a loaded conscience, it was a difficult struggle trying to keep up a happy façade with Aunt Eleanor. All Theresa wanted was to get through the day and return the stolen goods haunting her continuously. She felt physically ill when her aunt steered her toward the handbags in Simpsons to choose her birthday gift, something in previous years she thoroughly enjoyed. Today, the smell of leather nauseated her, grabbing the first wallet she saw; her motion didn't go unnoticed.

'I've never seen you make a decision so quickly,' Aunt Eleanor said pointedly. 'Last year we stood here for almost an hour, remember? You just had to open and close each and every wallet before deciding. Oh well. It gives us more time to enjoy our lunch. Happy birthday,' she said, handing her niece the bag.

During lunch, Aunt Eleanor made a concerted effort to draw her favourite niece into conversation, though her one word responses were discouraging to say the least. It soon became apparent something was troubling her and rather than take it personally, chalked it up to Theresa's age. Thirteenth birthdays marked the beginning of teenage struggles with parents, school and boys. Rather than pursue what was troubling her, she decided not to make an issue, enjoying the remainder of the day.

Theresa was never more thankful to see her house. Though most of the day had been a total blur, she managed to get through it. Stepping out of the car, she thanked Aunt Eleanor profusely, vowing to be more fun next year. She stood in the driveway waving until her aunt's car disappeared around the corner.

When the parking lot came into view, Theresa ran even faster. Leaning against a parked car to catch her breath, she stared at the red Towers sign mounted on the front of the store with a sense of dread, chastising herself for being so stupid in the first place. *It wasn't Janet's fault I stole the stuff. I had the choice and made the wrong one.*

She entered the store with her heart beating in her throat, moving toward the handbag section. Quickly she searched for the handbag buried at the bottom of the bin. She attached the strap, placing it on top.

Moving cautiously around the cosmetic section, she replaced all the stolen articles, the last being the two pencils Janet had tucked in her purse.

'I remember you.'

Theresa grasped the pencils tightly.

The young girl said, 'You were here a few days ago with your friend. I just love her long blond hair. I wish mine was long too,' she said, pulling the ends of her neatly trimmed black bob. 'I managed to locate the green pencil she was looking for, but she was gone when I got back to the counter. It would look great on her eyes.' She noticed the pencils Theresa was holding. 'What colours do you have?'

Her throat was so parched; she found it difficult to speak. 'I have...'

'Black and dark brown, so passé,' she interrupted, pulling the pencils out of her hand, placing them on the rack. 'I'm sorry. Did you want to purchase them?'

Theresa's reply was barely audible. 'No, I was just looking.'

'Well then, do you want to surprise your friend with a green pencil?'

Theresa shook her head. 'If she wants it she can buy it.'

She tucked the empty handbag tightly up under her arm, exiting the store crying tears of relief.

After supper, Theresa sat on the edge of her bed, admiring the wallet Aunt Eleanor had purchased for her. She was surprised at how nice it was considering it was little more than an afterthought when she grabbed it. She breathed in the scent of new leather, abruptly stopping with the knock on her door.

Dad sat down beside her. 'How did it go?'

She sighed deeply, assuring him the strap was back on the purse; thankful he didn't press her for any details.

He looked her in the eye, 'I hope you have learned a lesson.'

She nodded confidently. 'I will never steal again.' She would never forget the hell she had put herself through.

'I am very proud of you. It takes a big person to admit they were wrong, and an even bigger person to remedy it.' He moved toward the door. 'This will be our little secret,' he smiled.

Theresa felt the weight of the day dissipate completely.

Chapter Twenty-Eight

LIKE A WOUNDED fisher, Janet shrieked into the phone so loudly Marcie had to hold the receiver at arm's length. 'I can't understand what you're saying,' she yelled, over her best friend's hysteria.

After what seemed like an eternity, she said dejectedly, 'We are fucking moving again.'

She wondered where Janet's parents were as she continued her foul rant. After several minutes, Marcie got a word in edgewise; she'd be right over.

Theresa got the call from Marcie shortly after ten, wanting her to hurry over to Janet's. She hadn't seen or spoken to Janet since their stealing spree at Towers. Apprehensively, she agreed.

Marcie and Theresa stood at the curb eyeing the for sale sign in the middle of the lawn. 'She called me this morning screaming obscenities about moving.'

Shrugging indifferently, Theresa was thankful she hadn't gotten the call.

Janet, eyes swollen and red, continued to rant about not wanting to move again. 'My fucking parents, I hate them. I want to stay here and go to high school with my friends, not go live in fucking Sudbury. It's so fucking dead up there. No one fucking lives in Sudbury.'

Marcie raised her hands, silencing her momentarily. 'Where are your parents?' It was obvious they weren't at home.

'In fucking Sudbury, buying a fucking house,' she hissed, crossing her arms across her chest. 'Well I'm not fucking moving there.'

After more tears and ranting, Janet settled down. Wiping her eyes she said, 'I've got a solution. Mars, I could live at your house. There's plenty of room.'

Marcie's mouth opened but nothing came out. Her parents were definitely not keen on her. Ever since they had become friends, her parents didn't hesitate to voice their objection. They felt she wasn't good enough for their daughter. They even went so far as to forbid the friendship.

For the first time since their arrival, Janet smiled broadly. 'You've got four bedrooms in your house,' she said excitedly, mentally choosing the one she would occupy. 'Mars, you are my best friend. Problem solved,' she said, rubbing her hands together. 'Just talk to your parents. You can have anything you want. I'm sure they would welcome me with open arms, like another daughter. I haven't seen your mom in ages, but I know she just loves me. We could be sisters *and* best friends.'

Marcie turned to Theresa. 'Sorry, there's no room at my house,' she said emphatically. 'I'm stuck sharing my bedroom with my yappy sister; not that you're yappy, Janet,' she added, thankful for the first time ever she shared the room.

Theresa and Marcie left shortly after Janet settled down. On the way out, Marcie invited her to lunch at her house.

Not only was Theresa totally caught off guard by the invitation, she was even more shocked she hadn't invited Janet.

Marcie said, 'you know something, T, I'm glad Janet is moving, and far away. It was all her idea to steal stuff; I went along with it because I wanted her to like me. But after your talk about having a conscience and all, it got me thinking you were so right; it's not the way to go. I haven't stolen anything since. And as far as Janet moving in with my family, there's not a chance in hell my parents would agree to her very nervy suggestion. They can't stand her. I say good riddance.' She smiled warmly, 'now we can be best friends.'

Theresa couldn't agree more.

Endre sat down at his desk for the last time. He had had an early morning meeting with his employees, informing them that as of September 1^{st,} Herczeg Movers would be under new management. As expected, those that had remained loyal to him and the company voiced their opposition, in that, management was changing hands too often and they were fed up. He assured them this would definitely be the last time and thanked them for their loyalty. 'Without all of you, Herczeg Movers would not be the successful business it is today. For that, I am deeply grateful.'

Very reluctantly Etika had agreed to a meeting with his brother. They hadn't spoken since the judge awarded Endre sole ownership of the company.

Before he left for the meeting, a terrible row with Joyce ensued. *How can you trust that no good bastard after what he did to you, to us! He uprooted our whole lives and now you're going to meet with him like nothing happened.* She had ended the confrontation with a threat to leave him should he pursue a meeting with his heartless brother.

Endre had chosen his favourite Hungarian restaurant. At one time, Etika and Endre frequented *Leticia* to celebrate their success with family and friends. Today, it played host to two brothers with a distant past and no future.

He waved from a table for two located near the back of the restaurant when he saw Etika come through the door. 'You're looking well, my brother,' he said, rising from his seat.

Etika ignored his outstretched hand, sitting down on the rickety old wooden chair across from him. He was not interested in formalities, hoping his brother would get to the point swiftly; seeing him once again had given him a nasty taste in his mouth.

'The place hasn't changed much, eh Etika,' he said turning toward the nearby bar. 'Leticia, bring me a bottle of your best champagne.' A middle aged woman working behind the bar nodded once.

Endre smiled encouragingly as she expertly popped the cork without spilling a drop of the precious liquid. 'Ah Leticia, you are so talented, and beautiful I might add. But not as beautiful as my wife, Rosza.'

'Flattery will get you nowhere. Save it for your wife,' she said in fluent Hungarian.

Etika had heard recently from his children that Uncle Endre was back living with Aunt Betty but assumed it was just talk. He raised his hand halting Endre's attempt to fill his glass.

Endre looked at his brother questioningly. 'Do you not remember the good times in this restaurant? We would sing, dance and toast our success with endless bottles of wine,' he smiled, swaying his airborne glass back and forth. 'Today, dear brother, when you hear what I have to say, the champagne will flow once again,' he said, topping up his glass.

Etika was quickly losing patience. 'Get to the point of this bloody meeting. I have to leave shortly,' he said irritably, regretting the choice to meet with him.

Endre sipped the champagne, savouring the taste. 'You will regret your choice to abstain. This really is the best champagne I've had in a very long time. Are you sure you won't join me?' He watched Etika stand, pushing back his chair in one motion.

'You will never get an offer like this again,' Endre said, halting his hasty exit. He sipped his drink waiting for him to sit back down. 'Etika, you are unemployed, and have been for some time now.' He slid a key across the table; stopping at the fingertips of his brother's outstretched hand.

'What's this?' he said crossly, refusing to be part of his silly little game.

Endre half smiled. 'It should look familiar to you, little bro, surely you haven't forgotten.'

Etika grabbed the key, gave it a once over then slid it toward the center of the table. 'It's the key to your company; so what.'

Endre sipped his champagne. 'No Etika. It's the key to your company.'

He furrowed his brow. 'What do you mean?'

'I mean, the company is yours. Your employees are anxiously awaiting your return.'

Etika was aware of the pulse beating against his skull. 'Endre, if this is some kind of sick joke…'

'It is no joke,' he interrupted. 'I have transferred all rights and ownership of Herczeg Movers into your capable hands,' he said, watching his brother pick up the key. 'I know now, I had no right to take the company we both worked hard to establish away from you. I have done some pretty stupid, selfish, inconsiderate things lately, of which I'm not proud. All I want to do is make things right again,' he said, handing him a large manila envelope. 'You will find all the necessary paperwork authorized and signed by me and my lawyer.'

Etika quickly glanced through the documents. 'It's true. Herczeg Brothers Moving Co. is in my name. Still, I question your sudden change of heart. What about you? What are you going to do?'

Endre sipped his champagne. 'Don't worry about me, little brother. I will always get by. *Pezsgo.*'

Chapter Twenty-Nine

FRANK AND MAXINE'S wedding, officiated by the minister of Frank's church, was a small, intimate affair attended by a few of their closest friends. A reception, courtesy of the minister's wife and parishioners, followed in the church basement. The one room hall was decorated tastefully with white linen tablecloths and centerpieces of pale pink carnations, baby's breath tied together with pink satin ribbons.

The guests were treated to a roast beef dinner, complete with all the trimmings prepared lovingly by the women's auxiliary. Everyone raved about the delicious meal.

After glasses of champagne were poured, Frank stood to address their guests. Overwhelmed with gratitude, he thanked everyone for making their day so special; the newlyweds would be forever grateful.

He turned to face his bride. 'This is truly a day of celebration. I would like to propose a toast to my beautiful bride, Maxine.' He felt his eyes tearing, gazing down at her beautiful smiling face. 'To my wonderful wife and mother of my child,' he said with quivering lips.

Maxine, dressed in a short ivory empire dress, placed her hands on her large, swollen abdomen, smiling warmly at her loving husband.

'You, my dear, have made me the happiest and luckiest man in the world. I love you with all my heart. Thank you God for this beautiful woman. I will love you forever and ever, Maxine, my wife.'

Marcie and Theresa chatted amicably over the delicious lunch her mom had prepared. She put the dirty dishes in the sink, inviting her downstairs to the finished basement.

'This is amazing,' Theresa said, thinking of the bare concrete walls in her basement. She followed Marcie into a separate room.

'This is called the entertainment room,' she said, opening a solid oak door. Theresa's eyes widened when she saw the grand piano taking up much of the space. 'Oh my god! You are so lucky, a grand piano no less!' For years she had begged her parents to buy a piano for her to practice on but her parents stated they couldn't afford such a luxury, not to mention the cost of lessons.

'I had a classmate once, Wendy Andrews, who reluctantly went home after school every day to practice. I envied her so much. Piano is by far my favourite instrument; second only to the banjo,' Theresa smiled.

Marcie furrowed her brow, discovering something new about her friend, wishing she had given her more of a chance when they first met. 'I didn't realize you were so musically inclined.'

Theresa shrugged. 'Most people don't know that about me. I look forward to the day when I can get myself a piano.'

Marcie shrugged using the same tone Wendy used. 'You aren't missing much. I have to practice all the time. Hey, seeing you like piano so much, we can practice together.'

Theresa's eyes bulged. 'That would be amazing. Thanks Mars. You're the best.'

Sitting down at the dinner table, Tammy announced Herczeg's house would be going up for sale in the near future.

Before Theresa could protest, Bea confirmed it was true. 'I had a chat with Betty over coffee last week. Apparently, they're moving to the east coast.'

Dad said, 'Sounds like a pretty drastic change for Betty. I thought she really liked living here on the Crescent. What about her job at the doctor's office? I see Endre has moved back home.'

Bea raised a brow cutting into her ham.

Betty was totally caught unawares when Etika paid her a visit at the doctor's office with an invitation to lunch. She hadn't seen her brother-in-law or his family since the separation.

He chose a quaint Hungarian delicatessen, requesting a quiet table for two. 'You look very well, Betty,' he smiled, helping her with her chair. He noted her weight loss and her new complimentary hairstyle.

Betty felt her face flush. 'Thank you, Etika,' she said, tucking a lose strand of hair behind her ear. It felt awkward being here with Endre's brother; she couldn't help but wonder what the impromptu lunch was about.

He must have read her mind. 'I'm sure you're wondering why I suggested this luncheon.'

A partial smile crossed her face. 'It is unusual.' Previously, when the families gathered for special occasions, other than courteous exchanges, she had never spoken to him. In both their households, the men stuck together while the women prepared the feasts.

After the waitress brought their sandwiches, Etika spoke in hushed tones. 'I'm sure you are aware of Endre's latest endeavour, naming me sole owner of Herczeg.'

Betty nodded, biting into her pork cutlet sandwich.

He proceeded to tell her about his meeting with Endre and how when it was over he had driven straight to the company for verification. As Endre predicted, he was greeted warmly by all the employees ready and willing to begin working for him once again. 'I can honestly say there have been no issues. Things are running smoothly. Ironically, it's like I'd never left. But I have to admit I was, and still am to a degree, apprehensive about Endre's complete turnaround. After all, it's not every day a man gives up the company he fought so hard to take away from me in the first place.'

Betty too, had been very apprehensive when she invited Endre back into her home. The kids certainly had no objections, acting like he had never been away. Their sleeping arrangements remained the same with Endre in the basement. He has done a complete about face, in that; his family is all that matters now.

She looked up from her sandwich. 'So far, Endre has been an exemplary father.'

A concerned look crossed his face, 'And what about where you are concerned? Is he a good husband?'

She averted his eyes. 'We are taking our relationship one day at a time.' Endre's love child continued to haunt her. He continued to profess his role in the child's life would be financial only. Maxine was now married to Frank and the happy couple were expecting a Christmas baby.

Etika sighed deeply. 'I hope things continue to get better for you, Betty. Can I assume you are okay with his decision to transfer ownership of the company to me?'

A truly genuine smile crossed her face. 'Yes, I'm very happy with his decision; definitely one of his better moves. Pardon the pun.'

He glanced up from his lunch. 'What will he be doing with his time? If I know Endre, he will not be content to stay home and keep house forever.'

Betty rolled her eyes, 'He knows this new domestic lifestyle of his can't go on indefinitely so he's in the process of starting up another moving company.'

A confused look crossed his face. 'Why the hell, excuse my profanity, would Endre give me the moving company he worked so hard to regain, only to start up another? It just doesn't make sense. His mind must be warped or something,' he concluded, visibly shaken about competing with his brother.

Betty patted his hand. 'You don't have to worry, Etika. Starting a new moving company won't happen until after we are settled on the east coast. We are moving to Newfoundland. Endre decided we all needed a fresh start, somewhere far away from the familiar.'

It was obvious Etika had no idea of his brother's sudden interest in the east coast. 'This is all too much,' he said, anxiously. He was surprised at how upset he felt, knowing he may never see them again. After all, this is family. 'Are you okay with all this?'

She stared off into space. *No actually, I'm not. But I'm willing to try anything once.* 'You know your brother, Etika. Once his mind is made up, it's all or nothing. He wants to get as far away from his sordid past as possible. You and your family are welcome to visit anytime. Endre has purchased a big house and there's plenty of room.'

Etika said, 'Maybe I should consider driving the east coast runs once again. That way I can visit and have a place to stay.'

'You will always be welcome,' she smiled, glancing at the new gold watch Endre had given her recently. 'I'd better get back to work.' She had thoroughly enjoyed dining with her brother-in-law, thanking him profusely.

Etika sat in the parking lot feeling melancholy about the company he and Endre built together from the ground up; a business he was now the sole proprietor of. He was still trying to digest Endre's unselfish offer and subsequent move to the east coast. He rolled up the car window smiling. *Endre's not such an asshole after all.*

Theresa stood at the living room window watching the movers pack all the Herczeg's belongings into the back of a moving van that was so long, the cab was stationed in the middle of the road. She thought of all the families that had moved away, this year in particular, and now the Herczeg clan. Long ago she had decided Mr. Herczeg, her first real crush, was even more handsome than Elvis Presley.

Sharon, Danny and Charlie, each with a pillow tucked under their arm, bid a tearful goodbye to the neighbours then piled into the spacious backseat of the caddy for the long journey to the east coast.

Mr. Herczeg locked the front door one last time, handing the key to the real estate agent standing nearby. He watched fondly as Renee and Ian hugged Betty, gushing about how lucky they were having them as neighbours. 'Renee, I don't know what I would have done without you. Thank you from the bottom of my heart for looking after my kids. They love you to pieces, me too,' she said, wiping tears with a tissue.

Renee gave Endre a tearful hug. 'When Ian gets his transfer next year, we will be moving to Regina.'

Theresa, standing nearby, covered her face and cried hearing Renee's totally unexpected announcement.

'There, there,' Mr. Herczeg said, hugging her tightly. 'I don't like to see my girl crying like this,' he said jovially.

'Everyone is moving away from the Crescent,' she sobbed.

He put his hands on either side of her face, looking her in the eye. 'My dear young lady, life is about change. It never stays the same. One day you too will leave the Crescent to make a life of your own,' he smiled, wiping her tears with his thumbs. 'And I have started the ball rolling for you by moving out. Mark my words, there's a handsome, young guy moving in that you are going to marry.'

On the last day of the Labour Day weekend, Theresa walked home from Marcie's. They had spent the better part of the morning practicing piano and trying to decide what to wear on the first day of high school. Tomorrow marked the beginning of a new chapter in her life; she looked forward to the new experiences with excitement and a dash of apprehension. *Life is about change. It never stays the same.*

Rounding the corner, Theresa spotted the mid-sized moving van parked in Herczeg's old driveway. Though it had been a couple weeks since their departure, she was still upset about their sudden move so far away.

A blue Chevy Nova with three occupants came to a stop in front of Herczeg's. Theresa assumed they were the new neighbours, and slowed her pace. She watched a heavy set woman and tall thin man exit the car, followed by a young, good looking guy with sandy blond hair. They chatted briefly beside the car, taking in their new surroundings. The couple walked up the driveway; the young guy turned, meeting her gaze.

Theresa felt her face flush staring back. The truth was she couldn't take her eyes off of him. He smiled cordially, offering a quick wave before joining his family.

Theresa, with a noticeable spring in her step, walked up her driveway, silently thanking Mr. Herczeg.

Tammy rolled her eyes, standing at the living room window. 'Oh brother. You're not going to believe what just happened, Mom.'

Bea continued ironing Ken's white shirts. 'I'm sure you'll tell me,' she said dryly.

She proceeded to relay an accurate description of the guy moving into Herczeg's old haunt. 'He's probably a couple of years older than Theresa. Anyway, they just waved at each other with that stupid gaga look on their faces. You know the kind of look you see in the movies just before people kiss or something; the silly yucky look movie stars get paid for. I could never be a movie star.' She turned to face her mom. 'What do you bet she comes in sporting a goofy grin, goes straight to her room and puts on her stupid Summer Place record.'

Shortly after Edson's untimely death, she had put it away for good. All the family, including her father, had been ecstatic.

Theresa, grinning from ear to ear, stepped inside, offered a brief greeting to her sister and mom before moving quickly down the hall, closing the bedroom door.

Bea cursed under her breath when the opening bars of *Theme from a Summer Place* filtered into the living room.

Tammy covered her ears and ran toward the front door. 'Told ya.'

www.ingramcontent.com/pod-product-compliance
Lightning Source LLC
Chambersburg PA
CBHW070908260626
47162CB00007B/2594